Winds of Change

BOOK 5 IN THE BELLEVILLE FAMILY SERIES

J MARY MASTERS

First published 2025 by PMA Books, A divn of Peter Masters &
Associates, ABN 72 172 119 877
Unit 111, 1 Halcyon Way, Bli Bli Qld 4560, Australia
This edition 2025.

A catalogue record for this
book is available from the
National Library of Australia

ISBN 978-0-6458637-5-8

This book was written on the land of the Gubbi/Gubbi people.

Cover design: J D Smith Design, UK
www.jdsmith-design.co.uk
Author photo: Sheree McArthur
www.shereemcarthurphotography.com.au

www.pmabooks.com
Tel + (61) (0) 488 224 929
Email enquiries@pmabooks.com

Winds of Change

BOOK 5 IN THE
BELLEVILLE FAMILY SERIES

J MARY MASTERS

WWW.PMABOOKS.COM

 About the author

J Mary Masters (Judy) was born in Rockhampton, Queensland, Australia in the 1950s, the youngest of four children and raised on a cattle property.

For more than twenty years, she was involved in the magazine publishing industry as a senior executive. Having now given up full time magazine work, Judith is devoting her time to her writing career, with an emphasis on writing for women readers.

Her stories feature a mix of town and country settings, drawing heavily on her early country life.

She is a member of the Queensland Writers Centre (QWC) and the Australian Society of Authors (ASA). She has also completed a fiction writing course with noted literary agency Curtis Brown.

Judy now lives on Queensland's Sunshine Coast with her husband Peter.

Readers are invited to contact Judith through the following channels.

Website	jmarymasters.com
Instagram	@jmarymasters
Blog	jmarymasters.blog
Facebook	www.facebook.com/JudithMMasters
Email	jmarymasters1@gmail.com

Belleville series

BOOK 1 Julia's Story
BOOK 2 To Love, Honour and Betray
BOOK 3 Return to Prior Park
BOOK 4 Heirs and Successors
BOOK 5 Winds of Change

Philippe Duval series

BOOK 1 First Born Son
BOOK 2 Price to Pay

Prologue

In *Heirs and Successors,* Book 4 in the Belleville series, we left the family heading into the new decade of the 1970s. As we take up the story in *Winds of Change,* the fifth book, it is now 1976 and life has moved on for the family.

Of the three Belleville siblings, **Richard**, the eldest, has remarried his first wife, **Catherine**, the mother of his two sons, **Paul** and **Anthony**.

Paul has been married to **Amanda Robinson**. They have a son, **Andrew**. Anthony has almost finished his architecture studies in Sydney. **Susan**, Richard's daughter from his second marriage to Kate, is beginning to ask awkward questions of her father.

William, younger than Richard by two years, remains married to his wife, **Alice**, formerly Fitzroy. Their daughter **Marianne** married **Alex Fraser** and made them grandparents with the arrival of **Melanie**, affectionately called Little Mel.

Julia, her divorce from Philippe Duval finalised, spends more and more time at Prior Park but Sydney will always maintain a hold over her through her daughter with Philippe, **Pippa**. Now married to **Dr Joel Tynan**, Pippa has a baby daughter **Jessica**. Julia's son **John** continues to live on the neighbouring property Mayfield Downs with his father **James Fitzroy**, Julia's first husband.

Life seemed settled for the Belleville family until the betrayal within their midst is laid bare, threatening the very stability of the family.

And from the past, the unlikely origins of the family and the man who built Prior Park are all revealed in a dramatic discovery which rewrites the history of the Belleville family.

I hope you enjoy this final chapter in the Belleville story.

— Judy Masters writing as J Mary Masters

Key characters

BELLEVILLE FAMILY (Prior Park)

Richard Belleville	Elder son of the family
Catherine Belleville	Richard's wife
William Belleville	Younger son of the family
Alice Belleville (formerly Fitzroy)	William's wife
Julia Belleville	Only daughter
Paul Belleville	Richard & Catherine's son
Amanda Belleville (nee Robinson)	Paul's wife
Andrew Belleville	Paul and Amanda's son
Anthony Belleville	Richard & Catherine's son
Susan Belleville	Richard's daughter (2nd marriage)
Marianne Fraser (nee Belleville)	William & Alice's daughter
Alex Fraser	Marianne's husband
Melanie Fraser	Marianne & Alex's daughter
Pippa Tynan (nee Duval)	Julia & Philippe's daughter
Joel Tynan	Pippa's husband
Jessica Tynan	Pippa & Joel's daughter
James Fitzroy	Julia's first husband
John Fitzroy	Julia & James's son

OTHERS

Murray Anderson	Paul's school friend, solicitor
Lachlan Bell	Anthony's uni friend
Victoria Bell	Lachlan's sister,
John Bertram	Richard's friend, Qantas pilot
Tony Bland	Manager, Robinson Properties
Nathan Flynn	Project Manager, Prior Park
Larry Kent	Aircraft Maintenance Engineer
Linda Kent	Larry's daughter
Leonard King	Librarian, research library, Brisbane

BERRIMA

Daniel Harrington	Architect, Kate's 3rd husband
Kate Harrington	Richard's second wife
Tim Lester, Nancy Lester	Kate's son & daughter, 1st marriage

FROM THE PAST

Louis Belleville	Grandfather, Richard, William, Julia
Adeline Prior	Louis Belleville's wife
Henry Prior	Adeline's father
Francis Belleville	Father to Richard, William, Julia
Elizabeth Belleville	Mother to Richard, William, Julia
Alistair McGovern	Francis Belleville's natural son

ENGLAND

Sir Edward Cavendish	Catherine's 2nd husband
George Cavendish	Catherine and Edward's son

1

RICHARD BELLEVILLE FELT PERFECTLY fit and well, despite having just celebrated his fifty-sixth birthday.

But still, an annual medical check up was an essential requirement to continue his life insurance policy so he submitted, without complaint, to the doctor's probing and innumerable questions until the older man, who had been the Belleville family doctor for years, declared himself satisfied.

'You're in good shape for a man of your age,' Alan North declared, as he signed the insurance forms.

'Just lay off the whisky,' he added, not because he suspected Richard of imbibing too freely but because he was remembering Richard's father Francis and his premature death. 'Your father was pretty fond of the whisky bottle as I recall.'

Richard smiled and nodded, aware the warning was well intended.

'He was, Alan,' he replied. 'I've taken a lesson from that, don't worry. Is that the only thing you're concerned about?'

Alan North took a moment to answer as he carefully screwed the top back on his favourite fountain pen.

'Your personal life has been a bit up and down, if you don't mind me saying so. How are you coping? Are you seeing your youngest child?'

Richard had not raised any of these issues with him, but his doctor was aware of the gossip. *There's more to a man than his physical health*, he would often say to anyone who would listen. He waited patiently for Richard to break the silence that ensued, ignoring the impatient shrug of his shoulders.

'Getting to see Susan has been something of an issue,' Richard said cautiously, 'but having an argument with my ex-wife about it is just likely to make matters worse.'

He hesitated. He knew Alan North could be trusted but did he really need to go into it all? Did he really need to say Susan had adopted the name Lester and seemed entirely happy to be part of the growing Lester clan at Berrima Park?

'But Susan is old enough to know her own mind now surely or is that the real problem?'

'You hit the nail on the head, Alan,' Richard said, as he got up to leave. 'Her half-sister Nancy is married and had a baby girl. Her half-brother is about to get married. She feels part of that family, not part of the Belleville family. I see her in Sydney occasionally but rarely up here.'

He paused. It was time for honesty.

'It's a battle I've lost I'm afraid. It's a battle I knew I would lose once my ex-wife's son had more influence over her than I have.'

The doctor laid his hand on Richard's arm in a gesture of reassurance.

'You've done what you can. Marriage breakdown has no winners in the end I'm afraid,' he said. 'Besides you have a mischievous young grandson I noticed waiting impatiently for you outside. I saw your niece Marianne yesterday with her little girl. It's quite remarkable how much alike the two children look. It put me in mind of your father. I remember his unusual pale blue eyes, a bit faded though when I knew him. I wonder if that's who they take after?'

Richard inhaled sharply, the shock of the doctor's observation registering briefly on his face before he regained his composure.

'Probably,' he murmured, before shaking hands with the doctor and heading back to the waiting room to collect Andrew, who, surprisingly, had been well behaved according to the doctor's receptionist who had been asked to keep an eye on him.

'Milkshake time now, Grandad,' Andrew reminded him as he skipped ahead. 'Remember you promised if I was well behaved. And I was well behaved.'

Richard smiled. The boy had a way with him that endeared him to Richard. But still, the cloud remained. How much less would he look like a Belleville in the years to come, he wondered?

Deep in thought, he did not see Alex Fraser approach as they walked along the street. But Andrew saw him and yelled a greeting. Alex stopped and knelt to hug the boy.

'Where are you off to, young Andrew?' he asked. 'Is Grandad taking you out to Prior Park?'

He nodded enthusiastically.

'He is but he's buying me a milkshake first,' he declared.

Alex laughed and looked at Richard as he stood up.

'The boy is setting out his priorities, making sure you don't forget.'

Richard nodded.

'It's a reward for sitting quietly in the doctor's waiting room for half an hour,' he said. 'Apparently Marianne was there yesterday with your little one. Any news I should know about?'

Alex smiled.

'There is indeed. We're finally having our second baby. She's telling her mother today.'

Richard shook his hand and murmured the expected congratulations.

'The year for babies it seems,' Richard said.

'It is indeed,' Alex replied. 'Amanda told me she's desperate for it to be over when I called in to see her last night.'

'She's a few weeks off her due date yet, isn't she?'

For just a moment, Alex hesitated.

'She is but I was concerned about her being by herself. Don't forget Andrew came early when he was born. Took everyone by surprise. I just wanted to make sure she's OK.'

To Richard, it seemed as if Alex believed he was the only one concerned about her.

'It was bad timing for Paul to have to fly William out west. Hopefully they'll be home the day after tomorrow. She can call me anytime too. I told her that. Or Marianne.'

'She's very independent. You know that. She doesn't easily ask for help.'

Except from you, Richard wanted to say. *Except from you, Alex.* But he simply nodded and remained silent.

Six-year-old Andrew finally let out a small yelp of discontent at being kept waiting.

'Milkshake, Grandad,' he said, tugging at his arm.

Richard rolled his eyes and laughed.

'There are some important things that won't wait, Alex,' he said, as he began to walk away.

Alex laughed, relieved to bring the encounter to an end.

But the encounter had troubled Richard afresh. He began to wonder how frequently Alex visited Amanda when Paul was off flying around the countryside, mostly ferrying his Uncle William to their far flung rural properties. At those times, he knew Marianne and little Melanie would often be at Prior Park keeping her mother Alice company.

He shook his head to rid himself of the troubling thoughts and instead began fishing around in his pocket for the change he would need to pay for the strawberry milkshake Andrew had already ordered at the nearby milk bar.

Over a thousand kilometres to the south, Richard's wife Catherine sat alongside their son Anthony at Doyle's at Watsons Bay, the restaurant famed for its view of the outer reaches of Sydney's famous harbour. It was a warm day but mild compared with the heat and humidity of Springfield where they had been just a few days earlier to celebrate Andrew's sixth birthday.

'I've told your father nothing will induce me to travel north of Sydney in the middle of summer in future,' she said, fanning her face vigorously with the lunch menu. 'I don't know how they live up there all year round.'

Anthony laughed. He wasn't surprised at his mother's distaste for the heat. It didn't suit her pale English skin whereas he hadn't minded that his own pale skin had not survived very long after his return to the warmer climate.

'So that means you won't see the next baby until the winter?'

'Until the winter,' she said, emphasising her determination to avoid the extremes of the Australian climate.

'Does it work for you and Dad?'

'Does what work?' she asked although she understood exactly what was behind the question.

'Not living together full time. Is he happy with the arrangements?'

She paused. They had remarried nearly four years ago, this time at Haldon Hall, with a reception that included all the families who relied on the estate for their living. And the Belleville family who had made the trip to England for the event. It had been a lovely July day.

'Yes, I think so. We knew it would be like this, Anthony.'

'But it didn't work when Paul and I were children.'

'That was different,' she said. 'Very different. You're both adults now. You don't need your parents around you constantly. And travel is easier too.'

'I wonder though if George is disappointed you aren't in England all the time.'

It was only the mention of her youngest son that could make Catherine feel slightly guilty but then, she reasoned, he was away at school most of the year.

'We are taking a holiday to Greece in his summer vacation. He's looking forward to it. He wanted to come and visit me here but his father won't let him. But I told him he'll be eighteen soon. He can make up his own mind then.'

Anthony wasn't surprised at his father's refusal to allow George to travel to Australia but he was disappointed all the same. He liked his half-brother George but he had seen very little of him since his mother's divorce and remarriage.

'Now where are these friends of yours?'

She glanced at her watch. They were certainly late.

'Lachlan can be a bit casual when it comes to meeting times,' he conceded, 'but not the visiting lecturer. I'm surprised. Could be the traffic. He's taking Lachlan and me around one or two of the historic houses this afternoon. I thought you'd like to meet him.'

'And here I was thinking you were simply idling away your summer holidays. But this visiting lecturer, does he have a name? You haven't said.'

At that very moment, a shadow fell across the table.

'Anthony, good to see you. And Mrs Belleville,' he said, extending his hand. 'My name's Daniel Harrington. It's a pleasure to meet you. And I apologise for being late. More traffic than I expected.'

In that fleeting moment, Catherine understood exactly why Anthony had never mentioned the name of the guest lecturer, whose speciality – historic homes – was the subject that most interested Anthony.

'Well, as awkward moments go, Mr Harrington, I think this is right up there,' Catherine replied. 'My son didn't tell me your name. I understand why now but he has extolled your virtues as an architect of some note.'

In their first brief exchange, Daniel Harrington glimpsed in Catherine all the aristocratic breeding he had heard about from his wife Kate, Richard's ex-wife. But he was reassured by her smile.

'Sorry, Mum,' Anthony mumbled, not quite knowing what else to say. How complicated could one family get, he mused.

As Daniel Harrington sat down in the chair Catherine indicated, Anthony understood instinctively how his father would react to the meeting if he knew. Nothing could sugar-coat the fact that the man joining them for lunch was his half-sister Susan's stepfather, a role he relished according to what he'd been told. More disturbing still was the knowledge that Susan loved him in return. And in doing so, her own father had become an almost forgotten figure in her life, which saddened Anthony and his older brother Paul, who now rarely saw her at all.

He was brought back to the present by the noisy arrival of his friend, Lachlan Bell, who remembered just in time the manners his mother had hammered into him.

'How are you, Mrs Belleville?' he asked. 'It's very nice to see you again. You've chosen a lovely day for a harbourside lunch.'

Anthony looked sideways at his friend. He wondered how long his friend had been practising what was obviously a well-rehearsed greeting.

A small smile hovered on Daniel Harrington's lips. He wasn't surprised the imposing Catherine Belleville would have this effect on a young man. He quickly calculated her age. Probably early fifties, he decided. But she was a woman who would still turn heads. He wondered idly if she was indeed the reason he had been able to romance Richard Belleville's second wife. Before he could pursue the thought further, he heard her voice cutting through his reverie.

'So, is my son making progress, Mr Harrington? Will he be ready to turn the world of architecture on its head soon?'

He smiled. She was no different from any of the other mothers he had met in wanting her son to be the best. He was relieved he did not have to be evasive in his answers.

'Your son will make an excellent architect, Mrs Belleville,' he said. 'He's very enthusiastic and he's already wanting to challenge design concepts and ideas. That's a good start.'

He paused.

'And please call me Daniel.'

She nodded, apparently satisfied with the answer or acknowledging the invitation to call him by his first name. He wasn't sure.

'I'm pleased to hear it. By the time he is fully qualified and practising, Haldon Hall may well need a restoration. At least he will be able to oversee it as a professional.'

'But I'll be doing Aunt Julia's project first,' he reminded her.

'Your first professional commission?' his mother asked.

He nodded enthusiastically but Daniel Harrington laughed

'I think Anthony is in danger of getting ahead of himself on this. First step is to research the plans of the original house which burnt down, I understand, many years ago.'

There was silence for a few moments at the table. Daniel Harrington turned towards Catherine.

'He made need your help, Mrs Belleville. He's told me he was too young to remember the house.'

He paused then. Hadn't Anthony told him he was living with his mother in England at the time of the fire? He had been a very small boy.

For Catherine, the memories were not all good. She had never felt at ease in the house. Never felt she belonged, remembering how it was ruled by Richard's mother, Elizabeth Belleville.

She smiled and inclined her head.

'It was a fine house,' she conceded, 'but out of place in its setting. Surely Julia isn't going to build an exact replica?'

Anthony shrugged his shoulders.

'We haven't talked about it yet. But Mr Harrington is right. I need to research the plans of the original house which are held at a university library in Brisbane. A lot of work to do first,' he said, as they all settled to the important task of ordering lunch.

2

FOR THE FIRST TIME in a very long time, Julia Belleville felt at peace with the world. Approaching her fifty-second birthday, she still retained the natural beauty of her younger years but the naiveté was gone. Her world had been shattered by the breakup of her marriage to the man who had been her first and enduring love. Her life looked different now.

She doubted anyone really understood how much his betrayal had hurt her. Or that she had been shattered by the realisation he hadn't loved her the way she had loved him. The ease with which he moved on still hurt her deeply. A scheming, conniving seductress, that's the trap he'd fallen into, she told herself. And he had been powerless.

But in her clearer moments, she knew, deep down, their relationship had been doomed, not by the woman who usurped her, but by her mother's determination to keep them apart.

And then, when they met again, it was too late. They had never quite been able to recapture the love that had once been theirs. Except that somewhere in a forgotten corner of her heart, a small flame continued to flicker as if it refused to be extinguished. As if, somehow, the connection could never quite be severed. Not entirely. Did he feel the same, she sometimes wondered? Had Karen's baby son made the difference she supposed it had? She would never know, not for sure.

She smiled and held out her arms to take baby Jessica.

'She always wants to see you whenever she wakes up,' Pippa said, having brought her daughter onto the verandah at Prior Park.

Jessica's birth the previous year had been a delightful surprise for Julia after the devastation of her marriage breakdown to Pippa's father.

Looking at baby Jessica she could easily imagine how Pippa would have looked at the same age. Fair hair. Blue eyes. She had never known, of course. The tragedy of giving Pippa up for adoption at the time of her birth had never left Julia. She was grateful fate had intervened to allow her to meet her daughter. And now they were close. And despite everything, Pippa was close to her father too.

'It's a pity Joel couldn't get any time off to come up with you,' Julia said. 'He works too hard.'

Pippa shrugged.

'The life of a doctor, I'm afraid.'

You should remember what that was like, she was about to say, but hesitated. She had learnt to be careful about what she said. It was almost as if the life she had lived with both parents was now off limits, knowing that mentioning it was too painful for her mother.

Pippa leant against the verandah rail, gazing in the direction of the pile of weed-covered rubble that was all that remained of the grand mansion that had once stood proudly at the end of the long Prior Park driveway.

'Are you really going to rebuild it?' she asked.

'Yes, I am,' Julia said, the determined note in her voice leaving no room for doubt.

Pippa was about to ask why bother but something stopped her. Was this what her mother most needed? A project to occupy her mind. And she remembered her cousin Anthony's enthusiasm at the prospect of his first architectural commission. The more she thought about it, the more she came to see the benefits.

'What will he work from? Uncle Richard said the plans of the house were in the office and were lost in the fire.'

'We knew that,' her mother replied, 'but Richard remembered being told the history of the house and who the architect had been. Apparently, the architect's papers are with the University of Queensland library. Anthony hopes the plans will be among those papers because it was a significant commission.'

'You've got it all worked out then?'

She had never seen the house. There had been one surviving photograph of it taken by the local newspaper that she had seen years ago. It had never featured in her life the way it had featured in her mother's life or in the lives of her uncles. She always considered the practical country home built to replace it was exactly the right thing for Prior Park. It was welcoming with its wide friendly verandahs and cosy, busy kitchen.

'Not quite, but it soon will be.'

Was this just an expensive folly, Pippa wondered? She had never asked and never been told just how much of his fortune her father had settled on her mother with their divorce but it hadn't had any noticeable impact on her father's lifestyle and ambitions for his philanthropy.

'And Uncle Richard and Uncle William. Are they happy to let you build on Prior Park land? How do they feel about it?'

Her mother shrugged and smiled.

'It's mine now too,' she said, waiting for the expected look of surprised enquiry.

'Yours? How come?'

'Your uncles agreed to me buying into Prior Park Holdings. I'm now an equal shareholder with them.'

'Money from my divorce,' she added somewhat unnecessarily. 'And when I'm gone, it will be John's. I hope you don't mind.'

Pippa nodded. It made sense. With what she would inherit from her father, she didn't need her mother's legacy. Besides, she knew nothing about running rural properties. She was happy for her half-brother John to be added to the beneficiaries and for herself to be excluded.

'I've promised I won't interfere with Richard and William and how they run things. It gives them a chance to expand more quickly but they said they would consult me.'

'Uncle William might be worried you and Uncle Richard could gang up and outvote him though.'

It was the one thought that had occurred to Pippa. The younger of her two uncles was much more conservative.

But her mother dismissed the idea.

'William is very sound in his management of the rural properties. I'm happy for him to just get on with it.'

As they were chatting, they watched Richard's car negotiate the driveway and come to a stop in front of the house.

'Here's trouble,' Pippa chuckled as young Andrew slammed the door of the car and headed at full speed for the front steps.

Little Jessica, startled by the sudden arrival, snuggled closer to her grandmother as if for protection.

Pippa caught the young tearaway and scooped him up.

'Not so fast,' she said as he squirmed to be let go.

'I'm going riding,' he declared. 'I've got to get my riding boots.'

Everyone knew he was proud of his riding boots which had been a gift from Santa. They were now lined up in the boot room at Prior Park alongside all the other boots.

Pippa raised a questioning eyebrow in Richard's direction.

'I can't put him off any longer,' he sighed.

And they all laughed. Julia could see her brother was enjoying the role of grandfather. Like her, he had been through a painful divorce but unlike her, he had gone back and remarried his first wife. Even though she refused to spend much time *in the wilds* with him, as she described their life in the tropics, the marriage seemed to be going well the second time around.

'How's your little one?' he asked Pippa. 'A bit young for riding lessons yet. And Marianne? She's not here?'

Julia shook her head.

'Alice expects her soon, apparently. Why do you ask?'

Richard smiled.

'No reason. I ran into Alex in town and he said she was headed this way.'

He looked at his sister closely. To him, she appeared more

settled. Was it the fact that she now had her own stake in Prior Park, that she was no longer just a visitor. It was as if she actually had a purpose in her life now.

'William and I are meeting with the accountants tomorrow. You should come along,' he suggested. She had been an equal shareholder since the beginning of the year.

'Good idea,' she said. 'I'll keep an eye on you and William.'

He laughed. He had never revealed William had been less enthusiastic about her participation, worried, as only William could worry, that she might interfere. Richard had settled the matter with a sharp reminder. *You owe her this, William. You owe her this.*

William hadn't needed reminding of the part he had played in separating her from Philippe during their wartime love affair. He had simply nodded and signed the agreement without further comment.

Belleville Holdings now belonged to three people – Richard, William and Julia. And William was content. The next generation – Paul, Anthony, Susan, Marianne and now John – would step up when the time came. But Richard had added a provision. Paul would be custodian of Susan's share. William had made no comment beyond a nod of approval.

'We're pleased John is being added in as a beneficiary.' He smiled at Pippa. 'No disrespect, Pippa, but John will work well with his cousins. Your Dad isn't going to leave you poor.'

And then he wished he hadn't mentioned Philippe. Mentioning his name was still off limits at Prior Park.

'It's fine, Uncle Richard,' she said. 'John will be the right man in the right place. At this rate, Belleville interests will extend to the far horizon.'

He laughed. There was something to be said for that, he thought. Paul's wife Amanda now controlled her father's holdings, including nearby Armoobilla, since his death nearly two years earlier. John would inherit Mayfield Downs, next door to Prior Park, from his father James.

'That's how rural dynasties are made, Pippa. Wasn't that how kingdoms were advanced in the old world? Marriages between royal families.'

Pippa considered this for a few moments.

'It was your grandmother who brought Prior Park into the family, wasn't it?'

Richard nodded. He had been interested enough when he was younger to ask his father about the history of the property. And of the house.

'She did. It was the dowry my grandmother Adeline Prior brought to her marriage to my grandfather Louis Belleville. It was land her father had selected as the area was opened up for settlement. But there was no big house in those days. My grandfather apparently promised her family he would build a good home on it.'

He paused, digging deep into his memory for half-forgotten information he'd had no reason to recall for years.

'Louis Belleville was a man of grand gestures, I remember my father telling me. He had made some money in Victoria in the early days, so he used a substantial amount of it building the house. From what I was told, my grandmother couldn't cope with the heat. She liked the house but not the area. I believe she spent most of her time at their house in Melbourne. When my father married, she insisted it be given to him and his new bride. Within a few years, both my grandparents were both gone. My father was their only child.'

'You never knew them?' Pippa asked.

He shook his head.

'No, they both died within months of each other when I was a baby I was told.'

He remembered the heavy framed photograph of his grandparents. It too had been lost in the Prior Park fire. There had been nothing left to remember the family or their history. Nothing left to remind them of the earliest days of Prior Park. It was a loss still keenly felt.

Andrew, having stood quietly beside his grandfather, finally lost patience and tugged at his trouser leg.

'We're going riding, Grandad. We're going now.'

They all laughed. He could be a persistent child.

'We are indeed,' Richard said with a smile as he patted the boy's head. 'We are indeed.'

Together they headed towards the boot room.

Alex hesitated. He was about to head back to Prior Park. Should he check on Amanda again? She had seemed out of sorts the previous evening when he had called to see her. Or was he imagining it?

Would she, like him, always feel like an outsider in the Belleville family? Not quite belonging. She at least had her own properties. He still felt the lack of ownership himself. Marianne might have taken the name Fraser but she would always be a Belleville. It was her name that would eventually appear as a shareholder in Belleville Holdings, not his. Is that why he was still drawn to Amanda?

He stopped in front of her house and hesitated for a few moments. He noticed the front door was open. Just a quick stop, he promised himself, as he headed towards the front stairs. He peered through the open door and called out to her when his knock went unanswered.

Silence.

He called out again.

This time, a muffled voice called out a greeting. He walked down the hallway to the kitchen where he found her sitting at the kitchen table. A discarded crumpled letter lay in front of her.

And then he noticed her face. She had been crying. He walked quickly to where she was sitting and sat down beside her.

'What's up? What's the matter?'

His voice was quiet but his words were urgent. He had rarely seen Amanda cry. She was strong. Independent. Resourceful. Wilful. She was all of those things and more. But he could see something – or someone – had upset her.

He pressed her again.

'What's the matter? Tell me what's up?'

She thrust the crumpled letter into his hands.

'This is what's up. For my entire life, my father – my adored indulgent father – lied to me. He said my mother was dead.'

She sobbed loudly.

'I believed him. I never questioned him.'

Alex read the letter quickly, skimming some parts of the long, rambling story.

'When did this arrive?'

'With the post a couple of hours ago,' she said.

He glanced at the letter again. He was beginning to understand exactly why Amanda was upset. And angry.

'She says she agreed with your father to tell you she had died because she couldn't continue to keep in touch with you. She had married again. Her new husband didn't know she'd already had a child.'

He was beginning to make sense of it now. He tried to remember what he'd heard about Amanda's mother as he was growing up.

'But why is she contacting you now, after all this time?'

Amanda shook her head.

'She doesn't say specifically but she says her husband died a few months ago. And she had seen a newspaper report of my father's death, she says.'

Alex put his arm around her.

'I can see it's been a shock to you,' he said gently.

'More than a shock,' she admitted, 'but why tell me a lie? Why not tell me the truth?'

He shrugged.

'Your father probably had his reasons for going along with the plan,' he offered.

Is that what had drawn him towards Amanda, he wondered? Her loss of a mother. His loss of a mother. Was it because they had this in common. But in his case, he never knew for sure who his father was. A bastard child no one had laid claim to.

He almost never thought about it now. After all, his life was secure. A lovely wife who doted on him. A delightful young daughter. Work he enjoyed. None of this he ever thought would be possible. Not until he met Marianne.

But he had made a sacrifice too. Willingly. But sometimes – just sometimes – he wished for something he could not have. He tried not to let himself dwell on what might have been.

He had slipped up once – only once – and the guilt had never left him. And the fear too. The fear that a young boy – a Belleville heir of the future – would turn out to be what? A cuckoo in the nest? He prayed it wasn't so. But he knew there was one other member of the Belleville family who harboured suspicions. Apart from Amanda, that is. Silence was the only possible response, he had decided.

Amanda shook her head slowly from side to side.

'What do I do about this?' she asked, waving the letter. 'She wants to meet me. She writes that she is sorry about what happened. Sorry that she had to leave me behind.'

For the first time he could remember, Alex sensed uncertainty and indecision in Amanda. She had always been so sure of what she would do and quick to make decisions. He had never seen her like this before. Vulnerable. Unsure of herself.

'What do *you* want to do about it?' he asked. 'That's the important question.'

He could see she was struggling to take everything in, including the enormity of the lie her father had perpetuated. Was it for her protection? Did he do that to protect her from the disappointment of having a mother who hadn't cared about her? Not cared enough to fight for her. Or was he being unfair in even thinking that?

'There were so many times when I was growing up that I was desperate for a mother,' she said after a long pause. 'Away at school, all the girls spoke of their mothers. Everywhere I went. All the other girls talked about their mothers. I seemed to be the only child without a mother. It made me different. It made me stand out.'

Tears flowed then in a way Alex had never seen before, as if the memory of all the deliberate snubs and cruel comments had suddenly bubbled to the surface, suppressed for too many years.

'I had no idea,' he murmured. 'No idea at all. You always

seemed so confident. So much in control. It was what I loved about you.'

It was an admission he made without thinking. And then he wondered if he too had added to her feeling of abandonment.

'Loved?' She looked up at him, the challenge in her words implicit. 'If you had really loved me, you would not have deserted me the way you did. Am I someone people desert? First my mother. Then you. Will Paul desert me eventually too?'

Her question shocked him. He had never considered the possibility her marriage to Paul Belleville would not survive. Were there early signs he hadn't noticed? Paul seemed happy. Contented. A doting father.

He shook his head. What could he say? It was a conversation they should not be having. Not now. Had she forgotten why he had chosen Marianne instead of her? Had she forgotten how vehemently her father had opposed their marriage? Or how she had said she wouldn't go against her father to accept his proposal. But it was hardly the time to remind her. And Paul? What was it in their relationship that made her doubt him?

'Of course Paul won't desert you. He loves you. You know that. He worships you and little Andrew.'

She shrugged. He guessed nothing would convince her at that moment that she was loved and cherished.

He picked up the letter again. Her mother's life had been unremarkable. Married to a man who worked for the railways. She had given birth to three more children, two girls and a boy, but one of the girls had died in infancy.

One paragraph caught Alex's eye.

'Times are a bit tough now that I'm a widow,' she had written. 'Sadly, I never received all the money your father offered me to stay away from you.'

He began to speculate. Now that Amanda was in full control of her father's wealth, had her mother decided the time was right to push for a settlement from the daughter she had abandoned. Did Amanda's father really offer her money to stay away from Amanda? Or was it meant as a generous gesture to help her settle into a new life? Was it really the cold, calculated transaction she was suggesting? It seemed to Alex to contradict what she had written earlier in the letter.

He sat back in his chair. He remembered then his earlier encounter with Richard.

'Richard was close to your father in his last years. Why don't you ask his advice? There's always a possibility your father confided things to him he didn't share with you.'

She was doubtful but she did not dismiss the idea, as he feared she might.

'Do you think he would know anything?'

'Not sure, but I know he'll help if he can,' Alex replied confidently.

Of the two brothers, he knew Richard was the one who might be able to guide her. For once in her life, it seemed to Alex that Amanda really needed advice.

She shifted in her chair then and smoothed her hand over her stomach.

'I'm hoping he comes early,' she said quietly. 'I need him to come early.'

He ignored her remark. It wasn't a conversation he wanted to encourage.

'I'm heading back to Prior Park now. Richard will be dropping Andrew back home this afternoon. Why don't I have a chat to him on the quiet?'

She nodded. Perhaps Alex was right. She liked Richard. And she knew her father had liked him too. Perhaps he could help her decide. Should she agree to a meeting with her mother? Or should she write back, telling her she wanted no contact with her?

'I'll talk to Richard,' she said finally as she walked with Alex to the front door.

3

LATER THAT AFTERNOON, Richard knocked on the front door of Amanda's house but without the expected six-year-old alongside him. He greeted Amanda warmly.

'Your little boy declared he wanted to spend the night at Prior Park. I saw no reason to say no to him. He'll get fussed over alongside little Melanie. They're great pals.'

Amanda laughed quietly.

'I've noticed how he trails around after little Mel,' she said as she led the way into the kitchen. 'I suppose Marianne was out there because your brother is away.'

He simply nodded, not sure if he should be the one to reveal the reason for her visit to Prior Park.

'Alice doesn't lack for company at the moment. You know you're always welcome to go out and stay at Prior Park too when Paul's away.'

The offer had been made repeatedly but she had never taken it up. She could never escape the feeling she was less important than Marianne. But in her rational moments, she knew that was only to be expected. Marianne had grown up at Prior Park. It might be the centre of Belleville family life but it was also her parents' home.

'Ready for a beer?' she asked, having already taken a cold bottle from the fridge.

Richard accepted it with alacrity. It had been a hot day with no breeze.

'How did the riding lessons go?'

She had been a little nervous. At just six years old, she thought riding lessons could have waited another year. But Andrew had been insistent. In the end, she had agreed. After all she trusted Richard to be careful with him. She knew there was a docile mare at Prior Park kept especially for the purpose of the children's first riding lessons.

'He went well,' Richard said. 'Impatient of course. He wanted to manage the horse himself but there was no way I was allowing him to do that. We just did a few circuits of the yards. And I showed him how to take care of a horse, which he was less enthusiastic about.'

She smiled. Hearing that did not surprise her. It was the way she had been taught too.

'Alex tells me you've had some surprising news.'

He looked at her enquiringly across the kitchen table, unsure whether she really wanted to confide in him. He noticed she hadn't got a beer for herself. Instead, she was drinking a glass of lemonade.

She put her glass down on the table and picked up the letter which lay open in front of her and held it out towards him.

'Surprising is one way to describe the news that my mother – the mother I thought was long dead – is alive. My father lied to me, Richard,' she said, with more emphasis than she intended.

Richard was cautious. He had been the recipient of certain confidences from her father. Was this the time to share them? How would she react to finding out he had known for years that her mother was still alive? But he knew he had to risk her anger. Hadn't he told Howard Robinson everyone has a right to know about their parents?

'Your father told me about your mother when you and Paul were getting married. I think it troubled him towards the end. I think perhaps he felt he'd made a mistake in telling you she was dead, but then he couldn't undo that mistake. Not without risking his relationship with you, which meant everything to him.'

'You meant everything to him,' he said, wanting to be sure she

21

understood what her father had done was what he thought was in his daughter's best interests.

She listened in silence. And then she spoke.

'And you never thought I deserved to know? You never thought it was right to tell me?'

There was an anger towards him she had never shown before. What could he say in his defence? He hadn't thought it was his place to reveal what her father had told him. But that excuse sounded lame. Who else was ever going to tell her the truth about her mother, once her father had died? Who else knew the truth?

'Tell me exactly what he told you,' she demanded, not waiting for an explanation. 'Tell me exactly what he said. Every word.'

He proceeded to tell her the story he had been told – that her mother had been twenty, her father forty years old, when she was born and that the age difference and the remote living had proven too much for her mother. Her father had forbidden her mother to take Amanda with her.

'He didn't tell me how they met,' Richard said. 'He only told me the bare facts. That she had remarried, her new husband didn't know she'd already had a child so she wrote to your father to say it wouldn't be possible for her to keep in touch with you. It was then she suggested your father should tell you she had died. I imagine she thought it would be better than you thinking your mother hadn't made the effort – or couldn't make the effort – to be part of your life.'

It was all he knew. Just the simple facts. He looked at the letter she held out to him and read through it quickly. Was it a remorseful letter, apologising for the deception? Or a hopeful letter? His immediate reaction was to worry it might be nothing more than an appeal for money from the newly-wealthy daughter she had walked away from all those years ago. Could Amanda cope with such a disappointment, he wondered? And then a thought occurred to him. It was a long shot but worth asking.

'Was there any private correspondence included in your father's papers? Any personal papers?'

She shook her head.

'Surprisingly little,' she said, 'but of course most of the early stuff was probably at Isla Downs.'

Richard remembered his conversation with her father. How the old housekeeper at Isla Downs had sought her father out. Is it possible she would know more? He hesitated. The mention of the old housekeeper might lead to other, even more unwelcome revelations, but was he right to withhold the suggestion?

'Another time, your father was telling me he met the old housekeeper – whose name I can't remember – from Isla Downs. I think it was around the time you and Paul were getting married. I don't know if she would know anything about your mother but he told me she now lives here with her sister. She might be a good age though if she's still alive. Do you remember her?'

Amanda nodded and smiled, as if the memory of the old housekeeper was a happy one.

'Elsie. That would be Elsie,' she said. 'She rather mothered me when I was around. As she did Alex too. She'd make us special treats. We were always hanging around her kitchen.'

Her mood brightened.

'I wonder if we could find Elsie. She would know. She would know so much. About my father. About my mother probably.'

She frowned then, as if trying hard to remember.

'I don't know her surname. But Tony Bland has been around a long time. He would know. He might even know where she lives now.'

Tony Bland, her one-time suitor, had become a loyal and dedicated manager of her properties. It had suited her for him to take over most of the responsibility of managing the properties her father had left her.

Richard had endorsed her decision to elevate Tony Bland to oversee everything. He's a good cattle man, he had said approvingly. Richard was relieved he hadn't harboured any ill-feelings when Amanda had turned him down. He had simply moved on and married a country girl. Together they had turned out to be the ideal couple to take charge of the Robinson rural properties.

For Richard, Amanda's keenness to meet with the old housekeeper raised another concern. But perhaps it was unfounded, he decided. Would the old lady suddenly volunteer what she knew about the identity of Alex's father without being prompted? He hoped not. But having mentioned her name, there was no way now to curb Amanda's enthusiasm to meet Elsie again. He would just have to hope the topic of Alex never came up.

It was only a matter of days later that Amanda sought out the modest cottage Elsie Graham shared with her sister Gertrude. The old lady beamed, recognition spreading across her weathered features.

'My little Mandy,' she said, reverting to Amanda's childhood name. 'It's lovely to see you. Come in. Come in.'

At eighty-one, the old lady, now permanently stooped, used a walking stick but otherwise she appeared sprightly.

'I was so pleased to hear from you when you rang. I didn't know if your father had ever mentioned I lived here now, God rest his soul,' she said, looking towards the heavens. 'He was a good man. A tough man but a good man.'

Amanda hesitated. Should she tell her it was Tony Bland who had told her where Elsie lived now? She decided against it.

'I was in hospital when your father died,' she said, as if she needed to explain why she hadn't been in touch. 'Broken hip. I didn't find out about his passing until months later. Too late then to get in touch. I knew you'd got married though. You're Mrs Belleville now, I understand.'

Amanda smiled. She was Mrs Belleville. But she still felt she was Amanda Robinson. She still signed cheques, Amanda Robinson.

Elsie led the way to a small, neat sitting room.

'This is my sister, Gertrude,' she said.

Gertrude smiled a greeting.

'Elsie has told me so much about you Amanda,' she said sweetly. 'Such a pretty girl, she said, and she's right.'

And then they both began to fuss as they realised the advanced state of Amanda's pregnancy.

'Your second baby, if I'm not mistaken,' Elsie said, pointing

Amanda in the direction of the most comfortable armchair. 'We shouldn't keep you standing around in your condition.'

Amanda protested she felt fine but sat down to please Elsie.

'Gertrude will pour some tea and you can tell me why you were so anxious to see me. Something about your mother, you said.' And then she shook her head. 'I'm not sure I can help you very much but I will try.'

For just a moment, Amanda hesitated. How to begin? She was suddenly very unsure. Elsie filled the silence.

'Your mother Rose was a vivacious girl. Full of laughter. Spirited you might call her. We called her Rosie. Your father was besotted with her.'

Amanda, startled by the sudden mention of a name she hadn't heard out loud in years, almost dropped the cup and saucer Gertrude had just handed across to her. She took a deep breath. This had to be the start of the story, she decided. It had to start at the beginning. Or at least at the beginning of her mother's relationship with her father.

'Where did my father meet my mother?' Amanda asked. She realised so much detail was missing from what her father had told her over the years. Was he trying to protect her? Or had he thought none of the detail was important? Or likely to be of interest to her.

'It's all a bit vague,' Elsie admitted, 'but I think she was visiting friends or relatives in the area. She hadn't long left school in Melbourne, that I do know.'

And then the realisation hit Amanda. She knew nothing about her mother, beyond her name and the one photograph of her parents on their wedding day. What seemed like a thousand questions crowded her mind. Who were her parents? Did she have siblings? Where was she born? Was there more to the story of the marriage breakdown than her father had told her?

'How long had he known her before they got married?' Amanda was curious. Her father had said her mother was only twenty when she was born. That much she knew. 'Did they marry quite quickly?'

Elsie smiled as if Amanda should already have guessed they married quickly.

'Yes, it was very quick,' she said. 'Less than a year after they met, I would guess. She wasn't showing though, that I do remember.'

'Showing?'

And then the truth dawned on Amanda. Her father had married her mother because he had got her pregnant.

'You didn't know, did you?'

Amanda shook her head.

'No, he was always vague about when they actually got married. Said he couldn't remember for sure. He said she couldn't handle the isolation and that when I was a toddler, she told him she wanted to leave him. She did leave but he refused to let her take me with her. But she left anyway. And then he told me a couple of years later she had died. And that was that.'

Elsie nodded, the sadness in her face hard to miss.

'He told us all the same story at Isla Downs. His wife had left and he was getting a divorce. You were to stay with him. He hired a nursemaid initially. And then a few years later, he said, very offhandedly one day, that your mother had died. No details. No discussion. Just that your mother had died.'

She paused, remembering the scene. Remembering the sadness they had all felt for the little girl.

'And that was that. Nothing more was ever said. But we all knew the real reason she had left of course. It was nothing to do with the isolation of Isla Downs or Glenmoral where they lived a good part of the time.'

Amanda looked up, startled by the revelation. It was what she had always believed. Her mother couldn't cope living at the isolated properties. What else could it have been?

There was silence then. Elsie began to fuss with the tea table, pressing more cake on Amanda. Why did I say that? She began to berate herself silently. Did Amanda really need to know the sordid truth about her father? But Amanda was not easily sidetracked.

'What was the real reason she left, Elsie? Tell me. What was the real reason?' she demanded. 'I'm old enough now to know the truth.'

'Elizabeth Fraser was the real reason your mother left, I'm sorry to say.'

'Elizabeth Fraser? Alex's mother? What has she got to do with it?'

Elsie sat very still. Should she really be the one to tell Amanda the whole truth? The unvarnished, ugly truth behind her parents' marriage break up.

'Do you really want to know this, Amanda?' she asked, in a firm quiet voice. 'It's all so far in the past. You have a good life. Your father has left you well provided for. Your future is assured. My advice is to let the ghosts of the past rest in peace.'

Amanda shook her head slowly from side to side.

'It would haunt me, Elsie, not to know the truth. If it's something bad, I can handle it. I promise I can handle it. It's not knowing that's the worst.'

Elsie took a deep breath.

'Your father and your father's cousin Arthur were both very taken by Elizabeth Fraser. She was a gentlewoman in every sense of the word. Well spoken. Well educated. Charming. Very refined. But the family in Scotland had fallen on hard times so she had come out to take a job as a governess to Arthur's son, Alan. I think your father fell in love with her. As did his cousin. And I think your mother found out and confronted your father. And he didn't deny it. That was enough for her. She wouldn't stay with a man who didn't love her anymore.'

This was all new to Amanda.

'I don't remember it but was this the time he was sent to one of the Robinson family properties up in the gulf? What was to happen to me?'

Elsie let out a deep sigh.

'Yes, he was sent there by his cousin, against his will. Getting him out of the way, I would think. Your mother left and returned to Melbourne. You remained at Isla Downs in the care of a nurse-maid and Arthur's wife, Maureen. And of course, by this time Elizabeth was pregnant.'

'To my father?'

Elsie noticed the quick intake of breath, at first misunderstanding the reason for it. And then realising what Amanda was thinking.

'No, Arthur was the father of her baby. I know that for sure. She confided in me. But I do know your father thought it was possible he was the father.'

Amanda buried her head in her hands and let out a shuddering sob. It all made sense now.

'My father vehemently opposed any thought of my marrying Alex. Is that the reason? He thought he might have been Alex's father. Do you know?'

Old Elsie sat back in her chair, tired by the revelations, concerned by them too. Would she have been better to have stuck to the bare bones of the story? But there was something about Amanda now that demanded honesty.

She nodded slowly.

'About the time it was announced you were marrying Paul Belleville I got in touch with him. Something was niggling at me. I knew you and Alex were keen on one another. And I heard on the grapevine before I left Isla Downs that your father was keen to get rid of him. Then I heard Alex moved up this way and then you and your father moved too.'

She paused, looking at Amanda for the silent confirmation that Alex's move had prompted her to come to the area. She went on.

'I contacted your father and asked him straight out if he had been opposed to your marrying Alex because he was uncertain as to who Alex's father was. He said that was the reason, so I told him what I knew. That Elizabeth Fraser had confided in me that Arthur was Alex's father. When she and your father … well, you know what I mean … she was already pregnant.'

Elsie gave a shake of her head, remembering the sadness of that time.

'And then she died a few weeks after Alex was born, before your father could get back from the gulf. It wasn't easy in those days. And Alex was brought up as something of an embarrassment. A poor orphan child with no parents. And no prospects. And you and your father spent more time at some of the other properties although we saw you during the holiday times.'

Amanda sat for a long time, not moving, not speaking, but

taking in everything she'd been told. And the father she had loved and adored? He was not the man she thought he was. Lying to cover up his own shortcomings. Telling her an enormous lie that had blighted her life. And then separating her from Alex.

'Why the interest all of a sudden?' Elsie asked quietly, feeling perhaps it was the question she should have asked in the beginning.

Amanda pulled the crumpled letter from the pocket of her dress and held it up.

'I received a letter from my mother a few days ago,' she said. 'As you can see, she isn't dead as my father told me she was.'

Elsie gasped, not knowing what to say. What could she say? She'd had no idea they had all been lied to. She waited for Amanda to go on with the story.

'She told me her husband had died. She went on to have three more children, two girls and a boy but one girl died in infancy. She said her husband hadn't known she'd had a child previously and that's why she couldn't keep in touch with me. She didn't say anything more than that.'

There was silence in the room for some time after Amanda finished speaking. And then Elsie spoke, her voice breaking with emotion.

'My poor girl,' she said, as she got up and awkwardly put her arm around Amanda. 'What an awful shock for you.' She let out a long sigh. 'A terrible shock.' And then she corrected herself. 'A terrible shock but good news really.'

But then she began to wonder. Was it really good news for Amanda? Had Rosie lived a good life after leaving Howard? Or had life not been kind to her? Either way, she would be a much different person from the lively young girl of Elsie's memory.

She was cautious. Should she warn Amanda? Or simply share her excitement that her mother was alive?

'She'll be a lot different from the girl I remember,' Elsie said quietly. 'You know she may want some money now if her husband has died. Her circumstances might not be so good.'

Amanda nodded. Would her mother really write for that purpose, and that purpose only? And why shouldn't she share some of the Robinson inheritance anyway? It seemed she had left with nothing. Or almost nothing.

'What was she like, Elsie, when she was young?'

'As I said, she was vivacious. She liked having fun. She liked flirting with the young men. I don't think your father had ever met anyone like her. But I think the differences in their temperaments were always going to lead to trouble in the end. It just came a bit sooner than anyone expected.'

Amanda let out a deep sigh. She pulled herself out of the armchair, the weight of the baby suddenly feeling heavier than usual.

'Elsie, I'm so grateful to you for telling me everything. There was so much I didn't know.'

The elderly woman smiled broadly. Whatever happened, she was satisfied. She had simply told Amanda the truth. And she said a silent prayer that everything would turn out well, because, above all else, little Mandy deserved to have a happy life.

'Not long now by the look of it,' Gertrude said. 'Another bouncing boy perhaps?'

'Probably,' Amanda said, as if she had suddenly lost interest in the impending birth. Paul had pressured her to have another child. There would be no more after this one.

But one thing was for sure, the name Howard wouldn't feature among the new baby's names. The revelations of the morning had shattered the carefully manufactured myth her father had created. And that would take her some time to come to terms with.

She was now set on a definite path. She would write to her mother as soon as she got home. And she would send money. Wasn't that the very least her mother deserved? And her father? How would she hold him in her memory now? On that point, she was still undecided. Very undecided.

And Alex? A wave of disappointment engulfed her. What might have been had they known the truth? She tried to shut out the thoughts from her mind. It was too late. All too late … Alex married to Marianne; she married to Paul. It would tear the Belleville family apart to upend their marriages.

I love Paul, she reminded herself, I love Paul. But Alex haunted her dreams still …

31

4

AMANDA SAT AT HER kitchen table, numerous sheets of writing paper discarded on the table around her, all of them failed attempts to reply to the letter from her mother.

She grabbed her chequebook. That at least she could do easily. But how much to send? Or should she send anything at all? Would her mother regard it as an insult? The thought had only just occurred to her. In the end, she decided against sending money. It might get everything off on the wrong track.

As she sat deep in thought surrounded by a pile of discarded paper, she did not hear Paul walk through the house until he called her name. She turned around, startled.

He put his arms around her and kissed her lightly.

'What's all this?' he said, pointing to the crumpled balls of paper.

She put down her pen. She was pleased to have him home. Someone to talk to about it all. Well, perhaps not all of it. Not about Alex.

'How was the trip?' she asked. He had been away longer than expected. 'I thought you'd be home sooner.'

He rolled his eyes.

'Trouble at the place out near Longreach. In the end, Uncle William had to sack the manager. He seemed to be the source of the problem, not the workers.'

'Did it get nasty?'

He shook his head as he reached for a cold beer from the fridge.

'Mutual agreement. He agreed he wasn't suited to the life out west. Uncle William gave him a fair settlement. I think he was relieved in the end.'

'And a replacement?'

'A young bloke who was brought up on one of the neighbouring properties. He's been working on our property out there for a year. It's a step up but we think he'll do a good job. But it all took days longer than we expected to sort out.'

She was thoughtful for a moment.

'In twenty years' time, do you realise this will be your job? To take control of everything.'

He laughed as he flipped the lid off his beer.

'I'll send Marianne to sort it out.'

'Not your architect brother?'

It was a regular joke. No one could quite see what role Anthony would fulfil in the Belleville family rural business in the years to come. Paul knew though that his father had hopes of him taking over running the commercial interests which he had overseen for years.

'Or maybe John?' he suggested. No one much mentioned Susan in these discussions. Through her absence, she had become Paul's forgotten sister

Amanda shrugged. That was more of a possibility. She knew Paul was happy his cousin would now be included in the Belleville inheritance. It put them all on an equal footing.

'It's funny, isn't it, in a strange way. In the end, John will be the one to benefit from your aunt's divorce settlement.'

Paul smiled. She was right, he thought. Life has some strange twists and turns. They were all happy their Aunt Julia had moved on from the two-timing American. Except Pippa, of course. But still, Paul remembered, with immense gratitude, the expert medical care he had received under Philippe Duval's supervision. He doubted he would have survived without it. Whenever he was in the pilot's seat now, he was on heightened alert for birds. The fear of bird strike would never leave him.

He looked around.

'No Andrew?'

He had expected to be greeted by an excited shriek as he came through the house but it had all been quiet.

'Still at Prior Park,' she explained. 'Your father took him out there a few days ago. He's having his first riding lessons. Alice and Marianne are looking after him.'

'Spoiling him, you mean,' Paul said with a smile. He knew Amanda would be quite relieved by the arrangement, even though she wouldn't admit it. He had come to accept she didn't enjoy the day-to-day work of looking after a small boy. Much like my mother really, he thought.

'He's happy out there,' she said. 'Anyway, he'll be off to school next week. The last days of summer freedom.'

He laughed. There had been a great fuss acquiring new uniforms.

'And you? How have you been?' he asked finally. 'You look tired. And you haven't explained what all this is?'

He pointed to the mess of discarded attempts at letter writing strewn across the kitchen table.

She let out a long sigh of frustration.

'I'm trying to write to my mother,' she said simply, as if there was no other way to begin the story.

He looked perplexed.

'But your mother's dead.'

And then he noticed the slow shake of the head. She held out her mother's letter. He read through it quickly.

'But your father …'

And then words failed him. He knew the story. She had told him of course. Or perhaps someone else had told him. Maybe it was his father, he couldn't be sure now. But somehow, he knew the story. That her mother had left her father when she was a toddler and then later, her mother had died. That was it. She hadn't even had a name. It was almost as if she was not a real person because she had never been a real person in Amanda's life.

He struggled to take in this news. His thoughts immediately went to his own mother. How old was he when his parents had split up? Eleven or twelve years old? He couldn't remember now for sure. But it had felt like a loss. It had almost felt like a death in the family at the time. But now they had remarried, and he and his brother were delighted. And yet still there were parts of his growing up she had missed because of that separation. How must Amanda feel, he wondered, never having shared anything she could remember with her mother? And now this.

'Yes. My father told me she had died. But the truth is, she couldn't keep in touch with me because she married again. Her husband didn't know she'd had a child to her previous husband. So she and my father decided between them to tell me she had died. My father would have thought it was the easy way out.'

She hesitated, thinking back to the scant details of the story and how evasive he had been about how she had died.

'I just accepted the story. Didn't question it. I could never imagine my father would tell me such a lie. It never occurred to me.'

Tears began to flow unchecked. Paul reached out and held her in his arms, wanting to comfort her, trying desperately to understand how she felt. He knew she was angry with her father but was she pleased? Or was she in two minds? Had it been easier to imagine what her mother might have been like than to find out she was still alive and all the uncertainty that came with that knowledge?

'What are you planning to say to her in the letter?' he asked finally.

'What do you think I should say?' she asked.

Her question surprised him. She almost never asked his advice as if she never needed it. But he sensed there was something different about this. It was as if the shocking news had undermined her very sense of herself. Was she worried her mother would find her wanting in some way? He worried, in turn, she would find her mother wanting.

'I think you should write back and ask her to come for a visit,' he said, his voice reassuring and calm. 'Be honest with her. Tell her why you can't travel at the present time. She'll understand.'

'She may not be able to afford the plane ticket,' she said, immediately thinking of the practicalities.

'Then send her a cheque but make the offer first. Besides it would be better if she came after the baby is born.'

He wondered if this second baby would surprise them and come weeks early as Andrew had done. There was no way of knowing. Secretly he hoped for another boy. There had been two Belleville boys in each generation, his father Richard and his Uncle William and himself and his brother Anthony. He hoped Andrew would have the companionship of a brother too. Someone to share the load with. Or at least he hoped Anthony would share the load with him in future, just as his Uncle William had shared the load with his father.

'We haven't talked about names,' he ventured. He hoped it would distract her to think about possible names for the new baby.

She shook her head.

'I haven't thought about names because I named Andrew. I always thought you would name this baby. It could be a girl you know.'

He shrugged.

'Adam, perhaps, for a boy. Sarah for a girl.'

'Andrew and Adam. Too much alike,' she said with a smile, immediately wanting to overturn his suggestion. 'What about Matthew?'

'Let's wait and see,' he said. 'You're probably right about Adam though. Now what are you going to do about this letter?'

She turned back towards the table and began to write on a fresh sheet of paper. This time she managed the letter without feeling dissatisfied with it. He read it through over her shoulder.

'That's good,' he said. 'Post it tomorrow and we'll see what happens then.'

But there was a part of the story she didn't tell Paul. She had breathed a sigh of relief he had never probed the reasons for her mother leaving her father. He had simply accepted the story of her mother's unhappiness with the remote living.

But Alex? How would he react to knowing the real reason why her father had kept them apart? How would he feel? How did she feel? Did it matter now as it might once have mattered? It was a question she could not answer. Not truthfully.

She was happy with Paul. As happy as she expected to be in a marriage. Or rather, as happy as she expected to be within the constraints of marriage and motherhood. But there were times she regretted the loss of her independence. But had she ever really had independence?

Not for the first time did it occur to her that she had gone from being her father's constant companion to being a wife and mother, with all the expectations that entailed. A marriage she hadn't wanted. But pregnancy had forced her hand. Had made it necessary. No, more than necessary. She knew, deep down, her pregnancy had made marriage essential. And Paul idolised his son.

At Prior Park, Richard relaxed on the verandah with his brother William and his wife, Alice.

The heat had just about gone from the day. Another day without any sign of rain. Baking heat had sapped most of the remaining moisture from the paddocks around Prior Park.

'Alex thinks we should lighten the cattle load here,' William said, as they gazed out on an horizon devoid of storm clouds.

'He's probably right,' Richard agreed. 'Are you going to book some cattle into the meatworks before they lose too much condition?'

'I'll do it tomorrow,' William said. 'It depends on whether we can get a slot.'

'It's not too much for you having the little tearaway is it, Alice?' Richard asked, aware that Alice was once again being expected to look after a small child who wasn't her own. With William back home, Marianne and little Melanie had headed back to their own home that afternoon.

Alice shook her head.

'Like old times, isn't it?' she said, good-naturedly. 'Remember when Catherine suddenly headed to England when her father became ill and you were left with two little boys to look after.'

He smiled. As a family, they owed Alice a great deal.

'I do, Alice, and I've always been eternally grateful to you. I know Amanda's grateful too, especially with what's just happened.'

He paused then. Should he tell them her news? But having hinted at it, the ever alert Alice raised her eyebrows.

'What's happened with Amanda? Not something to do with the baby, is it?'

He shook his head, unsure then how to tell the story.

'Remember when I asked you to help with Amanda's wedding dress? You asked me then about her mother and I told you the truth – that Amanda didn't know she was still alive. She had been told she had died.'

Alice nodded.

'I remember thinking how sad for the girl, not to have a mother to take care of her.'

Richard sighed deeply.

'Well, that mother she thought was dead has written to her. She got the letter a few days ago. She asked my advice because she knew I had been on good terms with her father.'

Both William and Alice expressed shock at the unexpected news. William, inevitably, was the first to voice his concerns.

'Amanda's a substantial heiress now. I wonder if the mother knew that. Or is that too cynical?'

Richard was cautious in his answer.

'I was inclined to think that was a possibility too. I don't think the mother's well off. She told Amanda her husband passed away a few months ago. That's the reason she could write and finally get in touch with Amanda. It may be well intentioned.'

'And how is Amanda going to respond?' Alice asked.

Like William, she thought such a bolt from the blue raised more questions than it answered.

'I don't know for sure,' he said, 'but I told her about something her father hadn't obviously told her – that the old housekeeper from Isla Downs, the Robinson property next door to Glenmoral, had retired up to these parts and was living with her sister. I said if she was still alive, she might be able to shed some light on things. She would have known Amanda's mother, I would think.'

Both William and Alice nodded.

'Good idea, brother. The old housekeeper may know what sort of person she is.'

'I hope so,' Richard said, 'although I'm hoping she doesn't volunteer information on another topic.'

'And what topic would that be?' William asked.

'Who Alex's father really is.'

Richard could see he had their full attention now, at the mention of their son-in-law's name. They had not been happy when their daughter Marianne had become pregnant to him, but they were happy now. The marriage seemed to be going well and they had a lovely little granddaughter. And now, finally, there was another baby on the way.

'Are you going to keep us in suspense?' William demanded.

There was a long moment of silence before Richard spoke.

'Howard told me the story himself, around the time Paul married Amanda. Alex's mother Elizabeth had apparently confided in the housekeeper. The old housekeeper had come to see Howard. It was Howard's cousin, Arthur Robinson, who was Alex's father. Couldn't acknowledge him, of course. He was already married with a son.'

'And the housekeeper suddenly told Howard this without prompting?'

It was Alice who had asked the question Richard didn't really want to answer.

'Well, not without prompting,' Richard admitted. 'She had heard Howard opposed any match between Alex and Amanda. She guessed the reason, Howard said. That Howard himself might have been Alex's father. I urged him to tell Alex but he said he didn't want to. He said it was too late.'

'Too late is right,' William said sharply. 'My daughter is happy. He might get ideas if he knows the truth.'

But Richard defended him.

'Alex hasn't put a foot wrong since he married Marianne. You must admit that,' Richard said, hoping he was right. 'He's fitted in well here.'

William agreed but he would always be a cautious man.

'I don't think he needs to know,' William said finally. 'Let sleeping dogs lie. That's what I say.'

Richard was inclined to agree. But he worried then the decision might not be theirs to make. If Amanda came to know about it, then he was sure she would tell him. And he could do nothing about that. Nothing at all.

Besides, hadn't he said that every man has the right to know who his father is. Was it fair to think Alex should be the exception?

With that thought he downed the rest of his beer and went in search of another one.

5

FOR SOME TIME AFTER Amanda had left, the two elderly sisters Elsie and Gertrude sat together reminiscing about the past, remembering everything as if it was only yesterday.

The warm memories of their early lives made conversation easy between them now. Elsie hadn't liked the man Gertrude had married but he was long dead and no longer a barrier between them. Elsie had never married, preferring instead her work as a housekeeper. That had been enough for her.

Elsie reached beside her chair and pulled up her knitting basket.

'Looks as though I should be knitting a matinee jacket,' she said, pulling out the half completed cardigan she had long promised her sister and setting to work.

Gertrude harrumphed in her usual way.

'I imagine she has drawers full of baby clothes left over from the first one,' she said. 'Besides you wouldn't know whether to knit a blue one or a pink one.'

'That's true, Gert,' she agreed. Her sister was always sensible. Eminently sensible.

But she was kindly too, offering Elsie a home when she wanted to retire. We'll be company for one another, she remembered Gertrude saying, and that was true. Elsie was grateful. But once again she had begun to feel like the little sister, always under the watchful – occasionally critical – eye of her older sister.

41

And then Elsie froze, knitting needles poised ready for the next stitch.

'I forgot about it, Gert. I forgot about it.'

'What did you say?' Startled, her sister looked up from the embroidery she had taken up. 'What did you say? What did you forget?'

Elsie let out a long sigh of frustration and annoyance.

'Just before she died, Alex's mother Elizabeth entrusted me with a small keepsake box that she kept underneath her bed. She made me get it out. And then she made me promise I would keep it for Alex and give it to him when he turned eighteen.'

Her sister frowned. Surely Elsie hadn't misplaced it.

'What did you do with it? Did you ever give it to Alex?'

She shook her head from side to side slowly.

'I forgot about it, Gert. I really forgot about it. He was only a couple of weeks old when she died.'

'But you must have done something with it, Elsie. It must have been a reasonable size. You couldn't have thrown it out. Could you?'

Elsie shook her head.

'No, of course I didn't throw it out. I did something with it, I remember, because it was quite heavy. It had a key. She gave me the key too. The box was well made. Lovely polished timber. She must have brought it out from Scotland with her.'

'Do you remember what you did with it?' Gertrude asked again. 'You must remember. It could be important.'

Elsie closed her eyes as if remembering the scene. And then she let out a small squeal of delight.

'Of course, I put it in the back of the store cupboard off the kitchen. Right up the back on a high shelf. I wrapped it in a piece of hessian first. I thought it would be a hiding place where no one would ever look. It had big cans of fruit and vegetables in front of it. And the big canisters of sugar and flour we used to buy.'

Gertrude shook her head from side to side.

'And then you forgot about it. I can't believe it!'

'I clean forgot about it, Gert. It was a busy job you know. And then Alex went away to school. We didn't see so much of him. And then he went to work on Glenmoral. There was nothing to remind me. What do I do now?'

'There's only one thing you can do, Elsie. You know that. You've got to get in touch with Alex. You're too old to travel out to Isla Downs but he could. He could go and see if it's still there.'

'Do you think so? Or should I just tell Amanda?'

But Gertrude shook her head.

'This is to do with Alex, not Amanda. Alex deserves to be told. Find his address in the phone book and write a note to him. Then it will be up to him. You'll have to come clean and be honest. Tell him you forgot until now. There is nothing else you can do.'

Elsie sighed. How had she been so forgetful? But still, better to remember now than never. With that, she set her knitting aside and got up from her chair.

'I'll write a note now, Gert. You're right. That's the way to do it.'

And with that she went in search of the local telephone directory.

Days later, Alex was surprised to receive the note Elsie Graham had written him.

Marianne, of course, had examined the envelope closely when it had arrived but the return address had provided no clues beyond the obvious. Everyone she knew named Elsie was old, well, older than sixty. It wasn't a name for a young girl. Anyway, she reasoned, the only girl she had ever worried about was Amanda and she was safely married to Paul.

'A mystery letter for you on the table,' she said, as she herded little Melanie towards the bathroom. 'Who's Elsie Graham by the way? A jilted girlfriend I don't know about?'

But Alex remembered exactly who Elsie Graham was.

'She's the old housekeeper from Isla Downs,' he said. 'Not sure why she's writing to me though. But she was good to me when I was a kid.'

He might have said she was good to me and Amanda when we were kids, but he generally refrained from mentioning Amanda's name to Marianne, unless he couldn't avoid it. He worried the old suspicions might still lie very close to the surface. He didn't always tell her when he dropped in to see Amanda when Paul was away, but that was only to see she was getting along alright, he told himself. He was being neighbourly. Being a friend. Nothing more.

He ripped open the letter.

Dear Alex

I hope you are getting on well. You'll see from the address I live only a few streets away from you now.

Amanda came to see me the other day. She had some quite startling news she might have told you about, but I won't say what that news is. It's up to her to tell people, or not, as she sees fit.

After her visit, all the memories of the past came flooding back. Memories of her mother Rosie. And memories too of your mother Elizabeth.

My sister Gertrude – I live with Gertrude now – and I were sitting discussing everything after Amanda left and then I suddenly remembered something I should have remembered years ago.

Your mother left a small trinket box in my care for you to have when you turned eighteen. I am so sorry but over all the years I forgot about it. I apologise from the bottom of my heart. It's yours and you should have it. I do have the key still.

You should come and see me and I will tell you where to find the box at Isla Downs (and give you the key). I have no idea what is in the box, but it could be some precious keepsakes of your mother's, which I am sure you would want. I know you have no memory of her nor anything to remind you of her.

Arthur Robinson was a tough man. He had her room cleaned out. There was absolutely no trace of her after she died. It was as if she never existed. Except for you, of course. I don't know if he wrote to her family in Scotland. I hope so. But perhaps there will be letters from your Scottish relatives in the box. But I am only speculating because I don't know.

She may even have written a letter for you, confirming who your father is, which would confirm what she told me although I know your birth certificate lists 'father unknown'.

It would be good if you came to see me one morning. We usually take a nap in the afternoons.

Yours sincerely,

Elsie Graham

He sat for a long time, head in hands, the despair of his early life coming unbidden to his mind. He remembered the desolation of not having a family. Of not having anyone who cared about him. Until Amanda had taken an interest in him. She had changed everything about his life. He had been about twelve years of age. Whatever improvements there had been in his life were down to her. Because no one would say no to Amanda.

Beyond loving her as he had – still did, if he was honest – he would do anything for her. Well, almost anything. He knew he had broken her heart when he married Marianne. But it was an opportunity he couldn't deny himself. He couldn't deny himself the security marrying Marianne offered him.

But now this. This connection with the past. And the knowledge he would finally know for sure who his father was. Was he a Robinson as he had always suspected? As everyone had whispered.

'Can I read the letter?' Marianne asked quietly. She knew, just looking at him, he had received devastating – or at least unexpected – news.

He held the letter out to her and then he pulled his bright eyed little daughter, fresh from her bath, onto his lap. She giggled with delight.

'That's a lot to take in,' Marianne said finally. 'First Amanda's news about her mother. And now this.'

'What news about Amanda's mother?' he asked, desperate to hide the fact Amanda had already told him.

'I was talking to my mum on the phone this morning,' she replied. 'Uncle Richard told them Amanda had received a letter from her mother. Her mother did not die years ago as her father had told her. She's written to Amanda, now that her husband has died, wanting to get in contact.'

He was careful in what he said.

'That's shocking news for Amanda,' he said. 'Good news though I hope. Is she going to meet her mother, do you know?'

Marianne shook her head.

'I think she was undecided but Uncle Richard knew about Elsie Graham apparently and he advised her to go and see Elsie. You see Elsie mentions her visit in her letter. It seems to have stirred up a lot of old memories.'

She handed the letter back to him.

'You'll be keen to see Elsie now. She says she knows for sure who your father is. How do you feel about that?'

He answered honestly.

'It matters less now than it once did,' he replied, 'but it would be nice to know for sure. The gossip was that Arthur Robinson, Howard's cousin, was my father, but no one could say for sure.'

Marianne moved away from the stove for a moment and came to sit alongside him. She put her hand on his.

'You must go and see Elsie tomorrow. First thing. You must hear what she has to say.'

He leant forward and kissed her lovingly.

'I will,' he said, 'and then I'll head out to Isla Downs as soon as I can.'

'You'll need to tell Amanda though,' she reminded him.

'Of course.'

Marianne added a note of caution.

'Once you find out where the box is hidden, you shouldn't tell anyone where it is. You don't know all the people on Isla Downs now. Someone might get wind of it and think there's something valuable in there.'

He agreed. Marianne was always very clear headed and sensible. He was grateful for that. She was no longer the naïve young girl he had romanced so successfully. She was now taking an active part in the Belleville business, keeping track of the accounting and administration that became more and more complicated as the business expanded.

He watched her don an apron, a clear signal she was about to start cooking dinner. When she was busy in the kitchen, his job was to take care of little Mel and keep her out of mischief but on this particular day he stayed, watching her move around the kitchen. It was reassuring. Despite how his life had started out, he had a good life now. Would knowing who his father really was change any of that? Not now, he thought, not now.

'You're right. I'll go and see old Elsie in the morning,' he said, as he turned his attention to little Melanie.

If there had been a moment in time – or a place – where Alex Fraser had imagined he would finally come to learn the truth of who his father really was, he would not have believed it would be in a cosy little sitting room in between two elderly women, one of whom was very eager to apologise to him.

'Alex, I'm so sorry,' she said, for the umpteenth time. 'How I could have forgotten about what your dear late mother entrusted to me is quite beyond me.'

'Well, at least you remembered now, Elsie, before it's too late.' What else could he say? He knew she was genuinely sorry. It hadn't been malicious.

'So it's in the kitchen storeroom, on a high shelf at the back where the surplus stores are kept?'

He was repeating back to her what she had already told him, to be sure he understood. If she had forgotten about the keepsake box, maybe she had been mistaken about its location. But she was adamant.

'Yes, that's where it is. No one would see it unless they looked for it. I needed to get up on the small step ladder to put it up there. I remember now.'

'Well, let's hope it's still there,' Alex said.

He examined the brass key she had given him. A small sliver of narrow ribbon was still attached to it. His mother would most certainly have been the one to add the ribbon to the key. Would it unlock some mysteries for him? He tried not to speculate.

'And there was something else you said that intrigued me. You said you knew for certain who my father was. How did you know? No one else was sure. It was all conjecture.'

He sat very still, holding his breath, wondering, at the last, if he really wanted Elsie to answer the question.

She took a deep breath. She knew instinctively what she was going to tell him was vitally important to him.

'Your mother told me just before she died that Arthur Robinson was your father,' she said. Her voice was so quiet Alex struggled to hear her.

'Did you say she confirmed Arthur Robinson was my father? Did I hear that correctly?'

Elsie nodded.

'You did, Alex. The gossip was true.'

'But he was already married with a child,' Alex said, trying to make sense of why his mother would accept such a man.

Elsie could see the troubled look on Alex's face, wondering what sort of a woman his mother had been. Was she an adventuress?

'I think he took advantage of her, Alex,' she said. 'I think she was ashamed of being pregnant out of wedlock. I had an idea she might have thought Howard would marry her because his marriage had broken up. I know he thought, until I told him only a few years ago, that he might have been your father.'

And in that moment, everything about his past life made sense.

'And that's why Howard Robinson was desperate to separate me from Amanda,' he stammered.

It wasn't a question. It was a statement of fact. He could see everything clearly now. Howard thought he had no way of knowing for sure until Elsie had confirmed it to him.

'When exactly did you tell Howard?' he asked.

Elsie paused, thinking back.

'I don't remember exactly but it would have been around the time when you married Marianne Belleville or when Amanda married Paul Belleville. I don't remember exactly but I went to see him. I had heard he was desperate to separate you from Amanda. I guessed the reason. But it was too late, wasn't it?'

He nodded slowly.

'Yes, Elsie. It was all too late.'

He got up quickly. He could no longer stay in the airless little room.

'Thank you for this,' he said, holding up the key. 'I'll let you know how I get on at Isla Downs. Hopefully the box is still where you left it.'

'I hope so too, Alex,' she said as she walked him to the front door. 'Your mother was a lovely young lady. She deserved more in life but she would be proud of how you've turned out.'

'I hope so, Elsie, I really hope so.'

6

SEVERAL DAYS LATER, Tony Bland stood on the verandah of the Isla Downs homestead and watched as Alex negotiated the final section of rutted road that led up to the house.

Give Alex access to whatever he wants. Those had been Amanda's orders to him in a telephone call a few days earlier. *He's hoping to find anything to do with his mother in the station's archives.* She hadn't been specific about what he would be searching for and Tony hadn't asked.

Amanda had given Alex a separate commission – to search for any old letters her father had kept. He guessed the reason. She was hoping to find letters her mother had written her father, letters that may have been kept and forgotten about in the dusty boxes that she remembered seeing on the shelves in the office at Isla Downs.

It had, in fact, taken Alex some time to convince Amanda she could not accompany him on his quick trip to Isla Downs. He had pointed out, reasonably, she was only a few weeks from having her baby and the risk would be too great.

Tony Bland greeted Alex with a friendly wave as he got out of the car. The two men shook hands. It had been some years since they had met.

'Life's been good to you since you left these parts,' he said. 'You found yourself a pretty heiress by all accounts. I missed out myself.'

'But I make up for it.'

Alex held out his hand towards the young woman who had spoken.

'My name's Stella. I've heard a lot about you, Alex,' she said, looking him up and down with keen interest.

She didn't elaborate on what she had heard about him but he knew, of course. In these parts, he would always be known as the unacknowledged bastard old Robinson hadn't wanted for his only daughter. Never mind that he had made a brilliant marriage to Marianne Belleville. Never mind that he was now a vital part of managing the Belleville cattle empire. He had been right to leave. None of this mattered now in the new life he had carved out. He was treated with respect. Treated as an equal. Marrying into the Belleville family had seen to that.

'It's nice to meet you, Stella,' he said politely. He thought she was probably just what Tony Bland needed in a wife. She looked as if she was ready to jump into the saddle and join the mustering at a moment's notice if they were short-handed. 'Are you from these parts?'

She nodded.

'My Mum and Dad moved up to these parts from New South Wales when I was a teenager to manage a property not far from here. I decided to come with them and then I met Tony. It would be after you left these parts.'

He realised then it had been more than six years since he'd left. Much had changed. But he was relieved to see the house was exactly as he remembered it.

'I've been gone a few years,' he said, without being specific, 'but I spent a lot of my childhood here.'

'And this is where your mother passed away,' she said sympathetically. 'Tony told me the story. It must have been hard being brought up without a mother.'

He simply nodded, reluctant to discuss the topic with a stranger.

'We've put you in the guest room along here,' she said briskly, realising he didn't want to say anything more about what had brought him to Isla Downs.

Tony had warned her. *Treat him well. He's a special friend of Amanda's. How special?* She had asked. *Very special before they both married other people. And now?* She got no reply except a shrug of the shoulders, which could mean anything.

'We have dinner early. In half an hour so you might want to wash up first after your trip.'

He thanked her and headed down the verandah to the bedroom she had indicated. The house was very similar to Glenmoral but, for him, it would always be a place of mixed emotions. It was where he had been born. It was where his mother had died. And in amongst the sadness, he remembered Amanda. A wild impetuous teenager who had become so important in his life.

He was tempted to run straight to the kitchen and find the small storeroom that adjoined it, but he knew it would be a busy place at that time of day. He decided instead to take Tony Bland into his confidence. Amanda had suggested it. And he knew she was right. *Tony values his job and he will help,* she had declared. *Not because he cares about my quest,* Alex had responded, *but because he cares about pleasing you.*

As the overall manager of all the Robinson properties, Tony Bland had hauled himself up from an unpromising beginning – an alcoholic father and a neurotic mother. He was respected now. He had a position he had worked hard to get. Keeping Amanda happy was the only part of it that really mattered now. Which meant doing a good job and if that meant helping Alex on some fruitless search, he would do it without comment.

But, deep down, he had always envied Alex his closeness to Amanda. He knew they had been lovers because he had spied on them. He wondered idly if that was all in the past for them.

As the sky lightened and the morning sun rose above the horizon, Isla Downs came to life. Alex was up early. Early enough to escape much scrutiny as he made his way through the kitchen to the storeroom, which was just as old Elsie had described it.

It did not take Alex very long to retrieve a solid wooden box from the top shelf where it had stayed, undisturbed, for nearly three decades.

Within minutes, in the privacy of his room, he had unlocked the box his mother had left for him. And there at the very top of a pile of letters – a letter addressed with the one word Alexander in a handwriting he had never seen before.

His hands shook as he carefully opened the envelope and removed the contents. There would never be another moment like this in his life.

As he read through the letter, he felt like the helpless child he had been. No, that was wrong, he decided. He felt like the motherless child he had always known himself to be. She had only ever been an idea in his head, never a real person. Never a flesh and blood person. Simply a person of whom he knew so little. And yet she was so important to him. He read and re-read the letter.

My dear son,

As I write this, I know I am not going to recover from your birth. I don't know how much longer I have but I feel weaker every day.

But my heart aches, not for myself, but for you, my child. For you will never know a mother's love nor a mother's guiding hand.

I have spoken to Arthur – Arthur Robinson, that is. He is your father. Even though I know he won't want to acknowledge you, he has promised he will see you are educated. That is important to me. After that, you must try to make your own way in life.

I'm sorry to say Arthur was not the gentleman he should have been. He put me in a very vulnerable position. I had no money to speak of. I had been promised marriage back home in Scotland – a good marriage to a man of property – but it never transpired. He turned out to be a scoundrel.

My mother was in despair. My father had died young and there were three younger children, all girls, to be provided for. I said I would take up a post as a governess to make things easier for her. Money had been more plentiful when I was growing up, at least plentiful enough for me to be well educated. For all the difficult circum-

stances she found herself in, she was a proud woman from a proud family. They did not like the idea of me working for a living, so I sought a post abroad.

You can read the family letters I have kept. But there is one thing you should know. They did not know I was having a baby. A warning you should heed if you ever want to contact them because they would, I know for sure, take a poor view of an illegitimate child.

With Howard's marriage breaking down, I had hoped he might accept you as his son. Like his cousin, he seemed to be keen to seek my company. That may be why his wife Rosie left him and dear little Amanda. I do not know for sure but I was hoping against hope for the respectability a marriage would confer on me and on you, my son.

But it is not to be.

All I can hope for is that you grow into a fine, honest man and that you occasionally give me a thought.

Your loving mother,

Elizabeth Fraser.

He sat for a long time, imagining his mother, her strength failing, writing the last few lines of the letter. And his life and who he really was? It was like a puzzle slowly coming together to form a complete picture.

He picked up the first letter from the top of the small pile and read it through. It was from Agnes Fraser. The address in Scotland meant nothing to him.

My dear daughter, it began.

It is so hard to imagine you so far away from home but we are so pleased you have settled into a good post.

The war, of course, made everything more difficult than it might otherwise have been. Fancy you being on Isla Downs. A good Scottish name, to be sure.

You should ask how the property came to be named. Robinson is more an English name, but perhaps there was a Scottish wife at one stage in the family.

Little Annie has grown so much since you left, you would hardly recognise her. Bridget is doing well and declares she wants to be a nurse, which I think would suit her very well, given that she must work to support herself, but my big news is that Margaret is engaged to be married.

For all that we are not as prosperous as we once were, our good name still means something and Margaret is so charming. His name is Archibald Gray and he was serving with our kinsman Lord Lovat in the Special Air Services regiment. He will never speak about what he did. It was very secret war work, that's all we know. We are just thankful he survived the war and is now keen to talk of wedding dates. She will make such a pretty bride, which is, of course, what I had hoped for you with your golden hair and your lovely demeanour.

But the less said about the scoundrel who broke his promise to you, the better. I do not speak to his mother if I see her. Or to his sister. But that does not help you. And it does not help you get beyond the disappointment of knowing your wedding dress will remain here, unworn. It was such a lovely gown.

I must go now. I have very little help in the house these days and I must take on many tasks I was never accustomed to doing. But the Good Lord sends these things to try us, I believe. I pray for better times.

Your loving Mother.

He checked the date on the letter. It was written in late 1945. Less than a year later, he was born. Had there been later letters that were destroyed, he wondered? Had there been a final letter to Agnes Fraser telling her of the sad death of her daughter? What reason had they given, he wondered?

There were several other letters in the box. And two photographs. One of his mother as a teenage girl and one of her mother and sisters. And nestled in the corner of the box he found a fine gold pendant. He carefully opened the locket attached. On one side, a photo of his mother but the other side of the locket was empty except for the jagged edges of a torn photograph. There was no doubting whose photo that would have been, Alex thought. The scoundrel who had let her down. But then if the scoundrel hadn't let her down … his thoughts trailed off.

'Looks as though you found what you were looking for, Alex.'

The voice startled him. He quickly placed the contents back into the box and shut the lid with a slight bang.

'Sorry, mate, I didn't mean to startle you,' Tony said. 'Private stuff by the look of it. From your mother?'

Alex nodded.

'It is,' he replied, hoping not to have to elaborate. 'And some letters from her family, a couple of photos and a gold chain that belonged to her.'

'I hope it answers some questions for you.' He said it as if he meant it.

Alex shrugged. Would Tony Bland really care about what he had discovered? And then he smiled to himself. If I had been acknowledged, I might now be your boss alongside Amanda, he wanted to say, but he refrained.

In any case he knew most people, Tony Bland included, had assumed Arthur Robinson had been his father. Having it confirmed was neither here nor there, not to them. But to Alex it was everything. And it was nothing, he decided, because everything had gone to Amanda.

'Amanda wants me to check out some old files in the office too,' he said, without being specific.

'Help yourself, mate. You know the way. You and Amanda still close, are you?'

It was said with a half-knowing smile, which immediately annoyed Alex.

'She's married to Marianne's cousin, Paul. We see one another a lot. She and Paul live a couple of streets away from Marianne and me.'

Tony Bland was about to say, all very cosy but he stopped

himself. It was a line he shouldn't cross and he knew it.

'We're off to do some mustering now. Got some new calves to brand. Are you planning to head straight home or going to stay another night?'

Alex looked at his watch. It was still early morning.

'Another hour and I'll be gone, Tony,' he said. 'Thanks for your help.'

'No worries, mate,' he said as he extended his hand towards Alex. 'I'm not sure what Amanda wants from the office but take whatever you think she wants. Everything is hers, of course. And tell her I send my regards. My wife too. I hope we see her not too long after the baby comes.'

'I think she's impatient for that to be over with, knowing Amanda.'

Tony smiled. Even far removed from the events, he had known that Amanda had been rushed to the altar to marry Paul Belleville only a few months in advance of the birth of her first baby. He wondered how disappointed Alex had been at that development. But then, how disappointed had she been when he had married Marianne Belleville? Disappointment all round, Tony thought, as he headed out in the direction of the stockyards. There was a hard day's work ahead of him and he was suddenly impatient to get started.

7

SEVERAL HOURS LATER, after a long drive, Alex pulled up in front of Amanda and Paul's house. He had a box of dusty files and a bundle of old letters on the seat beside him, having decided it was easier to scoop up what looked old rather than waste time sifting through everything himself.

She greeted him at the front door.

'You look tired,' she said as she led the way into the house, calling for Paul to come and help.

'That was a quick trip to Isla Downs, Alex. Did you find what you were looking for?' Paul asked as he took an armful of old files from Alex.

'I did. An old trinket box with some letters and a couple of photographs,' he replied, without being specific. He was reluctant at that moment to discuss what he had found with Paul.

He noticed Amanda glance at him with an unspoken question in her eyes. He merely nodded. Further discussion could wait. In any case, he wondered if there was any point now in lamenting her father's mistaken idea about his parentage and how that mistaken idea had shaped their lives irrevocably. It was a conversation for the two of them. But not today. Not with Paul present. But what would be the point anyway? He would never leave Marianne even if Amanda was willing to leave Paul.

He turned then and headed back down the hallway. He would

share what he had found with Marianne. He knew she would share his pleasure – and his pain – in finding out more about his mother and the sadness of her final days. The sadness of a life unfulfilled.

'Your mother's letter really set off a chain of events,' Paul said as he began to look through the old documents from Isla Downs. 'I feel sorry for Alex. I hope he found out something more about his mother and about his birth.'

Paul, having been brought up in the security of the Belleville family, could not imagine the life Alex had lived on the periphery of everything. Not belonging. But feeling that he did belong. Or at least that he should belong. No mother. No father. No one caring for him as a young child apart from hired help. Compared with the fuss that had accompanied his own birth and childhood, Paul knew he had no means of understanding the world Alex had inhabited as a child.

But for all that, Paul liked him. Only occasionally now did he give way to suspicion of Alex's relationship with Amanda. Most times he convinced himself it was all a thing of the past. Their relationship had settled into a comfortable routine.

But now, hearing this news of her mother, she had become unsettled.

'Where do you start?' he asked, casually flicking through some old papers. 'There's lots of useless stuff here.'

He held up a faded invoice for three new saddles. It was dated fifteen years earlier.

But Amanda wasn't listening. Instead, she was focused intently on a letter written more than twenty-five years earlier. It had taken only a few minutes of searching to find it.

'Have you found something?'

She nodded slowly and looked up at him.

'It's from my mother,' she said. She began to read aloud.

> *Dear Howard*
>
> *Thank you for your short letter letting me know how Amanda is getting on. My heart aches for her but I can't be a mother to her.*

I have met someone else and I'm about to get married again. The wedding is tomorrow, in fact. He is a good man. He knows I was married for a short time but he does not know I have already had a child. I don't think he would marry me if he knew that.

Perhaps it's better as Amanda grows up that she believes I have died. That would stop any awkward questions and her wanting to see me. I must make a new life for myself. If you tell people I have died, that will also satisfy people on the station who remember me. They won't go on asking you questions.

I think it would all be for the best.
Rosie

'I wonder why he kept it. He must have known one day I would find the letter.'

'Perhaps that's why he kept it,' Paul suggested, sitting down alongside her. 'Perhaps he wanted you to know but he couldn't bring himself to be the one to tell you because he knew he had told you a lie. And that he had continued to lie to you for all those years. I guess he hoped you would forgive him in the end. Do you forgive him? Or your mother?'

She looked up quickly but she did not answer immediately, as if she was, for the first time, asking herself how she felt about the deception.

'Seeing this,' she said, waving the letter, 'seeing this makes me angry. But I don't know who I'm angry with the most, my father for agreeing to the plan or my mother for suggesting it.'

Paul understood the rising tide of anger and hurt in her. Like Alex, she had been denied a mother's love. But he knew her father had doted on her. He spoke quietly, calmly.

'I feel sorry for your mother. She had to make a new life for herself. And your father wouldn't let her take you, so she had to make a choice. A tough choice. I think she made a choice she thought was in your best interests.'

'And hers,' Amanda retorted, the bitterness still not fully spent.

'Well, I hope you get a chance to ask her, finally,' Paul said.

He knew she had not yet heard back from her mother. Would her mother have second thoughts about them meeting up? If she did, how would Amanda feel then, he wondered? But he already knew the answer. She would be devastated.

Melanie was the first to spot her father pull up in the driveway of their home. She ran down the front stairs to meet him, followed closely by her mother Marianne.

'I didn't know you'd be back so soon,' she said, as she tried to curb little Mel's excited chatter.

'I got what I went for,' he said, as he returned her kiss. 'There was no point in staying on.'

'Did you get anything for Amanda?'

He nodded.

'I dropped the stuff off to her on the way home. I just grabbed a bundle of old files and letters for her.'

And then she noticed the polished trinket box.

'It's a beautiful box, Alex. Have you opened it?'

She bent to pick it up to carry it up the stairs and into the house but he stopped her.

'It's heavier than it looks,' he said. 'I'll carry it.'

He looked at her closely. Her pregnancy was beginning to show. She would be having a winter baby.

'How's the morning sickness?'

'I think I'm over the worst of it,' she said. 'It's not as bad as the first time.'

She remembered back to the day, nearly seven years ago, when her morning sickness had been so bad she hadn't been able to hide her pregnancy from her parents any longer. And all the drama that had ensued. It was all in the past now. Never mentioned. The new baby would put a seal on their marriage. Just as she hoped Amanda's baby would tie her irrevocably to Paul.

No one would have dared breathe a word in her presence but she knew there were whispers about who little Andrew's father really was. In quiet moments, she had observed the resemblance between Andrew and Melanie. But she trusted Alex. And she had accepted Amanda's story that Andrew had been born weeks early, just as Paul had accepted it. Would Amanda's second baby come early too? That would surely decide it, once and for all.

But all these concerns and worries went unspoken as she watched Alex set the box on the kitchen table and open it. Together, they read the letters that revealed something of his mother and her family. And then she saw the look of grief on his face. He had never grieved for the loss of his mother, because he had never known her. But now, there was something to cling on to. She was real. And she had died after giving birth to him. It was a burden of knowledge he felt deeply. And Marianne understood.

'And she thought Amanda's father might be interested in marrying her,' she said finally. 'It's all so sad. If she had lived, you would have had a mother and possibly Amanda too.'

She hugged little Melanie tightly as if, at any moment, their lives might be upended and her little girl left motherless.

'Life is a fragile thing,' she said suddenly. 'Very fragile.'

He nodded. What could he do but agree. There was his mother, in the prime of life, not surviving his birth. He wept for what might have been for the first time in his life.

It was several days before Alex had the opportunity to call in to see Amanda. He had just come from Prior Park where Paul was continuing Andrew's riding lessons, but with less patience than his father with the task. Alex had wondered if he should volunteer. Except he had begun to try to distance himself from Andrew. He knew that, seen together, there was a chance – a remote chance – a resemblance that might or might not exist could be noticed. He would not run the risk unnecessarily.

He wanted to see her. But he was concerned about seeing her. What could he say? What would she say? In the past few years, they had tried to bury their feelings for one another, but the revelations of the past weeks had brought everything back into stark relief.

He took the front stairs two at a time and rapped on the front door. No answer. He knocked again. This time he heard a faint voice calling out. He pushed the door open. She was sitting at the kitchen table. She looked deathly pale.

'I think the baby's started,' she said, her face distorted with pain. 'I was hoping it was Paul.'

He heard the sharp intake of breath.

'Have you called an ambulance?' he asked.

Even as she shook her head, he was picking up the phone to make the call.

'It looks like another premature baby,' she said, with a slight smile. She was three weeks off her due date, according to the doctor.

How could he say to her he felt a sense of relief. It would make the story of her first baby being premature more believable.

Within minutes, the wail of a siren signalled the approach of the ambulance.

'Can you let Paul know,' she asked as she was helped out of the house.

He nodded.

'I'll get him to drop Andrew off to us,' he said, thinking ahead.

She smiled her thanks through a haze of new, sharper pains that demanded her attention.

It was a full twenty-four hours before another Belleville heir, howling in protest, made his way into the world. Matthew Belleville, small but perfectly formed, enchanted his father, satisfied his mother, delighted his grandfather and bemused his brother, who wondered what all the fuss was about.

Richard, seeing the baby for the first time several days after the event, breathed a sigh of relief. This time, surely, there would be no doubting the baby was a Belleville.

'He's like you,' he told his son. 'Your mother is delighted but she said don't expect her to visit again at this time of the year. In a few months when the weather has improved, she'll visit.'

Paul laughed. He'd already been warned.

'What does Andrew think of having a baby brother?'

'Not much,' Amanda said. 'He'll probably be jealous for a while.'

'That won't last,' Richard said confidently. 'They'll be good mates. Just like Paul and Anthony. Just like me and William.'

'And Melanie will probably boss them both around,' she said with a smile.

'Did Marianne bring her to see the baby yesterday?' Richard asked.

'She did. And she declared she didn't want her mother to have a boy. She wants a sister. Secretly I think Marianne wants another girl too. I think I've taken the pressure off her.'

'Two boys and two girls in the next generation of the Belleville family. A good balance,' Richard said.

No one was quite prepared to ask if he'd forgotten his fifteen-year-old daughter Susan. They all understood Richard's disappointment in not seeing her regularly.

'If you're thinking of the inheritance, there's John too,' Paul said, reminding his father that his cousin's children would also become Belleville heirs in the future.

'Well, he'll have to get married first,' Richard reminded them.

'I thought he was keen on your friend Diana,' he said, looking towards Amanda.

'I thought so too for a while but since she moved to Sydney, I think she's having too much fun to get tied down. I think they're still in touch though.'

Richard looked towards his son, seeking confirmation.

'He's still keen on her but he said to me the other day that city life has turned her head. She's heading overseas soon with a girlfriend. I think her mother has encouraged her to live an independent life, not get tied down too soon.'

'And are we planning to wet the baby's head?' Richard asked, remembering the gathering that had followed Andrew's birth, only this time Amanda's father would be missing. He would have been delighted though, Richard thought. Absolutely delighted.

'Tomorrow afternoon. The usual place,' Paul said, as his father turned to go. 'I thought Anthony might come up. Isn't he still on uni holidays?'

Richard shook his head.

'Right now, he's got his head immersed in the papers and documents the architect who designed Prior Park left behind.'

'In Melbourne?' Paul asked.

'No, Brisbane. At the Fryer Library at the University of Queensland at St Lucia.'

'What? Does he think he'll find the plans to the house there?' It was the first he had heard of Anthony's quest.

'It's possible. It was a significant commission for the architect around the turn of the century.'

'Does that mean Aunt Julia's going to rebuild it completely?'

Richard shrugged.

'I don't know what her plans are to be honest but Anthony is excited about it. His first professional commission. The visiting lecturer in architecture suggested the visit to the library as a first course of action. It will be interesting to hear what he finds out.'

'It will,' Paul agreed, remembering the chain of events the fire at Prior Park more than seventeen years earlier had set in motion. 'A lot has happened in the time since then. In the family, I mean.'

Richard nodded. That was something of an understatement, he thought.

'Let's look to the future,' he said finally. 'And perhaps Prior Park – and the family – can finally rise proudly from the ashes.'

8

ANTHONY BELLEVILLE LET OUT an excited yell. After what seemed like hours of fruitless searching through boxes of files and old documents, he had finally found what he was looking for. Several students looked up from their work. One or two glared at him. The librarian reminded him this was a quiet space and not to disturb the other researchers.

He murmured an apology as he eagerly opened the file marked, Prior Park – Plans. The inked label was very faded but the plans appeared to be intact. He began to clear the space around him to spread out the documents but first he decided to read the copies of correspondence on the file. For him, it was like reaching back into a past of which he knew very little.

He tried to recall what his father had told him. He had never known his grandfather Francis Belleville. He knew even less about his great grandfather Louis Belleville, who had commissioned the building of Prior Park.

Instinctively, he went to the back of the file to find the very first correspondence. He stared at the first handwritten letter for some time before carefully smoothing it out. It was a letter from the past. His past. His family's past. It took him some time to decipher its contents. It read:

Dear Mr Wilson,

I am writing to you with what I hope you will consider

to be an exciting and interesting commission. Further, I hope you will take up this commission, despite the inconveniences it may present to you, sir.

I have recently married and with the marriage, my father-in-law has very kindly agreed to make us, the happy couple, the beneficiaries of a substantial gift of land in central Queensland. The gift, though, is conditional upon me providing a decent home for his daughter, Adeline, on the property so that she may live in a style to which she has become accustomed in Melbourne, when she is with me at Prior Park.

The land is good grazing country bordering the Fitzroy River on its northern boundary. I have visited the property on horseback, alighting at the nearby river port. Do not be alarmed, sir. I believe the access will improve greatly in the next year or so as the town grows and the area attracts more settlers. I hear reports the nearby gold mine has brought a surge of prosperity to the region.

I know you will be familiar with the grand homes in Melbourne, especially in Toorak. While I appreciate the location of my new home will make it difficult to rival the style and amenity of these fine buildings, yet I hesitate to dampen your enthusiasm for the project. You must build me a fine home that will outlast me and my wife. I envisage it will become a home for generations of the Belleville family to come. My wife will present me with our first child very soon. I pray for a son who will follow in my footsteps.

I look forward to your reply in due course.

I remain, sir, your respectful servant.

Louis Belleville, Esq.

Anthony sat back. He let his mind drift back in time, imagining for the first time what the very origins of his family in Australia might have been. What did he know of their history? Almost nothing. Up until this point, he had lacked any curiosity beyond the obvious. His limited French was enough to decipher the meaning of the name – beautiful town – but beyond that, his knowledge was sketchy. To see a letter written by his great grandfather to the architect had been totally unexpected.

He turned back to the file. He wondered how the architect had replied to the letter but there was no copy on the file that he could find. Instead, there was a letter in a totally different handwriting.

My dear Alexander

How interesting to have your letter about an unusual commission you are considering. Like you, it strikes me that it is an extravagance to build such a fine house in so remote location, especially when its immediate neighbours are likely to be little more than wattle and daub huts with fire pits for kitchens. What woman used to refined society would live there? I wonder if Mr Belleville has asked himself that question.

I know the Prior family of which Mr Belleville's wife is the only daughter. I believe I have met her once in company with the family. She has pretty manners and a delicacy of countenance that befits a young woman. There was surprise that her father permitted the alliance with Louis Belleville. I am sure she had other offers but he does have a dashing swagger that appeals to the ladies, I'm told.

Now you asked me for my opinion as to whether he is a man you should be doing business with. In other words, I'm sure your question, so delicately put, is whether he has the funds to match his ambitions.

I'm told he is well off but exactly how he came by his money, no one is quite sure. Judging by his name and his accent (I have met him once or twice), I feel sure he will have connections in France. This accords with the little information I have, that he has been successful importing some wines and spirits as well as fine textiles from that country.

I think too, although I am reluctant to impinge a man's

honour and virtue without he has the opportunity to speak for himself, but I have heard that he is not universally admired in business circles. He has been accused more than once, I believe, of sharp practice. He does gamble, I have been told, and he has been known to pull a gun in a quarrel. I believe on one occasion the firearm discharged (he said later it was accidental) and shot a fellow in the arm. He could have been up on serious assault charges, or even murder charges had the injury been worse, but by this time he was already engaged to marry Adeline Prior and her father Henry Prior managed to get the entire episode covered up. Prior is an influential figure in Melbourne business circles.

There were even whispers that he had killed a business partner some years ago, but it is purely gossip I believe, possibly put about by other men interested in securing the alliance through marriage with the Prior family.

As a client, I suspect he will be capricious and demanding. But in the end, I am sure he would not renege on his obligations. He knows his father-in-law would take a dim view of shady dealings. I think he hopes the gift of land will be but the first instalment in the largesse he hopes to receive from that quarter. Prior's only requirement, I am sure, will be that he be a good and faithful husband to the daughter.

There was, I was told, several disappointed young women who had set their caps at him, despite his lack of family and his unknown origins. Some have even whispered of the stain of transportation. Not him, of course, but perhaps his mother or father. No one knows for sure. Others have said he may be the father of a child born to a young woman of good family. Once again, it was all hushed up, but for all its claims to sophistication, Melbourne society is quite small and almost provincial. And gossip greases the wheels of social discourse so well!

On the whole though, I would say you can go forward

with confidence in your dealings with him, my dear Alexander, but be sure you gain his agreement at each step of the way in what I am sure will be an exciting but exacting project for you.

When next you visit our southern parts, I will be keen to hear your report of progress in the matter.

Your affectionate friend

William Pitt

Once again, Anthony sat back in his chair. The letter to the architect from a Melbourne colleague had been an extraordinary find. An unexpected find. It had painted a picture of his great grandfather that was not entirely flattering. A womaniser and possibly not always honest in his business dealings.

He dismissed the idea he would have killed a man but a question remained: *had he been cynical enough to woo Adeline Prior for the dowry she would bring him?*

Yet she had obviously been in love with him. *Dashing swagger,* the words both troubled him and amused him. Was this a fatal flaw in the men of the Belleville family that had played out in subsequent generations, he wondered?

He thought, then, of his grandfather Francis. The man he had never known except through family stories. And then the final tragic epitaph to his life. He guessed his father had stopped short of the description he might have applied to his father – a man of fatally flawed character – in finally telling Anthony the full story of his father's betrayal of his wife. And of his children.

But, looked at in the cold light of day, from the safe distance of many years, how else could he be described, he wondered? How else could you describe a man who had kept a mistress and the child she had borne him secret from the rest of the family?

How disappointed and angry must his father have been to be confronted by his younger half-brother demanding rights within the family years after his father had died? No wonder my father threw him out of the house, he thought. It was not the person himself but the embodiment of all he represented. Betrayal of their mother. He had glimpsed in his father the deep visceral anger with his father who had gone to his grave maintaining the charade of a happy family.

And then the tragedy. Almost inevitable, Anthony thought. Revenge is a powerful motive. What irony was there in it all? The grand mansion his great grandfather had built with such ambitions reduced to rubble by a grandson who should never have been born. A grandson bent on revenge against the family who had rejected him.

And his own father? An honourable man in almost every respect, he decided. Except he had romanced another man's wife. Was that part of the flawed inheritance of the Belleville men? Had his father been responsible for the breakup of his marriage to his mother the first time around, he wondered? Or had it simply been the geographic circumstances that had come between them? But there would always be consequences, he decided. Susan, a half-sister he loved but he hardly ever saw. George, a half-brother he almost never saw.

And then there had been his brother Paul. Ditching a girl the day before he was to marry her because another girl was already pregnant to him.

He sighed out loud. He had always thought of relationships as straightforward, uncomplicated things. But that was far from the truth.

And now, deep within his soul, he wondered if he himself was in similar danger. He let the thought slide. For the moment, there was only one issue troubling him.

How would he ever find a way to tell his father that the visiting tutor he so admired was Daniel Harrington. Did he need to? But in some obscure way he was grateful to Daniel Harrington. Hadn't it been Daniel's pursuit of his stepmother Kate that had made it possible for his father to reunite with his mother?

It would not matter except he really wanted Daniel Harrington to visit the site of the old house. To offer advice. What part of it should be revived? How should it be altered to reflect modern building practice? And the demands of a modern home?

Would building a replica of the building simply be building a pastiche? Somehow, he wanted to put his own stamp on it. Yet the same question occurred to him as had occurred to William Pitt.

Did it really make sense to build such a fine home at what would be great expense in such a location? The houses around Prior Park were more substantial than the wattle and daub huts of the early days, but they were still the practical, wide-verandahed single storey timber homes suited to the climate, not stately mansions of brick and mortar with finely crafted finials and expensive furnishings designed for a totally different way of life.

He began to unfold the final, finished plans of Prior Park, surveying the large unwieldy document carefully with a professional eye, while marvelling at the draftsman's skill.

His own memories of the house were vague, just a few fleeting snatches of memory that produced no coherent picture at all. He would need to talk at length with his father, his Uncle William and his Aunt Julia to form a true picture.

But he knew for sure the original house had dominated the landscape where it stood just as it had dominated the lives of its inhabitants. It had shaped his parents' first attempt at a successful marriage. It had been a different life, his father had said. A different way of life that had died with the house, that had died with his grandmother Elizabeth Belleville who had been the fire's unfortunate only victim.

His father's words haunted him.

'She went back for a picture of my father that was hanging in the hallway, otherwise she would not have been burned. She would have survived,' his father had told him.

'She did not know what your Uncle William and I knew,' he had said. 'She did not know how my father had betrayed her. Betrayed us.'

He was remembering especially the sadness in his father's voice as he explained the terrible details surrounding his grandmother's senseless death. And the awful events that followed. But for an excellent shot by Prior Park's long time manager, his father would be dead.

Anthony had been sitting deep in thought for some time, the plans unfolded in front of him.

'Have you found something of interest?' the librarian asked quietly as he came up behind him.

The room had emptied out. Anthony hadn't noticed. He glanced at his watch.

'I have, yes, very interesting,' he said, pointing to the plans and the file in front of him.

'Looks like a fine old home,' the librarian said, peering over his shoulder.

'It was,' Anthony said. 'It was indeed. It was my home when I was a small child.'

'Not now?'

Anthony shook his head.

'Not now. No. It was burned down many years ago, when I was a small boy.'

The librarian uttered the expected words of sympathy.

'That's so sad,' he said. 'Burned down, you say? It looks solid. How did such an accident happen, if I may ask?'

'A madman,' Anthony said simply. 'A madman who hated our family. He put a match to it one night.'

'That's awful,' the older man said. 'That's really awful. I hope no one was injured.'

Anthony turned to face him. What harm was there in telling him the truth, painful as it was.

'My grandmother died as a result of the fire,' Anthony replied. 'I wasn't there. I was living in England with my mother at the time.'

'That was probably fortunate,' the librarian said, 'but it must be interesting to see the plans of the house.'

'It is,' Anthony agreed. 'It's very interesting. And some of the correspondence too. It's a pity I can't take the file with me. I'd love to show my father.'

But the firm shake of the head confirmed what he already knew. None of the material could be removed.

'Why don't you bring your father in to have a look at the material?'

'Good idea. I'll give him a call this evening. I'll see if he can come down. He lives up north.'

'Perhaps in his next holidays?'

Anthony smiled.

'My father's life isn't like that,' he said. 'He and his brother oversee the family business. They do what they choose when they choose. There's a flight from up there every day.'

Leonard King nodded.

'That sounds like a plan. I'll put these papers away now. But they'll be easily retrieved next time you come in.'

He watched as Anthony headed out the door, satisfied with his day's work and eager to speak to his father.

As Leonard King began to refold the large plan carefully to return it to the file, it was then he read the name: Prior Park. And the client's name: Louis Belleville.

Surely not, he thought. Surely not. It can't be.

He shook his head from side to side. It was too much of a coincidence. He didn't believe in coincidences.

He bundled the file into the box and quickly shut the lid. It had awakened memories for him too. Difficult memories. Not of the house. But of the family. And of a young man he had befriended. How long ago was it? He tried to think. Less than twenty years but more than ten.

No, it can't be. He was muttering and shaking his head from side to side. But it must be. It must be. It was then he felt a surge of anger at their privilege. The privilege they wouldn't share with one of their own. Just because there was no wedding ring on his mother's finger.

He stood at the window and watched as Anthony Belleville walked quickly across the quadrangle to the bus stop. Would he ever really need to work for a living or was his study of architecture just some passing fancy? Even now he guessed he was financially secure with a monthly income appearing in his bank account without him having to lift a finger. There was nothing about his appearance that spoke of a down-at-heel student struggling to make ends meet.

And his arrogant, entitled father? How will I feel coming face to face with him? Leonard muttered to himself. Alistair never got a fair hearing from him or his brother. That was something he knew for certain. They simply wanted to buy me off, he remembered Alistair telling him.

Deep anger rose in him unchecked for the first time in years at the tragedy that had unfolded. He remembered how angry Alistair had been. And he had seen for himself how it had tipped Alistair over the edge. And his mother Muriel? He remembered how she had coped in her own quiet dignified way. But he remembered too how she had been ostracised. Neighbours had crossed the street to avoid her. Except that is for himself and his mother. And his sister too.

He turned away from the window and sighed deeply. He was pleased all his colleagues had already left for the day. The memories were painful. Shocking too. It had taken a long time for him to come to terms with the fact he had befriended a man capable of such madness. But he had always believed Alistair had been provoked beyond reason.

Would he tell Richard Belleville his story if he met him? Or tell Anthony Belleville? Would they even want to hear the other side of the story? Would they even want to know he had known Francis Belleville too? Would they want to know how young Alistair had hero worshipped his father? His mostly absent, charming, feckless father. But his father, nevertheless.

Would they want to know how Alistair had talked endlessly about his father? About joining him on his property when he was older. His father had promised. Promised him the world, in fact, and delivered exactly what? Nothing.

And it had been too much for the young Alistair to cope with. His mother, quiet and self-contained in her grief, had offered little comfort. He had built a dream world in his imagination of inheriting the property when he was older. But he did not share any of this with his mother. And then that dream had evaporated as he had grown older and learnt the truth, until, finally, the last shreds of his dream turned to dust. And in a final, desperate act he had reached out to the family. And been rejected. Harshly. Without sympathy. Without hope.

As he left the library, Leonard King flicked off the bank of light switches, closed the doors behind him with unaccustomed force and headed out into the fading light of a Brisbane summer afternoon.

9

LIKE HIS SON, Richard too was intrigued by the discovery of the original plans to the fine house that had once stood so commandingly at Prior Park. Within days, he was stepping off the plane and heading to the terminal, grateful the intense rain of the previous week had given way to sunshine.

Even before he could pay off the taxi driver at the entrance to the hotel, Anthony was beside him, chattering excitedly, having first remembered, at the last minute, to enquire politely about his new nephew before launching into details about what he had found in the library archives.

'The plans are all there. Can you believe it! And letters too.'

That had come as a surprise to Richard.

'My great grandfather – your grandfather – wasn't always honest,' Anthony declared. 'A bit of a rogue, it seems. What did your father say about him? Did he ever tell you anything about him?'

Richard laughed as he grabbed his bag and headed to the reception desk.

'All in good time,' he said, knowing that Anthony would not be fobbed off with half a story. But what did he really know? His own father had been circumspect in speaking about his parents. Unusually so he had thought at the time.

He paused for a moment, looking beyond the front door of the hotel to the street outside, and beyond that, to the entrance to the

Botanic Gardens. It was a place that had featured in his life although he had rarely visited it.

Anthony's eyes followed his gaze. And then he realised. His grandfather had collapsed while walking in the Botanic Gardens. It had all happened more than thirty years earlier, long before he was born. His grandfather had been fifty-seven years old. And at his side had been his mistress. Francis Belleville had drawn his last breath with Muriel McGovern by his side, a fact Richard had discovered only years later.

Later, as father and son sat together drinking in the hotel bar, Anthony was mostly silent, listening intently to the history of the family at Prior Park, at least to those parts of the history Richard knew. He had always known Prior Park had come into the family via his grandmother Adeline Prior.

He remembered overhearing his own mother Elizabeth describe her mother-in-law as 'an insipid woman who had apparently been pretty enough in her youth.'

This he related verbatim to Anthony, laughing as he did so at the memory.

'My mother – your grandmother – was many things but insipid was not one of them. Commanding. Overbearing. Clever. A disappointed wife. A demanding mother,' he said, without a hint of rancour, 'but we all loved her. Respected her. It haunts me to this day I could not save her life.'

'And her family?' Anthony asked. 'They must have considered your father a suitable match?'

'I've always believed it was the Prior family that lent respectability to the Belleville name. Marrying Adeline Prior was a masterstroke on my grandfather's part. My father told me Prior Park was, as his father had hoped – and as the letter you read predicted – just the beginning of the generosity Henry Prior would show his only daughter. There was commercial property in Melbourne. And a house in Melbourne. Plus some shares in newly established companies. It was a strong foundation for the family. That is, until my father got reckless.'

'Was he not good at managing the family's interest?' Anthony asked, aware that he was treading on difficult ground as far as his father was concerned.

Richard gave a half smile.

'He was gullible. Invested in schemes that had no hope of success. He would have done better to let my mother manage everything. Her Dalrymple trust fund went from strength to strength. Your Aunt Julia inherited that. But I know my mother helped the family with financial assistance from time to time. I think it tells you everything. Her family was happy with the marriage up to a point but they made sure my mother would always have money regardless of what my father did. Well, her Dalrymple grandmother did in any case.'

Anthony sat very still for some time, thinking through everything his father had told him. It had been a more complex story than he had imagined. So many personalities. Yet in the thirty years since his grandfather's death, his father, together with his Uncle William, had made good decisions that had benefitted the family, including himself.

For him, there had been no anxiety over the cost of his university fees. For the first time, he began to see how fortunate he was. Both his parents were individually wealthy. In the cloistered world of Eton, he had mixed with other boys from well-to-do families but in the very different world of an Australian university, he had met a diverse cross section of students, some of whom would have been unable to attend university, except for the scholarship that had come their way.

As they sat discussing the family, one question occurred to him. A question he had never asked before.

'What role do you see me playing in the Belleville family business in the future?' he asked quietly. 'Or do you not see me needing to have a role?'

Richard sat back in his chair and studied his son carefully. He could see it was a serious question.

'There are five of you now to inherit the Belleville interests. I think between them Paul and John, with Alex's help, can manage the rural property portfolio. Alex of course only has a role because of Marianne. I think Susan will be a silent partner. Paul is currently her trustee. Marianne will run the financial and administrative side of things. Which leaves someone to understudy my role.'

He looked speculatively at his son.

'You mean the commercial interests?'

Richard nodded.

'Yes. Your uncle and I were totally unprepared for what was thrust upon us when our father died suddenly. It's important this is planned out now.'

'I suppose I should have been studying commerce or accountancy, not architecture?'

But Richard shook his head.

'No, I thought the architecture course was a good choice. You can learn the other stuff as you go along. But you will have professional qualifications, which will add to your standing.'

'So I'd better not fail my honours year,' he said with a laugh.

'You won't fail, son, especially under the guidance of Daniel Harrington. He's a good architect, I believe.'

'How did you know?' he asked, a look of consternation crossing his face. It was as if he'd been found out not being entirely honest with his father.

'Your mother told me,' Richard said, smiling at his son's shocked look. 'I know you want to bring him up to Prior Park to look at the site.'

He paused. What had happened between his ex-wife Kate and Daniel Harrington was nothing to do with Anthony, he had decided.

'Do it when I'm away from Prior Park visiting your mother,' he suggested.

Anthony nodded, pleased there would be no need for subterfuge. It was another hurdle overcome.

'And now, let's eat,' Richard declared as he headed towards the hotel restaurant.

Tomorrow, he and Anthony would head to the library so he could view the material his son had uncovered. He had no inkling then of what lay ahead. Of how the simmering anger of one man towards the Belleville family – and towards him in particular – was still very much alive.

Leonard King, ensconced behind a desk piled high with archive boxes, greeted both Richard and Anthony with a slight smile that faded as quickly as it appeared.

'I'm back, Mr King, as promised,' Anthony said brightly. 'This is my father, Richard Belleville. He's really keen to see the files I've been looking at on Prior Park. My father was brought up in the house.'

'Of course,' Leonard King responded. He had anticipated the request. The unwieldy archive box was already among those on his desk. He reached to pick it up, but his hands shook so violently he fumbled the box. It clattered to the floor.

Anthony reacted quickly, retrieving the archive box and the contents that had spilled out. It was Richard who could see there was something wrong. Something beyond clumsiness.

'Are you unwell, Mr King?' His enquiry was genuine. 'Is there something the matter?'

Leonard King shook his head.

If he had been a brave man – or perhaps a foolish man – he would have struck out at Richard Belleville to avenge his long dead friend Alistair McGovern. But he was neither of those things.

But still he was an angry man. Angry that the first born son Richard Belleville had grown up with all the advantages, all the privileges his family could bestow while his friend – Francis Belleville's misbegotten youngest son – had grown up in a fantasy land of promises that could never be kept.

His voice trembled when he did manage to speak. He was breathing heavily.

'I'm fine, thank you,' he said quietly, cursing himself for his weakness.

Father and son headed towards a table in the far corner of the room, well removed from other researchers.

Heads together, they began to study the old letters that Anthony had discovered, letters that had, inadvertently, illuminated their family history in ways they could never have expected.

'It seems to have taken a decade or more to build the house,' Anthony said, quickly making notes of key dates in the construction schedule.

'Easily explained, son,' Richard said. 'There was a very deep depression in Australia in the early 1890s. Banks failed. It's likely that may have affected my grandfather's financial capacity to continue with the build.'

'It wouldn't have been easy. The road isn't great even today but back then it would have been little more than a cart track,' he added.

They both began to see what an overly ambitious undertaking it had been. A folly really. A smaller, perfectly adequate house could have been constructed in a quarter of the time.

'My understanding is that my grandfather gifted Prior Park to my father on his marriage. I don't think he and my grandmother ever spent much time together in the house. After all, they had a house in Toorak. Much more comfortable. And civilised,' he said with a wry smile.

'So what happened to the house in Toorak?'

'It was sold, I believe, after my grandparents died. I think my father needed the money.'

'He was an only child, wasn't he?'

Richard nodded. He had a vague recollection there had been another child but she had not survived infancy.

'Was the remoteness of Prior Park a reason for my grandmother's disappointment?' Anthony asked. He knew his grandmother had been brought up in Melbourne. How different life at Prior Park, so remote in those days, must have been for her, he thought.

And then it struck him. His own mother had encountered the same frustrations. Limited society. A cultural backwater. These factors had to be the reason for the breach with his father. She had wanted to live elsewhere.

'In fact, Aunt Alice is the only woman who's been happy there.

And that's because she was brought up next door on Mayfield Downs. Am I right?'

'That about sums it up, son. Your mother certainly couldn't settle there. I think she felt she was missing out on life. At least on the life she had grown up to expect she would live.'

Anthony nodded. He knew the sort of life his mother lived in England. And then he laughed quietly.

'I'm surprised she stuck it out long enough to have me.'

He was, after all, more than six years younger than his brother Paul.

Richard smiled. It was a smile of genuine affection for his younger son. There was so much about him that reminded him of his mother Catherine.

'Well, I'm glad she did.'

In many ways, Anthony had been a whole lot less trouble than Paul, who had very nearly killed himself in a plane crash and then got himself into a romantic tangle all his own making. He hoped Anthony's life would be less chaotic.

Anthony turned back to the old archive.

'I'm going to photocopy some of these documents,' he said, pointing to a coin-operated photocopier in the opposite corner of the room.

'Good idea. But you'll have trouble with the plans.'

'I'll do what I can in sections,' he said. His pocket jangled with the coins he had brought with him for the purpose.

'Do two copies,' his father suggested, 'so I can take one copy back to Prior Park and show your Uncle William. He'll be very interested. He loved the house.'

'But he didn't want to rebuild it?'

Richard shook his head.

'It was under insured. And with our mother gone, it was time to live differently.'

'And now?'

His father shrugged.

'Perhaps it's Julia's folly,' he said. 'Or perhaps it will be a new landmark for the family. Who knows? Maybe its success will depend on the architect.'

With that Anthony let out a quiet laugh and headed off to copy the important parts of the Prior Park archive, including the letters.

With the work completed and Anthony weighed down with an armful of photocopies, father and son headed towards the desk to return the archive.

'Thank you, Mr King,' Anthony said politely. 'You've been a great help. My father was really interested in the history the archive revealed.'

As they turned to leave, Leonard King's anger could no longer be contained. He knew it was now or never. There would never be another opportunity to confront Richard Belleville. The library was largely empty.

'You killed Alistair,' he cried out. 'You killed my friend. You destroyed him. You're a cruel man, Richard Belleville. A cruel, heartless man.'

Leonard was breathing heavily, spent by the explosion of emotion so uncharacteristic of his nature.

Richard stopped suddenly and turned to face him. He had been quite unprepared for the attack. There had been nothing to forewarn him of the simmering anger of the mild mannered man behind the desk.

Anthony looked at his father. How would he respond? He seemed as if he was robbed of his voice for a few moments.

'My father did nothing. He didn't …'

But Richard put his hand out to his son and shook his head, as if to say, let me handle this.

In those few seconds, Richard regained his composure. It was essential he calm the situation.

'What you say isn't true, Mr King,' he said evenly, shaking his head, 'but we can hardly have this conversation here.'

He paused for a moment, considering his options. He could walk away but he knew the accusation, uncontested, would haunt him forever.

'But we must have this conversation. Later perhaps,' he said quietly, his natural authority asserting itself.

He waited for Leonard King to respond. Before him, he saw a man torn between a seething unresolved anger and a man appalled by his own behaviour. He was trembling still.

Richard leaned across the desk and put his hand on his arm. It was meant as a gesture of reassurance. Nothing more.

'Don't upset yourself further, Mr King. I'm sure we can talk about all this very calmly. I'm interested to hear what you have to say.'

He did not want Leonard King to think he would be treated with contempt. Far from it. His outburst had shocked Richard. He had known for a long time, deep down, the uncontrollable anger he had felt towards Alistair McGovern had its origins in the anger he felt towards his father, who was no longer alive to answer for his actions. It had been the ultimate betrayal of his family that had angered Richard. And Alistair McGovern had been the living, breathing evidence of it. And he had borne the brunt of his anger.

Anthony listened intently. The events surrounding Alistair McGovern had all happened so long ago. Only later had he been told the full story. And only because he had asked. He wondered how his father would handle a meeting with Leonard King.

He did some quick calculations. His father had just turned fifty-six. He had been told that Alistair McGovern had been fourteen years younger than his father which meant he would have been forty-two had he lived. The librarian he judged to be forty-seven or thereabouts. Had Leonard King acted like an older brother to the younger boy? It was possible, Anthony thought, especially if he didn't have a brother. He wondered idly if they had been neighbours.

Leonard King, his first flush of anger spent, shook his head.

'And what good would that do?' he asked.

'I think it would help you, Mr King, and I think it would help me too. What happened with Alistair was regrettable but you must know he came within a moment of killing me, having already killed my mother,' Richard said. 'These may be unpalatable facts but they are facts nonetheless.'

Leonard King nodded. He knew. Of course he knew. He knew Alistair had gone too far. He'd accepted that fact long ago. He berated himself silently. If only he hadn't lent him his car, he would not have had the means to get there. To do what he did.

'I finish work at five,' he said, leaving it open to Richard to suggest an arrangement.

'Come to our hotel. We can have a drink in the bar. In Alice Street, right opposite the entrance to the Botanic Gardens.'

'I know it,' he said. 'Probably half past five before I can get there.'

'We'll see you then,' Richard said, as he turned and motioned to Anthony to walk away with him.

'Wow,' Anthony said, as they moved out of earshot. 'That was unexpected.'

His father grimaced.

'You could say that. I think he's been harbouring a grudge against me for many years. I'm pleased he didn't have a pop at me like his friend.'

Anthony laughed.

'He'd have been no match for you.'

'I wouldn't have thought Alistair McGovern would have had a chance either but the element of surprise is never to be underestimated. You'd be fatherless if it hadn't been for Charles Brockman.'

With that thought hanging in the air, father and son walked on in silence in search of a telephone to call for a taxi.

10

THE HOTEL BAR WAS small. Richard looked around and chose a table in what was likely to be the quietest corner. He checked his watch as he and Anthony sat down. It was approaching five thirty.

'Do you think he'll come?'

Anthony was sceptical. He thought Leonard King had probably said all he had the courage to say back at the library. How difficult would it be for him to sit with them and have a civil conversation considering what he had said.

'I hope so, son,' Richard replied. 'I hope so. There's so much more to this story than I ever realised. Alistair McGovern had nursed his own hopes and dreams for the future. They might have been misguided but was that his fault?'

For the first time Anthony could remember, he sensed uncertainty in his father. He had always admired his father's air of calm reassurance, of strength and wisdom.

In all the years he had lived with his mother and her second husband, there had never been any chance Edward Cavendish would replace his father. Edward had, in the end, become a largely irrelevant figure in his life. The marriage breakdown had come as a relief to Anthony, just as it had to his brother Paul. Seeing their mother remarry their father had been, for both of them, immensely satisfying. The world had righted itself.

But the ghost of the long dead Alistair McGovern had always haunted the family, and especially his father. He knew that. They had rarely ever spoken about the whole tragic episode but he knew his father had always felt indirectly responsible for the awful events that had occurred. He had said it only once but his words had remained etched in Anthony's mind: *if only I had been more even tempered with him, negotiated with him, strung him along, the tragedy might have been avoided.*

It had been useless to try to reassure his father he could never have predicted what had occurred. It had been beyond anyone's wildest imagination, beyond anyone's understanding of what Alistair McGovern, bent on revenge, might have been capable of.

The barman placed their drinks on the table and Richard scrawled his signature on the docket. He felt like downing the single malt in his glass in one go but he resisted the temptation. He wanted to keep a clear head.

Despite the subdued lighting, Leonard King quickly spotted them at the table in the far corner.

Richard stood as he approached and held out his hand, which Leonard shook briefly. There was no strength in his grip, no warmth in the exchange between the two men.

'Sit down, Mr King,' Richard said. 'Leonard, isn't it? May I call you Leonard? Would you like a drink?'

He nodded, as if assenting to both questions. Richard signalled for the barman.

'A beer? Something else? Whisky perhaps?'

He waited for Leonard to respond.

'A small beer, thanks. Whatever you have on tap,' Leonard said slowly. He rarely drank. He knew he would not have been up to the task at that moment of nominating a preferred beer brand. He didn't even know why he'd come. What could Richard Belleville tell him that he didn't already know.

When it all happened, he had taken the train up north to retrieve his car which had been impounded by the police. It was then he had heard the story up to that point. It was only later, when Alistair had escaped custody, that the final act had played out. He always regretted he hadn't pushed harder to be allowed to see Alistair, but the police had been adamant: he wasn't family, he couldn't see the prisoner. Perhaps he could have talked sense into him. But in his rational moments, he realised it would have been unlikely. Impossible really. All reason had clearly deserted his friend.

'Tell me how you knew Alistair McGovern, Leonard,' Richard said, his voice calm and reassuring. 'Tell me what I should have known about him.'

It was an invitation Leonard could not refuse. When Anthony Belleville had first mentioned his father, he had expected a big, rough country man of loud opinions. Richard Belleville, he discovered, was none of those things. He was refined, polished and articulate. But most especially, Leonard could see how easily authority settled on his shoulders.

That afternoon, in the reference library, he had researched his war record. He hadn't been able to access the more extensive record available in Canberra but the brief information he found was enough. Richard Belleville, he had learned, was a war hero. Distinguished Flying Cross. Badly injured in a bombing raid over Germany, his skilful flying had saved the lives of his crew. He had been a brave man in war. And now? He was self-assured. A commanding figure. But a decent man all the same, he guessed. So why had he been so angry and unreasonable with Alistair?

'What can I say, Mr Belleville.'

'Call me Richard, please.'

'What can I say, Richard,' he said, correcting himself. 'I'd known Alistair since he was in nappies. I was about six years old I think when they moved in next door to us – to my mother, my sister and me. Well, my father was alive then actually, but he died a few years later, the after-effects of the first war.'

'That would have been tough for you and your family,' Richard said, his sympathy genuine. He had been a young man when he had lost his father, but losing a father as a child would be devastating.

He nodded. It was a long forgotten sadness. But was it really forgotten? Life had never been the same for the family.

'That's why my mother and Muriel McGovern got along so well. Muriel said her husband was absent so much because he was working on his property up north. It seemed like they were both widows. No one questioned that story. No one questioned Muriel saying her husband wanted her to stay in Brisbane so Alistair could have a good education and that he would see them when he could. It all sounded perfectly reasonable. She was living the role assigned to her – that of dutiful wife. No one, for one moment, ever thought Muriel wasn't married. Which meant, later on, she became a widow in the eyes of her neighbours. But all that fell apart after ...'

He couldn't finish the sentence. He couldn't find the words to describe what his friend had done and the terrible implications for his friend's mother. Instead, he reached for his beer and sipped cautiously at the pale liquid.

Anthony, transfixed by the story, glanced at his father and saw immediately what it had cost his father to sit and listen to Leonard King's story.

'And you were a friend to Alistair?' Richard asked.

Leonard nodded, remembering how, in the absence of a father, Alistair had turned to him.

'We did a lot of things together, especially when he became a teenager. His mother trusted me to look after him. She was relieved, I think. I took him fishing. I taught him to swim. We went to the pictures together, that sort of thing. And eventually I taught him to drive.'

'And it was your car he was driving on the two occasions he drove out to Prior Park?'

Again, he nodded. Alistair had pestered him and he had finally agreed he would lend him his car. He could easily get to work by bus. He had thought he was helping his friend.

'It was. I lent him my car. He told me what he had found out about the Belleville family.'

He hesitated. It was Richard Belleville's family. And Anthony Belleville's family. How much did they really need to know? But he pressed on. It was clear father and son both wanted to know more.

'He said to me. *I don't even have the right name. My father's name is Belleville, not McGovern. He never married my mother.* Everything came as a terrible shock to him.'

Leonard was shaking his head from side to side. He let out a deep sigh.

'His mother should have told him the whole story years before but I suppose she didn't want to run the risk of gossip. She was a respectable widow with a young son. If people found out the truth, which they did later of course, she'd be ostracised as a kept woman. As a disgraced woman. And Alistair would have suffered too. But she suffered anyway when the truth finally emerged.'

Richard sighed deeply and buried his head in his hands. His father had left a terrible legacy for which other people had paid a high price. His wife Elizabeth had paid with her life, as had Alistair, the son Muriel McGovern had borne him. Richard and his brother and sister had been left with an empty hollowness where there might have been a loving memory of their father. And Muriel McGovern? She had paid a high price too. Had she believed in the beginning his father was free to marry her? He didn't know.

But there was one more surprise to come.

'I'm not sure I should tell you this, Richard,' Leonard said quietly.

He had become aware how everything he said had further doomed Richard's father in his family's eyes. But he had to say it. He had to tell him how much Francis Belleville had cared about his youngest son.

'Go on,' Richard said, his voice barely above a whisper.

'I met your father Francis Belleville on a few occasions. It's not going to be easy for you to hear this but he loved Alistair. Alistair, of course, hero worshipped him. He was a charming man as I recall. I'm very much afraid your father created a fantasy world for Alistair. He talked to Alistair about how the two of them would work together on the property up north when he was older. Alistair's eyes would light up at the mention of his father's name and what they would do together in the future.'

'Bloody hell! What a bloody fool my father was!'

It was an explosion of disappointment. Of anger. Not at the boy or his mother. But at his father for his selfishness.

He had never, until that moment, understood the depths of his father's duplicity. Nor the full depths of his weakness. He had wanted to be loved and admired by everyone. And when his marriage had turned sour, he had sought solace elsewhere. But not with a woman who understood the limitations of such an arrangement but with a woman, naïve and trusting, who had wanted what many women want: a husband, a home, a family – and the respectability all this automatically infers. He hardly knew what to say. In this story, he could barely recognise the man he had known as his father.

'I'm sorry, Leonard. I'm shocked. I had no idea. Perhaps my brother William did. My father died while I was in England serving. He dealt with the aftermath. There was one overriding ambition for us. We were determined our mother would never find out about Muriel McGovern and her son. There was no way, at least while she was alive, we could ever countenance dealing with Alistair McGovern. He was the embodiment of my father's betrayal, not just of my mother, but of all of us.'

He paused. He was still trying to absorb everything he had been told.

'And then of course Alistair turned up on the night of my mother's sixtieth birthday. We had a house full of guests. We had tried again and again to get Alistair to settle for money. A substantial amount of money. We had two stipulations. He wasn't to contact the family and he was never going to be allowed to change his name to Belleville. But he refused our offer every time. And then he turned up at our front door on this important night for the family. What did he want us to do? Introduce him to our mother in front of all her friends and neighbours? Of course I threw him out. I was angry. With him. And with our father. I was beyond angry if you must know.'

Even now, remembering the dramatic scene that ensued, Richard's anger resurfaced.

'I understand,' Leonard said quietly.

In fact, he knew he was understanding everything for the very first time. He had only ever seen it from Alistair's point of view. But what more could Richard Belleville have done? He knew Alistair, by that point, would have been at the point of hysteria.

'It's a very sad business, Richard,' he said, as he drained his glass. 'A very sad business.'

Richard was calmer now. What purpose did anger serve now except to indulge his feelings of intense disappointment in his father?

'It is, Leonard. There are no winners. And how, may I ask, did Muriel McGovern cope with it all? Do you know?'

Leonard nodded sadly.

'She became almost a recluse. She and my mother remained friends. A Christian act, my mother said, but no one else in the street felt the same way. They would cross the road to avoid her. Some obscenities were painted on her front fence. I helped her scrub them off and repaint the fence.'

'She died a few years back, as I understand it,' Richard said, surprising Leonard – and Anthony – with that knowledge.

'Yes, she did. Cancer, I'm afraid. My mother helped nurse her. She maintained a quiet dignity right up until the end. I'm surprised you know about her death.'

It was now Richard's turn for revelations.

'My brother William is due some credit, not me. He had met her after our father had died. Just once, when he came down here to arrange for our father's body to be returned home. He visited her at her home. After he died, we arranged some money to help support Alistair. When he died, my brother, without consulting me, arranged for a quarterly payment to help Muriel McGovern. Not a lot of money but it was something. We were advised of her death by our Brisbane solicitors. We never asked what happened to the house though. We always assumed it was in her name.'

Leonard King let out a deep sigh. There was just one more postscript to the story.

'She left the house to me, Richard,' he said finally. 'I'm now living in the house your father bought for her and her son.'

He waited for a reaction. Would he hate the fact that a house bought by his father hadn't been returned to Belleville ownership? Would he feel it should have come back to the Belleville family now? Would they care?

But for the first time, Richard smiled. This time the smile was meant to be reassuring.

'I think she was rewarding you for the friendship you had shown her son,' Richard said. 'And the friendship your family had shown her. I have no problems with that. I hope it brings you happiness. I didn't ask before. Are you married?'

It was the first genuinely warm smile Richard had noticed on Leonard King's face.

'Yes. I got married quite late actually. Annie is my wife's name. And we have a son.'

Richard closed his eyes briefly. Please God don't let him have called the child Alistair.

'His name is Henry. Harry really. For my father. Inheriting the house was a godsend for us.'

Richard breathed a sigh of relief. Of course, he would name his son after the father he had lost as a child. Perhaps the house would now have an ordinary happy family living in it. He hoped so.

'I know you've been angry with me for some time, but I hope you see there are two sides to the story, just as I have seen there are two sides to the story,' Richard said. 'I hope you can see why we could never offer Alistair what he wanted. For all of us, he represented a betrayal of us as a family. We wouldn't ever have wanted to be reminded of that constantly. It was just never going to happen. I may have handled it better, but the outcome would have been the same.'

'You know what he most wanted?'

Leonard shifted in his seat, suddenly unsure as to whether he should say anything more.

'What was it he really wanted, Leonard?' Richard asked. Was there something he had missed?

'He wanted to take his place alongside you and your brother in the family. He was the third son. He thought that stood for something.'

It saddened Richard to hear this admission.

'He was completely deluded,' Richard said, wondering at just how twisted Alistair McGovern's mind had become. But he knew of course. And it seemed as if, at that moment, Leonard King needed to be reminded of it.

'And when he was denied this fantasy, he did his best to kill me,' Richard said, the echo of his long buried anger resurfacing. 'That's the plain fact of it.'

But he did not say more. To Richard, there seemed no point in recounting the shocking details of Alistair McGovern's final moments. One fatal shot had saved his life just as it had ended Alistair's.

'I know. I heard the story,' Leonard murmured. He too was keen not to revisit it. 'I know. It was all too shocking.'

He took a deep breath and then turned towards Anthony. He wanted to lighten the mood. He felt there was nothing more left to say about Alistair McGovern.

'And you, Anthony, have the final chapter to write – restoring the house, if I understand your mission correctly.'

Through all the revelations, Anthony had remained silent, unable to contribute but listening intently to everything that had been said.

'I hope so,' he said, with a sense of pride. 'This time the client is my Aunt Julia. She divorced her very wealthy husband a few years back. She's decided the family will have a new Prior Park mansion. She's financing the new build.'

'Will it be exactly the same?'

Leonard, too, had looked through the file. He had seen the letters questioning the wisdom of building such a fine house in so remote a location. Wasn't that still a consideration?

'Not sure yet,' Anthony admitted. He now had his own reservations. He chose to be non-committal. 'Building methods have changed of course so that impacts design but one thing is for sure, it will have very strong links with the past. It will be, in many ways, a phoenix rising from the ashes.'

'Sounds like a good project for a fledgling architect. I wish you luck with it,' Leonard said.

'Thanks. It'll be exciting. My first commission.'

But could anything he did now match the grand ambition of the man who had conceived Prior Park's magnificent house eighty years earlier, he wondered. That was the challenge.

'Let's drink to the new house rising from the ashes,' Richard said, as he signalled for the barman. More than ever, he needed another stiff drink.

But in a strange way it had been cathartic too. Revisiting it all had been painful but necessary. Now that chapter of the Belleville family could be closed. It was finished with. It was over.

The new chapter for Prior Park was something for them all to look forward to.

11

'HOW WAS THE TRIP to Brisbane?' Alice asked. 'Did Anthony find something interesting?'

She was standing in the garden at the front of the house at Prior Park, hose in hand, watering her favourite plants. The ambitious rose garden of the early years was long gone, replaced by hardier plants less susceptible to the heat and humidity of a tropical summer.

Richard walked towards her, a bulky envelope held out in front of him.

'He found the plans to the original Prior Park house in the architect's archive. It was quite a coup. He photocopied what he could.'

Alice remembered the house well. She had gone there as a young bride, nervous at the prospect of living under her mother-in-law's roof. But it had worked out well, in the end, as Elizabeth Belleville had gradually allowed her to take charge of the day-to-day running of the household. She knew, in doing so, she had usurped Catherine, Richard's wife, which she had never meant to do.

But Catherine hadn't seemed to mind. For all her early years as Richard's wife, Catherine had seemed like a visitor at Prior Park. She would take herself off to England at every opportunity. She wondered how things were going for them now, second time around. Catherine had made it plain she would only ever be an occasional visitor to Richard's house in town.

She walked to the tap and turned off the hose, wiping her hands on her apron.

'I'm keen to have a look,' she said. 'William will want to see them too.'

Just then, William appeared on the verandah and held a hand up in greeting to his brother.

'Did I hear you say you have the plans for the old house there?'

'And much more besides,' Richard replied, without elaborating.

The three of them sat down on the verandah around a small table where Richard produced the copies Anthony had taken.

William quickly read through the copies of the letters to the architect, including the letter from their grandfather and then glanced through the architectural plans, which Anthony had meticulously taped together to form a whole.

He laughed out loud.

'A man of grand gestures indeed,' William said. 'Whichever way you look at it, it was foolish to build such a house out here. And in my opinion, it's a foolish whim to rebuild it. Not to mention expensive. It won't add a cent to the value of Prior Park as a rural property.'

Richard shrugged. He noticed a quiet smile on Alice's face. They both knew William was a man entirely incapable of grand gestures. If he resembled either of their parents, Richard thought it was their mother, Elizabeth Belleville. He was practical and clear sighted. He was kind and generous to his wife and daughter and an indulgent grandfather but never extravagant. He queried every expense to do with the running of their properties.

'I hope you won't say that to Julia. Or to Anthony,' Richard cautioned. 'We agreed she could rebuild if she wanted to.'

He nodded but he was annoyed with his brother all the same.

'Of course I won't say anything to her. It's her money. She can sink it into a folly if she wants to. My only worry is that it will overshadow this house if it's as big and commanding as the original.'

He was very content in the house that had been rebuilt after the fire. It suited him and Alice.

'Perhaps we can encourage her to shrink the building footprint,' Richard said hopefully. He didn't want to raise William's hopes but it was exactly what he and Anthony had discussed after seeing the original plans.

'I hope so. That would make much more sense.'

He looked at his brother then, sensing there was something else he wanted to share with them.

'There's something else, isn't there?'

He knew his brother well. Too well at times, he felt.

Richard nodded.

'I don't think you'll believe this but a ghost from our past resurfaced. The librarian we dealt with was Alistair McGovern's good friend. His next door neighbour in fact.'

William was speechless. It was Alice who asked the obvious question.

'Really? How did he come to tell you this? Did the name mean something to him?'

'It did, Alice.'

He looked at William then, wondering if he should tell him. But he had a right to know.

'He recognised the name of the place when he was putting the file away after Anthony had accessed it. I think he was in two minds, but in the end, he wanted to say something to defend his friend.'

He proceeded then to recount the story, leaving nothing out, and seeing on William's face the same renewed sense of disillusionment and disappointment in their father he had felt.

But Alice's sympathy was for Muriel McGovern. She had been duped. She too had paid a terrible price for having fallen for their father's flawed charm and hollow promises.

'Poor woman. I imagine by the time she found out the truth about him, it was too late,' she said quietly. She didn't say it but she suspected he would have made an empty promise to divorce his wife once Muriel discovered she was pregnant and he wasn't free to marry her.

'And you say Leonard King is now in possession of the house she lived in?'

'A good thing to come from it all, I believe,' Richard said. 'He and his wife Annie have a son named Harry. Hopefully it will be a happy family home from now on.'

'I agree, brother,' William said. 'An interesting postscript to the whole affair. Let's hope we never need to speak of it again.'

But both men knew, deep in their hearts, they would carry the bitter legacy left by their father to their graves.

At the very time Richard was visiting Prior Park, Alex stopped in front of Amanda and Paul's house. He had not spoken to her privately following the revelations of who his father really was. This would be his first opportunity.

He knew Paul was going to check on the progress of the maintenance overhaul of the small plane he flew regularly, and little Andrew would be at school. It was the perfect time, providing baby Matthew was asleep.

'Hello, stranger,' he greeted her as she opened the door to him. 'I hope I'm not disturbing you.'

She smiled. She was always pleased to see him. He kissed her quickly on the cheek.

'You're looking well. Baby asleep?'

She nodded.

He followed her through the house to the kitchen.

'No housekeeper today?' he asked.

'She'll be here this afternoon,' she said. 'She prefers to work in the afternoon.'

He knew that domestic work was not Amanda's strong point. Having a housekeeper was a small price to pay to be relieved of the domestic humdrum she hated.

'Have you heard from your mother?' he asked. Up to that point, he had received all the news second hand via Marianne.

'Yes, she's coming up to see me in a couple of weeks' time.'

'How do you feel about that?' He knew it had been a big shock to her to find out her mother was still alive.

She shrugged.

'It's a good thing, I guess.'

'Paul thinks it's a good thing,' she added, as if he had made the decision for her.

Did she have any idea how much it would have meant to me to find out my own mother was still alive, he wondered? I would have been ecstatic. But then he had known neither a mother nor a father. Well, he had known Arthur Robinson. But not as a father. Rather as a man to be avoided.

She looked at him then, aware that he too was coming to terms with revelations about his own life.

'We know now why your father was so desperate to keep us away from one another,' he said gently.

She nodded. It all made sense now. Her father had thought it possible he was Alex's father.

'You know Arthur Robinson forced himself on her,' he said finally. 'She wrote as much in her letter to me. Your uncle was not a nice man.'

Amanda filled in the blanks.

'And then I suppose she slept with my father, probably knowing she was pregnant and knowing his marriage was rocky, hoping to be offered marriage.'

He nodded. That had certainly been her plan. But the plan had never been fulfilled. Howard, sent to one of their remote gulf properties, had found out too late.

For the first time it struck him that Amanda had possibly done the same thing. Except of course that Paul had married her. Willingly. But he would never speak such an idea aloud. Even privately between the two of them, it would always be her secret. And he would go on living with the uncertainty. And with the guilt. Not to mention the shame of having betrayed Marianne.

'Our lives could have been different,' he said quietly, 'but it's too late now.'

She looked at him critically.

'It is. It's too late. You made a choice anyway,' she shrugged dismissively. 'A choice for both of us.'

He understood. She would always blame him for choosing Marianne.

'But you gave me no option. You never said, let's wait and see or I'll try and talk my father around. He was adamant, remember. And you didn't want to go against him. That seemed to me to be an end to it. There was nothing more to say. I had to move on.'

She smiled as if remembering.

'I had no idea you were going to move on so quickly,' she countered.

What could he say except the expected thing.

'I fell in love with Marianne.'

'No you didn't,' she insisted. 'What you fell in love with was Marianne's future prospects.'

He didn't try to argue with her. What was the point? After all Marianne and the children were his priorities now.

'Time for me to go, I think,' he said. He was cautious. They were beginning to traverse dangerous ground. He couldn't risk being drawn back to her. 'We both have good lives. That's what's important. You have a good life with Paul. I have a good life with Marianne.'

But he sensed a restlessness in her. He wondered if she would ever really settle down.

She let out a deep sigh.

'Yes, we have a good life but if I'm honest I find life tough going at the moment,' she admitted. 'I envy Paul's freedom to get up and go about his job. I don't have that freedom. Not now.'

'Not now perhaps but once the kids are older, you'll be able to visit your properties and get more involved in running them.'

He knew that was what she most wanted to do. Not to be tied to domesticity. He could see she was frustrated but he could see no way out. Not while the children were small. But he was gratified she was confiding in him as she once had. He smiled encouragingly. Only time will resolve the issue, he thought, as he turned to go.

'You and I would have made a good team,' she said suddenly, her hand on his arm. 'I should have listened to my heart. I see that now.'

It was an unexpected admission. It caught him by surprise.

'I wish you had,' he murmured. 'I wish you had.'

He took her in his arms for just a moment, enjoying the feel of her body against his. And then he turned and walked away quickly, not looking back. Not seeing the tears flow unchecked down her cheeks. Not seeing her look of utter desolation.

And not letting her see how those few words had destroyed his peace of mind too. Is this how it will be, he wondered? Would their old feelings for one another keep bubbling uncomfortably to the surface? Would he go on being tempted by her?

He was desperate now to head out to Prior Park to get stuck into some hard physical work. He had to get her out of his system. Once and for all. Because every time he saw her, he wanted to be with her. And then it would take a supreme act of self will to shut out the memories of being with her. Of being her lover.

It was just a week later that Rosie Archer stood on the top step and knocked on Amanda's door.

'Hello, Amanda,' she said, her greeting almost inaudible, as her daughter cautiously opened the door.

'Hello.'

As the day for the visit approached, Amanda had struggled with how she should address her mother. She had rarely used the word 'Mum'. She doubted she could now.

'Call me Rosie,' her mother said, sensing her uncertainty. 'I think that's best. Can I come in?'

Amanda held the door open for her. She wondered if she bore any resemblance at all to the woman in front of her. Grey had overtaken her hair. Her skin bore the familiar hallmarks of too much sun but there was a lively twinkle in her eyes. Amanda could see, in her youth, she would have been vivacious and lively.

She was dressed in a simple cotton dress, belted at the waist. Straight from a pattern in a women's magazine, Amanda guessed.

Amanda led the way into the house. Not to the kitchen but to the living room. She was surprised there was no suitcase with her mother.

'I'd prepared the spare room for you,' she said, pointing across the hallway to a room in the middle of the house. It had been her father's room when he had visited them.

Rosie shook her head.

'I thought that was too much of an imposition,' she said. 'I'm staying at a local hotel. Just for a few days.'

She looked around her.

'A lovely home. Did Paul buy it when you got married?'

Amanda shook her head.

'No, my father bought it for me when we first moved here. Paul moved in with me.'

There seemed no point in explaining the reason. She had simply refused to move into the house Paul had bought with his former fiancée.

There was silence then. What do I say to her, Amanda wondered? There was almost too much to say. Potentially, too many recriminations.

Just then she heard little Matthew whimpering and got up to see to him. Her mother followed her into the nursery.

'Here, let me hold him,' she offered. 'He's a beautiful baby.'

She looked from the baby to her daughter.

'Does he favour his father?'

Amanda nodded.

'Very much so,' she said, as she watched her mother lay him down gently in his cot again.

She noticed then a photo on the wall of the nursery.

'Is this little Andrew with his baby brother?'

Amanda nodded. The photographer had captured the two of them just at the right moment.

'You have fine looking children,' she said approvingly. 'You're a very lucky girl.'

Was there just a hint of grandmotherly pride, Amanda wondered?

'Paul dotes on them,' she said. 'Spoils them really.'

Her mother let out a deep sigh.

'Better that than being too tough.'

It was the first glimpse of her mother's life. As a wife to another man. As a mother to other children.

'Was your husband hard on your children?' she asked. 'Was he a hard father? Is that what you're saying? Or was my father hard on me?'

She turned then and faced Amanda.

'No, your father wasn't hard on you as a baby. He loved you. He was hard in the way he dealt with me. But then he'd fallen out of love with me. My next husband was pretty hard on our kids, particularly if he'd had too much to drink. I did my best to protect them. I'd send them to bed early. They didn't really mourn him when he died. Neither did I, if I'm honest.'

Little Matthew had settled again so they headed towards the kitchen. Amanda had laid a tea tray ready to make tea.

'Let me do it,' her mother insisted. 'You're probably exhausted, taking care of the house and two kids.'

She watched as her mother completed the tea-making ritual.

'You have to tell me everything from the beginning,' Amanda said, sipping the tea her mother had put in front of her. 'I should tell you though I found the letter you wrote to my father telling him you couldn't keep in touch with me. And why.'

Rosie sat down opposite her daughter.

'It's time, isn't it, for you to know the whole story. But it was like I wrote, I had to think of my future. I had no skills to support myself. My family couldn't help. And then I met Ronnie Archer. He'd just returned from the war. He served in the Middle East and in New Guinea. He had managed to get a job on the railways. He ended up in quite a good job, as a supervisor checking the work on the tracks.'

Amanda waited for her to continue.

'We went on to have three children, two girls and a boy, but we lost one of the little girls when she was two years old. It seemed to tear the heart out of our little family. Ronnie was never the same after that. She was his favourite.'

'And what are your children doing now?' Amanda asked. She did not call them her siblings. She didn't know them. Didn't even know their names.

'Patrick is in his mid-twenties. He's gone into the navy. And Sally is twenty. She is training to be a nurse.'

She reached into her handbag and pulled out a photograph. A tall young man proudly showing off his navy uniform smiled back at her. A younger girl – his sister Sally, she assumed – stood alongside him, scowling slightly.

'The sun was in her eyes,' Rosie said, explaining away the scowl with a laugh. 'And she was running late to meet a girlfriend to go to the movies. I took it when Patrick was home on leave at Christmas.'

'Do they know about me?' Amanda asked, handing the photograph back to Rosie.

She shook her head.

'I've never told them I was married before I married their father. I wanted us to meet first. I thought it really has to be your choice. There's been a lot of water under the bridge. You might decide you don't want to have anything more to do with me. I'd understand that.'

Amanda sat in silence for some time. Is this how she imagined the meeting with her mother would go? Had it all come too late to be meaningful in her life?

She shrugged.

'I don't know what you want me to say,' she said. 'I think it's up to you really. It's your story. Did my father drive you away?'

At that point, she couldn't meet Amanda's eye. It was time for honesty.

'He probably thought I flirted with the other men too much. It was in my nature then. I just wanted to have a good time. Motherhood wasn't something I planned. And then of course I had to get married.'

With those words, without knowing it, she was echoing her daughter's experience.

'In my heart, I knew the marriage wouldn't last. We were such different people. And then I realised he was keen on Elizabeth Fraser. She died, didn't she?'

Amanda nodded.

'She died two weeks after her son Alex was born.'

'Perhaps I shouldn't ask this but was he your father's child?'

Amanda shook her head.

'No, it turns out his father was Arthur Robinson, my father's cousin. He took advantage of her.'

She nodded knowingly.

'I'm not surprised to hear that,' she said. 'He tried the same with me but I told him I was marrying Howard, so he backed off. I felt sorry for his wife. A nice woman.'

She thought for a moment.

'What happened to Alex, do you know? No mother. No father. It would have been tough for him.'

'He was brought up on Isla Downs. He and I became close.'

'Brother and sister close. Or boyfriend-girlfriend close?'

Amanda smiled to herself. How could she answer except with a lie.

'Brother and sister close,' she said.

'What's he doing now?'

'He married Paul's cousin, Marianne Belleville. They live a few streets away. He's done very well for himself. He's found himself a good role in helping manage the Belleville rural properties.'

She listened to all this and then nodded.

'That's good, I'm pleased to hear it. His mother was a lovely woman. Very refined. Very well educated. From a good Scots family that had fallen on hard times. That's why she came to Australia to be a governess.'

And then she looked searchingly at Amanda.

'He's not pushing Paul out of the role he should have in the family, is he?'

There was a hint of anxiety in her question but she was relieved to hear Amanda laugh quietly.

'No, Paul prefers aeroplanes to cattle. Paul's main job is to fly his uncle around their properties. He's a pilot. In fact that's where he is now. Their plane has just undergone maintenance. He wanted to do a final test flight to make sure everything was fine with it.'

'And Paul's mother and father?'

'So many questions,' Amanda said, not expecting to have to

endure an interrogation. I'm the one with the questions, she wanted to say.

Her mother smiled and reached across to grasp Amanda's hand.

'I just want to make sure you're happy. That you're respected. I know what it's like to feel like an outsider,' she said unexpectedly. 'I want to know that your life here is a good life. That your in-laws care for you. You don't have anyone else. Not now your father has passed on.'

'They're good people. Paul's father Richard has always been very good to me.'

'And his mother?'

'It's a complicated story,' she said. 'She doesn't live here with him much. They divorced when Paul was twelve but remarried a few years ago. She's English. She lives in England at her country estate or in Sydney, where Paul's brother Anthony is at uni. She and I get on well.'

'Unusual arrangements,' Rosie murmured.

'It works for them apparently.'

It was as if, at that moment, Amanda projected herself forward into her future. Could she live like Paul's mother Catherine? She realised it was Catherine's life, not Alice's life, that appealed. Yet the whole family revolved around Alice and William and the stability they offered.

But there was one more question Rosie was desperate to ask. She had to know. There was only one way to find out.

'Did your father do the right thing by you?'

'Meaning?' Amanda was uncertain. What did her mother mean, *the right thing*?

'Did you get his share of the Robinson estate when he passed? Or did he pass it all on to the boy? What was his name? The cousin's boy, I mean.'

And then, in a flash, it occurred to Amanda she didn't know. How could she have known? She'd had no contact with anyone for years.

'My cousin Alan drowned when he was a boy. His father died a few years later a broken man. There was no one else. It all came to me,' she said. 'My father had been preparing me for years. I now own all five rural properties.'

She noticed the look of relief on her mother's face.

'I'm sorry to hear about the boy but I'm pleased to know your father did the right thing by you. I was worried he would bypass a girl.'

Amanda smiled.

'Was he disappointed when I was born that I wasn't a boy?'

The thought had never occurred to her up until that point.

'He was,' she admitted, 'but then he just came to dote on you. I hope he was a good father to you.'

'He was. The best,' Amanda said, 'except for telling me the lie about you.'

'Don't be too hard on him for that,' Rosie said. 'That was my fault really. I had to make my marriage work. Your father wanted to give me more money but he couldn't get any more cash out of his cousin Arthur who controlled everything.'

Was this the time to ask her, Amanda wondered?

'And now? Could you use that cash now?'

Rosie shook her head.

'I get a widow's pension. I get Ronnie's small pension from his work. And he inherited a bit of money from his elderly mother when she finally passed. I have enough.'

'Are you sure?'

She nodded.

'Yes, I'm sure.'

She looked at her watch.

'It must be time you fed that baby,' she said.

Amanda nodded, heading to the stove to prepare a bottle.

'It's never ending at this age,' she said, pulling a face.

'You should get a nanny,' her mother suggested. 'You can afford it.'

'You tell Paul that when you meet him, will you.'

She laughed.

'I will,' she said, without hesitation.

12

IT WAS A BRIGHT warm day, a day when flying is a pleasure, although for Paul, flying was almost always a pleasure.

The aircraft maintenance engineer sitting beside him watched closely and listened carefully. The sole purpose of the short flight was to test the aircraft, not sightseeing, he reminded Paul.

But still, the young pilot could not resist the temptation to fly low over one of the islands off the coast with a more daring manoeuvre than the engineer was comfortable with.

And then Paul turned the Cessna for home, flying in a wide arc to take in Prior Park before expertly touching down at the airport and taxiing to the hangar.

'Thanks, Larry. It all sounds fine,' Paul said, as he clambered out of the cockpit.

'When's the next trip?' he asked, hoping Paul would be able to give him some precise instructions. It helped to know, he reminded Paul, so the plane was ready for take off without delay.

'Not sure, Larry. Possibly at the end of next week. I'll talk to Uncle William and let you know.'

'You haven't taken your father up in a while,' he ventured.

'Well, he leaves the rural stuff to Uncle William. He's more likely to be on a commercial flight south.'

'To see your mother, I suppose?'

Paul laughed. Was there nothing about the Belleville family's lives that was private?

'To attend board meetings,' he said, ignoring the question about his mother.

As he turned from locking down the aircraft, he was surprised to see a young woman, almost as tall as he himself, holding out her hand for the keys.

'Shall I put those away for you, Mr Belleville?' she asked.

'Sure, thanks,' Paul mumbled.

'Paul, this is my daughter Linda. She's just graduated from university,' Larry said, smiling proudly. 'She's helping me out here for a while. She's just qualified as a pilot too.'

'Nice to meet you, Linda,' Paul said, as he surveyed the young woman standing in front of him.

He noticed how her dark blonde hair tumbled around her shoulders but it was the intensity of her gaze that he would remember. For just a few moments, her deep blue eyes mesmerised him. He wondered idly what her degree course had been. Arts probably, he guessed. Wrongly, as it turned out.

'She finished in the top ten in her engineering degree course,' the proud father said. 'I don't know where she gets her brains from. Must be her mother.' But he smiled broadly. He would boast about his clever daughter at every opportunity.

'Sure it's not from you, Dad?' she asked with a smile.

Paul could see father and daughter were close. He patted her arm in a fatherly way.

'No, definitely your mother,' he said but the pride on his face was plain.

He turned back to Paul.

'Your brother's at university, isn't he?'

Larry Kent had heard about the Belleville family's goings on, not from Paul or his father, but from the local gossips.

'Yes, Anthony's studying architecture at Sydney uni,' Paul replied, surprised that a man who spent most of his life with his head in an aircraft engine would know what his brother was up to. He glanced at his watch. 'I must be going. See you next week but I'll let you know, Larry. Nice to meet you, Linda. Come up with me sometime and I'll show you the ropes.'

He turned and walked back towards his car parked on the edge of the general aviation area. He would have been surprised to know he was the subject of further discussion between father and daughter.

'Is he a good pilot?' Linda asked. 'Is he safe to go up with? I take it he's not just some rich boy playing with planes.'

Her father shook his head.

'No, he's always been mad keen on flying. He's a good pilot although he almost died a few years back in a crash. Not his fault. Hit an eagle. Out near Taroom. Now he ferries his uncle around, mostly to their properties out west.'

He noticed the appraising look on his daughter's face.

'Don't get any ideas, my girl. He's married with two kids. Married a girl who inherited five cattle properties recently from her father. Money begets money.'

Linda shook her head.

'You're getting ahead of yourself just a bit, don't you think?'

He chuckled, but he could see she was disappointed by the news

'Well, maybe you'll get a chance to meet the younger brother one of these days. Inherited wealth. That's what the Belleville family have. You can't beat it. But then they have mixed fortunes when it comes to their marriages. Maybe it's just as well to steer clear of them.'

'Mixed fortunes?'

She turned a quizzical eye on her father.

'Too complicated to go into now. Remind me to tell you sometime. They've been the source of a lot of gossip over the years. That I can tell you. And of course their big house was burned down by a madman, must be nearly twenty years ago now.'

'Wow. That's unbelievable. What happened?'

'I don't know all the details,' her father admitted, 'but Paul's grandmother died as a result of the fire.'

'And the madman?'

'He was in custody but escaped. Almost killed Paul's father Richard in a surprise attack, I heard, but their station manager shot him dead. One shot. Brilliant marksman apparently. It was all hushed up though. No charges were ever laid against Charles Brockman.'

'I wonder where Paul was when all this was going on. It would have been traumatic.'

'He was away at boarding school. Just as well too.'

'And his brother?'

'Living with his mother in England.'

She thought for a moment.

'So that's why Paul's mother doesn't live with his father?'

Her father shrugged.

'It's probably why they broke up the first time. It's their second go at being married. I think Paul would have been an early teenager or thereabouts when they divorced.'

Linda shook her head, thinking of the cosy comfortable relationship of her parents and the warm and welcoming home they had created for their children.

'That must have been tough on him,' she said.

'I think it was. Very tough. But he's turned out alright. He's very easy to get on with. They say his wife is pretty headstrong though. And besotted with his cousin's husband except her father wouldn't countenance a marriage when he was alive.'

Her eyes widened at this revelation.

'Does Paul know?'

Her father shrugged. The gossips hadn't been able to decide.

'So where do you get all this gossip from? Not from him, that's for sure. He was pretty tight lipped when you made that comment about his father visiting his mother.'

He laughed.

'No, certainly not from him. From your mother. She brings it all home. From her work at the hospital. And from her craft group. There's always some new titbit about the Belleville family.'

'So now you'll have to tell me everything,' she said. 'It all sounds like delicious gossip but I'm beginning to feel sorry for him, despite all his advantages.'

Her father paused.

They had reached his workshop and he had begun to tidy his tools away into their allotted spaces.

'Well, maybe you should first feel sorry for the girl he abandoned at the altar. Devastated she was, by all accounts. But her family found out he'd got another girl pregnant. As it turned out, he was off to the altar anyway in quick time, just with a different girl.'

His daughter was left open mouthed but wondering, all the same, how such a privileged young man had got himself into such a pickle.

'I bet there's more to that story than people ever found out.'

'You're probably right,' her father said, shouting to be heard over the clatter of tools and then the click of the locks as he secured the valuable items in his workshop. 'Right now, though, I'm focussed on that cold beer I'm going to have when I get home.'

'That sounds like a good plan,' she said, as they walked towards the car to head home. 'I'll have to start thinking about applying for jobs soon. I'll probably have to move away again.'

'No rush, my girl. No rush. You need a holiday after those long years of study. And your mother and your sisters love having you back home.'

He couldn't quite bring himself to say *and I love having my eldest daughter back home too*. But that was the truth of it. Their family was complete again. Just the five of them. He was a contented man.

He wondered idly if Paul Belleville was a contented man. But still he cursed himself for not having introduced his daughter to his young client years before. The fact is the idea had never occurred to him. And now it was too late.

Larry Kent would have been surprised to know, given Paul's path to marriage, how well he had settled into life with Amanda. At least most of the time. It was a more predictable life. But still there were times when he missed the single life and there were times he knew Amanda chaffed at the constraints of marriage and domesticity. They rarely argued.

The house was well kept; the lawns and gardens were tended carefully; their home life went along in an ordered way, but it was mostly down to the housekeeper and the gardener. He had quickly discovered how easily domestic chores bored Amanda.

And then her father's death had consumed her time as she dealt with the myriad legal issues and the big decisions that only she could make. She rarely asked his advice. He wondered if she discussed aspects of the running of the properties with Alex but he wouldn't ask. The fact is he wouldn't ask because he didn't want to know the answer. He suspected Alex was a regular visitor when he was away with his uncle but he hoped that was because of their long-standing friendship. Nothing more.

But since the birth of the second baby and the news of her mother, her mood had swung wildly between despair and frustration.

As he returned home that afternoon, he was anxious, wondering how the first meeting with her mother had gone. He knew Marianne had volunteered to collect Andrew when she picked up little Mel from school to relieve Amanda of the responsibility.

He found her in the kitchen, baby Matthew asleep in her arms.

'How did it go?' he asked quietly.

They had agreed she would meet her mother for the first time by herself.

'It went well,' she said in hushed tones. She got up then to head to the nursery to put the baby into his cot.

He waited for her to return. Not waking up the baby was the most important priority in the household.

'It went well,' he echoed. 'That's good, isn't it? What's she like?'

'Like a woman in her fifties,' she replied noncommittally. 'Not particularly mourning her husband Ronnie though. She talked about her children. Her son is in the navy and her daughter is studying to be a nurse.'

'And her circumstances?' He didn't know how else to ask the question.

'Not well off but she insists she has enough. She knew my father had passed away. She saw the funeral notice in the paper, but she didn't know I had inherited everything. She was worried he might have bypassed me for my cousin Alan. She didn't know Alan had died.'

He sighed deeply, the relief in his voice apparent.

'You thought she might have been a gold digger, didn't you?'

She was almost accusing him of disrespecting her mother.

'Didn't you? Just for a moment?'

She shrugged. He was right. The thought had crossed her mind.

'So what happens next?'

'It's Saturday tomorrow. She's going to come for lunch. She wants to meet you. And see Andrew too. And then she's booked on the train back to Brisbane on Sunday morning.'

He put his arms around her. He noticed she was close to tears, as if the disappointment of not having a mother as a young girl had only become more acute. Thinking her mother was dead had left her bereft but accepting. Finding out later she was alive and had chosen not to participate in her life had been like reopening an old wound. And now he feared that wound would take a long time to heal.

'I understand,' Paul said. 'I understand how you feel. Meeting her now doesn't make up for what happened in the past. For what happened when you were a child.'

She sobbed against his shoulder.

'I'm being ridiculous,' she said, 'but I can't feel anything for her. She might be a neighbour. Or someone I met casually sometime in the past. I don't see her as my mother, because she was never a mother to me.'

'And I suspect she hasn't told her other children about you either. Am I right?'

'No, she hasn't. And I don't want her to either. In fact I don't think she wants to tell them. Not now.'

He understood exactly how she felt. They weren't part of her life. And they would never be part of her life. And she wasn't part of theirs.

'Then tell her that,' he said. 'Be honest with her.'

She nodded in agreement. It was, after all, a door she wanted to keep closed. Beyond the lie her father had told her, she remembered their warm loving relationship. She had worshipped him. He had idolised her. But he had only ever denied her one thing: Alex. That too was a door best kept closed, she decided. Firmly closed.

There was nothing more likely to lift the Belleville family's spirits than a Sunday lunch gathering at Prior Park.

It was baby Matthew's first outing to Prior Park and he was admired by everyone as he lay contentedly in his carry cot.

The two tearaways Andrew and Melanie made conversation almost impossible at times until William issued a stern command to his daughter and his nephew to keep the kids quiet, which was only achieved through the timely intervention of Alice with large bowls of ice cream for each of them but not before they had run their fingers through the icing on Paul's birthday cake while Alice wasn't looking.

Anthony, a surprise guest, had flown up from Brisbane before his return to Sydney and his university studies so much of the talk was about the plans for the new house and what had been discovered in the architect's archive.

But through the chatter, Richard took Amanda aside.

'How was the meeting with your mother?' It was his first opportunity to ask her.

She answered cautiously.

'OK, I guess.'

'That's it. OK?' He wasn't satisfied with her answer. 'Surely there's more to it than that?'

'Well, she told me about her life, her two kids, her husband. I told her about growing up. She didn't know I had inherited all the Robinson properties from my father. That came as a surprise to her. And a relief. She thought he might have sidestepped me. But then she didn't know my cousin Alan had died.'

To Richard, it sounded like a catch up between two acquaintances who hadn't seen one another for years. It had none of the warmth of a parent-child relationship.

'Am I right in thinking you didn't warm to her?'

Amanda shook her head.

'I didn't if I'm honest, Richard,' she said, knowing that she could speak freely with him. 'She was never a mother to me. Not when I needed a mother most. We've agreed to keep in contact, probably Christmas and birthdays. But I think perhaps my father made the right decision. I grew up only knowing one parent. That was the certainty in my life. I can't suddenly rewrite that part of my life.'

'No, you can't Amanda. We can't change the past. None of us can change the past.'

She looked at him then and wondered what he regretted the most from his past. But she would never ask. He, in many ways, had taken her father's place. She was grateful for his friendship and guidance. There were times she wished Paul had more of his father's strength of character. In time, perhaps, she mused. In time.

Along the table, Marianne was quizzing Paul about Amanda's mother, asking much the same questions.

'Amanda isn't the type of person to suddenly embrace a mother she has never known,' he said, hoping not to have to elaborate.

'So she didn't like her? Did you?'

He shrugged.

'She came to lunch yesterday. But she didn't stay long. I think digging up the past was painful for her too. I said to Amanda later that I think she just wanted to be satisfied the little girl she had left behind was having a good life. They agreed to keep in touch. That's all.'

'I heard Amanda say she had other children but they don't know about Amanda. Is she going to tell them?'

Paul shook his head.

'I don't think so. She has a settled life. She doesn't know how her children would react to the news. I don't think she's wants to risk her relationship with them.'

To Marianne, it made perfect sense. Why take the risk of jeopardising what she already had?

'And how is Amanda with it all?'

'Relieved, I think,' Paul said. 'And she's grateful for your help with Andrew.'

She smiled.

'He's no trouble. Not when he's with Mel.'

'Except perhaps noisy,' Paul said.

At that precise moment, they both saw Alex grab each child by the hand and walk with them into the garden.

'I think Alex thinks your father needs a bit of peace and quiet,' Paul said, as he watched the two children walking obediently with Alex.

'Mel's been asking about where the new house is going to be built,' she explained, 'and whether she'll get to live in it, so I think he's taking them down to the ruins to show them where it will be.'

Paul turned to his cousin John Fitzroy who'd been listening quietly to their conversation.

'Your mother might have more house guests than she bargained for,' he said with a laugh. 'The kids think this is going to be great fun watching a new house being built.'

'Well, you know my mother. She gets an idea in her head and it's hard to shift it.'

He turned towards Anthony.

'You'll need to lower her ambitions a bit, cousin,' he said. 'Pippa doesn't care if she spends all her money. She'll get more money than she'll ever know what to do with from her father but that's my inheritance she's squandering.'

He said it with a smile. But Anthony wasn't having any of that argument.

'Don't be greedy. She secured your future by buying into Prior Park. Be happy she's got this project to revive her spirits.'

Anthony had a soft spot for his aunt and they all knew it. How badly could one woman be treated by the men in her life, he often said.

'So do you have any plans yet?'

He shook his head.

'Not yet. My uni lecturer is going to come and visit so we can discuss options. I think it's important. I want to get this right and he's an expert on historic houses.'

He was grateful no one thought to ask his name but his father, walking up behind him, had overheard the comment. He put his hand on Anthony's shoulder.

'Let's talk about that visit, son,' Richard said, indicating they should speak privately.

Anthony looked up, alarmed by his father's sudden appearance. He followed his father out into the garden.

'What's up? I thought we agreed he could come up while you were away?'

Richard held up his hands in a gesture of appeasement.

'Yes, of course I agreed. And then I got to thinking that it would be a good opportunity for us all to see Susan. She could come with her stepfather.'

It hurt him to even say the word *stepfather* but that was the reality of his daughter's life. And he couldn't change that. But he knew, if he didn't reach out to her, he would lose her, possibly forever. Perhaps it was already too late. How many times had he seen her in the past few years? He could almost count them on the fingers of one hand, and only twice in that time had she been to Prior Park.

For a few moments, Anthony was speechless. He had never expected such a complete change in his father's attitude. He put his hand on his father's arm.

'Will you be OK with it? With meeting Daniel Harrington?'

Richard nodded.

'I'll have to be, won't I? I will just have to be adult about the whole thing. They can stay here with Alice and William for a couple of days. When do you suggest?'

'What about Easter or close to it? That's if it suits everyone,' Anthony said, having already quizzed Daniel Harrington on his availability.

'Sounds fine to me,' he said. 'I'll check with Alice to see if she's OK with the arrangements.'

He turned back towards the house in search of Alice. He guessed, rightly, she would be busy clearing the table.

Paul, having spotted his father and brother in deep conversation, hung back until his father was out of earshot before joining his brother.

'A deep and meaningful with the old man?' Paul asked.

'You could say that. I didn't tell you the name of my lecturer. It's Daniel Harrington.'

He waited for the name to register with Paul, who groaned aloud.

'Oh, complicated,' he said. 'Very complicated in fact. I did wonder what all the subterfuge was about. I thought perhaps you didn't mention his name because it wouldn't mean anything to any of us.'

Anthony grimaced.

'It wasn't me who told Dad. It was our mother. She had lunch with us in Sydney. I couldn't find the words to tell her so she was taken by surprise. She reacted superbly. Gave everyone a master-class in good manners, I must say.'

Paul laughed. He could imagine it easily. In the limited society of rural Australia, her refined manners were often misinterpreted as superiority. But in awkward social situations, she could smooth troubled waters with just a few well-chosen words.

'So what is Dad suggesting? He'll make himself scarce while he visits? I might too in that case.'

'Actually, he's had a complete about face. He's going to suggest Daniel brings Susan with him. That way we'll get to see her and she'll get to visit Prior Park. Don't forget she belongs here too, just as we do.'

'Excellent plan,' Paul agreed enthusiastically.

For him – and for his brother too – there had been a silver lining with the breakdown of his father's second marriage to Kate, Susan's mother. Their mother and father had got back together again. But there was always the regret of not seeing very much of their half-sister Susan. For the two boys, having a little sister had been a delight.

But, personally, for Paul, there was that painful, awful memory of the day he had broken Kate's daughter's heart. He would always regret the way he had treated Nancy. Only the fact she had found someone else and gone on to marry and have a daughter had eased the burden of guilt he would always carry with him. He wondered at times if those events had somehow permanently tainted his marriage to Amanda. But whenever he began to think such thoughts, he would not allow the idea to form fully in his mind. He would instead dismiss it impatiently as ridiculous.

Together, the brothers headed down towards the ruins of the Prior Park house, to join Alex and the two young children who chatted excitedly about the big house that was going to be built and who would live in it.

As Andrew's hair caught the light of the mid-afternoon sun, Paul stopped mid-stride. Was it really possible he had fathered such a fair child? His own father had insisted Andrew's looks were a throwback to his own father but seen alongside Alex, the terrible suspicions bubbled to the surface again. He walked like Alex. In years to come, Paul feared Andrew would look more and more like Alex.

Beside him, Anthony had noticed the break in Paul's stride. He made no comment. But he knew what was going through his brother's mind because he and his father had discussed it. His father had warned him. *Say nothing. Make no comment if it ever comes up. But if you must say something, tell him he's being ridiculous.* Except deep in his heart, Anthony knew his brother was right to harbour suspicions.

He remembered too how his father had impressed upon him the risk of two marriages crumbling if the suspicion was allowed to take hold. And if the two marriages failed, his father had been clear about the consequences. He feared the Belleville family would fracture beyond repair. And a child's life would be unnecessarily upended.

And that, Richard had insisted to his younger son, would be a price too high to pay.

13

THE FOLLOWING DAY Paul dropped his brother at the airport to catch the flight to Sydney.

'It was good to see you, brother,' Paul said. 'We'll see you in a couple of months, I hope. You'll notice a big change in the baby next time'

'They sleep a lot, don't they?' Anthony said.

'Only natural at this age. You'll find out when you've got a brood of your own,' he replied, with a broad smile.

But marriage seemed a long way off for his brother. As far as he could tell, Anthony hadn't expressed any interest in girls, not that he had heard. His father had asked him outright, only to be dissatisfied with Paul's answer he had no idea if Anthony had a girlfriend.

Ask him, his father had demanded. For no good reason, his son's silence on the subject had begun to worry Richard.

Paul seized the opportunity to put the question to his brother only because it bothered his father. Privately, he thought Anthony was quite capable of keeping quiet about any romantic involvement until such time as he couldn't avoid telling them.

'Maybe next time you'll bring a girlfriend with you,' Paul suggested, hoping to draw his brother out.

He stopped and looked closely at his brother. The answer was longer in coming than it should have been. It was after all a simple question. Finally, Anthony shook his head.

'Too busy for girls,' he said flatly. 'I've got to get through this final year. That's all that matters.'

But for some reason Paul sensed it wasn't quite the truth. Had his brother been disappointed romantically? Had he fallen for the wrong girl? He hoped Anthony wasn't about to repeat the mistakes he had made.

But he wouldn't pry further.

'Well, I'm sure you'll pass everything with flying colours,' Paul said, as he bade his brother a final farewell.

Anthony was relieved to be spared the probing questions his brother might have asked. He knew he had told him a lie. He hadn't been too busy for girls. The fact was he had suffered a disappointment so deep he did not want to share it with anyone. It had suited him to be absent from Sydney for a few days. Because in being absent, he had a perfect excuse to decline a wedding invitation.

As he sat in the terminal waiting for his flight to be called, he let out a deep sigh. She would be married now and setting off on her honeymoon. Why hadn't he realised she would simply toy with him and then discard him?

He cursed Lachlan Bell for having introduced him to his sister. To his capricious, lively, gorgeous sister. And she had carelessly snapped his heart in two. Victoria. The name was etched indelibly in his mind. And the ultimate insult had been the gold-embossed wedding invitation. He had torn it to shreds.

And now he must endure the thought of her lying in another man's arms. Just as she had lain in his arms.

He got up and began to pace the small terminal. Would the pain ever stop, he wondered? Being with his family had given him a few days of respite. But alone again, he wondered how he would cope.

And then he heard the announcement of his flight and headed towards the departure gate, grateful for the momentary distraction.

Instead of turning back towards home, Paul detoured to the general aviation area, keen to see Larry Kent to confirm the next date he would be flying. But if he was being honest with himself, he hoped to catch Larry's daughter Linda, too.

He desperately needed a diversion. Disturbing thoughts lingered from the previous day. Did anyone else notice little Andrew's likeness to Alex? Or was he just imagining something that wasn't there? Why had it struck him yesterday when he hadn't noticed it on previous occasions? Was it because Andrew, as he got older, would come to look more like Alex? What would happen then? But he knew what would happen. The small group of people who doubted Andrew's parentage would go on denying Alex could be Andrew's father. Was that enough for his peace of mind?

He parked his car and was immediately rewarded by a smile and a wave from Linda, who was just coming out of the office in search of her father.

'An unexpected visit?' she said as he walked towards her.

'I was dropping my brother off at the airport. I decided to stop by to confirm the dates for our next trip. Is your father around?'

'Right behind you,' she said.

'Lovely day for a joy flight,' she added, glancing skywards.

'You're on,' Paul said, knowing he could spare an hour. 'That's if the plane's ready to go.'

'Yes, she's ready,' Larry Kent replied as Paul turned around to greet him. 'When are you and your uncle off next?'

'Thursday morning,' Paul said. 'Bright and early. We're flying down to St George. It's a while since we've been down that way. Uncle William wants to make sure everything is running smoothly.'

'And you'll be extra alert for eagles, I take it.'

'Yep. I always fly a slightly different route these days. But of course they can come from any direction. At least they don't come in a flock. That would be terrifying.'

'And what's this I hear about a joy flight now?'

Larry Kent frowned. He wasn't totally happy about his daughter going up with Paul. He knew the Belleville men by reputation. He knew Paul's grandfather and father had reputations where women were concerned. He wondered if Paul might head down the same path. But he could hardly say no, you can't go to his daughter. She was, he reminded himself constantly, old enough to make up her own mind and Paul was a good client.

'I've only got an hour to spare. I promised Linda I'd take her up. It's a great day for flying,' he said as he scanned the sky. It was almost cloudless.

But in truth he had jumped at the chance to fly. The weekend had left him unsettled. He needed a distraction. The distraction of flying, he told himself.

'Let's go,' he said as he turned towards Linda.

She smiled at him and just for a moment he held her gaze.

'Let's see if you're a better pilot than me,' she challenged.

'More experienced maybe?'

She pulled a face.

'Experienced at hard landings maybe.'

He laughed.

'Well, let's hope it doesn't happen to you,' he said. 'I hope you never find out what happens when an eagle and a propeller get in each other's way. It's not pretty.'

'So I heard,' she retorted. 'So I heard.'

An hour later, the Cessna touched down and came to a halt in its allotted space. They sat for a moment, the cockpit finally quiet enough to allow easy conversation.

'Did I pass your scrutiny as a pilot?' Paul asked with a smile.

Linda nodded. Like Paul, she was happy in the air.

'Definitely,' she said. 'That was fabulous. Maybe next time I can show you what I can do if you'll let me fly your plane.'

'Well, I'd better check the insurance policy first …'

But he was teasing her and she knew it.

'What, worried that it won't cover new pilots? I think you take more risks than I ever will,' she declared.

'That wasn't a risky flight,' he declared in his defence. 'That was textbook flying.'

She laughed.

'My father was a bit disturbed by your low swoop over the islands when you took him up on the test flight,' she countered.

'Your father likes two feet on the ground,' he said. 'He's good at maintaining aircraft but a nervous passenger.'

She knew what he said was true. But it was her father's job that had got her interested in flying. She wondered what route Paul had taken to his love of flying.

'And you? How did you come to love flying?'

'My father's good friend John Bertram. He's a Qantas pilot. He flew with my dad during the war. John would take me aboard the Qantas plane in Sydney sometimes before he headed to London. I thought it was all magic.'

'But you're content with a private pilot's licence? You didn't want to follow your dad's friend into commercial aviation?'

He shook his head.

'I was needed here, once we started adding far flung rural properties to the Belleville family holdings. My flying skills come in handy. Otherwise it's a long drive.'

'But not your brother?'

Paul shook his head.

'He spent more of his childhood in England than I did. He's doing architecture.'

'Not so useful then for running rural properties,' she commented.

'My Aunt Julia would disagree. She's paying for the rebuild of the Prior Park house. Anthony is doing the architectural work on it.'

'My father told me it had burned down many years ago. I'm surprised it wasn't rebuilt then.'

He sighed. How much more should he tell her?

'A new home was built, just not a rebuild of the original house,' he said, as they climbed out of the cockpit.

She was concerned then she might have offended him with her questions. Her natural curiosity had got the better of her. She put her hand on his arm.

'Sorry, Paul, I didn't mean to pry. I was just interested in …'

He cut her off.

'More gossip about the Belleville family?'

She sensed his mood had changed.

'No, of course not,' she said, shaking her head. 'I just wanted to get to know you a bit better.'

He relented. It wasn't her fault. There had been so much gossip about the family it had become a natural reaction for all of them to push back.

'Of course,' he said.

They stood together in silence for a moment.

'I've blown it, haven't I? You won't want anything to do with me in future.'

He shook his head.

'Of course not. I'll tell you all about my family sometime. Just not today.'

He leant forward, hugged her briefly and kissed her on the cheek.

'I must go now. When I get back, we'll go up again. And yes, I'll let you fly my plane. I trust you.'

With that, he was gone, but not before he registered the deep frown on her father's face.

'What's this? Kissing you on the cheek? He's married, my girl. Remember that. Don't encourage him.'

She smiled and shook her head at her father.

'I think there's something troubling him.'

'Maybe,' her father responded, 'but whatever it is, it's not something you need to worry about.'

He had already warned his daughter. Would warning her again make any difference? He began to doubt it as he looked at her. He would have to find other young men to put in her way. The last thing she needed was to get herself involved with a married man. But he wondered if it was already too late.

Anthony threw his bag into the back seat of his friend's car before settling himself in the front passenger seat.

'Thanks for picking me up, Lachie,' he said. He knew he should ask about Victoria's wedding but somehow the words wouldn't come, so he sat in silence.

'How was your family?' Lachie asked. 'How was that new nephew of yours?'

'Family's good. And the baby is asleep most of the time,' he said, 'but I had a chance to have a good look at the ruins of the old house. It will be a big job to clear the rubble.'

'So when is our esteemed lecturer going up to take a look?'

'Around Easter time I hope.'

'I want to have a look at the plans for the old house you managed to get hold of. That must have been exciting, finding them.'

Anthony nodded.

'Exciting is one way to describe it. Revelatory might be better though.'

Lachie risked a sideways glance at his friend as he navigated the traffic back to their student digs.

'How so? How can a set of architectural plans be revelatory?'

Anthony closed his eyes and sighed.

'There's a lot I haven't told you about why the house was burnt down in the first place. A family scandal years in the making. And it reemerged in a quite unexpected way at the uni library in Brisbane.'

He noticed Lachie's eyes widen.

'And I thought the only Belleville family scandal was our esteemed lecturer pinching your stepmother off your father.'

Anthony shook his head.

'No, there's lots more. I'll tell you some other time. Maybe you can write a book about it someday, Lachie,' he said, knowing his friend had recently developed an interest in writing fiction in addition to his architecture studies.

'Well, I'd start with my own family first, mate. Vic was really the sacrificial lamb for the family. She looked beautiful by the way. All white lace and satin.'

'Sorry, I should have asked,' Anthony mumbled.

'I'm just sorry you missed it. Everything went off beautifully.'

But the only words Anthony had really heard were *sacrificial lamb*. He had to ask.

'Why did you describe your sister as the *sacrificial lamb*?'

'It's complicated. Mark was earmarked as a future husband for Vic ages ago. It's been talked about between the families for years. Mark's father bailed our father out when he got into business difficulties a few years back. My father's company became a subsidiary. He was allowed to stay on as a director. I think the inference was that my father wasn't much of a businessman so it was a face-saving exercise. We've been beholden to Mark's family ever since.'

'But surely your sister had a say in the matter?'

He shrugged.

'Of course but she knew what was at stake. Mark's father can be difficult if things don't go his way. He likes Vic and was pleased she would become his daughter-in-law. He thought she would be a good influence on Mark who can be a bit wayward at times.'

Anthony listened in silence. He hadn't asked her about her fiancé because he hadn't wanted to know. She hadn't lied to him. She hadn't deceived him. In his rational moments he knew that. But he had hoped she would break her engagement. Except that she'd never suggested she would.

And now he understood why. She couldn't jeopardise the financial security of her family. And now his heart ached even more. Because he knew for certain she hadn't married for love. She had married for duty. Now she was out of reach, he would have to go on keeping the secret of their short, passionate affair. To protect her. To protect her family.

And then he heard Lachlan's voice cutting through his thoughts.

'They'll be back from their honeymoon next Saturday, just in time for our father's sixtieth birthday celebrations. You'll come, won't you? My mother put your name on the guest list especially.'

Of all his friends, Lachlan knew his mother preferred Anthony. He knew why, of course. As soon as he had told her his friend was a grandson of an English baronet, Anthony's status had been elevated above his other friends. For Lachlan's English-born mother, class still mattered. He had shamelessly teased his mother with the fact Anthony was distantly related to the Duke of Devonshire through his mother.

He had laughed at his mother's comment that Anthony would have made a good husband for his sister, if only Mark hadn't come along. *He's a good catch. I'm surprised he hasn't been snapped up by some social climbing family,* his mother had said. Since the idea had never occurred to Lachlan, he doubted it had ever occurred to Anthony either.

The sudden invitation had left Anthony struggling to find some excuse. He could survive the fact of Victoria being married. He didn't think he could quite so easily survive seeing her with her husband. He tried and failed to think of an excuse – any excuse – to decline the invitation. But he couldn't. All he could do was nod numbly.

'I'll pick you up at six on Saturday,' his friend said as he brought his car to a stop to let Anthony out. 'You probably wouldn't know the way so better that I drive you.'

'Suit? Black tie?'

It was the minimum he needed to know about the function. He had nearly a week to think of an excuse not to go.

'Suit's fine,' he said as Anthony closed the car door. 'It'll be a crush, knowing my mother.'

And with that he sped off towards his own apartment, leaving Anthony in a state of high anxiety.

As he inserted the key into the front door of his apartment, he heard the unmistakable sound of a ringing telephone. He dropped his bag inside the door and moved quickly to pick up the receiver.

He was relieved to hear his mother's voice on the other end of the line. The conversation was brief. But he was pleased at her invitation to dine with her that evening. He knew he could have lived with her in her spacious apartment but he preferred to be close to the university. Besides, he thought he was too old to be constantly under the watchful eye of his mother. Fortunately, she had agreed with him.

He slumped into a well-worn armchair, the silence closing in on him. The prospect of the silence stretching ahead of him depressed him. He knew there would be no more late night phone calls. No more secret assignations. No more thinking up excuses for his absence from the social events he was expected to attend.

He got up and went into his bedroom and pulled open the bedside drawer. Hidden carefully, turned face down away from prying eyes, was a framed photograph of the girl he loved. He read the cryptic greeting for the hundredth time except now he understood it. *My Darling, Love is not a choice. I wish it was with all my heart. Victoria xxx*

He replaced the photograph carefully and lay back on his bed. It was all he had of her. But she would never accept anything from him when he had suggested it.

Work and study, that's the only solution, he reminded himself, as he turned his mind to the forthcoming year. It would be his solace. He had even begun to wonder if the family were right. Was his aunt's ambition to rebuild Prior Park just an expensive folly? *Design her a house, by all means*, was the consensus, *but leave the grand gesture that had been the original Prior Park mansion where it belonged. In the past.*

That dilemma at least had given him something to think deeply about.

14

PAUL WATCHED CLOSELY AS Linda completed her pre-flight routine. He had been back only a matter of days from his trip with his uncle so she was surprised he had agreed to a flight so soon.

'I didn't think we'd be doing this so soon after your return,' she said. 'I thought you would have had enough of flying for a while.'

'It's a nice change of pace. Being with my uncle can be quite intense at times.'

'But you get on well with him, don't you?'

'Yes, I do. But there's never a light-hearted moment with Uncle William. He takes everything very seriously. And he doesn't like being away from home, so that doesn't improve his mood either. I've suggested to him I could do some of the trips for him in future, that he doesn't need to come along.'

'How did he take the suggestion?'

Paul laughed. He tried to mimic his uncle's deeper voice.

'*I'm not an old man yet* he said, but I could see he was thinking about it.'

She was about to ask what his wife might think of the idea but she stopped herself. They had never spoken of his wife or children.

'Anyway, we're not here to talk about me,' Paul said. 'You need to concentrate on what you're doing.'

For a few minutes, he watched her intently to make sure she

was doing everything by the book, in the same way he remembered John Bertram watching him.

Her pre-flight take-off procedure is perfect, he thought. No shortcuts. He wondered if her engineering qualifications lent an understanding of the need to follow proper procedure. He had known other newly qualified pilots who quickly developed sloppy habits in the cockpit. Or was it that, as a girl, she felt she had more to prove?

He relaxed as the plane lifted off and headed north. He admired her confidence. And not for the first time did he wonder if there was someone special in her life.

'You'll be wanting to get a job as a pilot,' Paul said, raising his voice to make himself heard.

She nodded her head enthusiastically.

'Do you know anyone who wants to hire a pilot? You're in the rural business.'

'Maybe,' he replied. 'What about your engineering degree?'

She smiled.

'Flying is more fun than civil engineering.'

He hadn't known until that point what her engineering specialty was. At least she's not going to ruin her hands in dirty machinery, he thought. Nor run the risk of her face getting covered in grease.

Just then the plane hit an unexpected pocket of turbulence. It lasted only a few seconds but Paul instinctively reached out and put his hand on hers to help steady the plane.

He could feel her shaking just a little from the experience. He had suffered similar incidents. For an inexperienced pilot, he understood it could be a frightening experience.

'Thanks,' she said, looking sideways at him. 'I didn't expect that.'

'It's happened to me before. But the more experience you have, the more confidence you'll feel.'

'Unfortunately, I won't get much chance once I get a job in an office,' she said, pulling a face. 'A job as a pilot is just a fantasy. I need more hours up. But I can't afford it until I get a job. And then I won't have the time.'

He wondered then how she had managed to accumulate the flight hours to qualify for her pilot's licence but before he could ask, she provided the answer.

'I had a boyfriend in Brisbane when I was at uni. His family had paid in advance for his lessons and flight time but he decided he didn't like it so I took his place. His father was livid with him. But he was happy for me to do the course. I think he thought I'd eventually marry his son.'

'Do I take it you're not marrying the son?'

It occurred to him she might have exploited the relationship to get something she wanted.

She shook her head.

'We were never that serious. We both knew we'd go our separate ways when it suited us. It was his parents who were doing the wedding planning, not us.'

'And now?'

He couldn't resist the question, despite the difficulty of making conversation in the noisy cockpit.

She looked around and shook her head.

'There's no one special.'

There was silence then as she began to concentrate on their return to the airport, doing repeated visual checks for commercial aircraft that might also be on a descent.

A short time later, she was taxiing the plane to its allotted parking spot on the outer edge of the airport. As she shut down the engine and flicked the necessary switches, Paul leant across to her.

'That was a great exhibition of flying,' he said. 'You can take the plane up any time you want.'

She impulsively kissed him on the cheek.

'Thank you,' she said. 'That would be great but will your family mind?'

He shook his head.

'No, I simply won't tell them,' he said. 'And if you're serious about wanting a job as a pilot, I'll ask around. You never know.'

He knew it would mean a trip to the next cattle sale but that was no bad thing. He needed to remind people he was the eldest of the Belleville heirs and he would have authority over the family's interests in the future. That authority would never rest with Alex.

'You'd do that for me?'

'Of course I would,' he said.

He leant across to her then and kissed her. It was the briefest of kisses followed by the briefest of caresses. He was treading on dangerous ground and he knew it. But he sensed too from her response it was dangerous ground she was willing to traverse.

He turned away from her abruptly and opened the door of the cockpit with more force than he intended. He had seen, out of the corner of his eye, her father approaching.

'How was the flight? How did my newly minted pilot perform?'

'Your daughter performed very well, Larry. She loves flying. Handled a bit of turbulence like an old pro.'

Her father nodded, satisfied with Paul's report.

'It's very good of you to take her up and let her fly your plane. I really appreciate it. She needs to keep her hours up now but flying is an expensive hobby I'm afraid.'

Paul paused for a moment. What would her father think of his offer? But it would be the only way she would maintain and improve her skills.

'I've told Linda she can take my plane up any time she likes,' he said, as she came to stand alongside them.

'That's a very generous offer, Paul,' her father said. 'Are you sure? Will your father approve?'

'Of course I'm sure and yes, of course my father will be fine with it,' he said. 'She needs more hours in the air if she wants to aim for a career as a pilot.'

He knew then he shouldn't have said anything. Her father shook his head.

'She didn't spend years at university to throw it all away. I don't think being a pilot is a career for her. I take it she didn't tell you she's shortlisted for a job in Brisbane.'

He held an envelope aloft and then handed it to his daughter.

'This arrived this morning. I hope it's a letter telling you about the job. I hope it's good news.'

Paul glanced at her quickly.

'No, I didn't say anything. I haven't got the job yet,' she said, aware of her father's eyes on her. Had he seen her intimate moment with Paul? She hoped not.

'You should open that letter,' her father insisted.

She tore open the envelope and read the short letter quickly.

'Yes, I've got the job,' she said. 'I'm to start in a month's time.'

Until that morning she had desperately wanted the job. And now? She wasn't so sure. Was it the prospect of a different career that had been dangled in front of her? Or was it the prospect of spending more time with Paul?

But in her heart she knew the answer. She wanted to spend more time with Paul.

As her father walked across to inspect the plane and its tyres for any superficial damage, she whispered to Paul.

'Thank you for today. I really enjoyed it.' And then she paused. 'I hope I see you again soon.'

'If you want to,' he said quietly.

'I do. Very much,' she said and then turned back and walked towards her father.

He stood for a moment watching her and then he turned and headed towards his car. He knew he was playing with fire but being with her lifted his spirits.

'She's just a friend,' he reminded himself. 'That's all she can ever be.'

But he knew he was being less than honest with himself. The fact was he wanted her to be more than a friend. But he knew there was a line he should not cross.

But a close friendship? That's possible, he told himself. And then he remembered the pleasure of their brief kiss. Wasn't that crossing a line?

He just hoped her father hadn't seen him kiss her because she would certainly face her father's disapproval if he had.

As it turned out, Paul was right to be concerned because nothing ever seemed to escape her father's eagle eye.

'I don't think you should be taking up his offer of flying his plane,' he said bluntly. He put his hand on his daughter's arm, gently but firmly.

'He's going to want you to show your gratitude, I reckon.'

'What are you talking about? Paul's not like that.'

She wanted to say he's very nice to me but she thought that would only reinforce her father's suspicions.

'Men are like that, my girl,' he said. 'You might think he's different but he's got history. The men in his family have history. And don't get the idea in your head he's going to leave his wife. I hear Belleville cattle are already being grazed on Armoobilla, one of the places his wife inherited from her father. They're building a rural dynasty that will be unrivalled. He's not going to give that up for a girl with nothing to bring to the table.'

She listened in silence. What could she say? But she felt she had to defend him.

'We're just friends. That's all. Nothing more.'

'Friends, eh? I saw his hands all over you. I saw him kiss you. Don't be fooled, my girl. His wife's probably busy with the new baby so he's feeling a bit neglected. I've seen the way he looks at you. It will be a good thing when you're settled in your new job in Brisbane, in my opinion.'

She sighed deeply but said nothing more. She knew she would never convince her father Paul was sincere in seeking her friendship.

Anthony had agonised all week about a credible way to decline the invitation to the sixtieth birthday celebrations for Lachlan's father but his imagination, on this occasion, had failed him.

He looked at the clock on his bedside table as he struggled with the Belleville cufflinks, a twenty-first birthday present from his family. He was finally ready with five minutes to spare.

There was nothing about the evening that appealed to him. He had met Lachie's parents a couple of times at university functions. His father Gordon Bell struck him as being full of self-importance, with a high opinion of himself which was probably undeserved. Louisa Bell, echoing her husband's self-belief, attempted to dominate any conversation she was involved in.

He heard a sharp toot of a horn and glanced out the window.

Lachlan, for once, was on time. Anthony banged the door shut and headed down the stairs from his first floor apartment, hoping he could simply hide in the crowd, if it was the crush his friend had confidently predicted.

As he slid into the front passenger seat of the small Renault, he noticed it was spotless.

'Clean car? That's unusual.'

Lachie sighed loudly.

'If my mother sees my car dirty, it's like I killed a bishop or something. I get the *we didn't buy that car for you so you can treat it like a trash can* lecture.'

Anthony laughed. He could well imagine Lachie's mother saying such a thing.

'Where are we off to? You didn't say.'

'Lavender Bay. It's the Hansen family home. A huge old mansion with a great view of the harbour. They insisted on hosting the birthday gig. Said it would be a welcome home party for Vic and Mark too. By the way I should warn you my mother is on the hunt for a husband for my cousin Beth. She might have you in her sights.'

'Really? I'm not looking for a wife. That might be a stumbling block.'

'I don't think that would cross my mother's mind. She thinks you have a lot going for you. Good pedigree. Prospects. All that sort of stuff.'

'And Beth can't find her own husband?'

His friend laughed quietly.

'They're worried if left to her own devices she'll marry someone totally unsuitable. She's brought a couple of long haired dropouts, as my mother called them, to her family home recently.'

'Perhaps she likes long haired dropouts,' Anthony suggested.

'She might but her family don't so they've set themselves a mission to redirect her interests, according to my aunt.'

'Well they can redirect their interests away from me. You might want to drop that word of warning in your mother's ear.'

Lachie did not reply. Instead he concentrated on reversing his car into a tight parking space on the street in front of the house. Having accomplished that feat, the two of them headed up the driveway to the house.

'I should have warned you. There's an intimate family dinner first. Just the two families plus my aunt Elena and Beth. Twelve in all.'

'Twelve?' Anthony counted quickly but he couldn't come up with twelve people.

'Mark has a brother Roger. He'll be there with his wife Connie. She's quite lively.'

Anthony felt miserable, as if he'd been outmanoeuvred at every turn. But he remembered his mother's advice about awkward social situations. Ask people about themselves. Without exception, they find their own lives endlessly fascinating. He hoped the advice would get him through the evening because he wasn't sure anything else would.

And then it hit him. He was being set up with the girl. Apart from Lachie, he was the only unattached young man attending the dinner. Clearly Lachie had been discarded as a potential match because of close kinship. Which left him as the main target of an ambitious mother. And aunt. He groaned inwardly. Could the evening get any worse?

By the time the main course was removed, Anthony had heard about Beth's father, who worked in the mines in Western Australia, Beth's friends, the university course she had dropped out of and her plans to head to Europe and return home via the hippie trail through countries Anthony had no desire to visit and thought were probably unsafe for a young woman. But he admired her spirit nonetheless.

Across the table, her mother smiled approvingly, mistaking Anthony's good manners for genuine interest in the girl, whose dress came either from a highly fashionable hippie boutique or an op shop. He couldn't decide which, except that if it had been intended to flatter her figure and her flaming red hair, it had failed on both counts, he thought.

Beth had been placed on his left. On his right, Connie Hansen chatted aimlessly and drank wine as if it were water with no apparent ill-effects. She had a brittle, high pitched laugh that carried along the table. It irritated her husband, Anthony noticed. An unlikely match. Roger Hansen was clearly the heir apparent. Probably ten years older than his brother Mark.

He wondered what cruel twist of fate had seated Victoria directly opposite him. He risked a smile in her direction and was rewarded with the faintest uplift in the corners of her mouth and an almost imperceptible shake of her head.

She was as beautiful as he remembered. But gone was the carefree smiling girl. Seated at the formal table of her in-laws, he could have been looking at a different person. Her blonde hair, which Anthony remembered cascading untidily over her shoulders, was carefully styled into an elegant chignon. She wore diamond earrings. Probably a wedding gift, he decided. Her dress was elegant and restrained. He noticed her father-in-law looking at her approvingly. He wondered if she would get to continue her work as an interior designer. He hoped so.

His gaze moved to her husband. There was nothing about him Anthony admired. He was too loud, too opinionated and clearly delighted at having been able to marry such a beautiful woman, as if his charm had been the sole reason she had chosen him. Anthony was sick to the stomach at the thought of him with Victoria. How could they condemn Victoria to that buffoon?

At that point, he would have got up from the table and made some feeble excuse to leave, except that he heard Beth chattering again.

'My cousin's beautiful, isn't she? I've always envied her. I'm not sure I do now, though.'

To Anthony, it was the most interesting thing Beth had said all evening.

'Not now? Why would that be?'

'Oh, come on, Anthony, use your eyes,' she said, her voice quieter. 'Her husband's a complete blockhead. He gambles heavily at illegal gambling clubs I've been told. I think they expect her to be able to keep him on a shorter leash.'

She dropped her voice to a whisper.

'I've even heard he's been known to visit brothels. I hope he's given that up.'

For once, Anthony was rendered speechless.

'You're shocked, I can see that. But then his old man makes his money in some seedy places, I've been told. That's how he gets access.'

Finally recovering the power of speech, Anthony began to quiz her.

'I was told Hansen senior had a big industrial company that invested in a number of businesses.

She laughed quietly.

'He does. But he makes more money out of illegal stuff than all the rest of it, I'm told.'

'Does her family know?'

She shook her head.

'No, they don't and you're not to say anything. I've had it all second hand from a girl I know whose father is a copper. Some of it could be exaggerated.'

But even if there's a grain of truth in it, Anthony thought, it still sounded awful. In years to come he wondered what the fallout might be for Victoria.

Finally, their hostess rose from the table, looking conspicuously at her watch.

'Our other guests will be knocking on the door very soon,' she said. 'Let's move out so the table can be cleared.'

Anthony breathed a sigh of relief and headed directly for the verandah. During the day, it was known to have a magnificent view of the harbour. At night a fairyland of lights glittered below, the harbour bridge dominating the vista.

As he stood there breathing in the night air, he felt a hand on his arm. Her voice was the same. Her perfume was the same.

'I didn't know you were coming with Lachie this evening,' she said quietly. 'It was a shock but it's lovely to see you again.'

He turned towards her.

'I couldn't get out of it,' he said.

She smiled.

'So you didn't want to see me again?'

'It's not that and you know it.'

She looked down as if examining her shoes but he could see she was trying not to cry. He wanted to reach out to her, but there were too many people around.

'I know,' she whispered. 'I know.'

And then she turned and was gone, melting into the crowd that had suddenly formed.

How would he ever find peace of mind again? How would another woman ever take her place in his heart? He couldn't begin to answer those questions.

And then he felt something rustling in the pocket of his jacket. A note.

'I need to see you,' it read. 'I'm onsite on Tuesday afternoon.' An address followed. There was no signature. Just the familiar V.

He put the note back in his pocket. What was the point of seeing her? She was off limits now. He remembered her parting words. *I can't see you again. It's better for both of us.* He wondered what had happened to change her mind.

But he would go and meet her. He was curious. Something had changed her mind. Exactly what, he could only speculate. And what good was speculation? It was no use at all, he decided. Absolutely no use at all.

15

ANTHONY CHECKED HIS WATCH. It was three o'clock on Tuesday afternoon as he pulled into a vacant car space at the front of what he recognised as a fine example of an art deco apartment block. He was in an unfamiliar suburb. The Sydney street directory lay open on the passenger seat.

He quickly headed to the stairwell and took the stairs to the first floor two at a time. She had been looking out for him and opened the door just as he was about to knock.

He was relieved to see she looked much as she had before her wedding, her long blonde hair floating freely, her face only lightly made up, her clothes simple and practical, with little adornment. He took all this in before even greeting her.

She closed the door behind them and then put her hand on his arm. He looked around nervously.

'There's no one else here,' she said, sensing his uncertainty. 'Just us.'

He kissed her then, enjoying the feel of her in his arms again. Was this what she expected? Or is she about to slap my face, he wondered?

'I thought we were never seeing each other again. Wasn't that the deal?' he asked as he released her from his embrace.

'I decided it was a deal that could be broken,' she said. 'I was fine until I saw you on Saturday night. What possessed Lachie to drag you along to my father's birthday party?'

He laughed. Hadn't she guessed?

'Matching making.'

'What?'

'Your cousin Beth is in need of a reliable husband, well not a long haired dropout apparently.'

'And they anointed you as the prime candidate?'

She giggled in an unexpectedly girlish way.

'Did you fall in with their plans?'

But he knew she was teasing him. He laughed.

'No, I think I disappointed the ambitious mother. Beth's not my type. The hippie dress and the red hair were a bit overwhelming,' he said.

'It was quite an awful dress, wasn't it? She's quite sweet though. I've always liked her even though the family have been very critical of her.'

'For her choices?' Anthony ventured.

She nodded.

'She has some questionable friends. Probably because she's very impressionable. Most of them seem to spend a lot of time talking and smoking marijuana and not very much else.'

And then he remembered what she had said about Victoria's husband. Should he say something? He let the thought slide. He wasn't going to ask but he hoped she would volunteer something about her marriage. Was she happy? Was he a good husband to her?

She took him by the hand then to show him through the apartment.

'I have the job of redecorating this for a client.'

He looked around. Walls were being stripped of their 1950s wallpaper. The table was piled high with expensive wallpaper ready to be hung in its place. He guessed the parquetry floor would undergo intensive restoration. Beyond the sitting room, an archway led to a sunroom that looked out across the rooftops towards the sea. Old broken blinds lay in a heap ready to be thrown out. There was a strong smell of fresh paint.

'It will be a great place when you're finished with it,' he said. 'I love the location. I hope your client has the budget to do it justice. And appreciates its character.'

He put his arms around her.

'You're a woman of many talents, my darling,' he said. 'We could have been so good together. Me helping your business. You helping mine. It would have been a perfect fit.'

'Except I had to go and marry someone else.'

She heard his sharp intake of breath. She moved away from him.

'Lachie said he'd told you the reason why I married Mark. I was surprised at that. Does he know about us? Did you tell him?'

Anthony shook his head.

'No, I didn't tell him. I told no one. And with all due respects to your brother, he's not the most observant of people. I don't think he knows about us. I think he was just being chatty.'

'I think you're right,' she said. 'I hope you're right. Mark would be insanely jealous if he ever found out. He asked me who you were on Saturday night. When I told him, he said you looked as though you were there under sufferance, that you looked as though you'd rather be anywhere else. A stuck-up Pom, he concluded.'

Anthony laughed out loud at the very inaccurate description of himself.

'For a start, I'm only half English. And if he ever saw my father's family together at Prior Park, he'd know there's no room in the Belleville family for people with attitude. It would be called out pretty brutally.'

She reached up and kissed him on the cheek.

'I'd love to see your family in that setting,' she said. 'They sound wonderful.'

'They are,' he said.

And then he had an idea. An idea that exploded in his mind.

'I must get you the contract for the interior design work on my aunt's house. Then you'll have an excuse to visit Prior Park.'

She knew what he was talking about. The rebuild of the big house.

'Wouldn't she be better off with a local interior designer?'

Anthony pulled a face.

'I don't think there would be such a person. And besides, she lives here in Sydney half the time because of her daughter Pippa and her granddaughter. It makes perfect sense.'

'Won't you need to consult your aunt? Won't she want competitive bids and all that?'

'I'll introduce you. I'm sure she'll take my advice to hire you. You'll get on with her like a house on fire. This is her passion project to revive her spirits. And I know she'll want to work with people she likes.'

'Reviving her spirits since her divorce? Didn't you tell me she recently divorced her husband?'

'Yes, she did,' he said. 'She got a big settlement. No one knows how much but he's a wealthy American. They seemed to be happily married until he inherited a massive fortune. And then he got his mistress pregnant. Humiliated my aunt in the end.'

'Wow. No one's life is straightforward, is it?'

'No, it isn't,' he agreed, 'but seeing you has lifted my spirits.'

He kissed her again.

'Seeing you has lifted my spirits too, my darling,' she said.

'But where do we go from here?' he asked.

He took her left hand in his and looked at the rings now clustered on her finger as if to remind her of what now stood between them.

'Can't we meet as friends?' she whispered

'Secret friends?'

'It has to be a secret, my darling,' she said quietly, 'but it's better than not seeing you at all. I can survive this marriage if I can see you. I don't think I can survive it if I don't. I realise that now.'

He saw the look in her eyes. Disappointment? Regret? Hope? He wasn't sure.

'How is he with you?'

He didn't quite know how else to frame the question, hoping she knew what he meant.

She shrugged her shoulders.

'Unpredictable. Like his father, he likes everything to go his way. But if I push back, he caves in pretty quickly. It's all bluster really.'

'Did he want you to give up your design business?'

'He said he did but in fact his father told him not to be so ridiculous. This wasn't the nineteenth century. I think my father-in-law likes to point to interiors I've done and say, *my daughter-in-law did that. Isn't she clever?*'

'That's helpful.'

'It is. I couldn't stand it without my creative outlet. His father has been sweet to me. He's found new office space for me which is being fitted out. He suggested Lachie should set up in the adjoining office suite when he completes his architecture degree.'

And then a thought occurred to her.

'Have you and Lachie discussed what you might do after you qualify?'

'Only in the vaguest terms. We could go into partnership. That might work. I will have to commit some of my time to my family's business interests in the future but probably just not yet.'

She looked at her watch, suddenly alarmed at how late it was.

'I must go. Some of Mark's business friends are coming over for dinner. He manages one of his father's companies.'

She pushed him towards the door.

'I'm going,' he said, 'I'm going. But when do I see you again?'

'I'll let you know,' she said as she ran ahead down the stairs to her car

He sat in his car for some time reflecting on what had occurred. Could he go on meeting her like this? Was it enough for him? Or was it better to make a clean break?

He was in two minds. And then he thought of what it meant to her to see him. Perhaps that was the most important thing. Not how he felt, but how she felt. Could their friendship bring her some respite from the husband she clearly didn't love? He hoped so. He really hoped so.

If Anthony's interest in Victoria Bell was indeed unknown by

anyone beyond the two of them up to this point, his brother Paul's flirtation with a certain young woman who shared his love of flying had quickly become the source of gossip. It had reached his father's ears in what seemed like record time.

The first inkling reached Richard through the news his elder son had attended the regular cattle sale that week, not something he very often did. Not, it seemed, for the purpose of reviewing the cattle put through the sale and to test industry sentiment about prices and the future direction of cattle prices. He learnt his son had been asking around among people he knew about any jobs going for pilots.

On hearing the news, Richard had at first thought his son was planning to branch out and perhaps hire out his services when their small plane wasn't being used. He was therefore surprised to learn Paul's enquiries were for quite another reason.

He confronted his son at Prior Park.

'Do you want to tell me about Linda Kent?' Richard asked his son, as they stood together at the stockyards watching some cattle being loaded onto a semi-trailer. The cattle were being more fractious than usual.

'What about her?' Paul asked, looking sideways at this father. It was an unusual question. He didn't know how his father had come to know about her. Had someone seen them together?

'A little birdie whispered in my ear yesterday that you were asking about pilot jobs for a young woman pilot you knew. I'm surprised I didn't know about her. I was told you looked to be on very good terms with her. I heard she was piloting our plane, not you, last week. That information was accompanied by what I can only describe as a knowing smile.'

'What's all that supposed to mean?' Paul demanded. 'She's Larry Kent's daughter and she's a nice girl. We get on well. It's fun to fly with her. I was helping her get some hours up. She's just qualified. That's all. End of story.'

But he was annoyed with his father for bringing it up at all.

'As long as that's all it is, son,' Richard said. 'As long as that's all it is.'

'That's all there is to it,' Paul snapped.

'Did you tell Amanda why you've been out flying so much. And with whom?'

Paul shook his head.

'No.'

'Meaning you think she doesn't need to know?' Richard persisted.

Paul looked at his father. After a long pause, he answered.

'That's right. She doesn't need to know. Just like I don't need to know how often Alex calls in to see her when I'm not around.'

Richard could see immediately he had touched a raw nerve. His son's jealousy of Alex would always be there, he thought. Under control most of the time but occasionally, something would trigger it. Richard didn't know what that might have been recently, deciding instead to change the subject.

'Still, from another perspective, it was good to know you went to the cattle sale. It was a good yarding, William said. Prices aren't too bad.'

'There were some good cattle through the sale. I decided it does no harm to remind people I'm the senior of the Belleville heirs,' he said. 'If anything happened to you or Uncle William, people would be looking to me for decisions.'

And it reminds people Alex has no real authority, Richard thought. That's the subtext. But he was reassured by his son's growing maturity. He just hoped the flirtation with the girl was just that. A harmless flirtation that meant nothing. And would lead nowhere. But still Richard decided to check things out for himself.

The following morning he dropped by the airfield unannounced and headed towards Larry Kent's workshop. He entered via the small office to be greeted, not by Larry Kent but by his daughter Linda

She looked up from the work she was doing. Richard guessed she helped her father with his accounts.

To Linda, there was something familiar about her visitor, but she was uncertain.

'You must be Linda,' Richard said.

She got up and walked across to the counter. In that time, she realised who the visitor was.

'Mr Belleville, it's nice to meet you,' she said, holding out her hand.

'Richard, please. Call me Richard. I hear you're quite a pilot in the making and that you can handle my plane very well,' he said with a smile, realising of course he had put her at a disadvantage.

She smiled at him, the slight colour in her cheeks telling him she had been caught unawares by his comment.

He too was struck by her deep blue eyes. It hadn't taken him long to realise how easily his son might have been captivated by her.

'It was very nice of your son to let me fly it,' she said.

She did not mention the offer Paul had made of allowing her to fly the Belleville plane whenever she wanted to. She had in fact flown it for half an hour the previous day.

'He was impressed,' Richard said, watching her carefully.

'With your abilities as a pilot,' he added.

'I was very nervous,' she admitted. 'He's a lot more experienced than I am.'

'We're all nervous in the beginning,' Richard said. He wanted to reassure her because he could see she was nervous now, talking to him. 'As you going to make flying a career?'

At that point, the door from the workshop opened and her father walked in. The two men shook hands.

'Richard, good to see you. We've seen a lot more of your son lately than you.'

And then he wished he hadn't said so, not quite in those terms. Had he given the impression Paul was visiting the airfield every day?

'I've not met your daughter before, Larry?'

'Been away at uni. Just finished her engineering degree. Now she's off to Brisbane at the end of next week to take up her first job.'

That was good news as far as Richard was concerned. Just by looking at her, he knew his son had been economical with the truth. Could his jealousy of Alex be behind his flirtation with the girl? How far had the flirtation gone? Would she willingly become involved with a married man? Richard couldn't decide. But one thing he had seen was her reaction to the mention of his son's name. Her face – and her eyes particularly – had lit up briefly. To Richard, it was a warning sign he couldn't ignore.

'Let's go and check out your plane,' Larry Kent suggested, opening the door for Richard to precede him. 'It's in good nick but I think it will need a major overhaul soon. Paul might have to take it south for that.'

Richard nodded. He had expected that. But would that be Brisbane? Or Sydney? He'd find that out in due course. Right now he could see Larry Kent was keen for a private conversation.

'I'll be blunt, Richard,' he said as they inspected the plane together. 'I need your son to back off from my daughter.'

There, he had said it. He had risked offending a good client, but his daughter was more important to him.

He heard Richard's sharp intake of breath. He was surprised Larry Kent would mention anything at all. He had to tease out the extent of the issue.

'I'm not sure what you mean, Larry,' Richard said. 'I don't think my son would overstep the mark with a young woman.'

'It depends on what you regard as overstepping the mark, doesn't it? I don't like seeing a young married man with his hands all over my daughter, kissing her and fondling her. It's what I witnessed the other day before they left the cockpit. And he said she can take your plane up any time she likes too. Pretty generous offer if you're not getting anything in return, in my opinion.'

He was silent then. He had said enough.

Richard drew in a deep breath. The accusations had angered him. He could not mistake the inference about his son. But he calmed down quickly. It was a father's prerogative to protect his daughter. A father's duty in fact. In reality, he knew he should be angrier with Paul.

Yet an obvious question remained. He was sure Paul wouldn't be going so far with the girl if his attentions were unwelcome. But it was something her father would never want to hear.

'I'll have a few words with my son, Larry,' he said, 'but if your daughter is going off to work in Brisbane soon, I don't think there's too much to worry about. Paul's happily married.'

Having seen Paul with his daughter, Larry Kent was inclined to want to question Richard's statement about the state of Paul's marriage, but he decided against it. Perhaps if his father has a word with him, that would be enough.

'I hope you're right,' he said, bringing the conversation to an end.

He did not want to make an enemy of Richard Belleville. That would serve no purpose at all.

'Anyway, the offer stands. Your daughter is welcome to take our plane up any time she likes. Tell her I said so. I was a young pilot once. Getting hours up is the key to improving your skills. She needs that.'

Larry Kent was satisfied. He'd said his piece. He hoped it would just be a short-lived flirtation that went no further. Unmarried, Paul Belleville would have been warmly welcomed as a potential husband for his daughter. But married with two children, he could see only one role for his daughter – as the plaything of a wealthy young man unsettled in his marriage who would be discarded when he got bored with her. Despite his father's protestations, he was sure Paul's marriage wasn't everything it should be.

But he was grateful to Richard Belleville for confirming the offer to his daughter to be allowed to fly their plane. He knew she would be delighted.

16

THE PARTY OF PEOPLE gathering to inspect the remains of the country mansion that had once dominated its surroundings at Prior Park had grown in size by the time they all gathered at the property several days before the Easter holidays.

Of the group, fifteen-year-old Susan Belleville was, in many ways, the most anxious about visiting Prior Park and the least interested in the project. The big house had never been part of her life. It had only ever been, in her memory, a pile of rubble which, as a child, she had been forbidden from exploring.

She hadn't exactly jumped at the opportunity to visit with her stepfather Daniel Harrington but her mother had approved the plan. You should go and see your father, her mother had said, as if she needed reminding of the obligation.

As soon as she arrived, disjointed memories had come flooding back. She had been nine years old when her parents' marriage had fallen apart. And now her family life revolved around a different set of people. Her memories of Prior Park from her childhood were vague. Her recent memories were sparse. She barely knew her brother Anthony, who had lived mostly in England as far as she remembered.

Her father had greeted her at Prior Park lovingly. She could see how delighted he was to see her. Did he notice her guarded response, she wondered? It had appeared as if he hadn't, but she noticed how the family watched the meeting between her father and her stepfather with apprehension. She didn't know what they were expecting to see. Angry words? Accusations? She had never seen her stepfather angry. Disappointed, yes. Frustrated, yes, when some of his projects proved more difficult than he expected, but never angry.

And her father? She eyed him cautiously. He was very different from her stepfather, she realised. More assertive. More commanding. Less approachable, perhaps. But as she saw the anxiety on the faces around her, she became anxious too. Did they think the visit was a mistake? She hoped not. She loved her stepfather.

Was it possible she loved him more than her own father? Or was it because her brother Tim Lester didn't like her father? Didn't like any of her Belleville family, in fact. Living with her mother and Daniel at Berrima Park with her brother Tim, it had been so much easier to let herself be known as Susan Lester and never speak about her other family. Her agreement to resume using the Lester name had pleased Tim enormously.

'That's what you were when you were born,' Tim had told her. 'That's how it should have stayed.'

Had she been older with more knowledge of past events, she might have marvelled at the ease with which Tim had convinced himself there was doubt that Richard really was her father.

Not for the first time did she regret overhearing a conversation she wasn't supposed to. From that point she had been in turmoil. But she told no one. She kept it to herself but how much longer could she do that? Someone must know for sure who her father was without her having to ask her mother outright. Or her father.

She hadn't been able to hear her mother's response to Tim's louder voice that had claimed she didn't look anything like the Belleville family so how could she be Richard's daughter. She was desperate to know what her mother had said in answer to his outburst.

She breathed a deep sigh of relief. There had been no angry words between her father and her stepfather. No raised voices just a brief business-like exchange of pleasantries. The general hubbub of conversation around her resumed, as if there had never been any cause for concern.

She looked around her. Across the room, her Aunt Alice smiled encouragingly at her. She remembered then her mother had particularly asked to be remembered to her aunt.

'It's lovely to have you at Prior Park, Susan,' Alice said, kissing the girl on the cheek. 'How is your mother?'

She was about to say we really missed your mother after she left but Alice decided against it. For some reason, she hesitated. Was it the right thing to say with Kate's current husband and ex-husband within earshot?

'Mum's well. She said to say hello to you,' Susan replied. 'She's always busy though. She spends a lot of time taking care of Amy.'

'Amy?'

Alice hadn't heard the name before.

'Amy is Nancy's little girl. Nancy married Ian a couple of years back. Amy was born a year later. Ian is my brother's stud master. He runs the stud cattle property. Nancy met him when he took the job a few years ago.'

'So is that property close by?'

Alice was trying to remember but her memories of Berrima Park mainly consisted of their hurried departure after the wedding plans fell apart so spectacularly with the revelations about Paul.

'It's about thirty kilometres away,' Susan explained. 'Mum goes over two days a week to help Nancy and then they usually come to Berrima Park for Sunday lunch. Tim's getting married too.'

'When is that happening, Susan?' Alice asked.

She did not have pleasant memories of Tim Lester but she accepted there was no reason why Susan shouldn't talk about him. On a day-to-day basis, he was part of her family. They were much closer to her now than her father's family would ever be.

'September,' she said. 'Her name's Margaret. She's very nice. I'll be one of the bridesmaids.'

Alice smiled to herself at how the fifteen-year-old rattled off information about her Lester family in a typically teenage way. No embellishments. Just the bare facts.

And then Alice noticed a worried look on her face. She put her hand on the girl's arm.

'Is there something the matter?' Alice asked quietly. 'I think there's something you're unhappy about.'

Alice remained silent, hoping the girl would speak without further prompting. She simply shrugged as if to say there's nothing troubling me but Alice wasn't convinced.

'Are you sure, Susan? Whatever it is you can talk to me. Your mother and I were once good friends you know.'

'I know. She told me,' the girl said.

'Come on, tell me what's troubling you?'

She let out a long sigh.

'If you must know, I overheard Tim talking the other day. He seems to be convinced my father isn't my father,' she said finally. 'He said I don't look anything like a Belleville. It's true. I look like my mother. I don't know what to do. Tim sounded convinced my father isn't my father.'

For once, Alice was lost for words. What should she say to the girl? What could she say that would convince her without telling a fifteen-year-old the salacious details of her father's affair with her mother Kate while she was still married to Gerald Lester.

One thing she knew for certain – if Richard came to know about it, he would be furious. And that wouldn't help Susan at all.

She put her arm around the girl and hugged her.

'You're staying here for a few days after your stepfather goes back,' Alice said. 'We'll have a private talk then but now is not the time.' She gestured around the dining room. 'I've got too many things to see to just now. But promise me one thing, you won't say anything to anyone else until we have a talk. Especially your father. And he is your father. Make no mistake about that.'

She looked at the girl for confirmation she understood.

'Thanks, I won't tell Dad, I promise.'

'Good, now go and say hello to Marianne and Amanda and meet the new baby.'

'What's his name?' she asked.

'Matthew. Matthew Paul Belleville. He's really starting to take notice now.'

She smiled.

'Dad told me Paul and Amanda had a new baby. He just forgot to tell me the name.'

'Well, that's men for you,' Alice said, as she turned to head back to the kitchen but not before she noticed Richard looking intently at her. She increased her pace to avoid him, because she knew he'd begin asking awkward questions as to why she and Susan had been in such an earnest conversation. It was not a question she wanted to answer at that moment.

She sighed, wondering how it was she often found herself being called upon to play the role of family confidante and peacemaker.

Lachlan Bell, on the pretext he could hold the other end of the tape measure and help record measurements for the proposed rebuild, had invited himself to the site inspection. In the back of his mind he thought perhaps it might be appropriate to accompany his sister, but he didn't say that to Anthony. Nor to Victoria.

But he was delighted with the opportunities opening up for her. Especially delighted because it was work away from the people who were in the orbit of the Hansen family. He was sure some of the money those people lavished on their homes came from dubious sources. He wanted Victoria to cultivate an entirely different clientele.

And it had begun with Anthony's Aunt Julia. Anthony had been right. His aunt had liked Victoria immediately and, as it turned out, the timing couldn't have been better.

Julia had just bought an apartment in the same block as her sister-in-law Catherine. On seeing it, he heard that Victoria had declared it a *crime scene*, which had amused him. A crime against interior design was what she had meant, of course. She was now busy updating the interior. But it would be a small job compared with the task of decorating the newly built house at Prior Park.

Lachie looked around him. He had now met most of Anthony's family. He envied Anthony. Envied him their strong family bonds and their obvious pleasure in each other's company. By all accounts, they were wealthy but there were no overt displays of wealth. No bragging. No over-the-top talk of the kind he was used to. They were very grounded in their country ways and their family traditions. He wondered how well Anthony fitted in, but he noticed how warmly he was welcomed. He fits in because he's a Belleville, he concluded. He belongs to them.

And he noticed the new generation emerging. Andrew, who had eyed him suspiciously and Melanie who had wanted to show him a bird nesting in the front garden. He noticed the baby too. And that there was another baby on the way.

This dining room will be at capacity in a few years' time, he thought. He began to wonder how it might be extended. For just one moment, he had thought Andrew and Melanie were brother and sister until he realised that would have been impossible. He assumed the Belleville genetic inheritance was a strong one.

Just then, he heard the slightly raised voice of his hostess, urging them all to the table. Food smells wafting from the kitchen had begun to penetrate the dining room. He realised then he was hungry.

Alice had in fact lingered in the kitchen to avoid Richard even though it was not strictly necessary. She had extra help and there was nothing for her to do but to check everything was on track.

As she ushered her guests to their seats, the food began to arrive.

In true country style, the table groaned under large platters of roasted meats and vegetables, to be followed by puddings and tarts. The preparation had occupied the kitchen for what seemed like days. The recently installed cold room had been left depleted of fresh meat.

There was a scrape of chairs. She had fussed over the seating plan, sitting Daniel Harrington as far from Richard as the table would allow. And trying and once again failing to ensure her son-in-law Alex didn't claim the seat between Amanda and Marianne. She wished her brother James and his son John had been available to add to the numbers but they were out west at a clearance sale.

He had lamented the timing but they were governed by the date of the sale.

As the lunch proceeded noisily under Alice's watchful eye, Richard looked along the table to where his younger son sat alongside Victoria Bell. He had been told she had kept her maiden name for her professional work.

But what Richard noticed particularly was Anthony's closeness to her. He saw them laughing, heads together at times, clearly enjoying one another's company. For Richard, these were all telltale signs. He sighed inwardly. He knew then why there had never been any mention of a girlfriend in Anthony's life.

And then an uncomfortable thought occurred to him. Was he sleeping with her? He couldn't decide, but there was one thing he was sure of. He wanted to sleep with her. And Victoria? He thought there was no doubt at all she wanted to be with Anthony. At that very moment, from across the table, she sensed Richard's eyes on her. She turned and whispered to Anthony.

'I think your father might be suspicious of us,' she said.

Very wisely, Anthony did not look at his father.

'Don't worry about it. I'll get a lecture on propriety later,' he said quietly, 'but you're worth it.'

Beside her, her brother was thinking the very same thing and wondering what would become of it. He wouldn't want to be in his sister's shoes if her husband found out but he realised the family had been wrong to push her to marry Mark Hansen. Very wrong. He knew his parents had been self-serving. He feared someday there would be a reckoning. Looking at her with Anthony, he was sure of it.

As the lunch concluded, a small group formed to walk the short distance to the site of the old house and to view what remained of it.

Both Andrew and Melanie, confident their presence was essential, set off too, only to be gathered in by each of their fathers determined to keep them out of the way. This intervention led to howls of protest which were ignored as they were returned to the house and told to play quietly.

Paul, having told an unhappy Andrew to behave himself, walked quickly to catch up with his father and uncle. Anthony had walked on ahead with Daniel Harrington and Julia, with Lachie and Victoria just behind them.

The grass in the immediate area had been mown the day before. William, ever cautious, had expressed the view they should still be wary of snakes, even though the snakes wouldn't be as active in April as they were in spring and mid-summer.

As Daniel Harrington stood before the wreckage of the grand home for the first time, he began to wonder how the Belleville family had coped with such a tragedy. He knew the fire pre-dated his wife's relationship with Richard. In fact, it had been her invitation to Paul through her son Tim, Paul's school friend, to stay at Berrima Park when he had no home to return to in the Christmas holidays following the tragedy that had brought about their meeting.

He noticed heavy chain link fencing had kept the site secure for years. It was in good repair.

'I've cut this panel of the fencing away,' William said, pointing to a section of the fence to Daniel's left. 'I thought you might want to get a closer look.'

'Thanks, William,' he said. He knew William had lived in the house until it had burned down. 'It looks like it was a big house. Tell me about it.'

But it was Richard who answered.

'It was a magnificent house,' Richard said. His memory of the house and the terrible night it had burned to the ground were indelibly imbedded in his mind.

He gestured to indicate the direction of the major ground floor rooms.

'From the front entrance of a few steps, a spacious hallway led to three reception rooms, the dining room plus my father's study with the hallway running the length of the ground floor to the back of the house where the kitchen and utility rooms were. Some of that was still standing but we demolished it after the ashes had gone cold.'

As they moved around the site, he continued.

'Upstairs, there were four bedrooms, several children's bedrooms, three bathrooms, my mother's sitting room and dressing room plus servants' rooms, accessed by two internal staircases. We survived because our housekeeper reminded us we could use the servants' stairs that came out in the kitchen. The grand staircase was well alight by the time we became aware of the fire. It had started at the front door and in the dining room via a window that had been left slightly ajar.'

It was the most Richard had spoken of the fire in many years and yet it was all fresh in his memory.

'Your mother died as a result of her injuries, I understand,' Daniel said. 'It must have been shocking.'

'It was,' Richard said. 'We were just pleased that none of the children were in the house. I tried hard to save my mother but, in the end, I failed.'

He could see that Richard still carried the burden of that failure.

As to the children, he guessed Paul had been at boarding school and Anthony would have been in England with his mother. But Marianne? He was about to ask when Richard spoke again.

'Marianne, William and Alice's daughter, was staying with Alice's mother in town to go to the local grammar school as a day pupil. There was just me, William and Alice, my mother and our housekeeper Mrs Duffy in the house that night.'

The whole group remained silent, each trying to imagine – except for William who was reliving the terrible night even as his brother spoke – what it must have been like to wake and find your grand home going up in flames.

'A tragedy,' Daniel said.

'It was,' William said.

He had noticed how much it had affected his brother to recount the events of that night.

'And then we decided to move on. Not rebuild it. Not clear it. Just leave it. There was nothing that was salvageable,' William said quietly.

'We buried our mother,' he said, as he pointed to the gravestones at a discreet distance from the house, 'and got on with living.'

'It would have been a commanding sight when it stood here,' Daniel said. 'A very formal house by Richard's description. I've seen places like it in Sydney and Melbourne, but hardly ever in Queensland, and certainly not up this way.'

William agreed.

'It was a very formal house. That was the way our mother liked to live. When she died, Richard and I decided it wasn't appropriate to try to rebuild it. We could never recapture that lifestyle without her. We decided to build the new house. It's far more practical,' he said.

Faced with the twin tragedy of the death of their mother and the complete ruin of the house, Daniel Harrington felt they had made a very sensible decision. He had read the correspondence Anthony had found in the original architect's archive. He found himself agreeing with the sentiment – *it is an extravagance to build such a fine house in so remote a location.*

He looked back towards the comfortable country house that William and Alice had called home for fifteen years or more.

In a low voice, he spoke his thoughts to Anthony. It was after all Anthony's commission. He was there simply to give advice, not make decisions.

'To rebuild an exact replica of what was here would be prohibitively expensive and then, in later years, costly to maintain. Houses like this need live in staff, otherwise they go to wrack and ruin in a very short time and no one is happy. The house had a very large footprint. It was indeed a grand gesture, not one that I think should be repeated. Perhaps your father and your uncle were right.'

He looked again towards William and Alice's house.

'And to rebuild it now, it would completely dominate its near neighbour, whatever you did.'

Anthony nodded.

'I've come to the same conclusion myself but I don't want to disappoint my aunt,' he said quietly.

'That, Anthony, is what architects must do sometimes. Disappoint their clients. Keep them from their worst excesses. Keep them from making costly mistakes. But I don't think we need to disappoint your aunt. I think we need to find a compromise solution.'

'So what do you suggest? I think you have an idea, don't you?'

'I do. If it was my job,' he said diplomatically, 'I would assess the site properly and then consider a scaled down version of the house. I would try to recover some of the building materials from the site such as the less charred bricks and incorporate them into the design, probably using them for a garden wall for example. They would provide a link with the original house.'

'Not a modern design surely?'

'No, a replica in a sense. Let's call it a tribute. You might want to think about shrinking the footprint of the building and then use the remaining space for the garden. Where's Lachie?'

He turned around.

'Didn't you come ready to do some measurements?'

Lachie smiled and held up the tape measure he had brought for the purpose and his notebook for recording the measurements.

'Good.'

He began to direct the two young men to the measurements he thought would be helpful. While Anthony and Lachie were busy following his instructions, he asked William about prevailing winds as he pulled out his small compass to confirm how the house would need to be sited to face north.

He guessed the old house had been built facing more to the east than north but it was accepted practice that houses should be built facing north in the southern hemisphere to get the best of the winter sun.

Through all of this, Julia had been silent. Listening firstly to her brother and his memories and then watching on as Daniel made suggestions to Anthony. It was as if it was a practical class for his students.

Richard, worrying she might be about to hear disappointing advice from the expert architect, put his arm around her.

'What's he suggesting?' Richard asked. 'I take it he doesn't think rebuilding the original is a good idea.'

But before she could answer, Daniel turned and approached her.

'I'm sorry, Julia. I just go a bit carried away there. I so quickly assume the role of lecturer. But this is more than a university project. I wasn't meaning to exclude you.'

His manners are impeccable, Richard thought. The ultimate diplomat.

She shook her head.

'What are you thinking?'

'Do you want me to be honest with you?' he asked.

'Yes, of course.'

'Then I wouldn't advise you to rebuild what was here. Not exactly. It would be expensive, costly for future generations in upkeep and it would dominate its neighbour.'

And then he drew her to one side.

'And you saw how your brother reacted when he spoke of the fire that night. I think he would find it difficult to see an exact replica in its place. It would remind him of what he couldn't do. He couldn't save your mother. It is better to keep the memory of it, I believe, but honour it with a new version.'

'A new version?'

He nodded.

'A similar design – a tribute, if you like – with a smaller footprint for the house and then use all the remaining land for a garden, perhaps a loggia on one side. I have an idea of using recycled bricks from the old house in a low wall around the back garden which will have a pathway leading to a back gate that would head towards the existing house. We will, of course, need to check the water supply situation. That would be essential for a reasonable garden.'

He looked around for William, who was helping the two young men as they struggled with the tape measure over the distance.

Victoria, who had listened attentively but said nothing, looked at Julia. Was she happy with the suggestion?

'Daniel seems to have taken charge,' she said to Julia, with a laugh. 'Anthony isn't going to be too pleased if he takes over completely.'

'I think Anthony will be relieved to have his advice. I think he'll agree with what Daniel is saying,' she said. 'Rebuilding the big house just as it was would be like a ghost rising from the grave. But building a tribute to it sounds more reasonable. It will be exciting. Are you up for the challenge of the interiors? It will give you a chance to work with my nephew. The two of you seem to get on very well.'

Victoria noticed just the hint of a smile on Julia's lips.

'We do get on very well. I'm hoping he and my brother will go into partnership. This could be a landmark project to get them started.'

'So you hope to be working more frequently with Anthony in the future?'

'I hope so,' she said. 'He has a good eye for design.'

Julia said nothing further but, like her brother, she had noticed the closeness between them.

'Nice girl,' Richard said as he stood beside Julia and watched Victoria walk across to join Anthony, Paul and her brother.

'She is. She's lovely. Shame about the wedding ring.'

Richard laughed quietly.

'I noticed that.'

'Do you think Anthony's in love with her?'

Richard let out a deep sigh.

'Possibly. I do think she's as keen on him as he is on her. I hope he doesn't fall foul of a jealous husband. She must have married quite young I suspect.'

They did not hear William come up behind them.

'What's this about Anthony? Don't tell me he's getting into trouble over a woman too,' William said, in his usual blunt way.

'I hope not,' Richard said evenly.

'Is Paul still asking around for a pilot job for Larry Kent's daughter? That caused a ripple of gossip. I didn't tell you someone saw him with her in our plane. They said he was kissing her. I said I didn't believe it. They must have been mistaken.'

Julia looked from one to the other. None of the gossip had reached her.

'Paul? Surely not.'

She waited for her brother Richard to deny it.

'I think there's something going on with him and Amanda. I don't know what. But I had words with him about Linda Kent. He virtually told me to mind my own business,' Richard said. 'I guess my influence is waning.'

The mention of Amanda had alerted William.

'I hope that girl keeps her hands off Alex. He's been a bit unsettled since his discoveries about his mother. And his father of course. I know Marianne thinks he's seen Amanda a few times he hasn't told her about. But I said to her I think it's only natural they would want to discuss what they found out about their mothers. After all, they have some shared history.'

It was, Richard thought, sensible advice.

'Marianne is very level-headed,' Richard said. 'She shouldn't let her imagination run riot. I think Alex and Amanda had a lot to discuss from what they both found out. Don't forget they shared a lot when they were youngsters.'

William nodded.

'I think you're right. Marianne said Alex has written to the address in Scotland he got from the letters left for him by his mother. He's hoping he eventually gets a reply.'

Richard felt reassured by William's explanation. But he knew Alex still had the capacity to make Paul jealous.

'I heard that Kent girl is working in Brisbane now,' William said, 'so that should be one problem out of the way.'

Richard sighed.

'I hope so, William, except that Paul is taking the plane down to Brisbane soon for a major overhaul. It's the first time I've ever seen him keen to go to Brisbane.'

He said nothing more but both Julia and William realised what was worrying their brother. Would Paul use the opportunity to see Linda Kent?

Julia had heard the latest news with growing concern. Her

nephews – two goodlooking young men – appeared to have inherited all the traits, good and bad, of the Belleville men, except for her brother William. She wondered what lay ahead for them. She hoped they would avoid the disappointment of failed relationships.

17

THE FOLLOWING DAY Prior Park was a far less busy place for which Alice was grateful. Susan, given the choice, had opted to stay at Prior Park rather than at her father's house in town. He too had stayed at Prior Park. Anthony was expected back once he had seen his visitors onto the morning flight to Sydney.

It was a perfect opportunity for Alice to speak quietly with Susan. Richard had opted for a morning ride with his brother. He liked to keep abreast of the situation with the cattle. Were they overstocked? Was it too dry heading into the winter for comfort? He knew William liked to discuss these issues with him. Julia, now more interested in the management of Prior Park, joined her brothers on their morning ride.

'Alex told me yesterday the Armoobilla manager had called him suggesting the stock we put in their paddock last month be moved,' William said. 'He's worried it's getting too eaten out. Alex is organising that today.'

'Well, it gave us some breathing space,' Richard said.

'It did. Fortunately there's another truckload of feed coming from our place down near Taroom next week. That will help ease the feed situation.'

He looked to the sky.

'We sometimes get good rain in April. The long range forecast actually predicts it for this year.'

'I hope you're right,' Richard said, although he had less faith in the long range forecaster who had predicted it than William.

Julia had listened to the conversation without making any comments but she smiled to herself. It was the same conversation she'd been hearing for decades. The weather. Rain. The lack of rain. Or rain at the wrong time. Or too much of it. She understood more than ever how the weather dominated the lives of country people in a way it would never dominate day-to-day life in the cities.

With the others out of the house, Alice sat with Susan in the kitchen. She could see the girl was reluctant to talk, and yet she needed to talk.

'Is it difficult at home with Tim disliking this family so much?' Alice asked, hoping she was approaching the problem in the right way.

Susan nodded.

'Sometimes. Just lately he seems to bring things up,' she said, without being specific. 'I agreed to use the name Susan Lester. I thought that would satisfy him. Mum said to do it to make him happy. So I did.'

'And now he's suggesting your father isn't your father after all? It sounds to me as if he is trying to undermine your relationship with your father.'

It's exactly as Richard predicted, Alice thought. It was what he had always been afraid of. She waited for the girl to answer.

'It's because he thinks I don't look anything like my father or other members of the Belleville family.'

'I don't think that means anything. Marianne takes after me. She doesn't look anything like her father,' Alice said, trying to draw a comparison Susan might understand.

Alice was at a loss to know what else to say. She had no idea how to refute the suggestion that Richard wasn't her father. It seemed so preposterous. But creating doubt seemed to be working just as Tim Lester hoped it would. Alice was sure he would have been happy for Susan to cut herself off entirely from her father and the rest of the family.

'They weren't married when I was conceived, were they? Mum was still married to Tim and Nancy's father, wasn't she? Were my parents having an affair?'

She paused.

'They must have been,' she said, answering her own question, 'but no one's told me anything of how I came to be born to a man who wasn't my mother's husband at the time.'

Alice took a deep breath. Her worst fears had been realised. The scandal she had hoped never to revisit had resurfaced because the child at the centre of it was old enough now to want answers.

'You're right, Susan, they did have an affair,' she said quietly, 'but you need to understand the circumstances. Your mother wasn't happy in her marriage. Her first husband didn't treat her well. But I don't think Tim would ever want to hear that about his father. Or acknowledge it even. His father died in a riding accident just as you were born. Otherwise you would have been brought up as his child.'

'And my real father wouldn't have been able to have anything to do with me? That means I would never have known him.'

Alice was pleased to hear her describe Richard as her real father. But she decided the girl needed to know the full story.

'Your father was always prepared to acknowledge you were his child. He wanted your mother to leave her husband and get a divorce so she could marry him but she wouldn't leave Gerald Lester because he would have cut her off from Tim and Nancy. It was really very difficult for her. But she made the choice to stay with him, knowing she was having another man's child, and then fate intervened. After a decent interval they were able to get married. You were very young, not much more than a baby. Your father had already divorced Catherine, his first wife.'

'And now he's married Catherine again,' she said. 'And Tim got his wish to have us back at Berrima Park. Why did my mother and my father not stay married?'

Did Susan not remember the dreadful scenes at Berrima Park? It was clear to Alice she did not understand what happened, even if she remembered them.

'You would need to ask them,' Alice said, deciding she had explained enough without going into details of another family scandal, 'but I think Paul letting Nancy down like he did disappointed your mother so much she couldn't get over it. Tim was very angry too. Your mother held your father partly responsible, I believe, because he hadn't intervened.'

'Intervened? What do you mean?'

Alice sighed deeply. How much further should she go in revealing the sordid details of Paul's deception?

'Paul was seeing Amanda on the quiet,' Alice said.

'And he got her pregnant, didn't he?'

Alice nodded. There was no other way to explain it to Susan.

'He did, but he didn't know that when he went down to marry Nancy. It was only that Alex revealed Paul's relationship with Amanda that stopped the wedding. He later found out she was pregnant.'

It was, Alice thought, the bare facts of the story. Unembellished. She was pleased Susan appeared to be satisfied with her explanation.

'So you don't think there's any doubt about who my father is?'

Alice shook her head.

'None at all,' she said, 'but I wouldn't tell your father what Tim's been saying. He and Tim don't get on. If Tim says that to you again, just tell him you don't believe him and leave it at that.'

The girl nodded, satisfied with Alice's advice.

'Does it matter that I use the Lester name down there?'

She looked at Alice enquiringly. She didn't want to hurt her father but it made life so much easier.

'No, it doesn't matter, Susan. If it makes Tim happy, then do it. That's the family you live with. The family you must get along with every day.'

Alice could see Susan was relieved.

'I miss my father at times,' she admitted. 'He was a good dad when we were together as a family.'

Alice was reassured to hear her say so.

'Of course you miss him. It's always difficult when marriages break up. It's often the children who suffer more in the end. You should come up and visit us more often. You'll soon be old enough to travel by yourself. Or come up with Aunt Julia or Anthony. There'll be a lot of trips backwards and forwards while this house is being built.'

'I will,' she promised. 'I will.'

Alice was satisfied. She had done what she could.

Anthony announced his return in a swirl of dust in the Prior Park driveway. His father, having just returned from riding, walked across to greet him, keen for a private word with his son.

'Our visitors safely on the plane south?'

'Yep, plane got away on time. I've been left with a to do list,' he said, holding up his notebook. 'First item of business is to talk to my client in detail.'

'About a smaller, more manageable house I hope,' Richard said, aware that his sister might be feeling just a hint of disappointment that her dreams of a complete rebuild were simply impractical. He was hoping there had been no late night change of mind.

Anthony nodded.

'When you look at it closely, it never made sense to build it here in the first place. It's not like it could serve an alternative purpose.'

He guessed Anthony was thinking of grand houses used as hotels or wedding reception venues to help defray the costs of maintaining them.

'No, it couldn't. I'd be afraid it would end up a ruin again in a generation because no one would spend the money on it to maintain it. If Marianne gets to control the purse strings eventually, I couldn't see her lavishing thousands of dollars on upkeep of a house that doesn't return anything to the family coffers.'

Anthony laughed quietly. He loved his cousin but he had noticed how much her attitudes had come to resemble her father's when it came to managing Belleville affairs.

'A chip off the old block, so to speak,' Anthony said, knowing no further explanation was required. He noticed the broad smile on his father's face.

Richard reached out then and put his hand on his son's arm as he was about to walk towards the house. Anthony knew what was coming.

'Victoria's a nice girl,' Richard said, looking intently at his son, 'but I'm not sure your behaviour yesterday was appropriate towards a married woman. I wasn't the only one to notice.'

Anthony shrugged. What could he say? He had predicted a ticking off from his father.

'That's all. Just a shrug? You don't have anything to say? No explanation?'

'That's right,' he said, the edginess in his voice betraying his annoyance. 'I don't have anything to say. It's between me and Victoria.'

'Are you in love with her, son?' Richard asked.

'What do you think, Dad?'

It wasn't so much the words his son spoke but the emphasis with which he spoke them. Richard heard the unhappiness in son's voice. The utter despair and disappointment.

'The fact I can't imagine my life without her should tell you everything you need to know.'

He paused and took a deep breath.

'Now leave it. Leave it be.'

He pulled away from his father's grasp and headed towards the house. Richard let him go. In those few words, he had learnt so much about his son. But almost nothing about the girl his son was in love with or how he had managed to tumble headlong into such heartache.

By the time the smaller group was being called for lunch into the kitchen, Anthony had filled several pages of his notebook with rough sketches and outlines of house plans that, in the end, began to look like an unintelligible mess to anyone who had not been involved in the discussions but Julia could see her dream already coming alive in the early pencil sketches.

Less ambitious perhaps but still, in her view, she would be honouring the extravagant gesture of her grandfather who had first conceived the idea of the grand house at Prior Park. And in doing so she would be restoring the site. It would no longer be a neglected shrine to the past, a constant reminder of a terrible event. Instead it would be a beautiful legacy for the family and the generations to come.

Alice, pleased to have a smaller group for lunch, stood over the stove, a pile of steaks ready for the pan. William, who considered he was better at cooking steak than his wife, took over the task. Dishes of vegetables and salad were already sitting in the middle of the table.

'William's taking up his usual role, I see,' Richard said.

'He doesn't like the way I cook steaks. That's fine by me,' she said, as she stood aside.

'I saw you having a chat with Susan yesterday. I had a sense you were keen to get me out of the house this morning. Was that so you could talk to her a bit more?'

Alice nodded, aware the girl might walk into the kitchen at any moment.

'She had some questions. Obvious ones,' Alice said, without being specific.

'Obvious?'

It was an unusual thing for Alice to say. What were the obvious questions?

'Richard, think about it. The girl will be sixteen this year. She's finally figured out you were having an affair with her mother when she was conceived. And she wanted to know why you split up.'

'So what did you tell her?' Richard was anxious.

'The truth. That's what I told her. What else was I to tell her?'

'It depends on how much detail you added,' he said.

She could see he was alarmed. The truth of their marriage failure was complicated. Complicated by things other than Paul's deception of Nancy. Alice was aware of almost everything that had contributed to the marriage breakdown so she was quick to reassure him.

'Don't worry,' Alice said. 'I told her just basic facts. I told her Gerald Lester had died just as she was being born but that, before she was born, you had wanted her mother to leave him and marry you. As to the breakup, I didn't speak about Daniel. Or Catherine. Or Tim's part in it all. I said Paul letting Nancy down was something Kate couldn't get over.'

'Thanks, Alice. I think that's all she needs to know, don't you?'

'I think so,' Alice said.

'I was worried Tim might be making her life difficult.'

'I think he has his moments. You know she uses the name Susan Lester down there.'

'I do,' Richard said. 'I can't say I'm happy about it but she's under Tim's roof. I suspect she doesn't want grief from him.'

Alice said nothing but Richard sensed then that Tim Lester was doing exactly what he had anticipated. And there was nothing, as Susan's father, he could do about it. He would not disrupt her life further by making a fuss.

'The children always suffer in marriage breakdown,' Alice said. 'I hope this younger generation is more settled.'

'I do too,' Richard said. 'I do too.'

And then he thought of Paul. And Anthony. Almost beyond his influence now. And certainly beyond taking any advice from a father whose private life had been anything but settled.

Richard accepted a plate barely large enough to contain the T bone steak his brother had cooked for him and sat alongside his daughter, who had opted for a dainty piece of fillet steak.

'It's really good you came up to visit,' he said. 'I really miss you.'

'I really miss you too, Dad,' she said.

For Richard, those few words felt like a small victory. At the time of her birth, he had been delighted to have fathered a daughter. But occasionally he asked himself how it was he had managed to miss large chunks of his children's childhoods, especially Anthony and Susan. She seemed more relaxed. He hoped it signalled a closer relationship.

'Should I ask how school's going?'

'If you like,' she said, without offering any response.

'And?'

She let out a deep sigh. Why must parents always ask about school?

'I'm going OK. Mum is happy with my results.'

'When you were in primary school, you said you wanted to go to the school Nancy had gone to in Sydney. I never knew if you'd changed your mind or your mother talked you out of it?'

In the nearly seven years since the marriage breakup, he had rarely spoken directly with her mother Kate. Messages were passed via her friend Angela or via their lawyers. Or via his occasional phone calls with Susan.

She shook her head.

'I decided I didn't want to go to Sydney to live. That's why Mum chose the local girls' school.'

'Do you like it?'

'It's OK,' she said. 'There aren't many girls with divorced parents though.'

He wondered if the scandal surrounding her birth was still the subject of local gossip but it wasn't something he could ask.

'Is Tim treating you OK?'

She shrugged.

'Of course he is,' she said but her father noticed how she looked towards Alice as she answered.

'And your future? Have you and your mother discussed it?'

'Not very much. She's been busy helping Nancy with Amy. And then helping Tim and Margaret plan their wedding in September. I'm going to be a bridesmaid.'

He tried again.

'Is there a career you'd really like to pursue?' he asked. 'Something you're really keen on?'

In asking these questions, he realised he didn't really know his daughter very well at all. What did she like? Was she like other teenagers obsessed with some pop star or other? Did she have a best friend? Did she have a boyfriend?

'I don't know,' she said. 'Mum said she'd discuss it with you at some stage. What you thought I should do because ...'

Her words trailed off but it was a blank her father could fill in.

'Because you won't inherit anything from the Lesters,' he said. 'Eventually you'll share in the Belleville estate with your brothers and Marianne. And John Fitzroy too.'

'Aunt Julia told me she is now a part owner with you and Uncle William. Did she do that so she could rebuild the old house?'

'Partly, I think,' her father said, 'but she's always loved Prior Park but she was left separate money by our mother. That's why she wasn't included alongside your uncle and me.'

She thought about this for a moment.

'Unlike Nancy. Nancy only gets some income but Tim got to own everything. I heard her discussing it with Mum. I think she always tries to stay in Tim's good books for that reason.'

'Well, your uncle and I decided girls should be treated the same as boys when it comes to inheriting the Belleville business.'

'Two girls, three boys. And I'm the youngest. I bet I won't get much of a say in anything.'

'Well, it's years off, I hope. So I wouldn't worry about it at the moment. Will your mother and Daniel go on living at Berrima Park after Tim is married?'

'I think so. They sometimes stay at Daniel's house in town. But Tim has always liked Mum to be in charge of the house at Berrima Park. I think Margaret is quite happy for her to stay in charge.'

'Your mother really belongs there,' he said, remembering the times he had returned to Berrima Park with her and the ease with which she had resumed her old life.

'Is that part of the reason your marriage broke up?'

'Partly,' he said. 'There were a lot of reasons, none of them to do with you.'

'Tim was one of the reasons, wasn't he?'

Richard nodded. He wouldn't lie to his daughter but nor would he tell her about the campaign Tim had waged against him. But he was curious. How well did Tim get on with Daniel Harrington?

'I think he gets on better with Daniel than he did with me,' Richard suggested.

She nodded.

'He and Daniel get on very well. He's very happy with the work

Daniel did on the house and he was delighted when Mum married him. Anyway Daniel's busy with his practice and his students so he's not around all the time so they don't really see much of one another.'

In other words, Richard thought, the perfect solution for Tim. He has his mother to himself for a good part of the time, running the household just as he likes it.

For the first time, Richard began to realise his daughter's future needed to be considered more carefully. She was living at Berrima Park because she had chosen to live with her mother and he had not objected. And that inevitably had predetermined her closest relationships.

But he knew her future would lie with the Belleville family. With her Belleville inheritance. He could no longer sit back and let other people make decisions for her. It was time for him to step up. Otherwise, he worried she risked never being accepted as a rightful heir to the Belleville legacy, as if her absence from their midst might undermine her entitlement.

For him, it became a new worry to add to his concerns about his sons.

18

Brisbane

PAUL LET THE HOT water from the shower cascade over his body. Is this how Alex felt, he wondered? Is this how he felt after being with Amanda? How he felt after betraying Marianne?

What had John Fitzroy told him after seeing them together? Alex had looked angry. Angry with himself. Angry with her, John had said. And Amanda? He remembered exactly what John had said. Amanda had looked happy. Triumphant. Like a woman in love. And now she's my wife, not Alex's. Does she love me like that? The question had begun to haunt him.

What am I feeling? Am I, like Alex was, angry at myself? Or just feeling guilty? Was this payback, he wondered? Because he knew – finally – that Amanda had lured him into marriage on a false premise. Or should I be angry with my father who refused to listen to my doubts? Who insisted I marry Amanda.

And now? Am I just a little less committed to her than before? He couldn't answer that question but each day, as Andrew grew older, he could see she had deceived him. Andrew wasn't a Belleville. Wasn't his son. The evidence was before his eyes.

But he could never ever say it out loud. He couldn't ruin a child's life. And he didn't want to ruin his marriage. Perhaps she had genuinely believed he had been her baby's father. Had she simply been unlucky? Had she been with Alex just the once? He didn't know for sure. Perhaps they were still carrying on behind his back even now.

He thought about Linda. How had he become so captivated by her? Those deep blue eyes had worked their magic on him.

And foolishly he had accepted an invitation to dinner at her flat. Hardly thinking what it meant. Not consciously. But he berated himself now. He'd known all along it was only ever going to end one way. Who had made the first move? He couldn't remember. Had he kissed her first? Had she kissed him? He was unsure. But the pleasure of holding her in his arms had been his undoing.

And then he realised what he was doing. He was deflecting the blame as he always did. Not taking responsibility for his own actions. Finding excuses.

He'd never seen Alex do more than kiss Amanda on the cheek since they were married. He seemed devoted to Marianne and little Mel. Had he slipped up just the once? But he knew for sure Alex visited often when he was away. Was he simply being friendly? Was it just his imagination that Amanda was still besotted with Alex?

He didn't know. But he knew the real reason why he would never accuse her. Or Alex.

Marianne. That's why I'm silent. And why I'll always remain silent. Marianne deserves happiness. No one else would ever openly raise doubts about Andrew's parentage for that single reason. So neither would he. Marianne was on a pedestal. However much others transgressed, she had not. She was entitled to keep her fairytale marriage intact. He wondered if she realised just how much Alex had been in love with Amanda. And now? He knew Alex tried hard to hide it. Tried hard to pretend it was all in the past. But Marianne must know, Paul decided. She must know. But then Alex chose her. And she was content in that knowledge. Secure in her marriage.

He stepped out of the shower and towelled himself vigorously. None of these thoughts had helped. It all seemed like a tangled web.

And then his mind drifted back to Linda. Lovely Linda. She had delighted him with her warmth. Seduced him with her passion. I've been honest with her, he thought. He remembered his words. *There's no future in a relationship with me* but she had simply shrugged.

'Of course I know that,' she had said laughingly, even as she had put her arms around him and kissed him. 'Let's enjoy the moment. Let's enjoy the time we have together.'

She had led him towards her bedroom. He hadn't the power to resist her. The truth was he wanted her as much as she wanted him.

Later, he had lain in her bed with her in his arms, caressing her and wondering how he would ever say no to her in the future, her body soft against his.

And he knew he would go on torturing himself for his weakness. But he wanted to be with her again. To make love to her again.

It was then a thought struck him. Was this a pattern in the men of the family? Except of course for his Uncle William. There was an awful moment when he realised how much his actions echoed those of his grandfather. Hadn't he kept a mistress in Brisbane?

No, I'm not that person, he decided. There won't be an unwanted child. She had assured him of that. But still he couldn't shake the parallels in their story.

But then he thought, *no, that's wrong. Linda knows I'm married. I never tried to hide that. She knows I won't leave Amanda. She understands the limitations of our relationship.*

The thought shocked him. Why was he thinking in terms of their relationship? But hadn't he promised her he would see her again?

He sat on the edge of his bed. Beyond the hotel, the streets were quiet. The city was asleep. But he knew in those darkest hours of the night, sleep would elude him.

The following day as he headed into the dining room for breakfast, the hotel receptionist handed him a note. He read it quickly. And groaned, almost aloud.

His father had called to tell him John Bertram was on his way to visit them. On finding out Paul was in Brisbane, he had decided to stop off in Brisbane and fly back with him. He was expected later that afternoon and he would stay over at the same hotel.

Paul screwed up the note and shoved it in his pocket. He looked forward to seeing John, who was, after all, the man responsible for his passion for flying. But he knew he would face the inevitable question from his father. He could hear it now. *Where were you all evening when I tried to call you?* And his father would guess. Unless he came up with a plausible excuse.

He reached into his wallet and took out a scrap of paper with a name and telephone number. It had been in his wallet for years. He went in search of a telephone.

The beer garden at the Breakfast Creek Hotel was unusually quiet for a lunchtime. Paul looked around and spotted his friend.

'Long time no see, mate,' Murray Anderson said. 'I was pleased to get your call though.'

Murray, noted for his prowess on the rugby field during their school days, crushed Paul's hand in his massive grip.

'Haven't got a legal problem, have you? Not getting a divorce, are you?'

Paul laughed. It was the Murray he remembered from his days at the Grammar School. It puzzled everyone as to how he had managed to pass law at university.

'No, Murray, nothing like that. How've you been?'

'Great,' he said. 'You have no idea how exciting commercial law is. And wills and estates, well it doesn't get any more exciting than that. And then there's the occasional couple wanting to scratch each other's eyes out. You get the picture.'

He pulled a face to emphasise his point.

'We all thought you were an unlikely lawyer,' Paul said, 'but I guess playing rugby isn't exactly a full time profession.'

'Pity about that, isn't it?' he said. 'What are you having? A beer?'

Paul nodded. He certainly needed one. He waited while Murray ordered their drinks.

'So is this just a catch up?'

He handed Paul his card.

'The Belleville family have always had a Brisbane solicitor, I understand, but if you think about changing at any time, give us a call. I do a lot of work with rural families. My old man put my name about to a few people. They don't always like to use locals. The whole town knows their business if they do.'

Paul understood exactly what he meant. Sometimes small places had their disadvantages. And the Belleville family, the source of so much gossip over the years, could certainly attest to that.

'Will do, Murray,' he said. 'My dad and his brother still handle most of the stuff, but that will change over time. My role is to act as a pilot to Uncle William who looks after the rural properties. I'm in the air a lot.'

'And your dad?'

'The Belleville family has commercial investments. My father handles that side of things.'

Murray's eyes brightened.

'There must be a lot of contracts involved. And the estate planning would be quite something, I should think. I hope your father and uncle have good people on it.'

'I'll put in a word for you, Murray,' Paul said as he sipped his beer.

'Thanks, mate. How's that younger brother of yours? Anthony, isn't it?'

'Doing his honours year at Sydney Uni. Architecture. He was up visiting us a couple of weeks ago.'

Murray nodded as he sipped thoughtfully at his beer.

'My mother said she saw your brother dropping some people at the airport a few weeks back. That tallies. She remarked at how grown up he is now.'

'He is. And he's about to launch himself onto the unsuspecting public as an architect.'

Murray laughed. Typical sibling comment, he thought.

'My mother also said she'd heard your sister was visiting. I remember her as a kid. She must be a good deal younger than you.'

'Susan. She's coming up sixteen this year. She lives with her mother in the Southern Highlands. We don't see her very much,'

Paul picked up the menu from the table. He wasn't keen to offer up more details about his family. Murray's mother was a noted gossip. He'd deliberately limited his answers to the basic facts.

'Do you come here often?' Paul asked.

'Bring my country clients here, mate. A lot of them come down at Exhibition time to show cattle or just to see the cattle. They prefer to have a chat in a comfortable atmosphere rather than in an airless meeting room. Not good with four walls, a lot of them.'

He grinned.

'It suits me too. I can take a few notes then correspond with them but the basic decisions get made over a beer and a steak. Suits everyone.'

'You've got it made,' Paul said laughing. 'Is there a Mrs Anderson yet?'

'Later this year,' he said. 'We've been engaged a couple of years. I said we could get married last December and go overseas on our honeymoon. We could have seen the Wallabies play Wales at Cardiff.'

'How did that suggestion go down?'

Paul couldn't imagine a new bride wanting to watch a game of rugby in the icy temperatures of a Welsh winter on her honeymoon.

'Not well,' he said with a grimace. 'We're going to Hawaii I've been told.'

'And what's your intended's name?'

'Serena. Serena Cameron. Her old man is president of the local rugby club I belong to. He's a lawyer too.'

'And Serena?'

'She sidestepped the law. She's a pharmacist. You married well, I understand.'

Paul was saved the necessity of replying by the waitress who stood waiting patiently to take their orders. He smiled to himself when his companion ordered the largest steak available.

He remembered standing on the sidelines of school rugby

matches watching his burly friend dominate the scrum. It was a game Paul had always been considered too slight to attempt. It was left to the big powerful boys in the school.

'So, we've had a quick catch up. I'm wondering what brought you my way today,' Murray said. 'I got the sense there was a purpose to this meet up.'

Paul took a deep breath. He would need to confide in his friend. But he was uncomfortable with it just the same.

'I do need you to do me a favour, should it ever come up. It might never come up but I'm being cautious.'

'What's up, mate? Happy to do anything in my power.'

'I brought our plane down yesterday. It's having an overhaul at Archerfield. My father rang my hotel last night and I wasn't there. He left me a message that I only got this morning.'

'And?'

'Last night I was somewhere where I shouldn't have been. With someone I shouldn't have been with, if you get my drift. He's going to be suspicious so I'm going to tell him I had dinner with you.'

Murray laughed out loud.

'Following in the fine tradition of the Belleville men,' he said. 'Pretty, is she? What time did you climb out of her bed?'

It was obvious Murray knew all about the history of the Belleville family. He had clearly heard everything from his mother. His parents were well known in the cattle industry.

Paul shifted uneasily in his seat. He wasn't sure confiding in Murray was such a good idea after all.

'I'm not going to go into details but you get the idea,' Paul said.

'Got it. And next time? Will I be the cover again? Are you sure you won't be needing a divorce lawyer? Your wife is pretty feisty I've heard.'

'She's never going to know, is she?'

Murray shrugged his muscular shoulders.

'Well, she won't hear it from me but these things have a habit of leaking out in my experience. I'd go carefully, Paul, if I was you. But then you always had the ability to charm the girls. Remember all those Grammar girls who made you their pinup boy? Stakes are a bit higher now though. I hope you haven't made any rash promises to this girl.'

'No, no rash promises,' Paul assured him.

'Except you're going to see her again, I take it.'

Paul shrugged. What could he say?

'I shouldn't. I know that,' he said.

'But you might.'

With that, Murray downed the rest of his beer and signalled for another, all the while contemplating how much trouble might lie ahead for his old school friend.

Paul checked his watch. It was now five o'clock and there was still no sign of John Bertram. He was sitting in the reception area of the hotel, expecting Linda to walk through the door at any moment. Her car keys were nestled in his pocket. She had lent him her car to get back to his hotel with the promise she would call in after work to collect them.

The arrangements had seemed fine. Innocuous even. With no risk. Hotel staff weren't interested in who he met. But now he worried that John Bertram, walking through the door and seeing him with Linda, would draw some very accurate conclusions. And he didn't want to risk that.

John would give him a lecture, that was for sure. But worse still, he would probably tell his father. And that was a lecture he wasn't prepared to endure. Not anymore. Not from a man whose own past could not withstand close scrutiny. And he, after all, had been the one who had forced him into marriage with Amanda. Maybe this was the result. Was there something lacking in his relationship with Amanda that he was seeking with Linda?

Deep in thought, he was startled by a gust of wind and the bang of a closing door. He stood up on seeing his father's good friend John Bertram walk into the reception area.

'Paul,' he said. 'Good to see you. How are you? Just let me check in quickly.'

John turned towards the reception desk. Paul waited, checking his watch again.

Linda is going to be walking through that door at any moment, he thought.

And then the door opened again. Linda, smiling broadly, breezed through and headed straight towards him. He gave a quick, almost imperceptible shake of the head and whispered urgently.

'John Bertram, a friend of my father's just turned up,' he said, indicating John at the reception counter.

She smiled and kissed him on the cheek.

'You'd better give me my keys quickly,' she said. 'He's the pilot, isn't he?'

But in those few seconds it took Paul to reach into his pocket, John turned and walked back towards him, just in time to notice a bundle of keys changing hands.

'I'm Linda,' she said, holding out her hand. 'I was just picking up my car keys. I'd lent Paul my car while he's here but something's come up and I need my car so I had to come and get it.'

John noticed immediately that Paul seemed incapable at that moment of saying anything.

'Nice to meet you, Linda,' John said, all the while taking in the little charade that was being played out for his benefit. 'I don't think we've met before.'

'No, we haven't. I only met Paul recently through our shared love of flying. My father services his plane up home. He told me about you. You're a pilot, aren't you? On real planes. I'd love to hear some of your stories.'

He could see she was keen to deflect his questions. But of course the one question in his mind was the very question he couldn't ask. Was this just a friendship? Because it looked to be something else altogether.

'Do you have time to have a drink with us,' John said, handing his bag off to the concierge. 'I could bore you for hours with flying talk but I promise not to do that. You need to tell me about yourself.'

Paul, who had said nothing up to this point, allowed himself to be propelled towards the bar. But the longer she stayed, the more certain he was his father's old friend would know his relationship with Linda was much more than mere friendship.

19

'NICE GIRL,' JOHN SAID as he and Paul watched Linda head in the direction of the carpark at the rear of the hotel.

'She is,' Paul agreed.

In the end, Linda had stayed only long enough to hear a couple of John's better stories of his flying career before excusing herself on the pretext of having to pick up a friend arriving by train from Sydney.

'You're playing with fire but you know that, don't you?'

'What do you mean?'

John shook his head slowly from side to side.

'Don't take me for a fool, Paul. You were with her last night, weren't you? She obviously lent you her car to come back here. Late at night, was it?'

Paul said nothing.

'Is that where you were when your father tried to call you last night? He rang me this morning before I left Sydney to tell me he hadn't been able to get on to you but that he'd left a message to let you know I was coming. So what are you going to tell your old man if he asks about where you were?'

'For goodness' sake,' Paul said, the exasperation in his voice evident. 'I'm thirty years old, not fifteen. Do I still have to account for my movements to my father?'

John conceded he had a point.

'You're right, of course. But he sounded worried about you. As if there might be something going on in your private life. That you're not entirely happy.'

'Well, he should stop meddling in my private life, if I'm being honest. He means well but …'

He didn't finish what he was about to say.

'But what?' John asked, wondering why Paul would suddenly accuse his father of interfering in his private life.

'It doesn't matter,' he said, draining the glass of beer that had sat too long in front of him. 'Let's have some dinner.'

He was annoyed with his father. It was as if his father was keeping tabs on him. He knew why of course. But that only increased his irritation.

That was one of the delightful things about being with Linda, he thought. There was no history. No links with the family. They could just be themselves.

After perusing the menu in silence for some minutes, John finally tossed it to one side and tried again.

'What doesn't matter, Paul?' he persisted. 'There's something bothering you, isn't there? Something you really need to talk about.'

He heard Paul sigh deeply. He remained silent, determined to force him to speak.

Paul lent forward, head in hands. After a few moments, he looked at John. Here was someone who knew all their history. His history. His father's. His mother's too. He'd proven himself to be a staunch friend. There was no one else quite like him. Close to them all, but not family.

'This goes back years, John,' Paul said finally. 'Years.'

'Whatever it is, you need to get it off your chest,' John said.

'You're right. I can't keep this bottled up. Not forever. And it's partly my father's fault.'

'Go on.'

He needed Paul to be honest with him. He wasn't going to try and second guess what he was about to reveal.

'I tried to tell my father but he wouldn't listen.'

'Tell him what, Paul?'

'That the baby Amanda was having wasn't my baby. That I wasn't the father of her child. I believed her pregnancy was too advanced for the baby to be mine. And as it's turned out, I was right.'

He saw the shocked look on John Bertram's face.

'Shocking, isn't it? But he assumed because I was having a relationship with her that I was responsible. He berated me for not living up to my responsibilities. For shaming the family.'

'How do you know for sure, Paul?' he asked. 'Surely there's room for doubt?'

Paul shook his head slowly from side to side.

'No doubt, John. For a start, Andrew looks nothing like me. Nothing like a Belleville. And very little like a Robinson.'

'That's not enough, Paul. Lots of kids don't look like their parents. They probably take traits from further back in the family. It's probably the case with Andrew.'

He knew it would take a lot to convince John Bertram.

'But that's not all,' he said, not looking at John. Not looking anywhere really. Because what he had discovered had left no room for doubt. 'I went to a doctor this afternoon. Just on a whim. I had a couple of hours to kill. It was about something I didn't want to ask our family doctor.'

He paused.

'Although our doctor's probably realised it too now. He's probably put two and two together. Andrew had to have a blood test a few weeks back. He'd have noted the blood type.'

'OK, so what's he probably put together. I've no idea where this is going,' John said. He was beginning to imagine all sorts of terrible diseases and incurable conditions.

'I asked the doctor about blood groups this morning. He confirmed that my blood group and Amanda's, which I already knew, couldn't have produced a child with an O blood group. He said, without any knowledge of who I was talking about, that the O blood group was very common in people of Scottish decent.

Andrew has type O blood.'

There. He had said it out loud. He had told someone.

'Say something, John. Say something. Anything. Tell me what I should do?'

John Bertram shook his head. Everything about what Paul had just told him seemed so shocking he'd lost the power of speech momentarily. How could he possibly advise him? It was beyond his experience. Beyond his imagination even. It was one thing to be suspicious. Quite another to have it confirmed in that way. Irrefutable.

'Shocking, isn't it? Perhaps I'd have been better off not confirming it. Living with the uncertainty. But I know now I'm bringing up Alex Fraser's child. Not my own.'

'And the new baby?'

It was the first question that had occurred to John. What if Paul hadn't fathered the second child either?

'No, he's definitely my child,' Paul said. 'He's got all the familiar Belleville characteristics. Looks like me when I look at my baby photos that I got from my mother.'

'And you're going to solve this problem by tumbling into bed with the first willing girl who comes across your path?'

'That's out of order, John, and you know it,' Paul snapped.

'Sorry, I apologise. It is out of order. She's a very nice girl. I just hope she doesn't get hurt.'

'She knows I'm married. And that I have children. She understands the limitations of our relationship.'

He heard John let out a deep audible sigh.

'Just at the present time, her friendship is something I really need. I'm not going to give it up.'

'I can see that Paul,' he said. 'And I'm never going to say anything to anyone, you can be sure of that. Your confidences are safe with me. But what will you tell your father? He'll ask. I know that for sure.'

'I've got a cover story all ready,' Paul said, smiling for the first time. 'An old friend from Grammar. Murray Anderson. I had lunch with him today. He's my cover story.'

John nodded. It was plausible. Paul wouldn't need to embellish it.

'But what choice do you have about little Andrew?' John asked, knowing he could no longer avoid the question.

'I decided, whatever the answer was about his blood group, I wouldn't run the risk of ruining a child's life by revealing the truth. I wouldn't ruin my marriage over it. I wouldn't want to ruin my cousin's marriage either, if it came to that.'

He took a long pause, thinking about what he would say next.

'I have to give Amanda the benefit of the doubt, don't I? She couldn't have been sure about Andrew's father. Not until later, after he was born. And by then we were married.'

He paused again.

'There's another possibility, of course. She and Alex decided between them I would make the ideal husband. I was the only other man she'd slept with. And Alex was already married to Marianne, who was about to have his baby. He didn't want to break Marianne's heart. And neither do I.'

'Oh what a mess,' John said, as he signalled for the waiter. 'I need a large whisky after this. And I thought it was only your father who had a special talent for messing up his private life. I'm sorry he passed that trait on to his son.'

'I think it's a Belleville family trait among the men, so my life is just running true to type, it seems.'

John wondered how Paul would feel about his marriage now. Could he really turn a blind eye to little Andrew's parentage and continue with his family life as if nothing had happened? Or would it eat away at his peace of mind?

'I have to ask this, Paul,' he said finally. 'Can you really put this to one side and make your marriage work? Will you be able to do that?'

'It is what it is, John. I've made the decision in everyone's interests, but it helped to talk about it. To say it out loud. And I do feel as if Andrew's my son, despite everything.'

'Will you tell anyone else what you've found out?' John asked.

'I don't plan to. I just plan to get on with my life. Pretend everything is as it was.'

Would that be enough? John wasn't so sure. Would he bring it up with Amanda if they had an argument? Would she ever admit it if he confronted her? He doubted it would be as easy to continue as normal as Paul made out. Was that why he was looking elsewhere, outside his marriage?

Even as John was thinking these thoughts, Paul began to speak again.

'I think maybe you'll understand now about my friendship with Linda.'

John nodded.

'I do, Paul,' he said. 'I do understand. I think the relationship offers you some type of consolation. But what if she falls in love with you and wants more? Starts to press for more from you than you can give.'

He sighed. He hadn't discounted the possibility. But then John hadn't considered the possibility he might fall in love with her. He might already be in love with her. But he was no longer the immature young man he had been when he romanced Nancy and then moved on to Amanda. He was sure he had learned from his earlier mistakes.

'I'll cross that bridge when I come to it. If I come to it,' he said quietly.

'Well, just make sure she doesn't come knocking on your door one day saying she's pregnant with your child,' John warned.

'That'd be the icing on the cake, wouldn't it,' Paul said, laughing quietly. 'I promise you that's not going to happen.'

'Well, I hope you're right,' John said, as he turned his attention to the important task of ordering dinner. 'It's your life. You must make your own decisions. Just don't get careless about Linda. You need to keep that very quiet or else Amanda will find out and then you'll be in a whole new world of trouble.'

'I will,' he said. 'Linda knows the boundaries. I won't be able to see her very often.'

'I hope she does,' John said, admiring his confidence but not sharing it. He knew secrets like that had a habit of leaking out. But he sensed Paul needed the relationship even more than he was willing to acknowledge. It was, John guessed, the safety valve relieving the pressure cooker his life had become.

'How did she perform?' Larry Kent asked as he greeted Paul and John as they alighted from the cockpit. He was already giving the plane a cursory inspection, as was his habit. 'I see you picked up a passenger in Brisbane.'

Paul performed the introductions.

'John Bertram is the reason for my passion for flying. He flies for Qantas. Long haul routes but he also flew in the war,' Paul said. 'Taught me a lot about flying too.'

The two men shook hands.

'You'd be a similar age to Paul's father then?'

'Yes, Richard was my pilot during the war. I was the navigator on his crew. Lancasters.'

'Now that's a real flying machine,' Larry Kent observed. 'I saw G for George in '44 when it was on its war bonds campaign being flown around Australia. I was maybe fifteen when I saw it. I had a look at the engines. I was amazed by all the technical stuff. That's what got me interested in aeroplanes. Well, in their engines anyway.'

'Larry's not a good flyer,' Paul explained with a chuckle.

'No, I'm ok. It's just that this young bloke likes to scare the heck out of his passengers. Takes deep swoops over the ocean. I couldn't wait to get my feet back on solid earth. I hope he didn't play any tricks like that with you, John.'

John laughed and shook his head.

'He knows better than that. I'd have taken him to task. I spent some pretty anxious hours searching for him when his plane went down a few years back. He knows better than to try any fancy flying with me.'

'My daughter Linda thinks he's a great pilot,' Larry said. 'I told her she didn't know many pilots to compare him with. Mind you, the chance to fly the Belleville plane to help keep her hours up rather coloured her judgement, I think.'

John was relieved, at that moment, to see Richard heading

towards them but he caught the tail end of a question Larry Kent had obviously been desperate to ask Paul.

'Didn't happen to see my daughter in the big city, did you, Paul?'

But Paul had been ready for his question.

'No, not this time, Larry. I didn't have much time. Next time maybe.'

The lie came readily to his lips. They had both agreed he would not say anything to her father.

'Here's my father,' Paul said. 'He's come to collect us. My ETA was good. Spot on.'

'That's good planning, Paul. Good flying.'

Richard greeted Larry Kent briefly and then the trio headed off towards his car. As he watched them walk away, he had the uncomfortable feeling that Paul Belleville had been too ready with his answer. It was too practised. It bore, Larry thought, all the hallmarks of a lie. A big fat one at that, he thought. But he expected he would get the same response from his daughter too.

'Oh, they're beautiful.'

Anika Larsen lifted her head from the massive bunch of yellow roses and looked sideways at Linda.

'So you saw him then?'

She hardly needed Linda to say anything. The smile on her face said it all.

'I told you I would.'

'So me being away was very convenient, am I right?'

She nodded.

'Very convenient. He left me an early birthday present too. He said I wasn't to open it until my birthday but I couldn't resist.'

She held out her right arm for Anika to admire the bracelet Paul had given her.

'It's gorgeous. And it has the sweetest little plane dangling from it too.'

'Unfortunately, he didn't get to give it to me in person. A friend of his father's turned up so I didn't see him again. But he sent this to my work,' she said, indicating the flowers and the gift.

'No card?'

'Yes, there was a card. Not going to show it to you though.'

'So I'll need to make myself scarce when he comes to town again?'

'Well, it fitted with your plans,' Linda said. 'Otherwise I wouldn't have expected it.'

'What did they think at work?' she asked, pointing to the showy bouquet of flowers. In her experience, work colleagues could be a nosy lot.

She laughed.

'That I'd got myself a rich boyfriend was the general consensus. At least that's what I overheard. Some pretty jealous girls in that tearoom.'

'I bet no one knows you got yourself a married boyfriend. How's that going to work out?'

She shrugged.

'He's been upfront. There's no future in the relationship. But he wants to see me again.'

'And you said?'

'I just want to enjoy our time together. Of course I want to see him again.'

'And the broken heart can be postponed to another day?'

'Yes, the broken heart can be postponed to another day.'

Anika looked at her. She had come to care deeply about Linda. They had been friends since their first day together at university. She sighed. Flowers. Gifts. There'll be more of that, she thought, but in the end, she'll find herself weeping into her pillow. Why couldn't she have fallen in love with someone else. Someone without a wedding ring on his finger.

20

IN THE RELATIVE COOL of a winter afternoon, Alex was happy to be in the kitchen, minding the two six-year olds while Marianne busied herself with cooking the dinner.

'Amanda asked me to pick up Andrew,' she explained. 'She had to take the baby to the doctor. She thought she might be late.'

'Nothing wrong, is there?'

Marianne shook her head.

'I don't think so. Just a check-up, she said. He seemed a bit out of sorts and she wasn't taking any chances. And Paul wasn't around.'

He was puzzled. Paul had left Prior Park around lunchtime, he was sure of it.

'Paul should have been home in time,' he said.

'Probably at the airfield she said.'

Marianne paused in the midst of stirring the custard she was making.

'She said he's spending a lot of time at the airfield lately. She doesn't know why he's doing that. But my father noticed he's been unsettled recently, as if he's got something on his mind. So maybe flying helps him.'

More like someone on his mind, Alex wanted to say, but he wouldn't repeat the gossip he had heard. Not to Marianne. She wouldn't believe it for a start. But he noticed how the gossip had gained a new lease of life recently. Especially since the recent long weekend.

But Marianne had heard things too. He was about to be surprised by her revelations.

'I was at a morning tea for mothers at the school yesterday. I overheard something I wasn't supposed to.'

'Which was?'

'Paul has been getting very friendly with the daughter of the guy who takes care of his plane. According to what I overheard, he took her up flying with him. They were away for hours one day. Her father wasn't pleased, they said. And someone else chimed in that a friend had seen them together over at the island. Having lunch together. He had his arm around her, as if she was his girlfriend.'

'Really? Does Amanda go to these morning teas? I hope she doesn't hear gossip like that if she does.'

Marianne shook her head.

'She's been to one or two but not since Matthew was born. I guess that's why they felt free to gossip about Paul.'

'And they said this so you could overhear it?'

She smiled.

'I don't think they knew I'd come back into the room. I'd been to the kitchen to top up the teapot with hot water. There were a few girls shifting in their seats and looking a bit sheepish when they realised what I'd overheard.'

'And what did you make of it? Of the gossip?'

She didn't answer immediately, the custard demanding her undivided attention. But as she shifted the saucepan from the hot plate, she turned back to face Alex.

'I think it sounds unlikely, in my opinion. Uncle Richard did say recently Paul had helped a newly qualified pilot to get more experience. It's an essential part of their licence apparently. Maybe he was just doing someone a favour and it's been misinterpreted.'

'Who was I doing a favour?'

Paul stood in the doorway to the kitchen. He looked from Marianne to Alex and then back again.

Marianne laughed and greeted him with a kiss on the cheek.

'The mothers at school have been gossiping about you,' she said. 'You want to watch out. They can take very flimsy evidence and create a scandal out of it.'

'What did they say?' he asked cautiously, although he had a fair idea. He knew that seeing Linda on the rare occasions she came home was always going to be risky.

'Some story about you having lunch with a girl over on the island,' she said dismissively. 'A friend of one of the mothers saw you and thought you looked as though you were with your girlfriend.'

Alex said nothing, preferring to watch Paul closely. He noticed a fleeting look of alarm cross Paul's face. He smiled to himself. So there is truth in the rumours. That much he understood. But what bothered him the most were the reports of Paul being unsettled. Was his pursuit of another girl a symptom of his state of mind or a result of it? He couldn't decide.

He looked across to Andrew, who hadn't immediately seen his father in the doorway. There was only one thought in Alex's mind as he looked at Andrew.

Why did he have to take after me? Why couldn't he have looked more like Amanda?

And then he looked towards Paul. *He knows.* The thought flashed through Alex's mind. He knows. That's why he's been unsettled. He's coming to terms with the fact he's raising my son as his own.

Then Andrew let out a screech and proudly showed off the paper plane he had been making to his father.

Paul lifted the boy off his feet.

'So have you been good? Behaving yourself?'

'Of course,' he declared. 'I want to be a pilot when I grow up.'

Paul laughed. Alex breathed again. Marianne rolled her eyes.

'Another pilot. Don't we need another cattleman?'

They all laughed and the tension in the room evaporated.

If Alex had one mission the next day, it was to see Amanda. He had to confront her once and for all about Andrew. He knew Paul would be attending a meeting with his father and uncle with the Belleville accountants. Marianne would be there too. He worried about that, with her so close to having the baby. But she had shrugged off his suggestion she shouldn't go, arguing she was still a month off her due date.

The front door stood open. He could hear Amanda on the phone. Turning around, she saw him and beckoned for him to come in.

'Problems?' he asked.

'Not really. Just Tony Bland giving me an update on everything. Getting workers is becoming a problem. Mine work pays better.'

He sympathised with that dilemma. Prior Park had the same problem as did the other Belleville properties. He had heard William complain frequently that the quality of the men available for the work had declined.

They walked quietly past the nursery.

'He's asleep now,' she said, holding her finger to her lips. 'Paul was up half the night with him. He's an erratic sleeper.'

With mention of Paul, he seized his opportunity.

'I've heard whispers Paul's been unsettled of late?'

He let the question hang in the air between them.

She smiled.

'Everyone's noticed, haven't they?'

'Have they?'

'I think so.'

'And?'

'What do you want me to tell you Alex?' she asked. She was on edge. He could see that clearly.

'Do you know why he's suddenly unsettled?'

She laughed but not with amusement.

'It's your fault,' she said quietly. 'Your fault entirely.'

'My fault? Why is it my fault?'

But he knew of course.

'I could have got away with it. Paul was convinced Andrew was his son. It was all fine until he got older. How do I explain a child who is the spitting image of you?'

'I'm sorry,' he said, 'but you seduced me remember.'

'So I robbed you of your capacity to say no. Is that it?'

He was remembering the encounter. The guilt he had felt. The pleasure he had taken. The consequences neither of them had expected. What could he say?

'I'd been in love with you since I was twelve years old. I didn't have the strength to say no to you. You took me by surprise.'

'And now I have a husband who knows he's bringing up your son. And a husband who is seeing someone else.'

Alex was shocked. How did she know about Paul? Why was she so calm?

'It could just be gossip about Paul,' Alex said.

'It isn't. I made some discreet enquiries. He's having an affair, I'm sure of it.'

'Have you confronted him about it?'

She shook her head.

'No, I'm just going to see what happens. I don't think he will want to break up our family.'

'Because of Matthew?'

She nodded.

'Partly. But I think he still loves me. I think he just needs space to come to terms with Andrew. If I make a scene, I might force him into having to make a choice.'

'Has he been any different with Andrew lately?'

'No, not that I've seen and that's good. Andrew worships his father.'

'And you? How do you feel about it all?' he asked.

She moved forward and put her arms around him. He could feel the warmth of her body.

'Disappointed with him. I wish he'd confronted me about Andrew. But that's not his way. He just decided to seek out someone else who'll tell him how wonderful he is.'

But Alex understood why Paul would be reluctant. If he challenged her to admit it, where would they go from there?

'You know it's better for everyone if he remains silent. If he openly accuses you, he might begin to think we conspired together to get him to marry you,' Alex said gently.

'And then the whole damn charade would unravel. Me with Paul. You with Marianne. As I remember you were keen for him to marry me. You feared what would happen if I wasn't married and I had a child. If I hadn't named Paul as the father, you would have been the prime suspect.'

'Yes, I knew what would happen. I didn't want it to happen,' he admitted

'Because of Marianne and her baby?'

'Of course. As I remember you were desperate for me to stop him marrying Nancy. I assumed you were desperate to marry him.'

'I was desperate to stop him because he wasn't in love with her. Do you know how many times I said no to him before we finally got together? The wedding had to be stopped for her sake, as much as mine.'

'Was he your insurance policy?'

'What do you mean?' But of course she knew what he meant.

'Did you get the feeling you might be pregnant very soon after being with me? Is that why you slept with him?'

'It sounds very cynical. I was attracted to him. It wasn't as callous as you make it sound.'

He laughed. She had previously accused him of being cynical in his pursuit of Marianne.

'And I was as jealous as hell,' he said.

'But you didn't know for sure, did you?'

'Not until I came to see you after Andrew was born. You shocked me that day. I couldn't acknowledge you were right. I was hardly even brave enough to look at him. And now as he's getting older …'

'Yes, as he's getting older, no one is going to have any doubts, are they? Except perhaps Marianne?'

'I hope she never realises it,' he said. 'We have a very good marriage. We love each other.'

She reached up and kissed him lightly on the lips.

'But if I said, right this minute, please make love to me, what would you do?'

He hesitated. He knew what his response should be.

'I don't think that would be a good idea …'

'Are you sure? I'm not.'

She kissed him again and this time he responded. She felt his whole body respond, his fingers tangled in her hair. She felt his passion for her. He felt the warmth of her body against his.

He pushed her away then, annoyed with himself. Angry with her. Angry with his own weakness.

'How does it make you feel to know you still have power over me?'

She laughed, delighted by his response. Finding herself loving him again as much as she ever had. Wanting him as much as she ever had. Confident of him again. Confident he still loved her. And in the future? The tantalising prospect they would become lovers again. With that thought she stepped away from him. Now was not the time.

'You'd better go. Paul may not be very long. If he finds you here, he won't like it.'

He said nothing but turned away from her, knowing he was playing with fire, knowing that the cold dead embers of their relationship had been reignited. Had Paul's pursuit of another girl given Amanda licence to enjoy her own freedoms within the marriage? The thought both excited him and appalled him. Could he resist her? He didn't know but there was one thing he was sure of. Marianne would despise him forever if she ever found out.

He sat for some moments in his car, head in hands. He had a clear memory of her response to the news he would marry Marianne. *You may marry Marianne but you will always be mine.*

He breathed deeply and slowly turned his car in the direction of Prior Park.

Paul opened the passenger door of his car for Marianne. At his father's suggestion, he had collected Marianne rather than have her drive herself. He noticed she was beginning to look uncomfortable, desperate for the baby to be born.

He slid into the driver's seat but he did not turn on the engine immediately, instead turning to Marianne. Should he raise the gossip with her? He had to know how widespread it was.

'I had no idea people were gossiping about me just because I've taken Linda Kent up a couple of times,' he said, playing down the number of times she had been flying with him. 'Don't they have anything else to gossip about?'

Marianne laughed, surprised he had brought the subject up.

'They mostly talk about the usual stuff. Husbands. Kids. Recipes. Who's getting married. Who's had a baby. The teachers at the school. The misbehaved kids. Never one of theirs, of course. Some of them talk about their jobs. Quite a few have part time jobs now.'

'And I suppose you talk about the complex accounting of Belleville Holdings and the accountant's plans to minimise our tax bill?'

This time she laughed heartily.

'Pretty boring, isn't it?'

'And here I was thinking you enjoyed it all.'

She shook her head.

'I enjoy being included. I appreciate not being excluded because I'm a woman. And I help keep the administration of everything on track.'

He noticed she didn't say *girl*. There was a new maturity about her. He wondered how much their cousin Pippa had been responsible for her realisation she could be more than a housewife and mother.

'You'll find it difficult to juggle everything once the second baby comes.'

'Well, I think I'll get some help. My mother knows a retired nurse who would like some part time work. She's happy to look after the children when I need her. I think that's what Amanda needs too. Someone she can call on to help with the kids. I don't think motherhood comes naturally to her, if you don't mind me saying so. After all she didn't have a role model, did she? She was brought up without a mother.'

'You're right, Marianne. She has been talking about it but I was lukewarm on the idea. But what you say makes good sense.'

Marianne was pleased he'd listened to her. Men can be so thoughtless at times, she decided.

'Getting back to the gossip, it is just gossip you know.'

'I know that,' she said with a confident smile.

'Linda's a good pilot. She can't afford the money for the private hire to keep her hours up so when she comes home, I take her up when I can.'

'Where does she live?'

'In Brisbane. She works at the city council. She's just graduated in civil engineering.'

'Unusual career for a girl,' Marianne said. In her experience, women opted for office work, teaching or nursing. 'You know her younger sister goes to the school. She's in grade six. I think that's possibly where some of the gossip has come from. Did you have your photo taken with Linda recently?'

He sighed.

'I did. Not my choice but I couldn't say no. The local aero club was celebrating another new fully-fledged member. I thought her father was in the shot too.'

But of course he knew there had been a photo of just the two of them.

'I think her nosy little sister saw it in her room,' Marianne said. 'She probably asked her father who you were.'

Paul reached over to start the engine to hide his nervousness. His cousin would be shocked to know the photograph now took pride of place on Linda's bedside table at her flat in Brisbane.

'My father said you have to take the plane back to Brisbane before your next trip with him. Why's that?'

'There's a recall notice on one of the parts they fitted. Larry Kent told me a couple of days ago. They want me to bring it back to have a replacement fitted. I'll probably do that soon. Fly down one Sunday so they can do it first thing on a Monday. They said it should only take an hour or two at the most.'

'That's a bit unfortunate,' she said. 'Will it be safe to fly the plane?'

'They assured me it's safe. It's just that the part might fail unexpectedly after only half the hours it's expected to last, so we're not taking any chances.'

He pulled into the kerb and got out to help Marianne out of the car.

'Thanks, Paul,' she said. 'I get the sense this baby is going to come sooner rather than later.'

'What's it going to be? Boy or girl?'

'It feels the same as little Mel. I think it's a girl.'

Paul smiled and breathed a sigh of relief. The last thing he wanted was a boy fathered by Alex. A boy who might grow up to look exactly like Andrew. He prayed for a girl. He hoped his cousin was right.

21

'I DIDN'T EXPECT TO see you again so soon.'

Linda turned in Paul's arms and reached up to kiss him again, reassured by the warmth of his lovemaking.

'It was a lovely dinner, thank you,' she said.

He kissed her.

'And the dessert was delicious,' he said, teasing her with the lightest of caresses. 'Why don't you spend the night with me?'

She shook her head.

'My flatmate Anika is expecting me home. She'll worry. She acts like a big sister to me.'

'Did you tell her where you were going?'

He looked at her enquiringly. He wondered who else was now aware of their relationship. The circle seemed to be widening.

'I did. It's a safety measure we have. Girls out alone at night are vulnerable, you know.'

He hadn't thought of that.

'Well, you're with me. And you're very safe.'

'In one way,' she said, 'but not in another.'

He laughed.

'My darling, you're as safe as you want to be with me. Or unsafe. However you want to look at it.'

She was thrilled by his use of the endearment.

'You mean as safe as I would expect to be lying in your bed.'

'Did I coerce you?' he asked, with mock concern.

She shook her head.

'Persuaded me, perhaps.'

'Persuaded? No, I'm not having that,' he said. 'I don't remember any persuasion. Not on my part.'

She laughed quietly.

'And I thought you were a gentleman, Paul Belleville,' she said. 'Are you saying I did all the persuading?'

'Well, there I was, a happily married man never looking at another woman and then you turned those deep blue eyes on me and hypnotised me.'

She hoisted herself up into a sitting position. It was the first time he had openly mentioned his marriage in such a way.

'That's just it,' she said, 'I don't think you are a happily married man. Are you?'

They had spoken about many things in his life. His childhood. His accident. His parents. His brother and his sister. But he had never spoken about his wife. Or his children.

He tried not to be annoyed with her for breaking the spell. This had been his safe place, where he didn't have to think about Amanda or Andrew or think about his real life.

'Actually, you're wrong. I am happily married. Up to a point.'

She sensed his change in mood. She bent over and kissed him lightly.

'Do you want to talk about it? Or would you rather keep the subject off limits as it has always been?'

He kissed her lovingly.

'Right now, I want to make love to you again,' he said, as he ran his hands over her body. 'We can talk another time. I'll tell you the sad tale of my marriage then.'

She held him for a few moments as if to reassure him before the urgency of their lovemaking overtook them both.

'Did you speak with Linda last night?' Larry Kent asked his wife at breakfast the next day. He had been so engrossed in the movie on television he hadn't noticed if she had gone into the kitchen to make the call as she usually did on a Sunday night.

It was a question Sheila Kent had hoped her husband wouldn't ask. But now that he had she had no option but to tell him the truth.

'She wasn't home. I talked to her flatmate Anika. She said Linda was out seeing a friend for dinner.'

Larry looked up from his breakfast at the news from his wife.

'Out on a Sunday night? She's never usually out on a Sunday night. That's when you feel sure you'll get her on the phone.'

'I said that to Anika and she said it was the only night this friend was in town.'

He turned to his two daughters also sitting at the breakfast table. He looked at his watch conspicuously.

'It's time you two girls headed out to school. Off you go. You can ride your bikes today.'

It was news they greeted with a collective groan. They had expected their father to drop them off on his way to work.

'It's cold and windy,' Theresa, the elder of the two, complained.

But their father was unmoved.

'Do you good. Just make sure Josie gets to her school in one piece,' he said, nodding in Theresa's direction.

The two girls dragged themselves out of the warm kitchen reluctantly, having decided that an appeal to their mother wasn't going to work either. Something was going on. They both sensed it. As they headed out the garden gate together, Josie let out a little snigger.

'Linda's in trouble, I bet.'

'What sort of trouble?' Theresa asked.

'I bet she was out with that bloke who was in the photo with her. The one taken by the aero club. I found it in her drawer before she went to Brisbane.'

Theresa shrugged her shoulders, none the wiser.

'Why would that matter?'

Josie stopped and looked at her sister.

'You haven't heard the gossip, have you?'

'What gossip? You shouldn't be listening to gossip. You're not even twelve yet.'

'My best friend Ann-Marie heard her mother discussing it. She told me because she thought I should know.'

'Told you what?'

'When Linda was back here for the long weekend a couple of weeks ago, he took her up flying in his plane. They landed at the strip on the island. My best friend and her family were staying there at the resort. They saw Linda with him. He had his arm around her. He was kissing her and everything.'

She pulled a face as if she couldn't imagine it herself.

'So, she's got herself a boyfriend. So what?'

This was such a delicious moment for Josie. She knew something her older sister didn't.

'He's married with two kids, apparently. One of his kids is in the second grade at our school.'

'That's shocking. And you think Dad knows about this?'

'Of course he does. He services the plane. He knows him well. That's where Linda would have met him, when she was helping Dad with his stuff. He won't be pleased about it.'

'Maybe he's getting a divorce?'

Josie shrugged. No one had yet even whispered that possibility as far as she knew. She began to wonder then if it was likely.

Meanwhile, back in the kitchen, Larry Kent let out a string of profanities that shocked his wife.

'Larry, what's up?'

'You know why Linda wasn't home when you called last night? She was out with Paul Belleville. The plane was recalled for a part to be replaced after the recent overhaul. He flew it down to Brisbane yesterday.'

'So you think she was out with him?'

'Don't you? It fits. And he was all over her, taking her flying last time she was home. They were away for hours one day. Don't you remember?'

She shook her head.

'I was at work, I think. I did some shifts on the public holidays recently if you remember.'

'I remember,' he said, his voice calmer now.

'You don't know for sure how far the relationship has gone. They might just be friends. There mightn't be any more to it than that.'

He shook his head, not persuaded by her argument.

'That first time he went up with her and she flew their plane, he reached over and kissed her before they left the plane. I didn't tell you. I hoped it would just be one of those spur of the moment things that never gets repeated. But as it's turned out, as nice as he is, he's really just another wealthy, self-entitled prick.'

'Well, I hope you don't say that to him. One word against you from the Belleville family and your business is ruined. You know that and I know that.'

'So you're happy he's running after our daughter, ignoring the fact he has a wife and two kids at home?'

She shook her head.

'Of course I'm not happy about it. Far from it. But she's entitled to her private life. To make her own mistakes. It's her life.'

Larry let out a deep, disappointed sigh.

'If you say so, Sheila, but I just hope the mistake doesn't present itself as a tiny bundle wrapped in a baby blanket that he doesn't want to know anything about.'

'You don't need to worry about that, Larry. I had a quiet word with her before she went away to uni. She's on the pill. I've seen too many unwed mothers come through our wards at the hospital. My daughter isn't going to be among them.'

'Well that's something, I suppose. But she's a warm, loving girl. She's going to be devastated when he gives her up. When he loses interest. Or when the gossip gets too hot for him and he has to back off.'

'Well, she's just got to go through that if she really is involved with him as deeply as you say she is.'

But it was fair to say, none of these things was worrying Linda the following morning, as her work colleagues admired the bouquet of creamy white roses that had just been delivered to her desk. She read the card and blushed, putting it back in the envelope quickly.

'You missed something.'

One of the girls clustered around her desk pointed to another small envelope tucked among the flowers. She opened it to find a new lucky charm for her bracelet. Her heart skipped a beat at the exquisite little heart with her birthstone embedded in the gold.

'Wow. Next thing it will be a diamond ring,' the girl said, her face a perfect picture of undisguised envy.

For Linda, it was as if a cloud just passed in front of the sun. Why did she have to say that? Why did she have to ruin the moment?

She dropped the card and the charm into her handbag and turned back to the problem of assessing the state of the public footpaths on the city's increasingly crowded streets.

Later that day, Larry Kent stood beside Richard and scanned the skies for the little Cessna. Richard checked his watch.

'He's a bit late, Larry. I hope nothing's wrong.'

'He might have been a few minutes late getting away. And the wind might slow him down today.'

He pointed to the nearby windsock, which was almost horizontal at times.

'It was a bit of a nuisance for him to have to fly back to Brisbane for this. I hope they got that part right this time.'

'Not their fault, Richard. It's the manufacturer. Perhaps it started failing early in other engines and they realised then they had a batch that wasn't up to scratch. These things happen. Better to know and have it replaced than to find out mid-air when your engine stalls.'

Richard said nothing. He knew it was the correct course of action.

'You know your son's seeing my daughter,' Larry said, looking down at his feet and kicking the dirt. He couldn't help himself even though he'd promised his wife he wouldn't say anything. 'I'm sure she was with him last night.'

Richard looked at him and sighed deeply. It wasn't a conversation he wanted to pursue.

'I don't pry into my son's private life, Larry,' he said. 'He's thirty years old. I can't treat him like a schoolboy. And your daughter is what, twenty-three? You can't control what she does, Larry.'

'That's pretty much what my wife said too, but I think there's gossip getting around too. Did you know? Doesn't do much for my daughter's reputation. And Paul's wife is likely to hear it too. How is she, by the way?'

'She's well,' Richard said cautiously. 'She's with her accountant at the moment. That's why she couldn't come and pick him up.'

'So who's looking after the baby?'

'She's hired someone to help with Matthew I believe. Normally Paul's cousin Marianne would help out but she's about to have her baby any day now.'

'The year for babies by the sound of it.'

'It is, Larry.' And then an alarming thought occurred to Richard.

'You're not trying to tell me something are you, Larry?'

'Well, I did suggest to my wife this morning that our daughter was making a mistake and I hoped that mistake didn't present itself as a tiny bundle wrapped in a baby blanket.'

He saw a look of panic spread across Richard's face.

'My wife assured me she'd given our daughter the right advice to avoid that situation.'

Richard breathed again.

'Sensible woman your wife.'

'Yes, she is, Richard. It's just hard to watch your kids make a mess of their lives and not step in.'

'Amen to that, Larry,' Richard said.

It was a conversation he did not want to continue but he knew he would need to have a word with his son. He remembered how John Bertram had hinted at Paul's personal problems during his recent visit. It was becoming clear to Richard his son was getting too deeply involved with Linda Kent. And that would be unfair on the girl. Very unfair, he decided.

And then they heard the familiar sound of the little aircraft as it approached the runway. By habit, Richard checked the windsock. It was limp. He was pleased to see that. The small plane didn't handle gusty wind well.

Within minutes, Paul had brought the plane to a halt and was heading towards the two men.

'Bloody wind,' he said. 'I hate flying in wind.'

With that, he gave the keys to Larry and headed off with his father.

Paul had been surprised to see his father waiting for him. He had thought Amanda would be picking him up.

'Where's Amanda?' he asked.

'A meeting with her accountants,' his father said. 'Have you ever been with her to discuss the Robinson business?'

He shook his head.

'She seems happy to keep that part of her life to herself. Just occasionally she asks my advice. We've discussed a few things over the years. But then, to be fair, she doesn't attend the Belleville meetings.'

Paul looked at his watch. It had just gone three o'clock.

'So who was picking up Andrew?'

'Alex volunteered, I understand. He had to pick up little Mel anyway. Marianne is likely to be put into hospital tomorrow if she hasn't already gone into labour.'

'Which means Sally Jones is taking care of Matthew?'

'Just for a couple of hours, I think. She's reliable, isn't she?'

'Yes, she's very nice. Matthew has really taken to her. She had to give up nursing. Back problems from lifting patients, she said. Her own children are grown up now.'

He noticed then his father was heading in the direction of his own house.

'Any reason we're going to your place first?'

'I need to have a private word with you, son,' he said. 'I thought maybe we could have a beer together.'

'Sure,' Paul said but he groaned inwardly. He guessed what was coming.

Paul accepted the glass of beer his father held out to him. He sipped it appreciatively. But he remained silent, forcing his father to speak.

'I know you're seeing Linda Kent on the quiet, son,' he said, holding his hand up. 'Don't deny it. For a start it's been all over town since you were seen together over the long weekend. Talk about indiscreet. And I know you saw her last night. So let me give you a word of advice. If you're determined to go on seeing her, then resist the temptation when she comes home. You'll just end up humiliating your wife. Just find a few more reasons to go to Brisbane. Have your fun with her there.'

'So that's what you're worried about? Me humiliating Amanda. What about Amanda humiliating me?'

'What do you mean, Amanda humiliating you?'

His father knew of course but he needed Paul to say it out loud. It was time for honesty.

'You know I tried to tell you her baby wasn't mine. But you wouldn't have it.'

He looked directly at his father. Richard could hear the suppressed anger in his voice. He had known later Paul had been right. But it was all too late then.

'I'm sorry, son,' he said. 'I wasn't in the best frame of mind myself as I remember, but that's no excuse.'

'I wanted to tell you she was too far advanced with the pregnancy. It didn't add up. But you wouldn't listen. And now I have to look at Andrew every day and see her deception. It won't be long before people start whispering about him.'

Richard sighed deeply. Why was Paul so sure?

'You can't be sure about Andrew,' he insisted. But they were hollow reassurances and he knew it.

'I am sure. Blood groups don't lie. According to a doctor I consulted in Brisbane, Amanda and I couldn't have produced a child with Andrew's blood type. Do you know what he said without prompting?'

Richard guessed what was coming, but he remained silent.

'Andrew's O type blood suggested he might be of Scottish decent.'

'Bloody hell, what a mess.'

'Indeed, what a mess. And every year he's just going to look more and more like him.'

He hesitated. Should he tell his father the worst of his suspicions? There was no point now in holding back.

'You know she's back with Alex.'

'What do you mean?' Richard was shocked. 'Back with Alex? He seems very devoted to Marianne.'

Paul laughed, a hollow cynical sound. Were they all just being naïve?

'Alex wears a very distinctive aftershave. It was all over her the other day after I got home from the meeting with the accountants. I don't know if they've become lovers again, but it's only a step away I reckon.'

Richard shook his head slowly from side to side. How is this mess all going to unravel, he wondered? Because unravel it most certainly will.

'I didn't think he'd do that to Marianne. To his children. For God's sake, Marianne is just about to have their second baby. Has he no morals at all?'

Paul shrugged.

'I don't think it's anything to do with Marianne and the children. I think he's just besotted with Amanda. Always has been. He's tried hard to hide it but I think she's thrown herself back into his arms. She knows I've been unsettled. Isn't that the word everyone's using? I'm sure she's confided in him. If he wasn't sure about Andrew before, he certainly is now.'

He noticed how his father shook his head slowly from side to side, trying to process everything he'd been told.

'Just think about it for a minute. He was with her just a few weeks after he and Marianne got married. I know because John Fitzroy saw them together. I think he was very angry with himself that he couldn't find the strength to say no to her. That's when she got pregnant,' Paul said.

'And then started sleeping with you so she could avoid Alex being identified as the father of her child. It might have worked if he hadn't looked so much like Alex. So where does that leave you, son? I'm sorry for my part in this mess. I had no idea. But I'm not sure raising another young girl's hopes is the answer.'

Paul smiled.

'Linda knows the limitations of our relationship. She enjoys being with me. I love being with her.'

His father heard the word *love* and looked up suddenly. Was this relationship more serious than he imagined?

'But you can't offer her a future, son. Not while you're married to Amanda. You haven't said that's going to change.'

'Linda's free to date other guys. She's free to tell me to get lost if she wants to. And I know she will eventually because she will want a permanent relationship but right now, she's happy with what I can offer her.'

'And your marriage? Your children? Because even if we know Alex is Andrew's father, he regards you as his father. He worships you. And then there's the baby. They deserve a stable home life.'

Paul threw back his head and laughed.

'Didn't Anthony and I deserve a stable home life, as you so nicely put it? I'm not sure you're in a position to lecture me on how to have a happy marriage and give my kids a stable home.'

Richard grimaced, knowing his son was right. He hadn't always put his kids first in his choices. Neither had Catherine if it came to that.

'Well, I guess as a flawed parent, you don't want to see your children making the same mistakes.'

Paul nodded. He understood that point of view.

'I don't plan to do anything rash. I love my sons. Both of them. And I love Amanda. I'm just going to give her space just like I think she's giving me space. I just hope I never walk in on her and Alex together. Hopefully with the plans she's putting together, they can spend their nights together under the stars at Isla Downs or Glenmoral. Away from me. Away from Marianne.'

He noticed his father look puzzled.

'What plans?'

'Before I went away on Sunday, she told me she planned to

restructure the Robinson assets into a new holding company with two shareholders, herself and Alex. He was robbed of his inheritance, she believes. I think that must be why she's having such a long meeting today. She wants it to take effect from the new financial year.'

Richard exhaled loudly. Such a move changed everything for Alex. Did Paul not realise that?

'You know what this means, don't you?'

'What do you mean?' Paul asked.

'It means Alex will no longer be dependent on his wife's family. For his job. For his future. It may even impact his marriage.'

'Well, I haven't thought much about it to be honest. I just thought it was a generous gesture on Amanda's part. I hadn't thought of it so much from Alex's point of view but you're right. It changes everything. For him. For Amanda. And I guess for Marianne.'

'And possibly for you, son.'

Paul shrugged.

'That why my friendship with Linda is so important to me,' he said. 'She's my safety valve.'

'Well, she's a very pretty safety valve, I'll give her that.'

But Richard's mind was now focused on the news about Alex. He had never thought it likely. Never even considered it a possibility. No one, of his acquaintance, had ever voluntarily given up half an inheritance – and a substantial one at that – to right an injustice. He admired Amanda for it.

'You're thinking about what this means for Alex, aren't you?'

'I am. For Amanda it's a good move in one way. Alex is familiar with three of her properties at least. He will want to have his say in running them now. Which means he's going to be less interested in earning mere wages from us. It elevates his status with the stroke of a pen.'

'None of this is going to please Uncle William,' Paul said. 'He's going to lose a capable manager at Prior Park and his daughter's marriage is going to move into uncharted waters.'

'Not to mention your marriage,' his father said. 'He's going to have legitimate reasons to spend a lot more time with Amanda.'

'I know,' Paul said. He had already considered what might lie ahead.

'Will you give Mum an update of what's happening next time you see her? Or will she be up here soon?'

He noticed his father did not reply immediately as if deciding how much really needed to be revealed.

'I'll tell her,' he said finally. 'She's taking George on a holiday in Greece in early July. I don't think we'll see her up here before August but I'm planning a few days in Sydney before she heads overseas. I think we should be honest with her about Andrew but it's your decision.'

He looked towards Paul for confirmation.

'If you think so,' he said reluctantly. 'And the state of my marriage?'

'She'll ask if I tell her about Andrew.'

Paul nodded.

'She will,' he said. 'She'll want to know everything then. And you'll have to discuss Alex's situation with Uncle William, I imagine.'

'I'll wait for Alex to tell everyone. It's not my place to do so. Or yours. But I know it will put William in a panic. We've come to rely heavily on Alex.'

'And Andrew?'

His father shook his head.

'It would take a braver man than me to tell him about Andrew. To tell him his son-in-law fathered a child with another woman weeks after marrying his daughter. He'd explode on the spot.'

They both laughed even though the issue was a serious one.

'We'll have to protect Andrew in the future,' Richard said. 'For his sake, you must try and forget what you know to be a fact. You must endeavour to be a good father to him just as I will be a good grandfather to him. He's a great kid. He deserves that. The less we talk about it the better, unless you really need to.'

Paul nodded. His father was right. Andrew needed the security and stability of a loving family.

22

TOO MANY PEOPLE WERE assembled in Marianne's hospital room as far as her mother Alice was concerned. Family. Neighbours. Friends. Her daughter needed rest, not chatter, after an exhausting labour, so she began to usher everyone out of the room except Alex.

The birth of Marianne's second daughter had been greeted with delight by everyone. Big sister Mel declared she would no longer be called *little Mel* because there was now *little Laura* and they couldn't both be *little*.

'She looks more fragile than Melanie did,' Marianne confided to her mother, who reassured her the new baby was perfect in every way. She was fair, blue eyed and already capturing their hearts.

William smiled at his daughter and kissed her on the cheek.

'Well done,' he said, beaming at her.

Alice, Marianne and her two little girls meant everything to him. He liked Alex but he could never forget how he had secured Marianne as his wife. There would always be a lingering suspicion in William's mind that his pursuit of Marianne had been a calculated move designed to improve his prospects.

As he headed towards the door, he held his hand out to his granddaughter and she grasped it happily. There wasn't much, if anything, her grandfather denied her. She knew she only had to shed a little tear for him to capitulate immediately to her demands.

Alice and Marianne were known to shake their heads and call him an old softie at heart which he always denied of course, despite the evidence.

'I'll have to have my own pony soon, Granddad,' she said.

William smiled, remembering how he had done the same thing for Marianne. He knew Alex had been teaching her to ride after she found out Andrew was learning to ride and she hadn't been included in the lessons. She had decided as she was older than Andrew she should learn to ride first.

But he knew Alex was concerned she was too small yet to be allowed to manage a pony by herself. William expected some tears when she found out her father had decided to delay her progression to her own pony.

So he told her the same thing he had told Marianne. He was looking for a suitable pony but they were hard to find. For the time being, she had believed him but he didn't imagine that excuse would be accepted for too long.

'A lovely little granddaughter, William,' Richard said as he fell into step alongside his brother. 'Marianne looks well.'

'She's beautiful, isn't she? Very much like this one here,' he said, indicating little Mel. 'Very much like their father in fact. Very fair and blue eyes.'

'And speaking of their father, I understand he told you his news from Amanda.'

William nodded.

'Probably not the time and place to discuss it,' he said. 'We've only had a very preliminary chat about it. About what it means. But he did say he'd always be happy to help out at Prior Park when he could.'

'But helping out won't mean taking daily responsibility for the running of the place,' Richard said.

'No, it won't. You're right there, brother.'

And then he felt the tug of a small hand in his.

'Ice cream, Granddad.'

William smiled.

'I've got more important priorities at the moment I'm afraid,' he said, as little Mel headed towards the hotel kiosk.

Richard laughed, pleased to see his brother enjoying the role of grandfather.

'We'll talk tomorrow,' Richard said.

And then little Mel spotted Andrew walking along the hospital corridor with Paul.

'You'd better make that two ice creams, William,' Richard said.

William nodded, reaching back into his pocket for more change.

'You know if someone looked at Andrew and didn't know that Paul is his father, you'd say he's Alex's child. There must be a Scottish strain in our family too,' William said. 'Probably the Dalrymple line. Our mother's family. That's a Scottish family name.'

'It is, William. He could well be a throwback of several generations. Our father had unusual blue eyes too if you remember,' Richard said, doing his best to find more evidence to support William's theory. 'There's probably some Scottish blood on both sides of our family.'

Paul heard the last few words his father spoke and raised his eyebrows in a silent question.

'I'll tell you later, son,' Richard said quietly, breathing a sigh of relief. Perhaps it would always be possible to shield his brother from the truth. 'Marianne said that Amanda came to see her and the baby earlier.'

'Yes, she did,' he said, 'but she couldn't stay long. She's still tying up all the legals. Lots of documents to sign. I think Alex is going to meet with her and the accountants tomorrow. Does Uncle William know?'

'He does, but we haven't talked about what it means for Prior Park in any detail yet. How did Alex greet the news? Do you know?'

'He was stunned. Delighted. And grateful, she said.'

'Well, it's a generous gesture and I don't think it's something he expected. Or asked for,' Richard said.

'No, it was all Amanda's idea,' Paul said.

'Did she actually ask your advice?'

'No, not really. She just told me it was going to happen. That she thought Alex had been treated badly. And it's hard to argue with that.'

'You're right. It is hard to argue with that.'

'According to Amanda, he's already got ideas about how to improve Glenmoral. I get the impression his first visit as co-owner will happen very soon.'

'But he's got a new baby?'

'According to Amanda, he said Marianne will understand and she has her mother to help.'

Richard heard all this with a growing sense of unease. Alex had always been so considerate towards Marianne. He hoped it didn't point to a change in his priorities. He'd be very disappointed in Alex if this was the case.

His first responsibility, Richard thought, was to his wife and his new baby daughter. A visit to Glenmoral should wait.

'We might have to get your backside reacquainted with a saddle,' Richard said as he navigated around a large pothole in the road. 'Just for the short term.'

'I knew that might be happening,' Paul said with a laugh. 'I'd still much rather fly a plane than ride a horse.'

'I know,' Richard said, 'but we're going to be shorthanded until we can decide how to handle the situation with Alex.'

'You know he's with Amanda today talking with her accountants and lawyers. It's all being signed off today. She's already talking about selling the two properties out west. She believes they're too far away. She wants to buy something closer to the other two. Or closer to Armoobilla. But we both agreed there wasn't anything of real value around here. I wonder if Alex will agree with her.'

'Well, given that you refuse to fly her anywhere, she may have a point. It's a long haul out west otherwise.'

'I know but I just think it's sensible the two of us don't fly together in the same small plane.'

'I agree,' Richard said. 'I know of couples who do but mostly their kids are grown up.'

'By the way, what were you and Uncle William talking about yesterday just as I arrived?'

Richard sighed. He had hoped Paul had forgotten the incident and he wouldn't be required to explain it.

'If you must know, your uncle said and I quote: *You know if someone looked at Andrew and didn't know that Paul is his father, you'd say he's Alex's child.*'

'Bloody hell! What did you say?'

'I didn't actually have to say much at all, just agree with him because he came up with what he considered to be a logical explanation.'

'Which was?'

'That we have Scottish ancestry via our mother whose family name was Dalrymple. He also decided there must be some on our father's side too because of the unusual colour of his eyes. My brother, bless him, doesn't seem to have alighted on the truth.'

Paul let out a long sigh. He was relieved his uncle had arrived at an explanation that satisfied him.

'I hope he offers Marianne the same explanation should she ever hear anyone raise doubts about Andrew's parentage.'

'Well, I'm pretty sure he's convinced he understands the reason for Andrew's looks so he's likely to say the same thing to Marianne if the subject comes up,' Richard said as he brought his car to a standstill in front of the Prior Park homestead.

As he got out of the car, he took a moment to look down the shallow slope to the remains of the original Prior Park mansion.

'I wonder how much longer it will be before we see action on the grand rebuild?'

'I was wondering the same thing myself. You'll have to ask Anthony when you see him in Sydney. I hope he's made some progress,' Paul said, as they headed into the house in search of William. 'Aunt Julia will be getting impatient.'

The two men found William sitting behind his desk in his study. It was uncharacteristically untidy. He made a half-hearted attempt to tidy up the desk as Richard and Paul walked in

'What's up, brother?' Richard said. 'You look like you have the weight of the world on your shoulders.'

'I'm missing Marianne. She usually tidies everything up for me these days. I've got out of the habit of dealing with the endless paperwork,' he said. 'She does such a good job. Draws all the cheques for me to sign. Enters the ledgers. Keeps everything in order ready for the accountants. I'm way past doing this now.'

'Why don't we get the accountants to send out one of their staff for a day or two?'

William looked up. Richard could see he was weighing up the suggestion.

'I might do that. In fact would you call them for me and organise it. Everyone will just have to wait a few more days this month for their cheques. That plane cost us a lot this month. And hotel bills. You clearly had dinner with someone at the hotel, Paul. A dinner for one couldn't possibly cost that much. Have they overcharged us?'

Paul couldn't look at his father at that moment. If he had he would have seen the look of wry amusement that accompanied his raised eyebrows.

'I caught up with a mate. A bloke I used to go to school with at Grammar. Murray Anderson. He bought me lunch the previous time. I was returning the favour.'

'I know him. Didn't he have hopes of making the Australian rugby team at one stage.'

'He did but his father told him to knuckle down and pass his law exams at university, that rugby wasn't going to pay the bills. He still plays on weekends.'

'Lawyer, is he? In Brisbane?'

'Yes but he has a lot of country clients via his parents putting the word out, I believe.'

'That's good to know. It's always useful to have a new contact. I think the firm we used previously has been absorbed by a bigger outfit. Always good to know someone else.'

'I did say I'd put in a good word for him,' Paul said, breathing a deep sigh of relief his cover story was convincing.

'Is he married yet?'

'Later this year, he told me. He wants Amanda and I to go down for the wedding. His wife to be is a pharmacist.'

'You should go down for the wedding,' his father suggested. 'It's always good to keep up a connection like that.'

'Well, I hope he bought you a good lunch, that's all I can say. Champagne! Really! I wonder if his fee schedule matches his expensive tastes.'

Richard was forced to turn away for fear he would explode into laughter at his son's expense.

'Caught out!' he mouthed to Paul who was only just beginning to regain his composure. 'Expensive safety valve.'

But unfortunately William heard him.

'Expensive safety valve?'

'Yes, they're expensive to replace in small planes but they're essential,' Richard said, hoping William wouldn't ask for further details. 'It would have been replaced in the overhaul.'

'Well, let's hope we don't have to do it too often,' he grumbled. 'And now we need to talk about Alex. I don't know why Amanda had to go and do what she did. He had a perfectly secure job here with us. We were all settled. He was doing an excellent job. And now, he's gone. And we have to find a new man.'

'Any ideas? Any candidates?' Richard asked.

'None that spring to mind. We only have four men here now and none of them are suitable. We should all go to the sale next week and ask around. There might be some young bloke there on the lookout for a step up.'

'Well, you're all a glum lot,' Alice said, as she put her head around the door.

'We wouldn't be if Alex hadn't suddenly been given half the Robinson estate,' William lamented.

But Alice was pleased for him.

'William, he's just getting what he should have been entitled to. Just because it's inconvenienced you doesn't mean it's not a good thing for him. And for his children.'

'His children would have been taken care of through Marianne.

They won't need another big windfall,' William declared, shaking his head.

But Alice persisted.

'It's changed his status. It's changed his life. He spent thirty years as an outcast. Unmarried mother who died when he was a baby. A father who wouldn't recognise him. I'm happy for him. I think it's a tremendous gesture from Amanda. They've always been very close.'

And then she realised it had been the wrong thing to say. The wrong thing to say in front of William. And in front of Paul too.

'And now they'll be closer than ever,' William growled. 'Sorry Paul. I shouldn't speak like that about your wife. I wasn't inferring anything.'

But something snapped inside Paul. Anger. Jealousy. Disappointment. In that moment all those emotions coalesced into an explosion of frustration.

'You can infer all you like, Uncle William,' he said, trying and failing to keep his temper in check. 'We all know they're besotted with each other. Why don't we just face the facts. What do you think they'll be doing when they're away together at Isla Downs? Or Glenmoral? It doesn't take much imagination, does it?'

His father put his hand on his son's arm, exerting enough pressure to get his attention.

'I think you've said enough, son,' he said evenly. 'Let's go and talk about this.'

Paul allowed himself to be ushered out of the room.

Glancing back, Richard caught the horrified look on his brother's face. And on Alice's face. As if the realisation had suddenly struck them. With the stroke of a pen, Amanda had ensured Alex would be by her side, whatever happened.

For some time it seemed as if both Alice and William had been robbed of the power of speech following Paul's outburst. And then William spoke.

'What's he saying? What's he implying?' he demanded, as if he didn't know, as if no one had ever alerted him to Amanda's lingering interest in Alex.

'For goodness' sake, William,' Alice said, exasperated with her husband. 'You must have known. Haven't you noticed them together?'

He shook his head.

'I thought all that was in the past,' he said. 'I thought they'd both settled down to married life. Alex with Marianne. Amanda with Paul. And that was an end of it.'

She let out a sigh of frustration mixed with disbelief. Men see so little, she thought.

'I think they both tried,' Alice said, her tone conciliatory. 'I think they really tried. I certainly think Alex tried his best to overcome his feelings. But with the revelations about their mothers in the past few months, I think that drew them back together. And then of course Amanda found out why her father was so opposed to her marrying Alex. And then there's Andrew getting older of course.'

'What's Andrew got to do with it?' William asked, perplexed.

'William, are you blind? You must know about Andrew. If you don't, then you're the last person to know.'

'What do you mean? What should I know?'

Alice shook her head slowly from side to side. In telling William she would be breaking confidence with her daughter, but it was inevitable now.

'Alex is his father,' she said bluntly, 'not Paul. I always knew there was something amiss with Amanda when she was getting ready to marry Paul. She'd been forced into it. By well-meaning people certainly but she was forced into it. I could see at times she wasn't enthusiastic about the idea.'

'You mean she didn't love Paul?'

'I mean she knew all along she wasn't carrying Paul's child. Whether she was in love with him or not, I couldn't really say. I'm not sure she could either.'

And then the truth dawned on William, but there was no explosion as his brother had predicted. Instead, he slumped in his chair, his head in his hands.

'Which means Alex was with Amanda after he married Marianne?'

Alice nodded. It had been a terrible realisation for her too. And for Marianne.

'Remember it was Alex she co-opted to stop Paul marrying Nancy. Alex must have known then she was pregnant. But she didn't tell Paul she was pregnant until much later. Probably so she could fudge the date of conception. In my opinion she married Paul to protect Alex. And it would have worked had Andrew not looked so much like him.'

'Does Marianne know?'

'Of course she does. She'll never admit it to anyone of course. It's too humiliating for her.'

'Have you discussed it with her?'

'Yes. It came out when we were talking about Paul.'

'What about Paul? Does he know about Andrew?'

'Marianne is sure he does. Why else would he be romancing another girl? And not very discreetly either.'

'What do you mean?'

But before Alice could answer, she heard her brother's voice.

James Fitzroy stood in the doorway. He held his hand up by way of apology.

'Sorry, I didn't mean to intrude on a private conversation. Didn't I just see Richard and Paul headed out to the stables? Paul didn't look particularly happy.'

Alice greeted him warmly with a kiss on the cheek.

'Well, let's just say our conversation touched a raw nerve. I was a bit careless in something I said.'

'What would that be, sis?' he asked. 'Would it be about the pretty blonde he's been paying a lot of attention to lately?'

'You know about that, do you?' Alice asked.

'I think the entire district knows about it. Someone I know just happened to be having dinner at a certain hotel in Brisbane recently when they spotted Paul. The girl was all over him. The champagne was flowing, apparently.'

William picked up an account from his desk and waved it in front of James.

'And he tried to tell me he had dinner with an old mate from

Grammar days. Murray Anderson.'

James laughed out loud.

'You mean the guy who had hopes of making the Australian rugby team? Champagne? Really. I don't see it myself. I think he'd crush a champagne glass before he got anywhere near to drinking from it. It's the sort of thing you buy for a lady. A lady you're trying to impress.'

William threw the invoice back on his desk in disgust. It was as if his settled world was disintegrating around him. He didn't like it. He didn't like it at all. Paul seeking consolation outside his marriage because he had been tricked into marriage. His own daughter ending up with a husband who was willing to break his marriage vows before the ink was dry on their marriage certificate.

Alice was watching him carefully. She knew how disappointed he was. And how angry he would be for Marianne. After a few minutes, she broke the strained silence that had descended on the room.

'Actually it wasn't about that at all, James, although Marianne did tell me the gossip. It's all over the school Melanie goes to because the girl's sister goes there too,' Alice said. 'Marianne has been telling people she doesn't believe the gossip. She's very loyal to him. I think she saw it as a way of protecting him.'

'So, if not Paul, you must be talking about Alex and Amanda?' James suggested cautiously.

He looked at William as he asked the question quietly of his sister.

'I made a remark about how close the two of them had always been without thinking of what that means now.'

'You mean now she's signed over half the Robinson properties to him?' James asked.

She nodded.

'Paul just laid it out really. Told us to use our imaginations as to what would happen when they went visiting the properties together.'

She could see her brother hesitate. Was there something he knew that they didn't?

'Well, she's obviously got a strong hold on him. I shouldn't tell you this but John said he's seen Alex's car outside their home quite often when Paul's away. It makes you think ...'

But Alice was quick to realise what those thoughts might be.

'I don't think there's any doubt about who Matthew's father is, if that's what you're about to suggest,' Alice said.

'No, I wasn't actually,' James said, quick to deny he'd considered the possibility.

He paused then, wondering if he should say anything further.

'Unlike Andrew,' Alice said quietly.

'You know then?'

'We do,' she replied cautiously. 'You obviously know. How long have you known?'

'Since he was born really,' James admitted. 'John saw them together, coming back from Fairy Lagoon one day. He said Amanda looked happy. Like a woman in love. Alex looked angry. Angry with himself, I'd say. John and I figured out the dates after we first saw her baby. We knew then that Amanda had married Paul to save Alex's marriage. Her baby needed a father. I take it Paul knows now?'

'We assume so, judging by his behaviour.'

'And Marianne?'

Alice nodded.

'She'll never speak about it. He's never admitted it to her. It's really only become obvious in the past six months or so.'

'And Richard? Does he know?'

William smiled for the first time, remembering the conversation he'd had with his brother.

'Well, he made an admirable case for Paul being Andrew's father when we spoke yesterday. But I'm sure he knows. He and Paul are very close. And he would certainly know about the girl.'

'Well, it's a fine mess, isn't it? What's going to happen?' James asked.

Alice shrugged her shoulders.

'I think we're just the audience, don't you? I don't know that we can influence anything. All I know is I wish I didn't know so much. I wish I was ignorant of it all. For Marianne's sake. For the children's sake.'

'Maybe they'll all settle down and resume their lives,' James said, trying to offer a crumb of comfort because he knew it would be their daughter who would suffer the most. She had put her faith in Alex.

'And in the meantime, we have to replace Alex,' William said, deciding to focus on the one issue he could do something about.

'If I hear of anyone suitable, I'll send them your way,' James said. 'I was just on my way to visit the new bub. I've got to stop at the jeweller's and pick up the little bracelet I've ordered for her. Like the one I got for Melanie, which I see her wearing a lot now.'

'That's a lovely thought, James,' Alice said. 'Marianne will love that.'

'Is there anything I can take for Marianne? Anything I can get for her?'

'I don't think so,' Alice said. 'Just make sure you never mention any of this in her presence. Remind John to be careful too. Don't humiliate her. She doesn't deserve this.'

'No, she doesn't, sis,' he agreed. 'Marianne doesn't have anything to answer for in this mess. The same can't be said for that husband of hers.'

'But we just have to go on as if we know nothing of this,' Alice said. 'For her sake. And she's the one I care most about. And Paul too. I just hope he can keep his temper around Alex in future. I think he's been badly hurt by Amanda's deception.'

'I think you're right, sis,' James said, 'but I'm sure everything will sort itself out eventually.'

A few words of reassurance. It was all he could offer. Like her parents, he was angry for Marianne's sake. She among the four of them had deserved better, he thought. She had been deceived just as Paul had been deceived. Could marriages survive that knowledge, he wondered? Despite his reassuring words, he very much doubted it.

23

AS JAMES FITZROY HEADED back down the Prior Park driveway, he was surprised to meet a car driven by someone he did not recognise heading towards the house.

He slowed and wound down his window, knowing the other vehicle would do the same. A stranger visiting Prior Park had once been the cause of a tragedy. He would not take that risk again.

'Can I help you, mate?' he asked as the two cars drew level.

'I've come to see Mr Belleville,' the stranger said.

'Which Mr Belleville?'

'William Belleville,' the reply came. 'Is he at home, do you know?'

James ignored the question.

'What's your business with him?' James asked. 'I haven't seen you about these parts.'

'My mother said I should call and see him. He might have a job going. I believe there's a vacancy for a manager at Prior Park.'

'News travels fast,' James said. 'So who's your mother? Who's given you the tip?'

'My mother is Edna Brockman. Her eldest brother Charles worked here for many years.'

'He did indeed,' James said, 'but the vacancy is only very recent. How did she find out?'

'She's friendly with Mrs Belleville's housekeeper I believe.'

James smiled to himself. Nothing was ever secret from house-keepers.

'And your name?'

'Charlie Weir,' he said. 'For my Uncle Charles obviously. I've been working out west for a long time but I really need a job closer to my mother now she's elderly.'

He extended his hand through the open window.

'Good to meet you, Charlie. I'm James Fitzroy. Mrs Belleville is my sister.'

They shook hands awkwardly.

'William is at home. Just give a shout out if they don't see you coming. He could be in his office at the side of the house.'

'Thanks, I will. See you round,' Charlie said.

Had providence delivered an easy answer to the problem of replacing Alex, James wondered? He hoped so for their sake.

By the time Charlie Weir had parked his car in front of the house at what he judged to be a respectful distance, William was already standing on the verandah surveying the newcomer.

He was not in the mood to welcome unknown visitors. But there was something about the cut of the man who alighted from the car that reminded William of someone. He just couldn't think who it was.

There was the erect carriage. The above average height. The purposeful walk. The swarthy complexion made darker by long hours in the sun. Yet the stranger's features, William noticed, were more refined than he would have expected.

'Mr Belleville?'

'Yes, that's right,' William said reluctantly.

'I'm Charlie Weir. You won't know me at all but my uncle was Charles Brockman.'

Recognition came instantly to William.

'Of course. I knew you reminded me of someone. I just couldn't think who,' he said, extending his hand to the newcomer. 'Your uncle served the Belleville family for decades. He was an excep-tional man. Really as close to us as if he was family.'

'Yes, when I was a lad, he used to tell me about Prior Park.'

'I remember he used to go and visit his sister in town from time to time,' William said. 'We met her once or twice as I recall. She came out here when we buried him on the country he loved.'

'She told me. I couldn't get down here then. I was sorry about that. It's a long way from Winton.'

'His death was a great loss to us,' William said, thinking back. He didn't say it but he could have said *my brother owes him his life*.

'Is this just a social call today?' William asked. 'Would you like to see where his grave is?'

'That would be good, Mr Belleville. I'd like to see where he's buried. But I actually came enquiring for work.'

William brightened.

'Well, let's go into my office and have a chat,' he said, gesturing for Charlie to follow him along the verandah.

'My brother Richard is out here today too. You can meet him. And his son Paul. Winton, you say. What work have you been doing out there?'

'How did you get a start out west?' Richard asked as they all sat down to a late lunch in the kitchen.

He and Paul had returned from their ride to the surprise news from Alice that William was interviewing a candidate for the job recently vacated by Alex.

'I was sent out west when I turned fifteen to work with my father,' he said. 'My mother and father were never actually married. I took his name though. They didn't live together for very long but he was always in touch. He had good jobs on stations out west. But it was a tough life for him, especially after a hard war. He'd been a prisoner of war.'

'Of the Japanese?' Richard asked.

'Yes. Changi. He wouldn't talk about it. He'd really suffered at their hands. That's why he liked the outdoor work. He didn't want to be confined. He was only in his fifties when he died a few years back.'

'So where have you been working most recently?'

'At Urquhart Downs. It's owned by Bill and Cora Anderson. You may know them.'

'Well, my son went to school with their son Murray,' Richard said. 'I've met his parents once or twice casually.'

He looked at Paul. A coincidence? It was as if the universe was toying with them, he thought.

'I had lunch with Murray in Brisbane recently,' Paul said, watching his uncle closely. 'He's a lawyer. Doing well too. I thought his father might have wanted to keep him close to help with the properties they own.'

Charlie Weir hesitated. And then he smiled.

'Big lad, isn't he? Probably not so suited to the work. His father jokes he sent him to university to spare his horses. I think his father hopes he's a better lawyer than he is a stockman.'

They all laughed.

'Murray would have needed a draught horse to carry him,' Paul said. 'It took my hand days to recover from his handshake.'

'Great rugby player though. Pity he didn't go on with it. His father of course was very set on him getting a profession,' Charlie said.

'That's probably wise,' Richard said. 'Anyway there are two other boys in the family I understand.'

'Yes. There's Ralph and Stephen. They're each managing a property. The best of the properties naturally.'

'We won't be in their good books if we pinch one of their good workers,' William said. He remembered Howard Robinson had been annoyed when they had offered Alex a job. He couldn't stop his mind going off into fanciful speculation. What if they had never done that?

'I did tell them I was looking for something closer to home with my mother getting older. They understand. They suggested I should call in here. They didn't know there was a vacancy though.'

'No, well, it's quite recent,' William said. 'Not something we expected.'

He had not told Charlie the full details only that Alex would no longer be able to devote the required amount of time to the job.

'I understand that,' Charlie said. 'One man's windfall becomes another man's opportunity. Am I right?'

'That just about sums it up,' William said. 'You seem to be very well informed.'

'I had a drink in the pub near where my mother lives yesterday. The Saleyards Hotel. I went there thinking it would be a good place to find out the local talk. Where the jobs are. Talk about gossip spreading like wildfire. Your son-in-law's good fortune was a hot topic of conversation,' he said, looking at William. 'And then my mother confirmed it. And filled in a few details. So that's how I came to be here today.'

He said nothing more, knowing the family would not want to hear the rest of the gossip. It had been generally agreed in the crowded bar that Alex Fraser had been extremely fortunate. There was, they decided, overwhelming evidence he had fathered Amanda Belleville's first child, not her husband. And that she had rewarded her lover to keep him by her side.

He looked across the lunch table at Paul. Did he know he'd been betrayed in this way? But like his uncle before him, he could keep secrets. He might listen with interest to the gossip but he would never repeat it.

Never gossip about the families you work for, he remembered his uncle telling him. They'll appreciate the loyalty. He knew his Uncle Charles had been rewarded by the Belleville family for his loyalty. He had been treated like a family member. And they had taken care of him until the end of his days.

Alex smiled at Amanda. He rubbed his right hand vigorously.

'I think it will take days for my hand to recover from all that signing,' he said, as they stood together in the carpark. 'I still can't believe you did that for me. No one else would have done it.'

She smiled.

'I was redressing a wrong, Alex. In more ways than one.'

'In more ways than one. What do you mean?'

'No one took responsibility for your mother, for what happened to her. And then they didn't want to acknowledge you. As if the lack of a marriage certificate was your fault. Once it was confirmed Arthur was your father, it seemed only right that you should share in the Robinson legacy.'

He turned towards her and kissed her lightly. It was meant as a sign of his affection, as a sign of his gratitude until it became a declaration of his love.

'Where would I be without you,' he said, putting his arm around her. 'I'd be nowhere. You are a remarkable woman. Even though I broke your heart you didn't abandon me.'

She kissed him again. She felt his arms tighten around her as he responded as she hoped he would.

'I'd never abandon you,' she said.

'You do know I still love you. That I've never stopped loving you,' he said, his voice just above a whisper.

'But you spent years denying it,' she said, the disappointment in her voice hard to disguise.

It was as if she didn't believe his admission. Was it possible she believed his declaration was nothing more than a surge of gratitude for her generous gesture? That he would regret his words later.

They stood together, not speaking for some time until finally he spoke.

'Where do we go from here?' he asked.

She shrugged. Her mind turned to practical matters.

'The first thing should be a meeting with Tony Bland to bring you up to speed on what's happening on all the properties. On what the strategy is. What role each property fulfils.'

He listened carefully. It was a good starting point.

'Tony's going to be surprised.'

'And as jealous as hell,' she said. 'As far as he's concerned, you're the wrong side of the blanket kid he never thought would amount to anything.'

He laughed out loud at her description of him. He could afford to laugh at it now. Once upon a time, he would have been humiliated by it.

'When can we do this?'

'As soon as you can get away for a day or two,' she said. 'It would be good to do it at Glenmoral or Isla Downs. But you can't leave Marianne and your new daughter the minute they come home from hospital. And you'll have to go on helping at Prior Park until they get a new manager, otherwise they'll be annoyed with us both.'

It seemed to Alex she understood his responsibilities almost better than he did.

'Sounds sensible,' he agreed, despite his eagerness to insert himself into his new role as co-owner.

He hesitated then. Should he ask the obvious question?

'And us?'

He risked the question, not because he expected an answer but because he knew Marianne would one day discover the truth about Andrew. And he was sure she would never forgive him.

'I expect my marriage to collapse eventually,' she said. It was as if she was speaking of a commonplace event that hardly warranted her attention.

'Because of Andrew?'

She nodded.

'Of course. Once it's out in the open there can be no more pretence, can there?'

'Perhaps he still loves you? Perhaps that will be enough?'

He didn't have the courage to ask if she still loved Paul. She gave a determined shake of her head.

'It won't be enough because I know he's devastated by the way I deceived him.'

He looked at her closely. Was she really so resigned to the collapse of her marriage as she appeared to be?

'But do you want your marriage to survive?' he asked.

He noticed her hesitate before she answered him.

'I always thought I did because I thought you were off limits,' she said, not looking at him. Part of her still expected him to pull away from her again. To reject her again. 'I've always thought you were totally committed to Marianne. She worships you. I suspect she's the reason why Paul hasn't said anything to me. He's protecting Marianne. The whole family will always protect Marianne.'

He sighed. It was the most honest discussion they had ever had. He wanted to be committed to Marianne. He loved his children. He had tried his hardest to be a good husband to her. A faithful husband. But he knew how hard it had been to fulfil that promise and now Amanda had become part of his life again, it would be even more difficult.

'I don't think she will feel like that about me when she realises I'm Andrew's father.'

Amanda looked up in surprise.

'I think she knows already.'

He looked at her, shocked she would even think such a thing.

'She's never said anything. And she's so good with him. She hasn't treated him any differently when he's been at our place to play with little Mel recently.'

'She wouldn't. She'd never take it out on an innocent child,' she said.

'I'm still not convinced. But if she knows, she hides it well.'

'That doesn't surprise me,' Amanda said. 'She's always played the role expected of her. Dutiful daughter. Loving wife. Indulgent mother. She's loved by everyone.'

'Dutiful daughter except for one fall from grace,' he said.

'But everyone blamed you for that. Blamed her naiveté. I bet her father was livid,' she said, laughing quietly.

'He was,' Alex said. 'And he's going to be livid again, I imagine. As will Paul.'

She closed her eyes briefly, thinking of the future. Of the fallout from their one encounter. How did one act of love create so much mayhem in a family, she wondered? But of course she knew.

'Paul was always jealous of you,' she said unexpectedly. 'Please don't provoke him unnecessarily.'

He sensed her uncertainty. Were either of them ready to disrupt their lives and the lives of their families?

'So we just wait for our marriages to fall apart under the pressure? Is that what you're saying?' he said, as he began to stroke her hair.

But she avoided answering the question. She had no clear vision of the future. Not yet.

'We need to talk further,' she whispered. 'About everything. But not just now.'

'You're right,' he said, as he kissed her and then released her reluctantly from his embrace.

As he watched her drive away, he sat in his car thinking of what had taken place. He doubted his marriage to Marianne would survive the revelations about Andrew. And then he thought of his two little daughters, the baby only days old. He resolved then to try for their sake. To go on as if nothing had changed. But he wondered how that would be possible because everything had changed for him.

Amanda had shaken the very foundations of his life. He was doubtful the foundations as they existed before could be rebuilt. Amanda. It was all down to her. Suddenly she was within his reach again. And now they would spend more time together. He was looking forward to it.

He took a deep breath banishing all thoughts of her from his mind. Marianne deserves my love and support, he reminded himself. And my daughters are entitled to a happy, stable home. For the time being at least, that's what he aimed to give them.

He shoved his car into reverse and pulled out of the car park to head to the hospital.

As Alex walked along the hospital corridor towards Marianne's room, he looked up to see her uncle James Fitzroy heading in his direction. He would have liked to avoid the encounter but he couldn't.

James held his hand out towards Alex.

'You have another lovely little daughter, Alex,' he said, shaking his hand in a grip that felt like a vice to Alex. 'Marianne seems well. She says she's going home tomorrow.' He consulted his watch. 'Is someone looking after little Mel? I didn't see her at Prior Park today?'

'No, we wanted to keep her in her regular routine. Sally Jones helps out with Andrew and with Mel if we need it. She's a retired nurse. She was taking care of Matthew today so she said she would walk up to the school with Matthew and pick up Andrew and Mel. It worked out well. Amanda should be back home now. We've just spent several hours signing documents.'

'Your windfall has caused quite a disruption at Prior Park,' James said. 'William's not happy. He thought everything was settled. He didn't have to worry. He's not happy with you. Not happy with Amanda.'

Alex pulled a face.

'He's never been particularly happy with me, let's face it, so not much has changed.'

'Well, he was happy with the work you did at Prior Park. You took on the responsibilities Charles Brockman had shouldered for years. He was pleased with that,' James said.

He paused.

'I'll give you a word of advice, Alex. Just keep your hands off Amanda. You have a lovely wife. Lovely daughters. You and Amanda may now be business partners but that's where it has to remain. Strictly business.' He took a deep breath. 'The two of you have already done enough damage.'

Anger rose quickly in Alex. What right did James Fitzroy have to lecture him? And what did he mean by *already done enough damage*? But he was, of course, another one of Marianne's protectors.

'I think you've said enough, James. Just keep your nose out of my business and my personal life.'

'Happy to do that, Alex,' he said, his tone far from conciliatory, 'but my advice is, if you can't keep your hands off Paul's wife, then make sure it's behind closed doors on one of those properties you're going to visit with her. Don't go riding across the Prior Park paddocks with her to Fairy Lagoon. Not unless you want to father another child with her. It seems to be a good place for that.'

With that, James brushed past him, leaving Alex open mouthed and, for a full minute, speechless.

24

Sydney

RICHARD SAT IN THE ARMCHAIR in his wife's bedroom, watching her apply the final touches to her makeup in advance of Anthony's arrival to have dinner with them.

'Greece is going to be hot at this time of the year,' he remarked. 'A dry heat probably but hot. I can't imagine that was your choice of destination.'

Catherine laughed quietly.

'No it wasn't but for some reason George decided he wanted to go there. I'm hoping we can spend just a few days there and then go to a resort. I haven't suggested that option yet.'

'Good luck with that idea,' he said. 'He'll probably think it sounds too dull.'

'Possibly but it would be nice. Then we'll go back to Haldon Hall for a couple of weeks. You should come over,' she suggested.

'Won't Edward protest about that?'

'He doesn't need to know, does he? George thinks it's ridiculous not to be allowed at Haldon Hall when you're with me.'

'Well, he'll soon be old enough to make up his own mind,' Richard pointed out. 'Mind you at least at his age he's not in the sort of trouble our two sons are.'

'So what is it I don't know about our other troublesome

offspring? I know Anthony's head over heels in love with a married woman.'

'You've met her then?'

'Yes, I have. With Julia. She's lovely. I think she should divorce that dolt of a husband. Anthony says her family forced her into the marriage to save the family's finances. That was too big a sacrifice in my opinion.'

'You've met her husband then?'

'Yes. He came to pick her up after a meeting with Julia. Julia asked me to join them to give my opinion on some of her ideas for the interiors.'

'I take it you didn't warm to him?'

'He's the type of man who likes to be the centre of attention. He's quite a big guy, full of bluster. I think Victoria is a little bit afraid of him.'

'God, I hope he never gets wind of Anthony's interest in her. He'll make mincemeat of him.'

She laughed nervously at the prospect. She knew it would be an unequal match. Anthony was neither as tall and strong as his father nor as athletic as his brother Paul.

'Maybe we should suggest he takes some self-defence lessons,' she said as she contemplated how much damage an angry husband could inflict upon their younger son.

'I might just do that. I learnt a few tricks during my air force training. It's come in handy a couple of times.'

'But not, fortunately, when Daniel Harrington visited Prior Park with Anthony. I'm told you were on your best behaviour.'

He shrugged his shoulders. It had all been very civilised.

'It was all water under the bridge by then but I noticed Alice seated us as far apart as she possibly could at lunch. She wasn't taking any chances.'

'Good for Alice,' Catherine said. 'I'd have done the same thing.'

'I hope Anthony can tell me what progress has been made on the big project,' he said. 'Everyone's getting impatient for something to happen. We need a distraction.'

She turned away from the mirror to look at him.

'And why do you need a distraction? You've been here for a couple of hours now and I know there's a topic you've been avoiding. There's something going on with Paul, isn't there?'

Her instincts were always unerring, he thought. He looked at his watch.

'There's plenty of time. Anthony will be late,' she said, knowing he was looking for any excuse to delay their discussion. 'You can depend upon it.'

Richard took a deep breath. How was he going to break the news about Andrew? About the state of Paul's marriage. About Amanda. About Alex. There was only one way.

'It's about Andrew,' he said. 'Paul has told me Andrew is not his child.'

There he had said it out loud.

'What! Not his child! Who's his father then?'

And then it dawned on her.

'Alex. Alex is his father, isn't he?'

Richard nodded slowly.

'It's become so obvious in the past six months,' Richard said. 'Paul confirmed it via Andrew's blood group, a blood type common to people of Scottish descent. He and Amanda couldn't be his parents, but Amanda and Alex ...'

His voice trailed off.

'And you pressured Paul to marry Amanda, didn't you? I suppose Alex and Amanda conspired to trap Paul into marriage to save Alex's marriage to Marianne.'

Like everyone else who had been told the news, she did some quick calculations.

'He was already married when he got her pregnant, I assume?'

'I figured that out. She always claimed the baby was very premature. He may have been premature but not by as many weeks as she claimed.'

'So what happens now?'

'It's like living with a ticking time bomb,' Richard said. 'Our son greeted the news by directing his amorous attentions elsewhere. And Amanda decided to share her inheritance with Alex.

Meantime Marianne's just had their second baby, another little girl.'

'Paul's mixed up with another girl. Is that what you're telling me?'

'The gossip is all over the district. He hasn't been very discreet,' Richard said.

'Who is she? What's she like?'

'Her father runs the aircraft maintenance business where we have our plane serviced. She's just finished university. Fortunately she has a job in Brisbane now so he can see her there away from prying eyes. Unfortunately I think she's really keen on him. She's a pilot too as well as a civil engineer.'

'And a little minx leading our son astray, by the sound of it.'

'I think it would be unfair to blame Linda,' Richard said. 'She's very nice. Very pretty. Her father is livid about it all.'

'So her father knows. And Amanda?'

'I think Amanda's been focused on rekindling her interest in Alex to be honest. He's given up his job at Prior Park. He's going to be helping Amanda run their rural properties.'

'That was a generous gesture,' she said, 'to share her inheritance with him.'

'According to Amanda, Alex had been denied justice. I think I told you his father turned out to be Arthur Robinson, Howard Robinson's cousin.'

'So that's going to throw Amanda and Alex together. Not ideal. I wonder if Marianne knows about Andrew.'

'I haven't asked. Everyone is tiptoeing around the issue.'

'And the new baby?'

'You mean Matthew?'

She nodded.

'He's definitely Paul's child.'

'Well, that's something. And Marianne has another little girl. She's well, I take it?'

'Everything is fine there. Alex is spending time at home with them at the moment. But I know he and Amanda are planning to visit some of the properties together soon.'

'If I were Marianne, I wouldn't let him out of my sight. Mind you, I think Marianne is more resilient than people give her credit for.'

'I hope you're right,' he said, as they headed towards the living room. 'I did try to give Paul some advice about putting his children first and providing a stable home for them. He didn't take it well. I was told in no uncertain terms I wasn't in a position to lecture him, given what we had done to him and Anthony.'

'Well, I guess he has a point. I take it he sees himself continuing as Andrew's father?'

Richard nodded.

'He does. I told him that Andrew regards him as his father. He just worships Paul. He's a good kid. It's a pity you don't see more of him.'

'It's a pity you don't live in a place with a more temperate climate. But as soon as I get back from England, I'll come up for a month or so.'

He put his arms around her then.

'I miss you when you're not with me, you know that don't you?'

'I do,' she said. 'I miss you too. When George is older, I think our lives will settle into a more regular pattern, but I have some responsibility towards him too. And to Haldon Hall.'

'I know all that,' Richard said, as if they hadn't already discussed it many times. 'I'm happy to spend more time with you but right now I don't want to not be there for Paul. One of these days the whole thing is going to explode. I'm worried he'll have a pop at Alex. Or he'll walk in on Alex and Amanda together. It will all get out of hand if I'm not around. It could tear the family apart. And I don't want that.'

'But you sound as if you expect it to happen?'

'Perhaps. Or perhaps it would be better if Alex and Amanda just keep their relationship private. When they're away together.'

'And Paul's relationship?'

'I think Amanda knows about it. I think she'll turn a blind eye to it if he turns a blind eye to her adventures with Alex.'

'My God,' Catherine said. 'That's a tangled web. A web of deception unfortunately.'

'And it will all unravel one day,' Richard said. What more was there to say? It all sounded so sordid.

'Are Julia and Pippa coming for dinner too?'

'Yes. Joel volunteered to babysit. Little Jessica is just a bit young yet for a dinner party,' Catherine said.

'That's good of him,' Richard said. 'He's a nice bloke.'

'He is. He and Pippa seem very well suited. Having them around has helped Julia a lot.'

'Helped her get over the two-timing American you mean.'

Catherine laughed quietly and raised her eyebrows at the comment.

'William's description of him. He never trusted him, you know. Always thought he'd pick up where he left off with Karen. It just took longer than we all thought it would.'

'I always thought he was very charming and sophisticated. When he inherited all that money, he would have had women falling over themselves to get his attention.'

He laughed.

'He did apparently. Joel told me on the quiet everyone was quite sure he'd had an affair with the woman he appointed to head up his foundation in America. She went on to marry his nephew but Joel thought the odds were the baby she had a few months after she got married might have been Philippe's.'

'So he wasn't quite so lonely over on Long Island while he was waiting for his divorce to be free to marry Karen after all?'

'Apparently not, but it's a topic completely out of bounds with Pippa.'

'Of course it is. Poor girl. For her it must be a tug of war of loyalty. Which parent does she favour? It's a tightrope for her.'

'That's why I'm pleased she has Joel,' Richard said. 'And little Jessica.'

'Indeed. Oh, by the way, John's coming tonight too.'

'I didn't know he was in Sydney. Visiting his mother?'

'Apparently. He arrived yesterday. Julia told me he's going to inherit her share of the Belleville interests, not Pippa. I think that's sensible.'

'Well, Pippa would hardly need it. And William and I are happy about it. Especially now Alex is less in the picture. John's got a good feel for cattle. And he's family.'

As they headed towards the dining room together, he could hear movement in her small kitchen.

'Something smells good,' he said.

'Yes, I get a private caterer in for dinners. I'm no cook, as you know. Or maybe a reluctant one.'

'But you're a great hostess,' he said, as he headed towards the front door at the insistent ringing of the doorbell.

Richard admired the ease with which courses appeared and disappeared as the six of them sat around the dinner table.

He noticed wine was being consumed at an astonishing pace except for John who hardly touched his wine, preferring the beer on offer.

'Lovely dinner, Catherine. Effortless.'

'It is, isn't it. That's the best sort.'

'So when will my sister be able to host effortless dinners at the new Prior Park house?'

He looked across the table at his son who smiled broadly.

'We're nearly there aren't we Aunt?' he said.

'I think Anthony's got an announcement about it,' she said. All eyes turned to Anthony.

'We appointed a local project manager today. Nathan Flynn.'

'Should I know him?' Richard asked.

'He's just set up a new branch of a national construction and engineering company up your way. Daniel knows him. He suggested that would be the best way to deal with the build. We need someone to handle all the Council stuff and the site works, then the build. He'll come out to Prior Park and introduce himself. Can you let Uncle William know when you get back home?'

'I will. He'll be pleased. That's good. That's progress. We need a distraction.'

'Why do you need a distraction?' Pippa asked. It seemed an odd thing to say.

Richard looked at Catherine, posing the silent question. *Should I tell them about Andrew? About Paul?*

But he was saved by Anthony.

'I think he's talking about the mess Paul's in, am I right?

'What mess?'

The question came from Julia but it had been on the tip of Pippa's tongue too.

'Anthony, why don't you tell us what you know?' Richard said, hoping to avoid the uncomfortable truth about Andrew.

'Which bit? That he's not Andrew's father? Or that Amanda is very close with Alex again? Or that Paul is seeking consolation elsewhere in the willing arms of a very pretty blonde?'

There was an audible intake of breath from both Pippa and Julia but Richard noticed John simply smile as if to say *it's about time it all came out.*

'I take it your brother has been in touch with you?' his father asked.

'Yes, he just needed to talk to someone. He's devastated about Andrew. Devastated about how Amanda tricked him into marriage. Beyond angry with Alex. Worried about Marianne. Worried about baby Matthew. And he's in danger of falling in love with a young woman who's probably already in love with him.'

If anything was likely to silence the conversation around Catherine's dinner table, it was Anthony's statement. He had summed up Paul's predicament precisely.

Julia looked at her son John.

'You don't look surprised John,' she said. 'Has he confided in you too?'

John shook his head.

'No, not directly. I've just pieced it all together with my father. We always knew it was likely Alex had fathered her first child. I saw them together in …' he paused then, searching for the right words.

'In compromising circumstances?' Richard suggested.

He nodded.

'I did tell Paul before I realised he was deeply involved with her. And Alex has always been keen on her of course. When we noticed how much little Andrew had come to look like Alex, it sort of confirmed what we suspected. And of course Paul's interest in Linda Kent is just common gossip now.'

No one spoke. Everyone sensed he had more to say.

'I saw her at a party a month or so ago. One of my cricket mates celebrating his birthday. She's a friend of his sister's. I particularly asked about her. He said, *don't go there, mate. Your cousin's already staked his claim.* My first response was Anthony? And the answer came back. *Not that simple, mate.* And then it dawned on me what he meant.'

Richard was the first to break the silence.

'Does Amanda know, do you think?'

'Of course she knows. But then she's concentrating on Alex at the moment I reckon. It was a very tender scene last time I saw them together. I think they'd just come out of the lawyer's office. Or maybe the accountant's. They were near that building anyway in the carpark. I wasn't spying on them. I just happened to be parked nearby.'

'Well, I'd appreciate it if you don't gossip about them, John,' Richard said. 'We need to contain this. I can't imagine what William and Alice are going to make of Alex's involvement with Amanda. I'm not inclined to tell them about Andrew.'

John looked up surprised.

'They already know. My old man called in to see them the other day on his way to visit Marianne in hospital. Aunt Alice already knew. She and Marianne had discussed it. I don't know why anyone would think Marianne hadn't noticed Andrew's likeness to Alex. He plays with little Mel a lot. They're inseparable. But I think Marianne's had other things on her mind just recently, like having a baby.'

'Which means William knows,' Richard said, letting out a deep sigh.

Through all this, Pippa had been strangely silent. And then, to the surprise of everyone, she spoke.

'Marianne has known for some time. She told me in a letter. She said she had to confide in someone.'

'What did she say about Alex? About her marriage?'

'Not much except that she knows he's Andrew's father. She's worried that Amanda might finally lure him back to her. She's sure he's always been in love with Amanda.'

Richard turned to his sister.

'Now you know, sis, why your project is suddenly so important. We need a distraction. Because we're all sitting on a ticking timebomb waiting for an explosion. One of these days, Paul will lose his temper and take a swing at Alex. That's my belief. And there mightn't be any way back from there. Not for the marriages, anyway.'

At this point, Catherine signalled for coffee as she began to quiz Anthony on the final designs for the house. His important announcement had suddenly been consumed by family gossip.

He smiled his appreciation at his mother.

'Well, I think everyone is going to be delighted by it. I have an exacting client you know.'

He looked at his aunt who smiled broadly. She had enjoyed the process so far.

'You and Victoria make a great team,' she said.

He nodded.

'We do. Maybe it will be the first wedding in the house,' he said.

There were gasps of surprise around the table.

'She's getting a divorce. Her husband has been sleeping with his secretary. She found out only recently. She moved out last week.'

Richard was concerned then. Was his son making assumptions? Or had he asked Victoria to marry him?

'Has she said yes?'

'Of course,' Anthony said. 'Of course she has. And she's happy to get married at Prior Park as I suggested. As far away from Sydney as possible. That was her only stipulation. I think Aunt Julia will be happy to oblige.'

Around the table, glasses clinked in unexpected congratulations. It was a happy ending to a night of traumatic conversation.

'I wish the silly boy had told me,' Catherine whispered to Richard. 'I could have invited her this evening.'

'Better not,' Richard said. 'There was a hefty airing of the family's dirty laundry. We don't want to alarm her.'

She smiled.

'Perhaps you're right. I think she's delightful. I'm so pleased.'

Anthony noticed the exchange and smiled to himself. His news, at least, had lightened the mood.

25

BACK AT PRIOR PARK, Richard sat alongside his brother William on the front verandah.

'You survived Sydney then,' William said, sipping his tea. 'How's Catherine? And Julia?'

'They're both well. Catherine should be in Athens by now. If you think Sydney is crowded, can you imagine Athens? It's probably ten times worse.'

'I take it the destination wasn't her choice but her son's? She should be up here at this time of year. It's nice weather today.'

'She's coming up when she gets back from England. She only plans to be in Greece for a short time before heading to Haldon Hall. She wants me to go across for a week or so while she's there.'

'Are you planning to?'

'No, not this time. There's a bit of uncertainty here. We've got a new man starting. I told her I didn't want to be away at the moment. She understood.'

William let out a deep groan that sounded very much like an expression of disgust to Richard, who turned sharply to look at his brother.

'A bit of uncertainty was understating it, don't you think?'

Richard wondered what he could say to William. Or rather what he should say. He stood up and leant against the verandah rail. He chose his words carefully.

'We had a family dinner while I was in Sydney. Julia and Pippa. Anthony. And John.'

'John visiting his mother, was he?'

'I think that was the only reason he was there for a few days,' Richard said.

'And what was the main topic of conversation at dinner?' William asked.

'Well, the progress on Julia's house. Anthony's forthcoming marriage.'

He saw a stunned look of surprise on William's face.

'I thought that nice girl he was keen on was married?'

Richard shook his head.

'Not for much longer. She's divorcing her husband because he was cheating on her. Anthony's on cloud nine.'

'I'm delighted for Anthony. They'll suit one another very well. So nothing else came up?'

'What do you expect might have come up, William?'

He wanted to be sure his brother really did know as much about Amanda and Paul and about Alex as his nephew had suggested.

'I would have thought my son-in-law being Andrew's father might have been discussed. You obviously know despite what you said previously. Or are you still hoping to keep it quiet? Pretending it's not an issue.'

Richard shook his head. None of this was going to be easy. There was a chance William would despise Alex forever.

'It was all discussed, William,' he said finally. 'Andrew's parentage. Amanda's continuing interest in Alex. Paul's disillusionment with his marriage. His dalliance with another girl.'

'And don't forget Marianne,' William growled. 'Don't forget my daughter who's at the centre of this farce. She's been let down badly. I told you he was an adventurer. We should never have brought him here.'

The conversation with William was every bit as difficult as Richard imagined it would be. He had been dreading it, knowing his brother would reach back to his decision to offer Alex a job at Prior Park.

'Imagine how I feel, William. I forced my son to acknowledge her baby as his and marry her. But if you think about it, the problem had its origins in her father opposing her match with Alex. If he had never done that, we wouldn't be having this conversation.'

William shook his head slowly. What was the use of going over the past? Nothing could change the facts as they now stood.

'Well, we can't deal in what ifs,' William snapped. 'What I want to know is what's going to happen? How do I keep a civil tongue in my head when I see Alex? I know I have to for my daughter's sake but I feel like letting him know exactly what I think of him.'

'Of course you do, William,' Richard said, 'but you have two lovely granddaughters. And a daughter you love. How is that going to help the situation if your relationship with your son-in-law collapses completely?'

'I know, I know,' William said, his disappointment on full display, 'but all I can think of is that he's going to be with Amanda more and more. You and I know what that's going to mean when they're at one of the properties together. Paul laid it out pretty plainly, if you remember.'

Richard chose to ignore him. He wasn't going to assume Alex and Amanda would become lovers again. He hoped good sense might prevail.

'Have you spoken with Marianne about it all?'

He shook his head.

'Alice won't let me. After Marianne and her mother had a talk, I just put my arm around her and told her we're always here for her and her daughters. Alice is better off dealing with it rather than me.'

'I think that's sensible, William. Remember that Marianne will feel she shouldn't have done what she did either, but she wasn't to know. I don't think Alex was honest with her about Amanda. I don't think he was honest with himself.'

'Honest!' He spat out the word. 'You're right. He hasn't been honest with anybody.'

Richard hesitated. Should he say more?

'I know it's probably no consolation but I think he was with Amanda only the once after he married Marianne. She was unlucky to fall pregnant from that one occasion.'

'But she knew,' William countered. 'Amanda clearly knew Alex was the father of her child, not Paul. Alice thought her behaviour was very strange when she was preparing for her wedding to Paul. She admitted she wasn't ready to be a wife and mother. It's clear now why she felt like that. She must have eventually decided to simply hope the baby looked like her and not Alex.'

'Which, unfortunately, he didn't. But, if you think about it, the alternative was just as awkward for Amanda. She knew without a husband she would be putting Alex's marriage to Marianne at risk.'

'It's a mess whichever way you look at it. And now your son is wining and dining another girl. Next thing she'll be pregnant to him and where will he be then,' William said, until another more shocking thought struck him. 'Or Amanda will become pregnant to Alex again.'

'Don't even think that, William,' Richard said, shaking his head, as if thinking about the possibility might actually make it a fact.

William shrugged his shoulders as if to say *anything is possible in this mess*. But there was, he decided, one issue his brother hadn't raised.

'There's one other matter none of us has yet considered. Andrew isn't a Belleville. What do you think we should do about that?'

'Nothing, William. Paul will go on being his father, which means he's a Belleville. So don't get any ideas he should be disinherited, because I'd fight that tooth and nail.'

'Fair enough,' William said, taken aback by the vehemence of Richard's defence of Andrew. 'I wouldn't want to punish the child either for something that he had no control over. He's a good kid. His little brother will need him in the future.'

'I'm pleased you see it that way,' Richard said with a finality that brought the discussion to an abrupt end.

'And what will happen now, do you think?'

'I have no bloody idea,' Richard said, his frustration getting the better of him. 'My one worry is that Paul will lose his temper one day and take a swing at Alex. And then the whole situation will likely implode.'

'I think you're right, brother. And you're right not to go heading off overseas. If that happens, you'll be needed here. And in the meantime, we just watch and wait.'

'Talking about waiting, where's this bloke we're supposed to meet today?'

William looked at his watch. It was nearly eleven o'clock.

'He should be here any minute. It will be good to talk to him and find out how this project is going to proceed,' William said, relieved to be talking about something else entirely.

Even as he spoke, they both spotted an unfamiliar vehicle driving slowly up the Prior Park driveway.

'This looks like our man,' William said, as he beckoned to the newcomer to park in front of the house.

Nathan Flynn held out his hand, first to William, whom he had expected to meet, and then to Richard.

'Thanks for making time for me today,' he said. 'We've got a tight timeframe on this build and a demanding client, I understand.'

He smiled as he said it.

'Yes, our sister got an idea into her head and now she's keen to get on with it,' William said.

'And the architect is your son, Richard. Is that right?'

'Yes, he's excited about his first commission. I hope he can produce a design that's achievable.'

Nathan Flynn smiled.

'I've worked with a lot of young architects,' he said good naturedly. 'We'll keep an eye on his ambitions and stop him if it looks like getting too ambitious. It will all be fine. Can we have a quick look at the site?'

The three men headed in the direction of the pile of rubble that was soon to become Julia's new house.

'A good site. It must have been a remarkable house. I've been to the local newspaper to their archives to see a photograph of it,' he said. 'What a terrible tragedy.'

He held up his hand then.

'There's no need to repeat the story of what happened. I've heard it,' he said, knowing what it must cost the brothers to speak about it. He had also seen the newspaper reporting of the fire and its aftermath.

Richard nodded, liking the young project manager immediately. He appeared to bring an air of calm authority to his work.

'A new role for you in this local office, I'm told?' Richard asked.

'Yes, I was in Brisbane but I was looking for a new challenge. My marriage just broke up.'

'I'm sorry to hear that,' Richard said. 'Marriage breakups are tough.'

'They are, although I have to say my ex-wife didn't get a settlement like your sister has obviously received.'

Richard smiled.

'Well, there aren't too many people around with the sort of wealth her ex-husband possesses. She decided to put it to good use.'

'I'm pleased about that. It will be an interesting project. We normally get to work on government buildings and the like. This will be a nice change.'

'We're looking forward to a new house emerging from the rubble. We've been looking at that for far too long,' William said, indicating the pile of charred and broken bricks.

'Well, it's certainly going to be a big improvement,' Nathan said as he surveyed the weed-covered site.

'How long before we see action?' Richard asked.

'Probably a week or so before we get machinery out here to start clearing, but we can't start building anything until we get council approvals.'

'We look forward to the end result,' Richard said, as they walked with him back to his car.

'He seems like a nice young fellow,' William said as they watched him drive away. 'Mid-thirties wouldn't you say? I wonder what happened with his marriage.'

'Who knows,' Richard said. 'Not everyone is as fortunate as you and Alice.'

'No they're not,' William agreed, 'but I did at least hope our own daughter would follow our path and have a long, happy marriage.'

'Who's to say it might not happen, William? Perhaps she'll forgive Alex his slip up providing he promises there'll be no more.'

'Perhaps,' William said, 'but she is bitterly disappointed in him according to her mother. And wary of Amanda. Very wary of Amanda, in fact. It won't take much for them to have a spectacular falling out either.'

Richard said nothing but he began to ponder just how much tension there might be at future family gatherings at Prior Park and what small spark might ignite the blue touchpaper with explosive results.

Several days after their conversation, both William and Richard would have been surprised at the apparently comfortable atmosphere in Marianne and Alex's home, had they been there to see it.

But for Marianne, the comfortable atmosphere had been achieved by pretending there was nothing troubling her which had in turn reassured Alex he had nothing to be concerned about.

He had suggested to Amanda that Andrew not come over quite so much. He had told Marianne he had suggested it while they were settling the baby into a routine, using the excuse that together the children were too noisy and would disturb the new baby. In reality, he worried the more Marianne saw of Andrew, the more likely she was to guess the truth.

As Marianne began her familiar routine of cooking dinner, Alex sat at the table, helping little Mel read her book.

'I think the baby seems settled now,' he said. 'Perhaps Andrew can come over one day after school for a little while to keep Mel company.'

If he had been more alert, he would have noticed Marianne

tense and her mood drop. She placed the casserole she had been stirring into the oven, banged the oven door closed and then turned to face him.

'Were you ever going to tell me about Andrew? Admit it to me?' she asked, her voice calmer than she felt.

'Admit what?'

He was shocked. The question had come so unexpectedly. There was no forewarning.

'I know Andrew is your son, Alex. It's so obvious now. Everyone's noticed it. Don't try and deny it. How long had we been married before you were unfaithful to me? I've tried to work it out. Less than a month, probably. And then you and Amanda conned Paul into marrying her when she found out she was pregnant to you.'

Her words came in a rush. If she paused for breath, she feared her courage might desert her.

She watched his reaction carefully. She saw only guilt. She wasn't sure she saw remorse. And in those moments, her trust in her husband evaporated. Had they been lovers since? Was Paul really Matthew's father? Was there a chance Alex was his father?

Alex drew a deep breath. It was the discussion he had always dreaded.

'Don't bother with a lie, Alex. I spoke to my mother. We had a heart to heart. And now she's told me everyone knows. It isn't a secret anymore.' She paused for breath. 'Everyone in the family knows.'

He sat for a long time, head in hands, watching his life with Marianne disintegrate before his eyes. To tell her it was just the once seemed such a lame excuse. And none of what followed had been as calculated as it now appeared.

'I'm sorry, Marianne,' he said as he got up from the table and walked across to where she was standing. He put his arms around her. 'What more can I say except that I'm deeply sorry. More than I can ever say. I didn't mean to hurt you.'

But he wouldn't lie outright. He wouldn't say it meant nothing.

'That's so easy to say. And now you're seeing her more and

more. You'll be going away with her too. I know what that will mean.'

'I promise you it won't,' he said, knowing it was a promise he would struggle to keep.

She laughed derisively.

'Don't make a promise you can't keep, Alex,' she retorted. 'She won't have any scruples about seducing you. She knows Paul is so devastated he's already cheating on her.'

Alex was shocked. This was a new and different Marianne. Gone was the compliant young girl he had seduced and married. The discussion was the toughest they'd ever had.

'So what do you want me to do?' he asked. 'I've apologised to you. I'm sorry for what happened. I've promised it won't happen again. What more can I do?'

She shook her head, trying desperately to stop the tears rolling down her cheeks. Everything about her marriage had seemed perfect. Until it wasn't. Until the ugly truth had revealed itself in the form of a child whose father should have been someone else.

But she had to ask one final question. If she didn't, she knew the uncertainty would haunt her forever.

'And Amanda's second baby. Will he turn out to look like you too?' she asked.

He looked at her. It was a deadly serious question.

'No, I promise you I didn't father another child with Amanda. Matthew is Paul's child.'

But he could see she only half believed him.

'It was only the once since we got married,' he admitted. 'Just the once.'

'But it wasn't the first time you'd been with her, was it?'

He shook his head.

'No, Marianne. It wasn't the first time.'

It was as if she was really seeing him for the first time and in doing so, she had exposed her own naiveté.

'I must have been such an easy target for you,' she said bitterly. 'Too easy really.'

He remained silent. What she said was true. She had been an

easy target. Cossetted and protected by her parents who never stopped treating her like a child, she had been vulnerable to his pursuit of her. It had been an opportunity he couldn't pass up. And then love and respect had followed, except it wasn't love in the all-consuming way he loved Amanda. In the way he wanted Amanda. And in the way Amanda wanted him.

'Just promise me I'm more important to you now than Amanda,' she said.

'You are much more important to me,' he said. 'You've been a wonderful wife and mother. I couldn't have asked for better.'

He heard her sigh deeply. He desperately wanted her to believe him. For the first time in their marriage, he felt uncertain. How would she respond? What would she decide? Would she press for a separation with the baby only a few weeks old? He waited for her to speak.

'My Uncle James regretted how he reacted to news of Pippa's birth. It ended his marriage. He didn't give Aunt Julia a chance to explain the circumstances. I don't want to know the circumstances with Amanda,' she said. 'I just want to know it's in the past. That I'm more important to you now than Amanda. I don't want our marriage to end.'

He kissed her lovingly, relieved by her decision.

'I don't want our marriage to end either,' he said quietly. 'I love you. I would do anything for you. And for our daughters.'

'Then we won't ever speak of it again,' she said but in the back of her mind she wondered whether he could fulfil his promise to her.

But she was no longer willing to say she loved him. The hurt was too deep, the wound too raw. The trust she had placed in him had been shattered. It would take more than a few words of apology to repair it.

Across the room, she noticed little Mel for the first time. Her eyes, big and startled, stared at her mother. And at her father. But she said nothing as if she knew instinctively this was no time for childish chatter.

'You'd better see to our daughter,' Marianne said quietly as she turned back to tend to the dinner she was cooking. 'She's never seen her parents argue before.'

Alex sat down beside his precious little daughter and put his arm around her. He felt her shiver so he pulled her on to this knee as he had when she was a toddler.

'It's alright, darling,' he said. 'Mummy and I just got a little bit cross with one another. But it's over now.'

'Are you sure?' she asked in her timid little voice.

'I'm sure,' he said as he began to read aloud to her as he had done many times before.

He understood then how important it was to protect her. To make sure she felt safe, secure and loved. He had never had that as a child. He was determined his own children would not suffer the same fate.

But it would be a memory little Mel would carry with her. As the other memories of her childhood slipped away, she would always remember the day she discovered Andrew, her best friend in all the world, was her brother.

26

THE SOUND OF HEAVY machinery cut through the early morning. Both William and Richard were on hand to witness the clearing of the site where the original Prior Park house had proudly stood for so long.

'I believe Anthony is coming up tomorrow to go over the plans with you,' Richard said, raising his voice to be heard above the noise.

Nathan Flynn, who was busy directing the workers, nodded.

'Yes. We're just doing this first clearing carefully. I believe there's a plan to re-use some of the bricks in a low garden wall. Many of them are too badly burnt and decayed, but there should be some towards the back of the house that will be salvageable.'

'It's good to see the work start,' William said. 'How long will approvals take?'

'Hopefully not too long. We'll do what we can to push it along.'

'So Anthony will have the final plans with him tomorrow. Is that what you're expecting?' Richard asked.

'That's what he's promised,' Nathan said.

Just then, they heard a shout from the machine operator. The bucket had hit the old broken front steps, some of which were still embedded in the foundations. But as the operator raised the bucket to scoop up the debris, he noticed a small iron box had been exposed by the demolition.

'Something there, boss,' the operator shouted, pointing to the rubble.

Nathan Flynn hurried over to the spot and collected the item, which apart from a small dent, appeared to be intact. He carried it awkwardly back to where Richard and William were standing at a safe distance from the worksite.

'Looks like this has been there since the house was built,' Nathan said, setting it down on the ground. It was too heavy for a man to carry too far. 'Did you have any idea this would be in the house?'

Both Richard and William shook their heads simultaneously both thinking the same thing. Had their father known and never told them? Perhaps he had meant to tell them but he had died suddenly before he could. Or perhaps he had never known.

'It's heavy,' Nathan said. 'I'll get a wheelbarrow. If you help me put it in, I'll transport it up to the house for you.'

'Good idea,' William said, having tested the weight of the box. 'The box itself is quite heavy but whatever is in it is heavy too, I'd say.'

Together William and Richard lifted the box out of the wheelbarrow onto a table on the verandah.

'Thanks, Nathan. We'll take it from here,' Richard said.

The commotion brought Alice to the verandah. And Marianne too who had been working in her father's office, dealing with the Prior Park monthly accounts.

'I was going to come down later and have a look at the work,' Marianne said, after being introduced.

'There's not much to see yet,' Nathan replied, 'although we didn't expect to turn up hidden treasure.'

She laughed.

'A treasure trove, is it?'

'Well, someone's left a surprise for whoever decided to demolish the house.'

'My great grandfather, I assume,' she said. 'I'm not sure how they're going to open it.'

'I think a wrench and a bit of muscle power will do the trick.

The hinges are quite rusty,' he said, as he started to walk back to the worksite.

'Anthony's up tomorrow, isn't he? With the plans? And my Aunt Julia?'

'Yes, they are. It will be good to get everything progressed. Your aunt is very keen.'

'We all are,' Marianne said. 'I remember the original house. I was in high school when it was burned down.'

'But you weren't here on the night I believe?'

'No, I stayed with my grandmother in town to go to school during the week.'

'It must have been awful for the family,' he said sympathetically.

'It was. And then he almost killed Uncle Richard when he broke out of jail.'

'I heard,' Nathan said. 'It must have been quite a topic of conversation at the time.'

'It was,' Marianne said. 'My parents tried to shield me from the awful truth. But we all had to know in the end. Can you imagine the scandal? Mind you, the Belleville family do scandals well. And regularly.'

He laughed.

'What's a family without a few scandals,' he said.

'Well, they're just a topic of conversation if they belong in the past and happened to people you don't know. But if they affect people you know and love, that's different.'

'Well, maybe there's another old scandal hidden in the box we've just unearthed,' he said.

She smiled.

'It's probably just a load of old rubbish. I don't think it will be hidden treasure.'

'You never know. It was heavy. It could be gold.'

'Well, I'd better go and find out,' she said.

As she turned to head back to the house, she paused.

'I'm really keen to see what Anthony has designed,' she said. 'My father sometimes talks about the new house being Julia's folly. I desperately want it to be a success. My aunt's been through a lot.'

He understood. He'd made it his business to enquire into Julia Belleville, his client. Her life must surely be one of the scandals Marianne was referring to.

And she was right. From what he had gleaned in the time since he had taken over the local office, the Belleville family was the source of a lot of local gossip.

And then he remembered the gossip had included Marianne's husband. It hadn't meant anything to him at the time but now that he had met her, he wondered if she had chosen badly. His instinct told him she deserved better.

Back on the verandah, William was busy forcing the old, rusted hinges from the heavy metal box.

Finally, the hinges gave way and the lid yielded to pressure from the wrench. While William held it open, Richard retrieved a small bundle of handwritten letters from the top. He set these aside for the moment as both he and William peered into the box.

What they saw brought a gasp of surprise from each of them, heavy gold bars loosely wrapped in hessian. Richard picked up one of the bars and tested its weight in his hands.

'What does it weigh?' William asked, staggered at what they had found.

'I'd say, at a guess, twelve pounds, maybe a bit more.'

He pointed to a stamp in the gold.

'That's probably two hundred troy ounces,' Richard said. 'And there's three of them. That's quite a treasure haul.'

'Well, that's a surprise,' Marianne said as she and her mother inspected the gold bars. 'I thought it would be a load of old rubbish.'

'No, I thought that was unlikely,' Richard said. 'No one goes to those lengths to hide something that's worthless.'

He picked up the handwritten letters then. 'This might tell us the story.'

He began to read aloud. He had already recognised the handwriting from the letter he had seen on the architect's file.

To my descendants

By the time you discover this box, many years will have passed since the house was built. I hope it is more than fifty years. I hope it is a hundred years or more. The house was built to last many generations.

I do not know what relation you, the reader, will be to me. A grandson perhaps. A great grandson. A granddaughter. Who can tell? Perhaps the Belleville family line will die out. But I am by nature optimistic. My wife Adeline has delivered me a child. A son. Perhaps there will be more children, but she is not strong. One child will suffice.

I am leaving this in a place where it will never be found unless the house is demolished. If the house is being demolished, it may mean that the family has fallen on hard times and can no longer afford the upkeep.

What this box contains is intended to keep the family going if it should have fallen on hard times.

I've known hard times. Through my wits and endeavours, I have worked to ensure my family will never know hard times.

I have secured the best marriage I could. I am sorry to have left another young woman desolate because I chose Adeline. It left me desolate too especially when I discovered later she was with child. Fortunately she married quickly and the husband accepted the child, a daughter.

There is more to my story, which I have written separately.

Louis Belleville

Richard set the letter aside and picked up the remaining pages.

'It looks like he has written about his life,' Richard said, as he began to read aloud again.

My Life Story

This may shock my descendants but I was not born Louis Belleville. I will tell you how I came by this name but first I will tell you what my real name is.

My name was Edward Simmons. My mother Louisa was not married. She was transported on the female convict ship Rajah in 1841 for a petty crime, which might have seen her sentenced to death had she not been pretty and the judge took pity on her. She was twenty years old. She obtained work as a servant in the household of a high born French family, who were initially in Van Diemen's Land, now Tasmania, before moving to the colony of Sydney. There were not many French people in the colony at that time, she told me.

The saddest part of her story is how I came to be born. She told me she tried desperately to fend off the son of the household but to no avail. Eventually, she became pregnant to him and they turned her off when they discovered her condition. We were desperately poor, she doing what work she could get and getting by on the kindness of strangers and the parish.

To her credit, she insisted I go to school and that I should understand the ways of a gentleman.

When I was sixteen, she died, broken down by hard work and illness. And I was on my own. Her last advice to me was to leave the colony of Sydney.

'Go to a place where no one knows you,' she said, 'and make a new life for yourself.'

I knew if I was to avoid her fate of dying in poverty, I would need to make something of myself.

By the time I was sixteen, gold was all the rage.

I worked first on the goldfields of New South Wales and then moved to the latest rush in South Australia. There I teamed up with a man of questionable habits but with an instinct for finding gold.

What you are looking at today as you open this box are the remnants of the treasure I helped him find and, in the end, took from him.

Goldfields were rough places. Too much grog. Too little law and order. I won't go into details. There have always been whispers I am capable of shooting a man, probably because I can lose my temper easily at any slight. But it is true I shot a man once. I shot my partner in the mine. He died instantly. But I did it in self-defence. He tried to shoot me but drink had rendered his aim unreliable.

We were deep inside a mining tunnel at this point, the alluvial gold having long ago run out. The shots caused a collapse in the tunnel. He was buried by tons of rock and soil. But he was already dead so it was pointless trying to dig him out.

I saw my opportunity. It was nearly dark. We had stashed our hard won hoard in a place where no one would find it. I quickly recovered the gold. We had invested in a cart and a horse, pitiful creature that it was. Under cover of darkness late that night, I slipped out of the encampment. No one saw me go.

I knew they would later discover the collapsed mine. I hoped they would assume we had both been buried by the collapse and that someone had stolen our horse and cart.

To cover my tracks, I changed my name at that point.

I remembered my mother telling me she had seen the name Belleville on a map of France in the house where she worked. And the name Louis of course honoured her name. Until my son was born, she was the only person I truly loved.

I moved on to Melbourne. I discovered I could use the gold as collateral with the banks, so I only ever sold a small amount. I became a merchant. I adopted a French accent, and remembering what my mother had taught me, I transformed myself into a gentleman, a man of means. I dressed in the best clothes. I was careful to give all the appearance of having been born a gentleman.

By the time the house at Prior Park was being built, I felt I no longer needed the reassurance of the gold close by. But I wanted to keep it. Except it could not be kept somewhere where others might find it in my lifetime, even in a bank vault. My wife was not aware of my real background. The bankers didn't ask too many questions in the early days. I made up a story that I had invested in several cargoes and the profits had been handsome, which I had turned to gold. But by this time they no longer needed such collateral from me.

By hiding the trunk in the new house, I knew I could always retrieve it if I ever needed it. It was, for my lifetime, my insurance policy.

And then I comforted myself with the knowledge it would be, at some far distant point, a windfall for my descendants.

I hope the Belleville family has prospered. I hope my son Francis has been a good provider and an honest man. Everything I did was for him. For him and his family to have a secure and prosperous life.

At some point when it no longer mattered, I wanted to be honest about my background. I was born a bastard. But I did not live as a bastard. I reinvented my life and my background. I threw off the cloak of poverty.

I became known for my flamboyant gestures. This house is testament to how I chose to live my life. With refinement. With flair. With an eye to the future.
Louis Belleville

No one spoke for quite some time. The story had been many things. Extraordinary. Revealing. Disturbing. And pitiful.

Finally, Richard broke the silence.

'Wow, that's a lot to take in,' he said, shaking his head. 'It's a lot to take in.'

Both he and William realised the vague stories their father had told them of the Belleville family origins were all a complete fabrication.

'So the little we were told of our family's origin was a complete lie,' William said.

'Apparently so,' Richard said, 'but I can't help but feel grudging admiration for our grandfather. All he had were his wits and his personal charm.'

'And a streak of ruthlessness,' William added.

'That too,' Richard agreed, 'for which we must all feel grateful.'

And then his mind turned to practical matters.

'What are we going to do with the gold bars?' he asked, looking towards William.

'Well, we'll have to tell Julia about them. But I guess for the time being one of us can take them into the bank and have them stored there. Probably the safest place.'

Richard agreed. If word got out there was a haul of gold bars at Prior Park, the house would never be safe when they were away.

'And the letter and the family history?'

'Well, everyone needs to see it,' Alice said. 'It can then be kept in the safe here. The safe is fireproof.'

'That sounds like a good plan,' William said.

'I'm not sure our father fulfilled his expectations,' Richard said, looking at William.

'No, I think he'd have been disappointed there. Our father would have cashed in the gold if he had known about it.'

Richard smiled. William had avoided mentioning the betrayal their father had perpetrated on the family. Had he inherited the tendencies of his unknown grandfather who had taken his pleasure with a young defenceless woman and walked away from any responsibility?

But that didn't fit either. His father hadn't walked away from Muriel McGovern. He had supported her. But he hadn't been honest with her.

'I think you're right. Fortunately, like our grandfather, he married well,' Richard said. 'No doubt his father's guiding hand was at work there.'

'You mean he didn't love our mother,' William said, 'even in the early days of their marriage?'

Richard drew a deep breath.

'I very much doubt it. I think he married for the same reasons his father had married. Financial gain.'

In an uncharacteristic display of affection, William put his arm around Alice.

'Well, it stopped at that generation,' William said. 'I married for love.'

Alice smiled. William was so rarely demonstrative she didn't know what to say.

'And you made a good choice, William,' he said, but even as the words were out of his mouth, Richard regretted them. He noticed a wistful look cross Marianne's face.

She had married for love but Alex might well have been making the same choices as her Belleville grandfather and great grandfather, Richard thought. He had married to improve his position in life. He possibly even convinced himself he was in love with Marianne.

Alice too had sensed the change in atmosphere.

'Let me go and make some tea,' she said. 'There's a lot to take in here.'

Tea and cake. Alice's remedy for everything, Richard thought, as he took one end of the heavy box to help William carry it to his office. It would be safe there for a few days until one of them could take it to the bank.

27

Glenmoral station

IT WAS LATE AFTERNOON. A chill had settled as the sun lost its power. For the very first time Alex sat in the living room – in the room from which he had been excluded as he was growing up – as an owner of Glenmoral. A low fire glowed in the fireplace. The fine glassware on the highly polished cedar sideboard sparkled in the gentle light. He took all this in with a growing sense of pleasure. But the pain of his early life would never fully recede.

'Literally lord of all you survey now Alex?' Tony Bland said, breaking into his reverie. 'Amanda has been very generous.'

His flicker of a smile might have been genuine pleasure at Alex's good fortune. Or it might have been a suggestive leer. Either way Alex no longer cared about Tony Bland's opinion.

'Yes, Tony. Lord of all I survey. You're right there,' he said evenly. 'With Amanda, of course.'

'Where is she by the way?' Tony asked.

'Enjoying the luxury of a long bath, she told me. I think you'll find the tanks will be empty when we've gone.'

Tony laughed.

'She's got used to town living. Turn on a tap and the water's there.'

'Well, I'm not going to say that to her, that's for certain. I think it's a relief for her to be away from the constant demands of her children for a while.'

'I understand,' Tony said. 'I think she'd find that part of motherhood a bit difficult from what I know of her. She'd love her kids but it would be the day-to-day grind she wouldn't enjoy.'

'That just about sums it up, I think,' he agreed. 'I don't think there'll be any more children.'

'Paul might be disappointed with that,' Tony said conversationally.

'I wouldn't know,' Alex said. 'I'm not privy to their private conversations.'

It was a discussion he wanted to close down. He knew too much about Paul and Amanda's marriage. Far too much. He knew it was teetering on the edge.

'It's a pity your wife isn't here, Tony? Everything alright there?'

'She's fine. Everything's fine. She's staying with her parents for a month to help out while her mother recovers from an operation.'

'You live mostly at Isla Downs?'

'Yes, she likes it there,' he said.

'Do you think these two properties should be operated together, almost as one?' Alex asked.

They had spent several hours riding around Glenmoral and talking about its operation. A visit to Isla Downs was next on the list, but not this time.

'I think there are lots of opportunities, given that the two properties share a boundary. But money needs to be spent here first. The stockyards need a major rebuild to bring them up to standard, not to mention the road needs proper repair.'

'I take it Amanda's father was reluctant to spend money?'

'He was part of the old make-do school. Get the stockmen to patch the rotten rails when they had some downtime. Call in a favour via the local councillor when they had a grader in the district. Things like that.'

'I'll talk with Amanda about it,' he agreed, as he accepted a cold beer from the housekeeper. He noticed a glass of wine on the tray, obviously intended for Amanda.

'Amanda shouldn't be too much longer,' he said.

'It was one of her father's favourite wines,' Betty Long said as she placed the glass on a side table. She had replaced the long serving Ada Williams five years earlier. 'We still have quite a bit of it on hand. I know she likes it too. Dinner is about fifteen minutes off. Should I hold it further?'

Alex shook his head.

'No, that's fine. If she's not here by then, I'll go and drag her out of the bath,' he said with a laugh.

Betty Long was about to say something and then thought better of it. She turned quickly and headed for the kitchen.

'I think you shocked your housekeeper,' Tony said pulling a face.

'I didn't mean to do that. I wanted to reassure her we weren't going to let her dinner spoil. That's all.'

'Well, there are some people who've raised eyebrows that Amanda is here without her husband and you're here without your wife. People remember how keen you were on each other once.'

'I think we'll survive the gossip,' Alex said as Amanda entered the room, her hair still slightly damp from the bath, her riding clothes replaced by a simple dress designed to flatter her figure.

Alex got up and handed her the glass of wine.

'We thought you must have drowned in the tub. I was about to come and pull you out. Betty Long was worried her dinner would spoil if she had to delay it.'

She smiled at him and whispered.

'You should have joined me. It would have been fun.'

'Tony says there's already gossip about us. Behave yourself,' he whispered back.

She turned towards Tony who had overheard their intimate exchange and smiled to himself. Playing with fire, that's what they're doing, he thought. And they're both enjoying it.

'Thanks for everything today, Tony,' she said, reverting to a business-like tone. 'We've got a lot of hard work to bring Glenmoral up to standard. I didn't realise my father had been so reluctant to spend money on maintenance. I think he must have wanted to make sure there was no debt when I took over.'

'I think you could be right,' he said, his tone conciliatory. 'It makes sense anyway. I knew it would take a while to get everything sorted after his passing, so I didn't want to start complaining about things.'

'And I appreciate that, Tony,' she said. 'Alex and I will have a think about it and decide what gets done first.'

As she sipped her wine, she looked around the room. It was unchanged from her father's day. For her, there were too many memories in the room. Alex noticed her drop in mood. He put his arm around her shoulders. It was a gesture of comfort, nothing more. But even that small gesture betrayed the closeness and intimacy of their relationship.

Tony Bland watched on silently. Her old man should never have separated them, he thought. They'll always find their way back to one another. Find a way to be together. She might stay married to Paul Belleville and he might stay married to Marianne Belleville but it was as clear now as it had ever been that they belonged together.

'I'll go and tell Betty we're ready for dinner,' Tony announced abruptly.

As he left the room, he was sure the arm around the shoulder became a tender embrace. He remembered the last time they were at Glenmoral together. Had the choice of the property been meaningful for their first visit together, he wondered? Everything pointed to it.

He shrugged. What happens at Glenmoral stays at Glenmoral, he decided.

And late in the evening as the old house creaked, reluctantly giving up the warmth of the day, he would not have been surprised to see Alex quietly opening the door to Amanda's room.

On Alex's part, there had been hesitation. Indecision. And then capitulation.

'You summoned me, I believe,' Alex said, as he closed the door behind him.

She laughed softly and put her arms around his neck.

'It wasn't an order,' she whispered. 'Just an invitation.'

'An invitation?'

'Yes, an invitation. You didn't have to accept the invitation,' she teased.

'But I didn't want to disappoint you.'

'You never disappoint me, my darling,' she said, as she nestled in his arms. 'Annoy me perhaps. Frustrate me. And make me doubt you. But you never disappoint me.'

'I'm sure that's not true,' he countered.

She laughed quietly. He had of course disappointed her but that was in the past. What she was now focused on was the present. And possibly the future.

'We've spent years denying each other,' she said, a hint of sadness in her voice.

'We have,' he agreed. 'We did make a mess of things, you must admit.'

'A spectacular mess. I never intended it to happen.'

'You mean you didn't think you'd get pregnant when you seduced me so unexpectedly?'

She shook her head.

'I didn't. It was careless of me. Very careless.'

'Not deliberate?'

'No, not deliberate,' she said.

And he believed her. He had never asked the question before.

'It seemed to me you didn't want to admit I was married.'

'I didn't,' she said. 'I didn't want to admit it at all. And then I decided I had to move on.'

'Did you always know I was Andrew's father and not Paul?'

She nodded her head slightly.

'I did know,' she said. 'But you're the only person I would ever admit that to. I won't ever admit that to him.'

'So what happens now?'

'We'll have to find our way out of this mess,' she said.

'Any ideas?' he asked.

She shook her head.

'No. I suggest we wait to see what happens.'

'Meaning that Paul might decide to leave you?'

'Yes, I think it's possible. We haven't discussed it but I know he's trying to live with the knowledge he's not Andrew's father. I think he's struggling. It's become so obvious he can't ignore it anymore. And Marianne?'

'She knows. She's angry with me. Angry that I let her down but she's trying to carry on as we were.'

'An impasse then,' she said.

'You could say that,' he said. 'And in the meantime?'

'We have each other,' she said. 'Away from them, we have each other.'

He kissed her then. Lovingly. Passionately. Without restraint.

'I love you. I will always love you, no matter what,' he said. 'You do know that, don't you?'

She nodded. His words were everything she wanted to hear.

'And I love you,' she replied as she let out a deep sigh of pleasure.

How long had she waited for this moment? Too long. But he would become her lover again and that was all that mattered to her. Should she feel guilty? Paul was doing the same thing. She didn't care. Not now she could have Alex.

For a brief moment, Alex hesitated, thinking of his promise to Marianne. But in his heart, he knew it was a promise he couldn't keep. He sighed. The end of his marriage was only a question of time. Because he could not turn his back on Amanda.

All thoughts and worries for the future vanished quickly from his mind as the pleasure of their lovemaking consumed him. And, later, as she lay contentedly in his arms, he began to contemplate the future. A future with her.

'What are you thinking about?' she asked.

'The future.'

'The unknowable future,' she said. 'The future will take care of itself. And in the meantime, we'll enjoy the present.'

He smiled to himself.

'We will,' he said as desire rose in him again.

It was early morning. Tony leaned against Alex's car as he began the task of filling the petrol tank from the station's fuel stocks.

'Amanda up yet?' he asked.

'Probably. I haven't seen her this morning.'

Which isn't a lie, Tony thought. He'd noticed Alex had ended the night in his own bed.

'You know I always wondered why her old man didn't want you to marry her. What did he have against you, apart from the obvious? Was there anything in what your mother left you to confirm who your father was?'

He was curious. It was a presumption to ask such a question. He worried then how Alex would react.

'I'm sorry if that's trespassing on your private life,' he added.

Alex did not reply immediately. It was a question he hadn't expected. He thought about his answer as he finished filling the car with petrol. What was the harm in telling him?

'The rumour always was that Arthur Robinson was my father. It turned out to be true. My mother confirmed it in a letter to me. But Amanda's father thought it was possible he was my father. Arthur Robinson forced himself on my mother. That's how I was conceived. Not very nice, is it? But it's something I have to live with. And she hoped Howard Robinson might offer her marriage but she died before he could get back from the gulf.'

He paused for a moment. It was all still raw. Still something he was coming to terms with.

'And my Scottish relatives don't want to know about me either. I wrote to them. They didn't know about me. Her very respectable sister wrote back to me and said she was sorry but the family couldn't cope with the disgrace of her sister giving birth out of wedlock. They hadn't known. They were never told. She said they were told my mother had contracted a fever and died before they could get medical help for her. She wished me a good life but told me not to contact them again.'

Tony was speechless. He hadn't meant to pry. He hadn't known half of it. Or even suspected that Alex's mother had been raped. Alex hadn't used the word – probably because he couldn't bring himself to say it out loud – but that was what had happened. He understood so much more now. Arthur Robinson had taken advantage of a vulnerable woman. There was nothing to admire in the man. And so Amanda had made amends in the only way she could. He admired her for it.

'I'm sorry, Alex, I had no idea. I shouldn't have asked such a question. It's obviously deeply personal. I apologise.'

Alex put his hand on Tony's arm to reassure him.

'It's fine, mate,' he said. 'Sometimes it helps to speak about it. It's hard for Marianne to understand. She was treated like a princess throughout her life. Amanda too. Her father doted on her. But she was the only one who took care of me. Looked out for me. Without her, I'd have amounted to nothing. And then she went one step further and made me her partner.'

'That was very generous of her.'

'It was,' Alex agreed. 'We didn't discuss it. She just did it and told me later. I was shocked. And once I got over the shock, I was delighted. It's strained my relations with Marianne's family though. They were happy for me to work at Prior Park, beholden to them, nothing of my own except through my marriage to Marianne. But I still felt excluded. You would know what I mean.'

'Yes, I know what you mean,' Tony said. 'I may run these properties for Amanda and now for you, but I would love to own them. Or own just one of them.'

'That I can understand,' Alex said. 'You do a good job. We're grateful for that.'

'If they aren't relying on you now at Prior Park, you could always move to Isla Downs or Glenmoral,' Tony suggested.

Alex shook his head.

'I don't see Marianne agreeing to that any time soon,' he said. 'Mind you, if she throws me out, it's where I'll end up.'

'You're kidding me, aren't you? You made a brilliant marriage. The Belleville family would be wealthier than the Robinson family ever was. And you've got two daughters with Marianne, I believe. Why would she throw you out?'

'My life is more complicated than it looks, Tony,' was all Alex was prepared to say.

Tony sensed there was more going on than simply the flirtation with Amanda. He wasn't a man to speculate.

Had he known more, he would have understood why both Amanda's marriage and Alex's marriage were teetering on a precipice.

'I've filled the car with petrol,' Alex said, as he sat down to breakfast opposite Amanda.

'You must have been up early,' she said brightly. 'Couldn't you sleep?'

He admired her boldness. She knew very well why he wouldn't have been able to sleep.

'I take it you slept like a baby,' he said. He would give as good as he got.

'Absolutely,' she said, with just the hint of a smile.

Did she ever feel guilty, Alex wondered? Or was that emotion reserved for him?

Tony watched the exchange in silence. There was a new level of intimacy between them. He wondered idly whose marriage would crumble first. If he was her husband, he'd have put his foot down and not let her travel about the country with Alex. Especially with Alex.

'So what's next on the agenda?' Tony asked, as he demolished the plate of hot food in front of him.

'When we can get away, we'll visit Isla Downs with you,' Amanda said. 'But we'll be in touch before that. There's lots to discuss.'

'Good,' Tony said. 'I'm keen to see some of the new ideas implemented.'

'Alex will keep an eye out for any sales of good stock,' Amanda said. 'My father was good at improving the quality of the cattle. But we'll need to do more on that front. Unfortunately I can't be away for very long yet.'

'How old is baby Matthew now?'

'He's only eight months. I have a nanny. She was staying the one night. Anything more is something of a stretch. And Alex has a younger baby at home. I don't think Marianne would be too pleased with him heading off for too long.'

For the first time, Tony realised what a tightrope Alex must be walking between the two women. His wife whom he should love. The mother of his children. And Amanda. The woman he had loved almost all his life.

Marianne should start preparing for a life without Alex, he decided. Amanda is going to want him, body and soul. And she won't be denied. Not this time, he thought. Not this time.

28

MARIANNE SCRIBBLED A NOTE, leaving it for Alex, before phoning the school to let them know Melanie wouldn't attend for that day and possibly the next. She gave no explanation.

She had spent a restless night, thinking of Alex with Amanda, knowing for sure he would break his promise to her. And knowing within a few hours he would be home and he would be telling her lies. She couldn't face it. Anthony's arrival had given her the perfect excuse to go to Prior Park.

She wanted to see what was proposed. She wanted to discuss the startling discoveries of the previous day.

But least of all she wanted to be waiting at home for an unfaithful husband who would lie to her the minute he walked through the door.

Alice greeted her daughter as she arrived at Prior Park. She was surprised to see both children with her.

'Is everything alright?' Alice asked, knowing of course that it wasn't. That it could never be alright again.

'Alex is due home today. I didn't want to be there,' she said quietly as her mother took little Mel's hand. 'I didn't want to be there having to listen to his lies about Amanda.'

'Mummy and Daddy had a big argument,' little Mel said, as if she wanted to explain why they were there. 'I found out Andrew is my brother.'

At that moment, the power of speech deserted Alice. Why had they argued in front of little Mel? What do I say to her now?'

Marianne held her finger to her lips.

'Darling, we don't talk about that. It's our secret.'

Little Mel nodded gravely. She would try to remember but she thought it was an exciting secret.

Alice gestured to William who had appeared from his office. They had expected Marianne. But not with both her children. And not so early.

'Take the children into the kitchen,' she said to him. 'I want to have a word with Marianne.'

William held his hand out to little Mel and picked up the carry basket. The baby had hardly stirred at all.

Mother and daughter sat together on the front verandah.

'What's happened?' Alice asked. 'Did you confront Alex?'

She nodded.

'I did. I couldn't stand it anymore. I wanted him to admit Andrew is his son.'

'And did he?'

'Not in so many words. He just said he was sorry. He assured me he's not Matthew's father. But I realised afterwards, thinking about it all, that he had lied to me about Amanda from the beginning. He told me they were like brother and sister, but he admitted he had been with her before … well, you know what I mean.'

'I know what you mean,' her mother said soothingly, 'but I think he genuinely had feelings for you.'

She shrugged offhandedly.

'I think so too, but not in the way he feels about Amanda. He won't have passed up the opportunity to be with her at Glenmoral. I'm sure of it.'

Alice reached out and held her daughter's hand.

'You have a decision to make, don't you? You need to decide whether you can stay with him and ignore what goes on between him and Amanda or you can leave him.'

'When we argued, I accepted his promise and said we wouldn't speak of it again. But I don't know how that's going to be possible.'

'You and Alex must work through this. Has he said he wants to leave?'

She shook her head.

'Not in so many words but am I just expected to wait around and hope he eventually loses interest in Amanda? Or wait around until Amanda and Paul's marriage collapses and then he'll go with her for sure.'

'I don't know,' her mother admitted. 'I've never been in that situation. I don't know what to advise you except to say it would be a disappointment to see a family broken up, especially with the baby so young.'

'So you think I should just put up with it for now?' Marianne asked.

Her mother gestured helplessly. How could she advise her daughter? How could she even put herself in her daughter's shoes? There was nothing in her experience to guide her except her belief in a stable, secure home for her two granddaughters.

'That sounds like the baby,' Marianne said as she heard a distinct cry. 'We'd better go in. Dad will be in a panic.'

Alice laughed. She was right. He would be in a panic. Before the two of them headed towards the kitchen, Alice gave her daughter a hug.

'There'll be a solution to all this,' she said reassuringly. 'You must put your faith in that.'

Later that morning a sizeable group gathered around the dining room table at Prior Park. Paul had dropped Andrew at school on the way, so he was surprised to see little Mel. He drew Marianne to one side.

'I didn't expect to see you here today. Is everything alright? I see little Mel is with you and the baby.'

She wished at that point she could have avoided a conversation with Paul. He was the last person she wanted to speak to.

'I don't really want to talk about it,' Marianne said. 'Not to you. And certainly not here.'

'Is it about Alex and Amanda?' he asked quietly.

She nodded.

'And Andrew,' she added.

'You know then.'

'Of course I know. I've known for ages. How long have you known?'

He let out a deep sigh of disappointment.

'I've suspected it for a while but I had it confirmed recently.'

'Bloody mess, isn't it?' Marianne said, shocking her cousin with her forceful language. It was so unlike her. He could tell she was angry. Deeply angry.

'That's one way to describe it.'

'Let's talk about it later,' Marianne said, as Anthony began to spread out architectural plans and drawings on the table. 'I want to have a look at what Anthony's done.'

'Hello again,' Nathan Flynn turned towards Marianne as she joined the group. 'Your cousin looks a bit nervous.'

'Well, this will be his toughest audience,' she said laughing and looking around the table at those who had assembled for the big reveal. William and Alice, Richard and Paul, Julia, and James and John Fitzroy, who had arrived late.

'A couple of people I don't know,' Nathan said quietly, nodding in the direction of the Fitzroy duo.

'My Uncle James Fitzroy, Aunt Julia's first husband, and her son John.'

'So your aunt's on good terms with her first husband but got a big settlement from her second husband?'

He looked at Marianne, hoping she would fill in the gaps in his knowledge.

'It's complicated,' Marianne said. 'Too complicated to talk about.'

At that point, little Mel inserted herself into the group, grabbing the table so she could get on tiptoes to see better. As she did so, she caught the edge of one of the plans and pulled it towards her.

'Your daughter?' Nathan asked.

'Yes, that's Melanie. She likes to be involved in everything. She forgets she's only six years old.'

He laughed.

'I have twin sisters, younger than me by a decade. I often had to look out for them when they were that age.'

He noticed all the chairs had been pushed back from the table so he grabbed one and brought it to the table and lifted up little Mel so she could stand on it to see everything that was going on.

'Is that better?'

She nodded, her little blonde ponytail bobbing up and down. Marianne smiled her thanks.

'I thought you'd be concentrating on the plans,' Marianne said.

'Time enough for that,' he said. 'I'll let Anthony have the limelight. Then he and I can go over it all in detail to see if there are any unworkable aspects of the design.'

'Do you expect any problems?'

She was curious. It was an unfamiliar process to her.

'Not really unless his client has pushed him to be over ambitious. Or his interior designer girlfriend.'

'You know about that then?'

He laughed.

'I do. We've had lots of discussions with Anthony on the phone. Some conversations have begun with *Victoria thinks it would be good* ... have you met her?'

'Yes, she came up when they were first looking at the site.'

'With Daniel Harrington? He's a noted architect when it comes to historic buildings. Anthony was lucky to have him as a tutor. He will really have benefitted from that.'

'It made for a tense visit though when he came up to see the site with Anthony,' Marianne said, before realising she should have remained silent on that topic too.

'Tense? Why was that?'

'Another complicated Belleville family story. Daniel Harrington is now married to Uncle Richard's second wife Kate. It's a complicated story. Too complicated to go into really.'

'Is that what the Belleville family is all about? Complicated family stories?'

'Well, we have history. You know that old trunk you unearthed …'

'I know,' he said, interrupting her. 'Your father said there were some historic papers in there.'

'That's one way of describing them. A confession you could probably call them. From my great grandfather.'

'Confession?'

'Another story too complicated to go into now,' she said quietly, as Anthony began to speak and the room fell silent.

Nathan turned his attention to Anthony's presentation. He surveyed the plans and the drawings with the eye of the project manager who's been tasked with bringing them to life.

Daniel Harrington's fingerprints are all over this, he thought. The young architect has been sensible enough to take advice from someone much more experienced.

As Anthony went through the plans and the artist's impression of what the site would become, he had saved the best to last.

To gasps – and then applause from around the table – he unveiled an artist's impression of the new house he hoped would stand for a hundred years at Prior Park.

Smaller in scale but recognisable, Julia and her brothers were transported back in time to their childhoods. The front elevation, although not as large as the original, revived the classic symmetry that had made the original house look so imposing.

In every respect, the design paid homage to the house they had known. Except that it was smaller, more compact, with a circular driveway at the front and a garden, defined by a low brick wall, at the rear of the building.

'That garden wall isn't going to keep anything out,' ever practical William said. 'If you have a green lawn, you'll have roos in there every afternoon.'

'I think we'll cross that bridge when we get to it, William,' she said.

'It's wonderful, Anthony,' his father said. 'It looks like you've achieved a great balance between the old and the new. We can all see the heritage in the design but it will be a new house, not just a copy of the old house.'

'Thanks, Dad,' Anthony said. He looked anxiously towards Nathan Flynn.

'What's your verdict, Nathan? Will you be able to build this?'

Nathan smiled and nodded.

'No worries, mate. If you consider what a task they had when the original house was built, this should be no problem at all, providing we can get all the trades we need. So is there a sct of plans for me?' he asked.

Anthony handed across a full set of architectural plans and artist's drawings.

'Thanks, mate,' he said. 'I'll get our team working on the applications straight away and the project plan. We've made good progress on clearing the site already.'

'Yes, I noticed as we drove past it,' he said. 'I'll drop into your office tomorrow morning and we can go through everything and come up with a build schedule.'

'Good idea,' he said, as he accepted the bundle of papers.

'Won't you stay for lunch?' Alice asked. 'William is going to put a few steaks on to cook.'

'Thanks, Alice, but no, I need to get on with this. I've got an impatient client,' he said, looking towards Julia who smiled and shook her head.

'Just anxious to get on with it,' she said. 'I want my own house.'

'We'll do our best to hurry things along,' he said. 'Your nephew has done a great job with the design. I promise you we'll do a great job with the building.'

'Thank you,' she said.

He looked around for Marianne but he couldn't see her. Probably gone to help her mother in the kitchen, he supposed, as he and Anthony headed to his car.

'Well done, Anthony,' he said. 'Looks like you've produced a good design that honours the old house while creating an entirely new one. It will be impressive.'

'Thanks, Nathan,' he said. 'I was nervous I must admit.'

'Families are always the harshest critics,' he said.

Anthony laughed.

'You're right there,' he said. 'I really wanted to do something they'd admire. And something that would free them from the tragedy of what had gone before.'

'Yes, once there's a new house there, the past can be put to rest.'

'I hope so,' Anthony said. 'I really hope so.'

In the kitchen, Alice had in fact brushed aside Marianne's offer of help.

'You need to see to the baby,' she said.

Marianne lifted her baby daughter out of her carry cot, testing the bottle for the correct temperature. Alice paused to beam approvingly at her little granddaughter.

'She looks so much like little Mel,' she said. 'She's adorable.'

'I'm not little Mel anymore,' an indignant six-year-old declared and they all laughed. She would always be little Mel to them. Her grandmother swept her up in a big hug.

If only Marianne can keep her marriage together, everything will be fine, she thought. But was it fair to suggest to Marianne she turn a blind eye to what Alex was doing with Amanda?

Except for the two little girls, she would have insisted her daughter leave him. But the two little girls changed everything as far as she was concerned. If Marianne could keep her marriage together, she should do so. But she knew in her heart it would be asking too much. Far too much of her daughter.

As the family gathered in the kitchen waiting for William to cook the steaks, Paul took Marianne to one side. She groaned inwardly. Did she really want to continue their earlier conversation? But there seemed to be no way to avoid it.

'What are you thinking of doing?' Paul asked quietly. 'I assume you've had words with Alex.'

'Yes, we've had a discussion.'

'And?'

'He promised me he …'

But she couldn't say it. She couldn't say to Paul that he promised he wouldn't sleep with Amanda again. But Paul understood what she had been about to say.

'And you don't believe him?'

Marianne shook her head.

'Do you?'

'No, I don't believe him.'

'What did Amanda say to you?'

'She's said nothing to me. We haven't spoken about it.'

'I'm surprised,' Marianne said. 'Everyone else in the family seems to be talking about it. About Andrew. About her and Alex.'

He let out a deep sigh.

'It's all a mess to be honest. I've even begun to doubt I'm Matthew's father.'

She looked at him and shook her head.

'Alex assured me Matthew is your son.'

'Well, that's something, I suppose. But they've both lied to us before. Can we trust what they say?'

She shrugged, a hopeless, helpless gesture.

'You're right. Can we trust them? They'll lie about what they got up to last night, that's for sure,' she said. It hurt her to admit it.

'It was inevitable really. Alex has visited a lot lately when I've been away or at least not at home.'

'I suspected that,' Marianne said, 'but I always knew they were good friends. I wasn't surprised by that. I didn't necessarily read anything into it. Until now. Is that why you turned to Linda?'

He smiled and nodded.

'She's lovely. I enjoy being with her. She's told me she's in love with me.'

'And you? How do you feel about her?'

'I'm being cautious,' he said. 'I can't forget I have two small kids. But then there's the realisation I'll never be the love of Amanda's life.'

'Just like I'll never be the love of Alex's life,' Marianne said. 'You know they were already lovers before she got pregnant to him. I suspect they had a lovely time together at Glenmoral that Christmas. You know when I mean.'

'I do,' he said. 'It wasn't my finest hour, that's for sure. I got carried away asking Nancy to marry me. I was young and foolish.'

'That makes two of us,' Marianne said. 'Disappointing my parents by deliberately getting pregnant.'

'But at least little Mel is your daughter. I have one son who isn't mine and can I really be sure about Matthew. I'd convinced myself he looks like me, but who knows. I thought that about Andrew too.'

'You do realise if one marriage fails, the other will fail too,' she said.

'You mean if Amanda leaves me, then Alex will leave you for her. And vice versa.'

'I think so,' Marianne said. It was a moment of clarity for them both. 'Is Linda pressuring you?'

He shook his head.

'Not yet. I always said she could just flick me when she got tired of me. I think that was me just pretending I could easily give her up. My father said I shouldn't raise a young girl's hopes without being able to offer her a permanent relationship but I couldn't help myself.'

'Are you in love with her?'

He paused.

'Yes, I think I am,' he said. 'But don't tell my father, whatever you do. I've had enough lectures from him.'

She nodded. She understood his dilemma.

'Mum won't let my father talk to me about any of it because she's sure he'll just make matters worse.'

In the intensity of their conversation, neither of them noticed their respective fathers eyeing them speculatively from across the room.

'What do you reckon those two are talking about?' William asked his brother quietly.

'It wouldn't take two guesses, William,' he said. 'How did we end up in this mess? Your daughter and my son. Both their marriages in trouble.'

'What can we do?' his brother asked.

'Nothing. Absolutely nothing. And you have to keep your temper,' Richard said.

'Don't worry Alice has already reminded me of that,' he said. 'I'd better get about cooking these steaks.'

'One worried father by the look of it,' James Fitzroy said, as he came to stand alongside Richard.

'You could say that, James. Amanda and Alex have been away together at Glenmoral. They're getting back later today. No prizes for guessing what everyone thinks they've been up to while they've been away together.'

'I think you're right unfortunately. William must be finding it hard to keep his temper. I had a go at Alex and was told to mind my own business.'

'Does that surprise you?'

'No, it doesn't but he's breaking Marianne's heart and it's hard to stand by and see that happen. Whereas your son is being consoled by a lovely young girl who the gossips say is head over heels in love with him.'

'I was afraid of that,' Richard said. 'I knew he'd be susceptible. But he's always been like that. It's in his nature. If he breaks up with Amanda, it's all over for Marianne's marriage too, I would think.'

'I think you're right,' James said. 'Pity for those two lovely little girls. They idolise their father.'

'Yep, no winners in marriage breakdown but you and I both know that.'

'We do, mate, we do.'

'Have you asked Julia to marry you again?' Richard was curious. They seemed to be on good terms.

'I have.'

'What's she said?'

'Well, it wasn't an outright no.'

'You could move in with her in her new house. Leave the Mayfield Downs house for John when he gets married. If he gets married, that is.'

'The thought had occurred to me,' he said. 'We'll see. We'll see how she feels about it when the house is built. She now has a greater stake in Prior Park than before. That might have changed everything.'

'I hope so,' Richard said. 'I was delighted she suggested buying into our business. It just feels right.'

'So the American's money came in handy after all,' James said.

'It did,' Richard said. 'And the irony of it is it will be your son who benefits in the end.'

James nodded and smiled.

'That thought had occurred to me too. I'm delighted. He's over the moon too. He's always got on well with Paul and Marianne. I think he felt he let Marianne down. That he should have protected her from a bloke like Alex. That she was an easy target for him.'

'Well, if anyone's to blame, it's her parents. They didn't see she was a young woman who might fall prey to a charmer. They thought she was still a child. And they treated her like that,' Richard said, 'but to be fair we all liked Alex and he did a great job for us, until Amanda got the idea to share her inheritance with him. It changed everything.'

'So how's the new bloke working out? I've run into him on the Prior Park boundary a couple of times.'

'He's going well. Very much like his uncle. Solid. Reliable. Gets on with the work. We were lucky he turned up.'

'Indeed,' James said, as he noticed William gesturing to them to collect the steaks he had just cooked. 'We'd better go and collect our steaks.'

'Yes, we don't want to keep the cook waiting. That wouldn't improve his mood,' Richard said.

James laughed.

'No, it wouldn't, would it!'

29

'HOW WAS THE TRIP to Glenmoral? Have you been home long?' Paul asked as he carried Andrew's schoolbag into the kitchen.

Andrew had run ahead of him to greet his mother, keen to show her his scraped knees.

She hugged the boy briefly and looked at his injuries.

'How did you do that?' she asked. 'Does it sting?'

He shook his head.

'Not now. I fell over in the playground.'

'How did that happen?'

He shrugged.

'I spoke to his teacher,' Paul said. 'She thinks an older girl pushed him when he ran nearby. She doesn't know why.'

'Perhaps, being a boy, he was just annoying her,' Amanda suggested. The damage wasn't serious.

'Mel wasn't at school today,' Andrew announced in a worried voice. 'Do you think she was sick?'

Amanda looked enquiringly at Paul. Did he know? Was it meaningful? Or had she just been off colour.

'She was at Prior Park with her mother,' Paul said evenly. 'Anthony was presenting his big plans today. Maybe Marianne was worried she wouldn't get back in time to pick Mel up.'

'But you did,' Amanda said, suspicious now there might be more to little Mel's absence than it had at first appeared.

299

'Well, she had baby Laura with her too. Maybe she didn't want to risk having to drive fast to get back to the school in time.'

'You could have picked her up,' Amanda said.

'I don't suppose she was sure of what our arrangements were.'

It's as if I'm being interrogated about Marianne's motives for pulling little Mel out of school for a day, he thought. And then he realised she had successfully sidestepped any discussion of her trip with Alex.

He watched for a few moments as she resumed the task of feeding baby Matthew a bowl of pureed fruit. She had already set out a glass of milk and biscuits for Andrew, which he consumed at lightning speed before heading out into the backyard yelling to his new friend next door as he went to come and play with his soccer ball.

'He seems to be happy playing with that new boy next door. He doesn't go to the same school, does he?'

Amanda shook her head.

'No, his parents are Catholic. He's going to the Catholic primary school,' she said, 'but he seems like a nice little boy. His name's Carlos. Andrew can play a bit rougher with him than he can with little Mel. She's such a dainty little thing. But she likes to be involved in everything of course.'

'She does. I've noticed. Nathan Flynn, the project manager, was standing next to Marianne when little Mel almost pulled one of the plans off the table as she was pulling herself up so she could see. He promptly stood her on a chair so she could see everything. I noticed him having quite a conversation with Marianne. I had the feeling he'd sought her out.'

Amanda raised her eyebrows.

'Really! What's he like?'

'Mid-thirties I'd say. My father told me he's divorced. A very thorough project manager is my guess. He seems very capable.'

'Good looking?'

'I don't know. What makes a guy good looking? He's not ugly. He's nicely presented. Not a rough worker-type. Tall and strong.'

He was about to say not as good looking as Alex, but he

refrained. Did he really want to open that conversation? He decided against it and reached into the fridge to grab himself a beer.

'Are you drinking anything?' he asked.

'Later,' she said. 'I brought some wine back with me from Glenmoral which my father had stashed there.'

'Your father indulged in the finer things in life as I remember,' Paul said.

'Yes, he liked his wine. Probably too much for the good of his health. But it seemed to be one of his few indulgences. He certainly didn't spend money on his properties.'

'Does that mean Glenmoral needs money spent on it?'

'Yes, Tony was adamant. The yards are in poor condition and the road in is terrible now. He just didn't spend on maintenance.'

'So what's the plan?'

'Alex and I are going to have a look at the cash flow and then draw up a plan with Tony for improvements at Glenmoral. Then we move on to Isla Downs. At which point I think we should consider selling the two far western properties.'

'And Armoobilla?'

'No, it stays,' she said. 'I like to have a place close by. Perhaps we can get another place closer in too. Now tell me about the new house. What's it going to look like?'

'A smaller version of the original house,' he said, describing the plans Anthony had revealed and the startling discovery of the unlikely origins of the Belleville family name, his great grandfather's unexpected confession and the hoard of gold that had been eye opening.

'Your great grandfather sounds like a piece of work,' she said, 'but you have to admire him. He didn't have a great start in life. Just like Alex in many ways.'

Paul tensed at the mention of Alex's name. Before he could even think about what he was saying, words he hadn't meant to speak came tumbling out of him.

'Speaking of Alex, were you ever going to tell me he's Andrew's father, not me? Or were you waiting for me to tell you I'd realised it?'

'It's hard not to notice, isn't it?'

'It is. Everyone knows, including Marianne. He lied to her about his relationship with you. Just as you lied to me about who the father of your baby was.'

'I wasn't sure, Paul,' she said. She knew she had to say that. To go on lying.

'And Matthew?' he asked, indicating his baby son who was sitting quietly in his highchair surrounded by the debris of his meal.

'Matthew is your child,' she said. 'Of course he's your child.'

He admired her calmness. Or was it coldness? Was she really as devoid of emotion as she appeared at times? Except, that is, when he was making love to her. But even that was rare now. He couldn't remember the last time he had made love to her. But he was sure Alex had enjoyed that privilege the previous night.

He was tempted to take the irretrievable step of accusing her of sleeping with Alex. But he couldn't do it. He wasn't ready for the upheaval in his life. And he was sure she would have accusations ready to hurl at him, which he couldn't deny.

In fact, he realised they had reached an impasse. He wanted to be sure of his relationship with Linda. She wanted to be sure Alex was ready to move on from Marianne.

But there was no time for further conversation.

Raised voices from the backyard demanded his attention. Somehow, a game between two small boys had blossomed into a game involving six boys, some of them bigger than Andrew and his little mate from next door.

It was time for Paul to bring order to the impromptu soccer match that looked like turning into a rugby scrum with the older boys showing no mercy to the two six-year-olds.

A few streets away, Alex had returned home to an empty house and a scribbled note which he screwed up and threw in the bin. He noticed the house had an empty, forlorn feeling as if Marianne had left for good, so he was relieved to hear her car finally pull up in the driveway.

As he walked down the front steps, his first thought was to help her with the baby who rewarded him with a smile. A wide-eyed trusting smile that tore at his heart.

Little Mel, worried she was being ignored, tugged at his free arm. She was full of chatter about the pretty picture Anthony had drawn of the new house which was going to be built at Prior Park.

'Anthony's going to do a picture just for me,' she said earnestly. 'Then I can see it all being built. Nathan said he'll mark the days on the calendar when important things are happening so I can be there to see.'

'Who's Nathan?' Alex asked. It was a name he hadn't heard before.

'Nathan's Mummy's friend. He's in charge of building the house. He lifted me up on a chair so I could see everything Anthony was showing everyone. I'm not tall enough yet.'

He turned then to greet Marianne.

'It was quite a turnout at Prior Park by the sound of it,' he said as he kissed her on the cheek.

'It was,' Marianne said, ushering little Mel ahead of her. 'It's all very exciting. Anthony has produced a design that looks like the original house but isn't the original house, if you know what I mean.'

'Smaller, I assume?'

She nodded, grateful to be able to discuss a neutral topic.

'Yes, more compact, with a big country garden at the back.'

'I'm sure it will be beautiful,' Alex said, as they climbed the front stairs together. 'Little Mel is certainly excited about it. I take it she's made a friend of the project manager already.'

'He was very nice to her,' Marianne said. 'He knew exactly what to do to keep her quiet. We'll have to be careful and keep her out of the site. She'll want to help.'

'Well, maybe he's got kids of his own,' Alex said. 'Maybe he knows how to manage children around building sites.'

She shook her head.

'No, he doesn't have children. He's divorced. Came up from Brisbane to manage the new office. He wanted a new start.'

'Not an old man then?'

'No, he's probably mid-thirties,' Marianne said.

'And on the lookout for a new wife probably?'

She shrugged.

'Probably. I don't know anything about his personal life at all. We talked about the design Anthony has presented and whether it was achievable.'

'So when does building start?'

'Not sure. A lot of paperwork to do yet but he's going to hurry it along. Aunt Julia is keen to have her new house.'

She realised then he had diverted conversation away from what he had been doing with Amanda. Clever really, she thought, as she busied herself with the baby.

'I think Mel is going to drive us mad wanting to be taken out there every other day once the building work starts.'

'Probably,' Marianne said. 'It will be interesting to see it getting built. I know my father will be pleased to see something happen with the site. He and Uncle Richard could never agree on what should be done.'

He watched in silence as she prepared to bathe the baby, knowing the inevitable questions must come soon. He was struggling to read her mood. Was she still angry with him? Or was she determined to put it all behind her? He couldn't tell.

'So how was your trip to Glenmoral?' she asked, glancing at him.

'It was good,' Alex said carefully. 'We spent a lot of time with Tony Bland riding around, having a look at everything. I didn't realise the property had become so rundown. The yards need a complete rebuild and the road into the property is in very bad condition.'

'I take it you weren't expecting that?'

He shook his head.

'No, but Amanda thinks her father hoarded the cash and wanted to make sure all the debt was cleared by the time she inherited it all.'

'So what happens next?' she asked as she concentrated on baby Laura.

'Isla Downs is next on the list once we decide how much money we can allocate for improvements at Glenmoral. I've got to start looking out for more cattle too. We probably need to improve the quality of the bulls and buy in some young females. That's my job, apparently.'

'Which means being away from home more?'

'Possibly,' he said.

'With Amanda?'

'Not always.'

Neither of them had noticed little Mel standing quietly in the doorway of the bathroom. She was listening intently.

'Our daughter announced to her grandmother today that Andrew is her brother. I told her she couldn't go around saying that. It's a secret.'

She glanced over her shoulder and noticed a look of alarm on his face.

'Paul told me he and Amanda haven't spoken about Andrew. Did you know that?'

He shrugged his shoulders. He was cautious. How could he recount the conversation he'd had with Amanda? It was too intimate. Too revealing. Marriage ending even.

'I'm not sure if they've spoken about it directly or not.'

'But she's spoken with you about Andrew?' Marianne asked. Her voice seemed to Alex to be devoid of any emotion.

'She has,' he said, without elaborating.

Say as little as possible, he reminded himself.

'Paul isn't sure now that Matthew is his child.' She turned to look at him. 'I reassured him he was. Was I wrong to do that?'

He noticed the edge in her voice, the unspoken accusation.

'No, he is Paul's child,' Alex said, his voice emphatic. He was trying to hide his annoyance the question had come up again. Even by asking him again, she was saying she didn't believe him.

And then he felt a little hand slip into his.

'Daddy, can you run me a bath?'

He smiled. Was there ever a more timely intervention from a child, he wondered?

The atmosphere that had grown tense relaxed. Marianne headed to the nursery with the baby wrapped in a warm towel. Alex filled the bath and tested the water until he considered the temperature was just right for little Mel. He assembled her favourite toys and sat on the edge of the bath while she splashed to her heart's content.

Had she realised the next question her mother was about to ask would almost certainly have burst the happy family bubble in which they lived? He balanced bubbles on her little upturned nose and she giggled. But then she became serious.

'Promise me you and Mummy won't argue any more,' she said. 'Please don't make Mummy cross.'

'I promise, darling,' he said, as he added extra bubble bath to create more bubbles and elicit more giggles. 'We love each other. Just like we love you.'

She smiled, satisfied. Her father would never let her down. She was sure of it.

30

'IT'S LOVELY TO HAVE you here,' he said as he hauled Catherine's suitcases from the boot of his car. 'The weather's great at the moment.'

His pleasure was genuine. Hers too. Being separated from him for months at a time wasn't her choice. Nor his. But they had accepted geography would keep them apart at times.

'Did you bring your entire wardrobe with you?' he asked with a laugh.

'No. Do you think I should have?' she teased as he struggled with her luggage.

'Come to think of it, no. I'd have to buy the house next door if you did that. By the way, did you see Anthony in Sydney?'

She shook her head.

'No, we just spoke on the phone. He was up to his neck in work, finishing his assignments and keeping up with the work on Julia's house. He said he'll be up here in a couple of days' time to check on progress and to celebrate his birthday. You hadn't forgotten his birthday, had you?'

'Of course not,' Richard said. 'We'll have the usual Sunday family lunch at Prior Park to celebrate. I didn't get a chance to tell you Susan is coming up too for a couple of days. She wants to stay at Prior Park though.'

'That's good,' Catherine said. 'It will be a full complement of our family then. I take it the shaky marriages are still trundling along.'

'For now,' he said as he headed to the living room to pour drinks for them. 'It's pretty tense at times.'

'Is our elder son still being wayward?'

'That's a nice way of putting it,' Richard said as he let out a deep sigh. 'At last count he's been to Brisbane three times in the past month.'

'And Amanda?'

'A couple of trips away with Alex in that time. Generally just overnight. I'm pretty sure she's enjoyed herself with him. It's getting to be obvious actually.'

'In what way?'

He shrugged.

'Just little things when I see them together, especially if Marianne isn't around. Or Paul. I was at the cattle sale earlier this week and one bloke said to me isn't that your son's wife? She seems pretty close with Alex Fraser.'

'What did you say?'

'*Yes*, and *do you think so?*'

She laughed at his retelling of the conversation.

'So it's obvious they're intimate, is that what you're saying?'

'Well, men don't usually notice things like that so for him to notice, I'd say Alex was getting pretty familiar with her, wouldn't you? I was trying to avoid them. So was William.'

'My goodness, William must be ready to explode at him.'

'He is,' Richard said. 'Alice has kept him on a tight leash fortunately. And the children are always with them when they visit Prior Park so they act as a buffer.'

'And how is Paul coping?'

'The way Paul copes. Head in the sand. Doesn't want to talk about it. Not to me anyway. I think he and Marianne chat a bit, which is good.'

'But this girl Paul is seeing isn't going to want the relationship to go on forever without having some clear future surely?'

'I wouldn't think so,' Richard said. 'I think our son is deciding if he's in love with her. I think he wants to be certain after the fiasco with Nancy and now Amanda. And he's still not convinced about Matthew.'

'Well, that's the problem, isn't it? Amanda deceived him once. What's to say she wouldn't do so again,' Catherine said.

'Why don't you ask her,' Richard suggested.

'Me? Ask her if she's lied to my son about whether he's Matthew's father? I couldn't do it.'

Richard shook his head.

'She wouldn't be like that. She admires you.'

This was all news to Catherine.

'Well, I'll go and see her tomorrow. And we'll see what she's willing to talk about.'

And then she looked him up and down.

'My mother would have been mortified to know you are descended from a convict woman,' Catherine said. Richard had written her a long letter about the discovery at Prior Park. 'And the French name of Belleville. Picked from a place name on a map. Your grandfather sounded like quite an adventurer.'

'I think he had to be,' Richard said. 'Without that spirit he would have been crushed by his circumstances.'

'I agree. Do you think your brother takes after the Prior side of the family?'

'Definitely,' Richard said. 'I was talking it over with William. I suggested that Louis Belleville had married for financial advantage and so had his son, our father. I think William was shocked by that but in the end, he agreed with me. I don't think our mother was the love of our father's life, sadly.'

'I guess that would have been his mistress,' Catherine suggested.

'I think so. And to think we have our own version of that in the family now.'

'You mean Alex and Marianne?'

He nodded his head slowly.

'I do. He's always been in love with Amanda. Don't forget I saw them together in the early days at Glenmoral after Paul's rescue. They just sparked off one another.'

'She should have got pregnant to him then. That would have resolved her father's issues pretty quickly.'

'Indeed. But she never wanted to go against her father. I think it was because he was the only person she really had. And meeting her mother didn't go so well.'

'Did you expect it would after all this time and the fact that she thought her mother was dead? It would be hard for her to insert herself into her mother's life now. And vice versa. Her mother wouldn't want to risk her other children reacting badly.'

'No, I guess not,' he said, letting out a deep sigh.

'You can't solve all the family problems, Richard,' she said.

He smiled. It was so good to have her to talk to. He'd missed that. More than he had realised.

'Anyway, how was Greece?' Richard asked. 'And George?'

'Greece was marvellous. I needed you there though. Because I was alone, I got propositioned at least once a day.'

'You weren't alone. You had George with you.'

'Sixteen-year-old sons don't count, apparently.'

'Were you tempted?'

She smiled, as if remembering an encounter, but she was teasing him.

'A Greek lover. Now, there's a problem I don't need. I don't think George would have approved. He would have reported everything about the holiday back to his father.'

'And you think I would have approved?'

She laughed quietly.

'Of course not,' she said, as he embraced her again. 'After a few days in Athens, we spent five days on Crete in a wonderful hotel. Picture it. The Aegean Sea sparkling in the background with beautiful food being served on an open terrace under a brilliant night sky.'

'Next time, I will come with you,' he said, 'whether George likes it or not.'

'I hope so,' she said. 'We can't put our life on hold because Paul's marriage might implode. Or because my ex-husband will worry that you'd exert a bad influence on George. Anyway, Edward has his own problems. A demanding wife, I'm told.'

'How does George get on with her?' Richard asked.

'He ignores her. Which infuriates her, he says. And she's annoyed George will inherit his father's title and not her son. Their son is only three years old. George describes him as the spare.'

Richard laughed out loud. He couldn't imagine thinking of his sons in that way.

'All that angst over a mere baronetcy. Just as well it's not a dukedom or George mightn't be safe from his wicked stepmother.'

Catherine laughed too at the absurdity of it.

'Anyway I'm pleased to see he's growing up to be his own man and not exactly in his father's image as I thought he would, which is a relief. He enjoyed himself on the holiday. Swimming and boating and chatting up a few English girls who were staying in the hotel. I let him have a drink too on the strict understanding he wouldn't tell his father. Europeans are far more relaxed about that sort of thing. He wants to come out to spend time in Sydney with me sometime in the future. He'd like to see Anthony especially.'

'If Anthony goes through with the wedding, he'll want to come out for that.'

'That wouldn't be a problem for you?' she asked.

'No, of course not. Apart from the fact that there were times I could have knocked his father out cold, I don't feel the same about George. He's just a kid. A bit like Andrew. He isn't responsible for the sins of the father, if you get my meaning.'

She smiled, relieved at Richard's attitude.

'He isn't, is he. He and his father have started to argue a bit. I don't think Edward realises that's the way with teenage boys, pushing back against their father's authority. Edward is always trying to pull him into line, he says.'

'Does that work?'

'What do you think? I suspect you're still trying to pull Paul into line. Has he told you to mind your own business yet?'

He grimaced.

'He has. In not very polite terms. He reminded me he's no longer a schoolboy.'

'Well, I understand why you try. He's a young man who seems to be capable of getting himself into trouble over women. A family trait, do you think?'

He laughed. She was teasing him. He had got himself into trouble over women, that was for sure. But he was settled now.

'Well, I'm not sure I should admit to having the family trait but the evidence is there if you care to look, I suppose.'

The daylight had faded as they sat together. He got up and turned on the lamps in the living room as nice aromas began to waft from the kitchen.

'Something smells good,' she said.

'Mrs Harper's cooking barramundi for us. Her son has just come back from a fishing trip up north.'

'You're lucky to have a reliable housekeeper,' Catherine said.

'Yes, I am, considering that my wife won't cook and keep house for me,' he said with a smile. 'That's the problem with marrying aristocratic ladies.'

She laughed and shrugged her shoulders.

'I can mix a great cocktail though. And make endless small talk to the most boring people. I do have some excellent qualities. They're just not related to being tied to the kitchen.'

He embraced her affectionately.

'And I wouldn't change any part of you,' he said. 'You haven't told me how things are going at Haldon Hall?'

'They're going well. I have a good agent. I hope you'll come across in the spring to spend some time there. I think it reassures my tenant farmers to see my husband about the place.'

'I will,' he said. 'I promise. Have you had any second thoughts about how you are leaving your estate?'

'You mean cutting George out of a share of Haldon House?'

He nodded. He had been thinking about it. Was her plan really the best one? Anthony was about to become an architect based in Sydney. Paul was very unlikely to swap Australia for England.

'I have actually. George raised it with me. He likes Haldon Hall. More than he likes Grantham Manor. There was no pressure from him but he did wonder if I might consider adding him into the trust with Paul and Anthony. He actually spent a week with me back in England and he met some of the tenant farmers. I was surprised. He seemed to have a good way of dealing with them.'

'Then you have your answer,' Richard said. 'Haldon Hall will need someone interested in it for it to continue as it is. You should discuss it with Paul and Anthony.'

'And the work you do with Prior Park Holdings? Who's going to take that over?'

'Anthony maybe. Or Paul and Anthony together. I've been discussing some new investment ideas with them. Paul thinks we have enough exposure to cattle. He's probably right. Julia's investment has paid down a couple of loans but there is a substantial wad of cash on the short term money market until we decide what to do.'

'With Alex involved with Amanda's properties now, who's going to take over William's role?'

'John Fitzroy, we hope.'

'Of course. He's going to inherit his mother's share. That was convenient. Did William object to having her as a partner?'

'Not after a little persuasion.'

'He doesn't like change, does he?'

'No, but he was happy that Julia doesn't want to interfere. She's done it for John, really. And he likes John.'

'I'll be keen to see the progress on her new house,' she said. 'Once Julia has a new house, she'll need a new husband.'

'Or a recycled one.'

'Is that still on the cards? She doesn't talk about it much. Not with me anyway.'

'It could be,' Richard said. 'James wants it, I believe. I think Julia is still undecided.'

'Well, whatever happens, I hope it's her choice. That she isn't pressured into it.'

'I agree. No pressure from me. I'm finished with meddling in other people's private lives. It's a very unproductive activity.'

'It is indeed,' she said, knowing all the while he would continue to worry about their son and the state of his marriage.

'How I envy you,' Amanda said as she placed baby Matthew on a rug on the floor. 'Your holiday sounds wonderful.'

'It was,' Catherine said as she sipped her coffee. She had kept her promise to Richard to look in on her daughter-in-law the next morning.

'I never got a chance to travel,' Amanda lamented. 'An elderly father to look after and then kids.'

'Well, they won't be small forever.'

'But you managed to travel when you were first married to Richard and the children were small. Paul said there were times he was left at Prior Park with his father.'

'Well, it wasn't practical in those days to travel with a small child. And Alice was so good at looking after him. And then Anthony. Better than me, really. All of us living at Prior Park made life a bit easier. And then eventually I didn't come back.'

'Was your marriage breakup difficult?' Amanda asked. It was almost as if she was testing the waters, trying to decide if she could endure the upheaval in her own life. 'Was distance the reason? Was it the life you were leading here?'

'The reasons were complex but I was unhappy here. It wasn't the life I was brought up to lead. I was missing my family and my friends. I was missing the social life I could have had in England.'

'Did you fall out of love with Richard?'

Catherine hesitated. She wondered how Amanda had managed to turn the conversation to focus on her and Richard, rather than on her relationship with Paul.

'For a time, I probably did.'

'I heard gossip he was unfaithful to you. Was he?'

'Why do you ask that?'

Catherine could guess but she wanted Amanda to spell it out. Her questions had been unexpectedly direct, prying into their private life in a way no one else had ever done. Except perhaps her mother.

'Because Paul is doing exactly the same thing his father probably did. He's stuck his head in the sand. Won't talk about things. But he's not even trying to hide his affair from me now.'

'I think he's disappointed in what he found out about Andrew,' Catherine said, sidestepping the question about Richard. It wasn't something she wanted to revisit.

'I know. But I didn't know for sure who Andrew's father was. Not until after he was born.'

Catherine looked closely at her, trying to decide whether she was telling the truth.

'But it's more than that, isn't it?' Catherine asked. 'You're not in love with Paul anymore, are you?'

She watched Amanda carefully. Had she been shocked by the question? Catherine couldn't tell. Or was it that she hadn't really confronted her own feelings until this moment.

A tense silence settled between them.

Catherine persisted.

'Richard told me Paul believes you're seeing Alex. I know he's your business partner now. But has he become more than that?'

'And if I answer that question, what happens then?' Amanda snapped. 'What will you do?'

'Me? I won't do anything,' Catherine insisted. 'I just want you to face up to what's happening in your life. And if you have to, to take the steps to change it, just as I did. Or you can go on with your life as it is and ignore what Paul's doing, hoping he'll extend you the same courtesy.'

'You know I'll pay a price either way.'

'Why is that?' Catherine asked.

'I'll always be seen as the marriage wrecker. Of my own marriage because everyone will believe I deliberately duped Paul into marrying me and then tried to pass off a child that wasn't his. And because Alex will eventually admit he wants to be with me and not Marianne. Everyone will be sorry for Marianne. They'll never feel sorry for me. They'll never see anything from my point of view. I never seemed to be allowed to make my own decisions.'

In that moment, Catherine understood more about Amanda than she ever had.

'You mean because your father wouldn't consider Alex as a potential husband and you felt obliged to please your father rather than yourself? And then, being pregnant, you had to cover up who the father was, again to please him?'

Catherine got up and sat next to her. She put her arm around Amanda.

'You didn't have anyone else, did you? If your father disowned you, you had no one.'

Amanda nodded, tears forming in her eyes.

'Do you have any idea what a lonely feeling that is? Only Alex understood that because he had no one either. But I was trying to pretend it didn't matter. No one in the Belleville family understands that. I always felt like an outsider. Just like Alex felt like an outsider. I think they all thought I was difficult.'

'Did having the children change that feeling at all?' Catherine asked. 'Do you feel more secure?'

'When they're older, possibly. But not yet. I sometimes wish I'd had a daughter.'

'Yes, well, I wasn't lucky there either,' Catherine said. 'My youngest son surprised me though when we were on holidays. He was very thoughtful.'

'I guess he's different from Paul and Anthony.'

'He is. Quite different. Their fathers are very different men.'

'So what caused your second marriage to fail?'

'Edward came to regard me as a trophy, not a wife. We drifted apart. He worked for the Foreign Office, then resigned but remained in their orbit working for them as they required on special missions. It was then I realised how much I still loved Richard and missed him.'

'Paul always hoped you and Richard would get back together when Kate left him.'

'I know. Does knowing my history help you in any way?' Catherine asked, unsure why Amanda wanted to know so much.

'Perhaps,' Amanda said. 'I'm trying to look into the future. Trying to understand how it might all work out. How did you decide what to do?'

Catherine looked at her and smiled.

'I let my heart rule my head.'

'Meaning?'

Catherine sidestepped the question. The truth was it had taken a bad decision on her part to realise where her heart belonged. But the parallels were startling between Richard and his son. Richard had closed himself off to her just as Paul had to Amanda. But there were differences too, she decided. Despite everything, she believed Richard had never stopped loving her. She was less sure about how Paul felt about Amanda. And the issue of Andrew's parentage would always come between them.

'All you need to do is ask yourself one question. Who am I in love with? Who is it I can't live without?'

'And if the answer to that question isn't your son?'

Catherine shook her head slowly from side to side.

'It doesn't matter what I think, Amanda. I didn't come here to plead Paul's case. If I have any advice for you at all, it's to follow your heart, but I think you're already doing that. Alex has become your lover again, hasn't he?'

'Yes, he has,' she said, without elaboration. 'Does that shock you?'

'No, not really. Richard told me how keen Alex was on you when he first met you both at Glenmoral. It's a shame your father was so against the marriage. I understand why but you should have taken matters into your own hands then.'

'You mean got pregnant to him?'

'Yes. Your father would have relented then.'

'I tried but it didn't work out.'

'And Alex was set on making a good marriage believing you would never have him as a husband.'

'Yes, that's right,' she said, 'and then I got pregnant to him too late.'

'You did, my dear,' Catherine said. 'And in doing so you created a whole world of trouble you didn't mean to. But spare a thought for Marianne, it must be difficult for her seeing Andrew and knowing her husband is his father.'

'I realise that. She hardly speaks to me these days.'

'And how does Alex feel? Have you asked him what he wants to do?'

'I think he's like all men. Doesn't want to take the tough decisions. It will be up to me. And to Marianne, I think.'

'Have you considered he may still love Marianne?' Catherine asked. She wondered if Amanda's confidence in Alex was misplaced.

She shook her head.

'I'm sure he has feelings for her but he doesn't love her in the way he loves me. But he's worried about his two daughters of course.'

'So will you put pressure on him to leave Marianne?'

She shook her head.

'He has to come to the decision to end his marriage in his own time. Or Marianne will.'

'You mean if Marianne realises he's involved with you again?'

'Yes. He could have said no to me. But he didn't,' Amanda said.

Catherine smiled to herself. Hadn't she and Richard reignited their passion for one another illicitly?

'You did the same thing with Richard, didn't you?' Amanda asked unexpectedly. 'You were still married. He was still married. So you'll know how it feels.'

'I do,' she said. 'I do know.'

All the while, baby Matthew had entertained himself and made some unsuccessful attempts to crawl off the blanket. Amanda picked him up and sat him on her lap.

'He's a fine looking child,' Catherine said.

'He is, isn't he? I'm still trying to convince Paul he's Matthew's father.'

'He doesn't believe you?'

She shrugged her shoulders.

'He thinks if I lied about Andrew I could lie about Matthew too.'

'He'll come to his senses,' Catherine said. 'If ever a baby looked like Paul, this is the one.'

'I know,' Amanda said. 'There's no chance anyone but Paul is his father. Will you reassure Paul for me please. You're his mother. He'll listen to you. I don't want him to think badly of me. I'm not a bad person.'

'Of course you're not a bad person,' Catherine said. 'I just hope the two of you get your lives sorted out. You both deserve to be happy.'

'We will,' Amanda reassured her. 'We will.'

They sat in silence for a few moments, each thinking about what had been discussed.

For Catherine it had revived memories of the tortured path she had taken to a settled life. Pregnant to Richard as the war ended, transported to the far side of the world as a bride, failing to settle, hoping another baby would make the difference, their marriage descending into bitter unhappiness until her return to England.

And then her realisation the marriage she had with Edward had become a sham and that her heart belonged to the man across the other side of the world. The failure of their second marriages had been a turning point.

As she thought about her life, a startling moment of clarity emerged.

'Your marriage to Paul really is over, isn't it?' she said.

After a long pause, Amanda finally broke the silence.

'Yes, it's over. It couldn't survive the revelations about Andrew. Paul tried but I knew he would never be able to cope with the knowledge that Andrew is Alex's son and not his. We just haven't had the final conversation yet'

Catherine smiled reassuringly. She had long ago decided that factor alone would be enough to end her son's marriage.

'I'm sorry it hasn't worked as we all hoped,' Catherine said.

'I am too,' Amanda said.

But in that moment, Catherine noticed Amanda smile as if a heavy weight had been lifted from her shoulders.

31

'I VISITED AMANDA THIS morning,' Catherine said, 'and met baby Matthew. He's a lovely baby.'

Her son Paul, sitting alongside her, groaned inwardly. He knew now why his father wasn't around. He guessed what was coming. Angry words formed in his mind. *Don't interfere in my life. I'll sort out my private life.* But he couldn't say those words. Not to his mother.

Still, he wondered if she understood how bitter he was at being forced into a marriage he always suspected had been based on a lie. And he had been proved right.

'Yes, he's a fine looking baby,' he replied. 'He had some restless nights early on but he seems settled now.'

He paused, waiting for what he knew for sure was coming next.

'He looks very much like you looked as a baby,' she said. 'You don't doubt he's your child, do you?'

'Did Amanda put you up to this?'

'Well, she's worried you don't believe her that you're his father.'

'So Amanda has suddenly become the most truthful person we know, has she? History would suggest otherwise.'

Catherine was shocked to hear the bitterness in his voice. It was unmistakeable.

'Let's calm down,' she said soothingly. 'Let me tell you the story of a young woman with limited options.'

'What do you mean limited options?' he demanded.

'You haven't thought about this, have you? You only see it from your point of view but she was a young woman, pregnant when she shouldn't have been, probably ninety percent sure the father of her baby was someone who was already married but she knew she would get pressure to get married so she named you as the father. Which meant you were getting pressure from your father to marry her. She was in a bind. I believe she went along with it, hoping the baby would look like her. It was the toss of a coin really and she lost.'

She paused for breath, surprised that he had said nothing. Instead he sat with his head in his hands for some time before turning to look at his mother.

'It's all a mess, isn't it? The result is I'm bringing up a child who isn't mine. As much as I try, I can't get past that fact. I see Alex in him every time I look at him.'

'And how do you feel about Amanda?'

The question had to be asked, Catherine decided.

Again he hesitated. He let out a deep sigh.

'I've been asking myself that question for some time,' he said finally.

'And the answer?'

'I think our marriage is over, if I'm honest.'

'Because you no longer love her or because of Andrew?'

'Both, I suppose,' he said. 'Andrew would always be there between us but it's more than that. It's obvious she prefers Alex. Compared with him, I feel like the consolation prize.'

'That's a brutal assessment of your marriage,' his mother said.

'Brutal or not, it's the truth,' he said.

'So is it serious with Linda?'

'Yes, it is. We get on very well. She's obsessed with flying too. We make a great team.'

His mother noticed the genuine pleasure in his smile as he spoke about her. Just like Amanda and Alex make a great team, she thought.

'Well, just don't get her pregnant,' his mother warned. 'Don't complicate your life further.'

He laughed, shaking his head. It's the sort of advice a mother gives an eighteen-year-old, he thought.

'No, she doesn't want kids. Not yet anyway. She said she'd had enough of her younger sisters when she was growing up.' He paused. 'Linda's father is none too pleased with me, I can tell you that.'

'Well, he's not going to be over the moon about a married man with two kids pursuing his daughter, is he? Will you marry her if your marriage ends?'

'I'm not rushing into a new marriage,' he said.

'Have you told her that?'

'I have. Of course I have. We'll go on seeing one another and live together when we can, but marriage isn't on the cards immediately.'

She thought about what he had said. It made sense. Far better for the relationship to become well established first.

'So what happens now?' she asked. 'Have you made any plans?'

'I have actually. Do you remember the house originally bought for me and Nancy but then I moved in with Amanda? The house has been rented since then. The tenants moved out two months ago. I suggested to Dad we keep it vacant. He agreed. It's been repainted and recarpeted and a new kitchen and bathroom installed. I plan to move in there.'

'So all that remains is to have a conversation with Amanda?'

'Yes, that's how I see it. Is that how she sees it? You obviously had a long conversation with her this morning.'

All of a sudden, it occurred to Catherine she was the one acting as the catalyst for change in the debacle that her son's marriage had become.

'Talk to her, Paul. You are two unhappy people at the present time. I think you can both move on with your lives, but whatever happens, don't treat her with disrespect. She's the mother of your child. You'll have to go on dealing with her in the future.'

'I'll talk to her. I still worry about Marianne though.'

'You must do what is right for you. Marianne and Alex must make their own decisions.'

'I know. But somehow, I can't help but feel Marianne is the innocent in it all and she's probably going to get hurt the most.'

'You're sure Alex will leave her for Amanda?'

'He will, I'm sure of it. I know he's already back in Amanda's bed when they go visiting the properties together. Marianne knows. She's turned a blind eye to it so far but she's worried he'll get Amanda pregnant again. I think that would be the ultimate humiliation for her.'

Catherine was surprised Paul had discussed so much with Marianne.

'Trust me, Marianne is stronger than you think. She'll get over it. She'll make a new life for herself and the children.'

He nodded. His mother was right. Marianne was sensible and resilient. He hoped she would find someone else.

'Thanks for the chat. And the advice. It's helped,' he said.

She smiled.

'That's what interfering mothers are for,' she said as she got up and turned to go inside. 'I know it's early but it must be time for a gin and tonic. It's been a trying day.'

'I'll join you,' he said, as he headed to the kitchen for a beer.

Having a social drink with his mother was a rare event. She brought a sense of calm to his life that no one else had ever been able to do. And he was grateful for it.

For the first few minutes at the building site at Prior Park, Anthony heard nothing. He heard nothing of what Nathan Flynn was telling him. Nothing of the detailed explanation of progress so far, of the milestones that had been reached and of what remained to be done.

He was focused instead on the new house finally emerging from the ruins, seeing, for the first time, his plans become reality. This moment would never happen again, he thought. Whatever he designed in the future, this was the first house. This would always be the benchmark of his work. Possibly his best work.

'I thought your aunt would be with you,' Nathan said, trying to gain Anthony's attention.

He shook his head and looked towards Nathan, acknowledging his presence for the first time.

'She'll be here later,' he said. 'I'll go over everything with her. It looks wonderful.'

'Is it how you imagined it would look?' Nathan asked.

In his experience, plans on paper and artist's impressions of houses sometimes bore little resemblance to what was built.

'Yes. It's better,' Anthony said. 'It looks as though it belongs here. Do we have a firm finish date yet?'

It was, after all, the question he had been asked repeatedly.

'Your family getting impatient, are they? Looks like there's a deputation about to descend on us,' he said, nodding in the direction of the existing house.

First in the group was Marianne with little Mel, who was tugging impatiently at her mother's hand.

'Your little cousin looks as if she's ready to give us her opinion,' Nathan said quietly. 'I've seen her and her mother here at the site quite a bit.'

As little Mel arrived, Nathan greeted her warmly. He lifted her up onto a small pile of bricks that had been used to create a platform for the sole purpose of giving her a better view of the site.

'I take it this is a regular part of her site visits,' Anthony said.'

Nathan nodded and grinned.

'She has her own little hard hat too. Watch this.'

She stood there patiently for a few moments and then pointed to her head. He had the hat hidden behind his back.

'It's our little game,' he said. 'She's a lovely kid.'

Marianne hugged Anthony affectionately. She was delighted to see him, having seen little enough of him as the two of them were growing up.

'How's life?' he asked quietly. 'I've been hearing things.'

'I'm coping,' she said simply.

'It must be tough, seeing Andrew often.'

'It is,' she said, as Richard, William and Susan joined them and the opportunity for further conversation was lost as Nathan began to give the newcomers a shorter version of the update he had given Anthony.

'I'm pleased to hear the build is going well,' Richard said. 'I think my sister is going to be very happy when she sees it.'

Ever cautious William had taken up a position beside his granddaughter, worried she would fall.

'Does she always get this preferential treatment?' William asked, with a broad smile.

Nathan looked at Marianne.

'Her mother thought it was a good idea to keep her from wandering where she shouldn't,' he said in a quiet voice.

'So what do you think, Mel?' he asked. 'Will it be a good house?'

She nodded gravely.

'It will be lovely but it should have a pink door,' she suggested.

But he shook his head, reminding her he had solved the pink door issue with her already.

'No, we agreed. The pink door is reserved for your house,' he said. 'Mel's house. It can't be on both houses.'

He knew not to call it little Mel's house. William looked around, first at Marianne and then at Nathan. This was something new he hadn't heard about.

'I've promised to build a little house for Mel in her backyard. We're going to use surplus timber and bricks. She's very excited about it.'

Her grandfather smiled broadly.

'That's a lovely idea,' he said enthusiastically.

'Is Mel getting her own tree house? I got a tree house at Berrima Park when I was a kid,' Susan said. 'Daniel designed it and had it built for me when he was doing renovations.'

Anthony knew it had been an innocent remark but he glanced at his father and understood instantly it might have been better left unsaid. He guessed it had been the means by which Daniel Harrington had ingratiated himself with Kate. And then a thought suddenly occurred to him. Was Nathan Flynn doing the same?

Had someone told him Marianne's marriage was in deep trouble? The parallels were striking, he thought.

'I've done a quick sketch for Nathan of Mel's house,' he said, producing his sketch pad for inspection while hoping everyone would ignore what his sister had said.

'It won't be a tree house,' Nathan said. 'Marianne says there aren't any trees big enough to support it, but we'll put it on a small platform. It's having white windows and a pink front door.'

Little Mel turned her attention back to the big house.

'What colour will the front door be if it's not pink?' she asked in a worried voice.

'It will be a pretty colour,' Anthony said, 'but it's all a secret at the moment until Aunt Julia makes some final decisions. You wouldn't want her making decisions about your house, would you?'

She shook her head, losing her little hard hat in the process which Nathan promptly restored to her head.

William drew Nathan to one side.

'You'll need extra cash for little Mel's house,' he said quietly. 'Just drop up to the house next week and see me. I want this to be special.'

'Well, we can pretty much cover the materials from this job, but I do need to pay for some labour if we're going to do it properly and get the little windows and door specially made.'

'Let's do it properly,' William said. 'Whatever you need.'

'The words of an indulgent granddad,' he said.

'Well, it gives me pleasure to see her happy so anything I can do to make the little girl happy, I will,' he said.

Nathan turned back to Anthony who seemed satisfied with progress so far.

'Uncle William just upped the specs on little Mel's house I take it?'

Nathan laughed.

'You're right. He did. I think she'll be able to get anything she wants from him in the future.'

'You seem to like her too?'

'She's impossible not to like. I've warned the men to watch their language when she's around but they all think she's a great kid too so they haven't minded. Quite a few of them have kids of a similar age.'

'And you? No kids?'

'No, never got around to it. My wife was too busy with her career in public relations. She was out most nights doing events. I could have gone with her but it wasn't my scene. We drifted apart. And you? How's the girlfriend?'

'Victoria is wonderful. We're being low key though. She won't be divorced until next year. What's our timeframe here?'

The house was well under way but there was still a lot to do.

'Six months, give or take.'

'So Easter next year?'

'That should do it,' Nathan agreed. 'Then we can pop the champagne corks.'

'There'll certainly be champagne,' Anthony said. 'It will be a milestone for the Belleville family. All thanks to my Aunt Julia.'

'And to her generous ex-husband,' Nathan said.

'Indeed. His money's been put to good use. Just a word of warning though. We don't talk about him at Prior Park.'

'Ah. Because it's one of the family scandals, I assume.'

'Indeed. And there'll be more too,' Anthony said.

'I got that feeling,' Nathan said cautiously.

'Must be something in the water,' Anthony said as he lifted little Mel down from her vantage point.

As Nathan watched them walk off, he began to speculate. Was it too much to hope that Marianne's marriage would collapse very soon? Was that what Anthony was referring to?

Each time he had met her, he had been drawn to her. They had laughed and chatted together so easily. He wouldn't let the opportunity slip through his fingers if she became single again.

The thought brightened his day as he tidied the site and finally headed home.

32

JULIA STOOD WITH HER daughter Pippa in front of the partially completed building listening intently as Anthony explained the intricacies of the building process and the work that remained to be done. She was flanked on either side by her brothers. Having arrived late the previous afternoon, this was her first opportunity to view the progress.

'Anthony, it looks wonderful',' she said. 'It's like a dream becoming reality. What do you think?'

She had turned to look at each of her brothers in turn, hoping they shared her enthusiasm. Apart from herself, Richard and William were the only ones who had known the old house intimately because it had been their home from childhood.

But for Alice and Catherine, who stood together a little apart from the others, memories came flooding back too.

'I remember the first day I arrived here,' Catherine exclaimed. 'It all seems so long ago. A lifetime ago. I remember what an uncomfortable trip it had been. And so hot.'

'What I remember,' Alice said, 'is how my mother-in-law was convinced the telegram was a mistake. It said something like *bringing wife*. She couldn't believe Richard would have the audacity to marry without her approval. It was the only time I ever saw her rendered speechless.'

William remembered too. He and Alice had already been

married for more than a year.

'We could never have foreseen what would happen in the future,' he said with a heavy sigh. 'Even now it's hard to believe.'

'I know,' Julia said. 'I just hope the new house will erase some of those painful memories.'

He shook his head.

'Nothing can completely erase them,' he said, 'but the new house will give us new memories and perhaps in time the painful memories will recede.'

As they turned to walk back to the house for lunch, Julia stopped and put her hand on Richard's arm.

'What's happening with Paul and Amanda? They seem very tense,' she remarked.

'I think their marriage is over,' Richard said. 'It's just neither of them has made the final move as far as I know.'

'And Alex and Marianne? She wasn't very talkative. Busy with baby Laura of course. Perhaps the baby gave her a bad night.'

'Same problem. Neither of them has made the final move. It's like playing chess. Someone is going to have to concede they've lost.'

'So this could be the final lunch before the winds of change blow through the family?'

'More than likely. Two marriages failing is something I hoped I wouldn't see in our children's generation.'

'Well, you and I survived marriage upheaval,' she said. 'They can too.'

But there was more to Richard's worries than the marriages.

'I worry what's going to happen with Andrew. He's not a Belleville. Will he continue to be brought up believing he is? Would it be unfair if he isn't? Will he feel excluded?'

'What do you suggest?' his sister asked.

'Not sure,' Richard said. 'Right now he seems to be unaware of the storm swirling around him. But that can't last. And it certainly can't last as he gets older.'

As the group approached the house, Richard stopped abruptly.

'Did you ever see a child who looked more like his father than Andrew does?'

Ahead of them, Andrew walked alongside Alex, heading back to the house from the direction of the stables. He had obviously been given an impromptu riding lesson. He was chatting happily with Alex.

Paul, beer in hand, was leaning over the verandah rail. He looked relaxed but Richard wasn't fooled. He strode out in front of the others in the group and quickly inserted himself between Paul and the path Alex would take.

'Don't do anything stupid, son,' Richard warned. 'Just get through the day.'

'I told Amanda I'm moving out,' he said, 'to make way for her lover. You know what she said.'

'I haven't a clue,' Richard said, not willing to play guessing games.

'Nothing. She simply nodded.'

'Has she said anything since?'

'Not much. Just that we probably need to consult a lawyer. And we should think about what it means for the children and Andrew in particular.'

'What did she mean by that?' Richard asked.

'I think she and Alex are planning to apply to have his birth certificate changed.'

'How do you feel about that?'

'Bloody disappointed if I'm honest. I love that little boy but you saw him just now. He's just a small version of Alex. He deserves to be brought up knowing the truth.'

'But it needs to be handled carefully for his sake,' Richard said. 'Not for your sake. You will learn to live with the disappointment. But he'll never understand if you abandon him completely.'

'I know,' Paul said. 'I won't abandon him but Amanda should never have put me in this position.'

'But she has,' Richard said. 'And you must deal with it the best way you can. Nothing will be helped by you having a swing at Alex to satisfy your bruised ego.'

Paul laughed, an unhappy chortling sound, and took a swig of his beer.

'No, the urge has passed,' he said. 'Let's enjoy lunch and celebrate us all being together.' He grabbed Anthony, who had followed his father onto the verandah, in a friendly hug. 'And celebrate the highly talented architect in our midst. Twenty-four today. Almost an old man.'

To Richard, it seemed like old times but he knew that was an illusion as fourteen people gathered around the table at Prior Park, not counting the children.

'Clever seating plan,' Richard whispered to Alice.

She had placed Pippa next to Paul and Amanda with Marianne and Alex on the other side of the table near James and John.

'I thought Paul was going to take a swing at Alex so I made sure he wasn't within punching distance,' Alice said, with a wry smile.

'I think I've settled him down,' Richard said, casting a glance across the room towards Alex who motioned to him. Richard walked around the table to join him.

'I think I owe you an apology, Richard,' he said as they walked onto the verandah together, out of earshot of the rest of the family, half of whom were already seated while others still hung back from the table.

'I don't think you owe me an apology, Alex,' Richard said evenly. 'I think perhaps you owe Marianne an apology. But apologies are probably too late, am I right?'

'Yes, you're right. They are too late. I never meant to break my promise to be a good husband to Marianne. But I discovered promises can be broken and actions have consequences.'

'You were wrong to pursue Marianne the way you did. She was an innocent. And you took advantage of that. You and Amanda were already lovers. You must have known, deep down, you were lying to Marianne. Lying to her for your own advantage,' Richard said, unable to suppress his simmering anger.

'I'm not as callous as you make me sound,' he said. He was clearly annoyed by the accusations. 'I love Marianne. I love our two daughters. It's just I can't live my life without Amanda.'

'Just tell me one thing,' Richard said. 'Amanda insists Matthew is Paul's child. Could he be your child? Is that a possibility?'

'I'm surprised you feel it's necessary to ask me that,' Alex retorted.

Richard hadn't missed the long pause that preceded Alex's answer.

'Well, I do find it necessary to ask,' he said testily. 'Or shall I put this another way?'

'What other way?'

'I know you visited Amanda often when Paul was away. Were they always innocent visits? Or did the two of you decide you would tell the same story? That you haven't been lovers since Andrew was conceived. Or do you want to tell me the truth?'

'I think this interrogation has gone far enough, Richard,' Alex snapped. 'I've given you my answer.'

'No, in fact you haven't, Alex. All you've done is cast more doubt. If you believe Matthew is your child too, please just tell me. We don't see it in him now but we don't want to have him get to age five or six and discover he looks like you. If you know, tell me.'

Alex relented and shook his head. He respected Richard. He had in the past been grateful to him.

'He's not my child,' Alex said finally.

'That's a relief,' Richard said. He paused before adding: 'I'm not unsympathetic to you and Amanda. I do acknowledge the two of you should never have been parted. Her father was wrong to do it.'

Alex sighed deeply.

'You're right. If her father hadn't objected so strongly, she would have felt she could win him over but he was so strident. That's why I left. He was making my life hell.'

'And then you met Marianne and decided she presented another opportunity for you.'

But he was keen to defend himself.

'I thought my past was behind me. I thought Amanda would move on from me. By the time I realised she wasn't moving on, I was already committed to Marianne. My pursuit of Marianne wasn't as cold and calculating as you suggest.'

'Well, the bottom line is none of that matters now. What

matters is that you and Marianne need to make a decision about your marriage.'

'I know,' Alex said. 'Marianne and I have talked briefly. I'm not sure she has come to terms with it all yet.'

'She will. So will Paul,' Richard said.

'I'm not concerned about Paul,' Alex said unexpectedly. 'He's never really been in love with Amanda. Infatuated yes. In love, I doubt it. He's found someone else, from what she tells me. He didn't even try to cover his tracks, according to Amanda.'

'He's very hurt about Andrew. That's why I was concerned about Matthew,' Richard said.

'I understand,' Alex said. He paused but he wanted to say more.

'I hope we can retain our friendship,' he said. 'I never set out to make an enemy of the Belleville family. We will always be connected through my daughters.'

Richard nodded. But at that moment he could think of nothing further to say. He was gripped instead by a feeling of desolation. If only Andrew hadn't looked quite so much like his father, he thought. But he dismissed the idea as fanciful.

The fact remained Marianne could not go through the rest of her married life, seeing Andrew and wondering when Amanda and Alex were last together. She had to move on. She deserved better. And he would have to live with his regret at the part he had unwittingly played in forcing his son to marry Amanda.

'Come and have some lunch,' Catherine said gently as she slipped her arm through his. 'Everyone is wondering where you are.'

She looked closely at him then.

'More bad news?'

'No,' he said, shaking his head. 'Just a sense of disappointment at how everything has transpired. I need a stiff drink.'

She had already anticipated the request, handing him a generous glass of single malt.

'You've got a daughter wondering where you are. She's growing up to be a nice young lady. You need to give her some attention.'

'I do,' he agreed. 'I do indeed.'

He linked arms with his wife and headed back to the dining room, ready to receive a plate laden with roast beef from his brother, who continued to wield the carving knife, only this time he was concentrating on dismembering a pair of roasted chickens.

'Paul and Amanda don't seem to be getting along,' Susan said as she looked towards her father. 'Something's going on with them. Everyone else seems to know but I don't.'

They were standing together on the front verandah following what had been a tense family lunch, except for Anthony's enthusiastic chatter about the progress of the building work and Julia's equally enthusiastic description of the extravagant plans Victoria had submitted for the interiors.

'Where do I start?' Richard said, as he savoured the single malt that had already been replenished several times.

'At the beginning,' his daughter suggested.

'No, I'll start at the end,' Richard said. He had no stomach for going into the details with his daughter. She wouldn't be sixteen until the following month. Did she really need to know the sordid details. Wasn't a simple explanation the best?

'They're separating,' Richard said.

'Is Paul seeing another girl?'

The question surprised Richard.

'Why do you ask that?'

'Because Tim always said he would turn out like that. I asked him recently why he was so much against Paul marrying Nancy and that's what he said. After a few years he'd be off romancing another girl. So is he seeing another girl?'

Richard hesitated. If he answered yes, he would have to explain it was only one part of their problems. If he answered no, he worried she would think later he hadn't been honest with her.

'It's complicated,' Richard said finally. 'He is seeing someone else but that's as a result of his marriage falling apart. It's not the cause of the marriage failing.'

'So what's the cause?'

She had always pursued issues when she wasn't satisfied with the answers. He smiled, remembering how she had tied him in knots trying to explain Julia's decision to live with James even though they were no longer married, which school gossips had described as *living in sin*.

'Maybe you should be a lawyer. Or a barrister,' he said, laughing quietly.

'Well?'

She was clearly not going to be sidetracked.

'Paul discovered he isn't Andrew's father.'

'It's Alex, I suppose,' she said.

'Yes. How did you know?'

She rolled her eyes as if to say, *really, that's a dumb question.*

'Because when you see him with Alex, he looks exactly like Alex. Which means Amanda conned Paul into marrying her. I suppose that was to save Alex's marriage to Marianne?'

'That's about it, I believe.'

'So what about Matthew? Maybe he's Alex's son too?'

'Amanda says he isn't.'

Richard noticed how she was mulling over the information, as if she was testing evidence.

'Do you believe her?'

'I think we have to believe her, don't you?'

'You mean in the absence of evidence to the contrary?'

Richard laughed out loud then.

'Have you been doing this sort of thing at school?'

'Yes, in Legal Studies,' she said. 'We had a Sydney barrister in class one day. We had a mock courtroom. I took part in that.'

'Did you enjoy it?'

'It was fun. The barrister was an uncle of one of the girls in the class. Seriously goodlooking.'

'But old enough to be your father probably.' He was guessing of course but he was keen to dampen his daughter's interest in the opposite sex.

'No he wasn't,' she declared. 'He would have been about thirty. All the girls just went ape over him.'

Her use of slang appalled him and then he remembered the

forty year gulf in their ages. So much had changed in the world around him since the war. Much of it he hadn't noticed until recently but listening to Susan, he suddenly felt old and out of touch.

'Well, if you want to be a lawyer, you'll need good marks to get into a good university,' he said.

She shrugged, wondering why parents always stated the obvious, as if she didn't already know that.

'Doing it easy,' she said.

Which could mean anything, Richard thought.

'What does your mother think of law as a career choice?'

'She's fine with it. She desperately wants me to have a career. She understands how the world is changing.'

'And you think I don't?'

She looked at him and smiled.

'You'll catch up,' she said. 'By the way I think I know what car I want you to buy for my seventeenth birthday.'

'Who said I was buying you a car for your seventeenth birthday?'

'Mum did. You could come to Sydney and we could go around the car dealers, see where we can get the best deal.'

'Let's cross that bridge when we get to it,' Richard said.

'Well, we'll get to it sooner than you think. Daniel is already giving me driving lessons. Tim too.'

'You're too young to go on a public road.'

'I know. Just around Berrima Park and around the stud farm. I'm quite good. I just need to learn the road rules.'

'We'll talk about it,' he said, as he noticed Catherine heading towards them.

'How are you getting on with Catherine?'

'Fine. She's great. Mum doesn't like her though.'

'Well, that's all in the past,' he said, hoping to head off a lengthy discussion about the merits of his two wives.

'Mum said you started seeing her again while the two of you were still married. You never really stopped loving her, did you?'

He hesitated. It wasn't a conversation he wanted to have with his daughter.

'We'll have that conversation when you're older,' he said, attempting to do what he had done when she was a child: use a certain tone of voice to bring an end to a conversation.

She suddenly noticed Catherine heading their way too and smiled.

'Saved by the bell,' she said. 'You'll have to tell me the whole sordid story sometime. It might as well be soon.'

He gave her a hug.

'You'll always win your cases. You'll badger witnesses until they break down and beg for mercy.'

'It's good practice, isn't it? Badgering my old man to reveal his murky romantic past.'

Catherine noticed the look on his face as she came up to them.

'Are you interrogating your father? I think he needs a break, don't you?'

Susan laughed.

'He's not a very cooperative witness but he has managed to sidetrack counsel.'

Catherine laughed heartily. The girl had spirit.

'Talking about being sidetracked, little Mel was looking for you to show you the bird's nest she's just discovered.'

'She's lovely, isn't she? She'll be devastated when she's older when she finds out about her father.'

'What do you mean?' Catherine asked, looking at Richard. Had she put Richard on the spot to explain the tense undercurrent at lunch?

'Well, he's obviously been screwing Paul's wife behind Marianne's back.'

'Susan!' Richard exclaimed. 'That's vulgar language I don't expect to hear from my daughter!'

'But it's true, isn't it?'

'True or not, we don't use language like that at Prior Park. I don't think you'd use language like that in front of your mother so I suggest you don't use it here.'

It was a belated attempt to exercise some control over his daughter who had, in a matter of months, changed markedly. He wondered if it was time to have a discussion with Kate about her.

She was saved by little Mel tugging impatiently at her arm.

'Go with Mel,' Catherine said. 'She's been keen to show you the new bird's nest all day.'

As Catherine and Richard watched the pair head into the garden, Catherine turned towards him.

'You've discovered the joy of teenagers in the modern age,' she said. 'The more you react the more she'll perform.'

'God give me strength,' Richard declared. 'I don't have the patience for this now.'

'You're starting to sound like your brother,' she chided.

And then he smiled.

'You're right. I just feel out of touch. And disappointed with everything right now.'

'So what was the discussion all about with Alex before lunch?'

He hesitated.

'He apologised to me but I told him it's Marianne to whom he should apologise. He said he wasn't Matthew's father and I believe him. But just looking at Amanda with him now, I'm sure they've become intimate again.'

'I know,' Catherine said.

'I think it's time for Alex to end his marriage to Marianne. He can't go on being dishonest with her. She might already know, of course.'

'After talking to Alice, I suspect Marianne knows more than she's letting on. Her mother thinks she wanted to maintain the fiction of a happy marriage with a faithful husband as long as she could. But she knows the marriage is over. Such a pity.'

Just then they heard raised angry voices. Richard groaned. He recognised his elder son's voice. And he recognised Alex's voice.

'You'd better go and sort it out,' Catherine said, 'before one of them gets seriously hurt.'

But William was several yards ahead of him.

'You are not fighting here. Not now,' he yelled as he gripped Paul's right arm which was poised ready to hit out at Alex. He had pushed Alex into the side of his car.

Paul struggled to free himself from his uncle's powerful grip.

'This finishes now,' Richard said, placing himself between the two of them. 'It's over.'

'It's over alright. He's ruined my marriage. And not content with that, he's fathered the children I thought were mine.'

'You don't know that for certain, Paul,' Richard said.

'Well, they lied about Andrew. Why wouldn't they lie about Matthew?'

'I don't think they lied about Matthew,' Richard said.

'But he often saw my wife while I was away. She's admitted that.'

'Admitting that is one thing. But that doesn't mean he's Matthew's father.'

Out of the corner of his eye, Richard spotted Marianne walking towards them.

She put her hand on Paul's arm.

'Don't do this, Paul. Please think of my feelings.'

He calmed down then, worried that he had upset his cousin.

'I'm sorry, Marianne,' he said. 'I just don't know how to cope with the uncertainty.'

She put her arms around him.

'I'd bet all my Belleville inheritance on Matthew being a Belleville,' she said. 'He looks nothing like Andrew. Nothing like my two little girls. He really is your son.'

He hugged her then and relaxed. Everyone heaved a sigh of relief.

'Thank God for Marianne,' William said quietly to Richard as they walked away together.

'Indeed,' Richard said, praying silently that Marianne's intervention would be enough to quash Paul's doubts once and for all.

'We need to talk,' Alex said as he closed the door of little Mel's bedroom.

He had spent twenty minutes reading to her and now she was fast asleep, exhausted by the day out at Prior Park.

'Is the baby asleep?' he asked, as he watched Marianne tidy away the last few things in the nursery.

Marianne nodded. Was talking really necessary?

'What's there to talk about?' she asked irritably. 'Do you want to tell me how many times you've been with Amanda since we've been married? Or admit that you only married me because of my expectations? I know you never loved me and that's very hard for me to come to terms with.'

He had never heard her so angry. There was disillusionment and disappointment in every single word she spoke.

'I know what it looks like,' he said quietly, 'but it doesn't look like that from where I'm standing. Of course I was in love with you. I love you still.'

She let out a strange sound that spoke only of her contempt for what he had just said.

'Alex, if you really loved me, you wouldn't be unfaithful to me. All I ask now is that you be honest with me. Is there a possibility Matthew is your child too?'

Why had she asked that question, he wondered? Hadn't he already declared he wasn't Matthew's father? And she had intervened to declare to Paul she believed Matthew was a Belleville?

'You told Paul you would stake your Belleville inheritance on Matthew being a Belleville.'

She laughed, an unhappy, cynical sound.

'I did that to stop our daughter witnessing the awful spectacle of a fight between you and Paul. It was the only thing I could think to say that would defuse the situation. But you haven't answered my question.'

There was silence then, as they stood in the hallway of the house they had shared for more than seven years.

'I've said it before but I'll say it again and hopefully you'll believe me this time. He isn't my child,' he declared.

'So you want me to believe you've only been unfaithful to me just once, when Andrew was conceived?'

He hesitated.

'Do you really want me to answer that?'

'No, don't bother,' she said.

She took a deep breath. Her worst fears had been confirmed. Alex shook his head slowly from side to side. What could he say?

'I'm sorry I let you down,' Alex said. 'I didn't mean to. I thought I could move on from Amanda and I had for years. I thought she had moved on from me.'

'And now?'

'I'm being honest. I would love our marriage to continue but I can't promise to give up Amanda.'

'Well, at least that's honest,' she said. 'Did you know Paul's moving out tomorrow?'

'I didn't know that,' he said. 'Did he tell you that?'

She nodded.

'He's already contacted his lawyer friend regarding a divorce.'

'And do you want me to leave?' he asked, but he already knew what her answer would be.

'Yes, I do,' she said. 'Our marriage is over. Have you thought about where you will go?'

'Well, I have a few options, but I thought I'd move to Armoobilla. It means I can help with the children. Glenmoral or Isla Downs are options too but I need to be closer.'

'That's a good plan,' she agreed. 'I'll consult a lawyer tomorrow. Divorce is easier now. Just twelve months apart and we can be divorced.'

Alex shook his head in disbelief. The discussion that had ended their marriage had been so unemotional. No tears. No recriminations. But he wasn't fooled by her calm demeanour. He put his arms around her. He felt her stiffen.

'Please don't hate me,' he said. 'I didn't plan any of this. I really loved you. Loved our life together. But for Amanda ...'

'But for Amanda ...' she echoed his words back to him as she turned and headed to the bedroom they had once shared.

In the darkness of the room, she pulled off her rings and dropped them into a keepsake box at the back of her top drawer. She'd keep them for Melanie. And then she lay down on the bed and wept.

33

'OK, SO LET ME see if I have this right,' Murray Anderson said after a long, satisfying swig of his beer. 'You want to divorce your wife. There's no need for a property settlement. She keeps what's hers, you keep what's yours, meaning your Belleville inheritance. You'll contribute to the upkeep of the children as needed.'

Paul nodded, emptying the glass of beer in front of him and calling for another.

'But there's something else, isn't there?' he asked, looking directly at Paul, as if he had sensed there was another issue he hadn't yet raised. 'Did she find out about your other interest? Did she throw you out? It's her house, after all, I understand.'

Paul shook his head.

'No, I moved out.' He paused. 'It's nothing to do with Linda really.'

Murray raised his eyebrows. In his experience, wives were not particularly understanding of husbands who were unfaithful. He wondered what else might be the reason for the collapse of Paul's marriage.

'It's the elder of our two children. He's not my son.'

'Bloody hell! You did get yourself into a mess. When did you find this out?'

'I suspected for a long time, but it was only confirmed as Andrew got older. He's the spitting image of my cousin's husband, Alex. Alex and Amanda had history.'

'As in romantic history, I assume?'

'Yes, except her father wouldn't let her marry Alex so Alex got my cousin Marianne pregnant and then married her. Not long after that he got Amanda pregnant which was at about the same time I was seeing her. She said the baby was mine.'

'Wow. So more scandalous goings on in the Belleville family. Is your cousin getting a divorce too?'

'Yes, she is. Alex and Amanda are together now, which they would have been originally if her father hadn't objected.'

'So why did he object?'

Paul proceeded to tell Murray a shortened version of the story.

'One thing though. For Andrew's sake I want him to go on thinking of me as his father, until he's older at least, so I will not give permission to have the name of his father changed on his birth certificate.'

Murray pursed his lips.

'Are they likely to ask for your permission?'

'It's possible. I think they've discussed it.'

'Have you thought about what this means inheritance-wise?'

'You mean the Belleville inheritance?'

'Of course. How many are there in your generation?'

'Me and Anthony, my sister Susan, Marianne and John Fitzroy.'

'John Fitzroy?'

'Yes, my Aunt Julia bought into Prior Park Holdings, which brings John in as an heir.'

'Not her daughter?'

Paul shook his head.

'No, Pippa won't need to add to the millions her father will leave her.'

'Wow, I'd heard your aunt's ex-husband was wealthy but I thought it was exaggerated.'

Paul shook his head.

'Believe me, it's not. That's where my aunt got the money from to buy into Prior Park. Her divorce settlement.'

'Wish I'd been in on that one. Would have been good fees for the lawyers I imagine.'

Paul laughed.

'Well, don't think I'm paying Sydney lawyer fees for what I need.'

Murray ignored the jibe. He was happy his friend had turned to him for help.

'Have you discussed the Andrew situation with your father?'

'I have and he's satisfied with it. He's very fond of the boy too. He doesn't want to stop being a grandfather to him. If we repudiated him, Andrew would have no one then, at least not until Matthew is older. No extended family. Amanda had no siblings. Alex had no siblings. Amanda's father is dead. She has no real contact with her mother. Alex's mother died when he was born. As far as we're concerned, Andrew will remain part of the family.'

'I admire that, Paul. I know you're putting the child's welfare ahead of your own feelings. I'm surprised you haven't had a go at Alex though.'

'I tried but my uncle and my father intervened. Anyway, what good would it serve? He's been besotted with Amanda since he was a teenager.'

'Just as well they didn't turn out to be brother and sister then, I'd say.'

He leant back from the table as two plates of sizzling steak were put in front of them.

'So how's Linda taken all this?'

'She's delighted, but I've told her I'm not getting married for some time.'

'How'd she take that news?'

'She's fine with it. Not sure her parents will be when she starts living with me.'

'When's that happening?'

'Around Christmas, I think. She's looking for a new job locally. I think I might have found her something actually.'

'Flying planes or doing civil construction?'

Paul laughed.

'She's not quite experienced enough to take on a job as a pilot but the company overseeing the building of my aunt's house at

Prior Park has interviewed her. I think a job offer is imminent.'

'Well, if she's with you, she'll get a chance to improve her flying. I hope that's not her only reason for wanting to hook up with you.'

Paul shook his head, smiling.

'You should meet her next time I'm down,' he said. 'She's delightful.'

'So next time might be for my wedding,' Murray said, as he handed Paul an invitation. 'I managed to hijack the invitation addressed to Mr and Mrs. Your invitation is now *and partner*.'

'Next month, isn't it?'

'Yep. Sixth of November. At St John's. My mother is trying to put her beak in. Unsuccessfully I might add. It's Serena's mother's shindig. I'm staying right out of it. I did make one suggestion only for it to be howled down so I know my place. Turn up in a suit on the day, not hung over, and do what I'm told.'

'Well, I suppose your mother doesn't have any daughters to fuss over for a wedding.'

'No, shame about that really. She saw your little cousin Melanie the other day. She said she's a delightful child. She saw her with her mother and a bloke she didn't recognise.'

'Ah, that would be Nathan Flynn.'

'So your cousin has got over her broken marriage too by the sound of it.'

'We're not sure. She's not telling anyone but I think he's keen. He's the one who looks like giving Linda a job, so I hope it doesn't go pear-shaped with Marianne. He's overseeing the rebuilding of the house at Prior Park.'

'How's that going?' Murray asked as he chewed vigorously on his steak.

'It's going well. Next time you're up our way come out and have a look.'

'I will. And I hear Charlie Weir has settled in well to take over his uncle's old spot. My parents thought that was a good move for him, but they said it through gritted teeth. They were sorry to lose him, but they knew the reason.'

'Right time, right place for him. And for us. I'm not particularly keen on stock work so I was pleased he happened along.'

Murray understood Paul's reluctance. He'd felt the same about the daily grind on his parents' properties. Not something he wanted to do long term.

'Anyway, how are relations with Amanda? Amicable, I hope.'

'They are,' Paul said. 'She's got what she wanted.'

'Alex?'

'Yep. He moved to one of their properties. Armoobilla. It's close to Prior Park. It's the last property her father bought. I know he spends time with her at her house in town so he can still see his kids. Little Mel doesn't really understand everything yet. Neither does Andrew if it comes to that. And the other two are babies. Their routine hasn't changed.'

'And life goes on,' Murray said, as he pushed aside his plate.

'Yes, life goes on,' Paul agreed. 'Life goes on.'

But even as Paul spoke the words, there was a hollow ring about them. Murray sensed the experience had left its mark. Paul had essentially been duped by a woman carrying another man's child. A brutal lesson, he thought. How much it must have hurt him to know his first born son wasn't his child Murray could only guess. It's an invisible scar he'll carry for a very long time, he concluded. A very long time.

A week later, Paul sat across from his cousin Marianne in her kitchen as she fed baby Laura. It was late afternoon. He hadn't expected to hear the sound of hammering drifting in from the back garden.

And then he noticed little Mel sitting on the back steps watching progress on her house, frowning occasionally as something unexpected happened.

'It's like Prior Park only in miniature,' Paul said, as he looked through the door. 'Nathan found some willing workers I take it.'

Marianne smiled.

'Mel is delighted. Nathan's father Brian came up to visit his son. He's just retired. I think his wife wanted him out of the house for a few days. He was a builder so he jumped at the chance to do the work with one of the other tradesmen from the Prior Park site, who's getting some extra cash I believe.'

'Probably wanted to check up on their son.'

'I expect so. I think the divorce was a bit painful for him. He hadn't expected his marriage to fail.'

Paul shrugged.

'Well, none of us expected our marriages to fail, did we?'

Marianne shook her head in a slow sad rhythm.

'Looking back, I can't believe I was so naïve.'

'You're not the only one,' Paul said. 'I should have trusted my instincts.'

'Meaning that you felt at the time Amanda's baby wasn't yours?'

He nodded and smiled ruefully.

'I'm sure Amanda told him she was pregnant and they hatched the plot then. No wonder Alex intervened at Berrima.'

'That's probably right,' Marianne conceded. She hadn't been present when he had tackled Paul a day before his wedding to Nancy but she remembered the pandemonium that followed. 'That was quite an experience.'

'I should never have proposed to Nancy in the first place. I got carried away.'

'And now? What's happening with Linda?'

'Not marriage. Not in the immediate future. She's going to live with me. Nathan has confirmed the job offer to start in the New Year.'

'That's great. There'll be a sharp intake of breath in some quarters about you living together.'

'Your father included,' Paul said.

She shrugged and smiled. She loved her father but even she conceded he was stuck fast in his old ways.

'I wouldn't worry about him but what about her father?'

'He'll be pretty grumpy with me too, I imagine. He'll get used to it. He'll have to. The world has changed. No one raises an eyebrow anymore at people living together.'

'How will she be with the kids?'

'Fine. She's got two younger sisters. She did a lot for them when they were little, she told me.'

'And your mother?'

'I've written to her at Haldon Hall to bring her up to date so she can share it with my father. I think they'll be heading back to Sydney in a couple of weeks' time.'

'I'd imagine England would be too cold for your father soon.'

'I think that's likely but he wanted to meet George, my stepbrother, at half term. I think there's moves afoot to change our inheritance from our mother.'

'In what way?' Marianne was curious. They hadn't really discussed his inheritance beyond their shared interest in the Belleville family.

'Years ago, my mother set up a trust for Haldon Hall with Anthony and I as beneficiaries with George to be given money and other things. But George has expressed an interest in Haldon Hall and the estate. She wants my father's advice as to how she should change things to include George.'

'How do you feel about that?' Marianne asked. She had visited Haldon Hall once when her uncle had remarried Paul's mother. It was a beautiful house but she had been glad to come home. She couldn't imagine Paul as master of the house. Anthony perhaps?

'I don't see myself living there. Honestly, my mother should do what is best for Haldon Hall. I think that's what my father will advise.'

'And Anthony?'

'Anthony loves living in Sydney. He's happy to visit Haldon Hall but he doesn't see himself taking up residence there. Blame our father if you like. I think the Australian part of us has triumphed just as he had hoped. George is born to that life. He's been educated to that life. He'll be the next baronet. He should have it.'

'Did you tell your mother that?'

He nodded.

'I did. We had a chat before she left. I told her Anthony agreed with me. I think it relieved her mind. After holidaying with George in Greece, I think she was beginning to think she was being unfair to him.'

'I'm pleased. We don't want more family discord.'

'No, we don't,' he agreed. 'You and I have caused enough trouble to last a generation.'

He got up then and went to the back door to survey the work.

'Another pair of hands, that's what we need,' Nathan called out as he spotted Paul. 'We want to lift the completed roof into place. One man on each corner will do it.'

Paul hurried down the back steps, carefully avoiding little Mel, who continued to study proceedings with a critical eye.

Nathan performed a quick introduction before assigning Paul to a corner of the structure. On a command, the four men lifted the roof structure into place. It wasn't heavy, so much as awkward but it took a bit of manoeuvring.

'It's really taking shape now,' Paul said, admiring the work.

'I'm making some little furniture to go inside it,' Brian said. 'Her grandfather has been generous with his funds for the project.'

'Uncle William is an absolute soft touch when it comes to little Mel,' Paul said.

He noticed Nathan's father turn then to look at little Mel sitting on the back steps.

'She's a darling little girl. I'd be a soft touch too if I was her grandfather.'

Paul looked at Nathan then who glanced away, rather than meet Paul's gaze. Was his father expressing a hope that Nathan might become Mel's stepdad?

'I think that's it for the day,' Nathan said. 'We'll do another hour or so on it tomorrow.'

As Nathan began to gather up the tools, Brian Flynn took Paul aside.

'Do you think my son has any chance with your cousin?'

Paul shrugged, unprepared for the question.

'I don't know to be honest. She's pretty shattered by what happened with her husband.'

'Yes, Nathan told me the bare facts about her husband and … oh! sorry, Paul. I should have kept my big mouth shut. It was just that …' He stopped then, realising the enormity of his gaff.

'That's fine,' Paul reassured him, despite a surge of irritation. 'Don't worry about it. I think Nathan just needs to be patient. Marianne had put her faith in one man. It turned out to be misplaced. She's not going to do that again in a hurry.'

'No, she's not. I agree.'

He looked at his son then who frowned a warning.

'I'm in trouble. I know that look,' he said as he began to collect odd bits of timber into a small pile.

'Thanks for helping with this little project,' Paul said. 'Marianne is very grateful.'

'No worries. It's a lovely idea. I'm happy to help,' Brian Flynn said, carefully avoiding any further mention of Marianne. Or his son.

With that, the work ended for the day as Marianne emerged to thank them for their efforts. She was nursing baby Laura, who at that moment, began to cry, so she headed back inside very quickly, leaving Paul in charge of little Mel who wanted to inspect the work at close quarters.

34

ON THE OTHER SIDE of the world, an unlikely trio sat down to breakfast at Haldon Hall on the first day of the half-term holiday.

George Cavendish looked warily at Richard. For all of his nearly seventeen years, he had been given an unflattering description of his mother's first husband.

A country yokel, his father had told him. Not one of us. A colonial. Supposedly a war hero but he had only done what countless others had done. A womaniser too.

Yet as he sat opposite Richard, George began to understand jealousy had been the driving force behind his father's dislike of Richard Belleville and his description of him.

His mother, he noticed, looked happy and contented. He had been disappointed at how quickly his father had moved on from his mother, as if, having achieved the prize he had long coveted, he no longer valued it quite so highly.

'I see your tan has faded,' she said, looking at his pale face.

'Well, it's hardly going to last stuck in a stuffy classroom studying Latin for hours on end.'

'Well, less than year to go,' his mother sympathised. 'What then? What does your father suggest?'

She remembered Richard having the same conversation with Anthony at the breakfast table at Haldon Hall years before.

Anthony's choice of architecture had surprised them at the time.

'How's Anthony going with architecture?' George asked unexpectedly, clearly hoping to divert his mother's attention from his own interests.

'He's going well, George,' Richard said, pleased to contribute. 'He's doing his Honours year and designing the rebuild of the Prior Park house for my sister Julia. It's well under way.'

'And after that?'

'He's opening a practice in Sydney with his friend Lachlan Bell. He's actually going to marry Lachlan's sister Victoria, once her divorce is finalised. She's an interior designer with her own practice.'

'Well, I hope his marriage goes better than Paul's.'

'So do we,' his mother said. She had already told him the news of Paul's divorce.

'Hopefully you'll be able to come out for Anthony's wedding,' Richard said. 'It won't be until next year. Probably in our spring. You'll be finished school by then.'

'That would be great assuming I can get my father's consent to travel.'

'I don't think he'll deny you that. Besides you'll be very close to turning eighteen and making your own decisions,' his mother said, hoping to bring the conversation back to what career he would pursue.

'I think my father had visions of me going into the Foreign Office,' he said, without enthusiasm.

'But it's not what you see for yourself, is it?' his mother asked.

He shook his head emphatically.

'No, it isn't.'

'What then?' she asked.

'Perhaps a course at the London School of Economics. They have some interesting programs.'

'Did you mention this idea to your father?' his mother asked, imagining that her former husband would have fixed views on their son's future.

'I mentioned it in passing. He hardly reacted,' he said.

'I think young Edward was throwing a tantrum at the time,' he added with a smile, 'so I didn't pursue it.'

He looked towards Richard then.

'Have you been around the farms here with my mother to see how everyone is getting on?'

'I have. Usual complaints,' Richard said. 'They want more money spent on upgrading buildings. They grumbled about the cost of everything but I've looked at the figures. They're doing alright. Like us at home, they can't control the weather.'

He could see George thinking about what he had said.

'Did they just use your visit as a chance to voice their grievances?'

'Not quite but they're never likely to say, *everything's going well*. They'd worry their annual rental would go up if they were too cheerful.'

'How do you think the estate should be managed in the future?' George asked, this time directing the question to his mother.

'Well, I think that's one of the discussions we need to have,' Richard said, heading off Catherine's response. 'Your mother initially thought you would inherit Grantham Manor from your father but there are competing claims for that now. And she said you expressed a preference for Haldon Hall?'

Richard left the question hang in the air.

'It's a much nicer house than Grantham Manor,' George conceded, 'but what about Paul and Anthony? They have equal claim as I have. In fact Paul as the eldest son has the strongest claim.'

Richard was pleased to hear him acknowledge his two half-brothers in this way.

'I've discussed it with them both,' Catherine said. 'Neither of them wants to reside in England. I'm afraid their father's nationality has won the day.' She smiled at Richard as she said it. 'We all agreed you would be a better custodian of the estate if that's what you want.'

George smiled broadly. He was clearly relieved. He hadn't thought it likely his mother would change her mind to favour him.

'Richard and I are going to the lawyer tomorrow,' she said. 'The trust will be amended. Paul and Anthony will benefit in cash terms but of course we need to leave most of the investments intact, otherwise you won't be able to afford the upkeep of the house. Once you take over, I expect you to welcome your half-brothers if they want to visit. And if you don't have heirs, then the heirs to Haldon Hall will be Paul and Anthony, or their children.'

Richard noticed how George listened intently, taking in every word his mother spoke.

'That's very generous of you, Mother,' he said, as he turned his attention to the plate loaded with bacon and eggs that had sat untouched in front of him.

Only then did it occur to Catherine to wonder if his father had been behind the push for his son to become the heir to Haldon Hall instead of Richard's sons.

But through mouthfuls of food, George quickly dispelled the idea.

'I can't tell you how relieved I am by your decision. I have a plan for my life that's probably different from what my father thinks it should be. This decision gives me an independence from him that's going to make all the difference. And of course Paul and Anthony will always be welcome here. Anytime.'

It was Catherine's turn to feel relieved.

'I'm pleased, George,' she said. 'We all need to follow our own paths in life. My parents didn't approve of me marrying Richard. My mother – your grandmother – was delighted when I married your father. It fulfilled her expectations. But in the end, it was the wrong move for me.'

'Apart from having you,' she added, as if to reassure him he wasn't her forgotten child.

'Well, I certainly plan to make my own decisions about my life. And I can assure you I'll be very cautious about marriage. Any girl who bears the faintest resemblance to my stepmother is a non-starter.'

Richard laughed out loud.

'I take it you don't get on with her?'

He shook his head forcibly.

'No, I don't. I just ignore her and remind her she isn't my mother. That I have a perfectly acceptable mother and I don't need another one.'

Catherine smiled at the unexpected compliment. It felt to her as if she had triumphed over Edward. He had expected a son to grow up in his own image but she could see George was determined to follow his own path. She was pleased she had made it possible for him.

'Hello, stranger.' Alice raised a hand in greeting to Richard from the verandah at Prior Park. 'It seems like you've been gone for months. You've been missed.'

He kissed his sister-in-law on the cheek and accepted a cup of tea.

'Well, not months, six, seven weeks I suppose. A lot of travel in that time.'

'How was your stay at Haldon Hall? Did you meet George? Did Catherine sort everything out the way she wanted? I must say you look a bit tired.'

Alice peppered him with so many questions he hardly knew what to tell her.

'I'm fine, Alice,' he said. 'A bit tired, that's all. And yes, Catherine sorted everything out. George turns out to be quite a pleasant young man. He seems to have inherited more of Catherine's father's temperament than his father's, thank goodness. And he's very fond of his mother.'

'I'm pleased to hear that,' Alice said. 'I think she'd be relieved.'

'She is. She's quite happy with the way he's growing up to be his own man. She changed the trust to ensure George can take control of Haldon Hall on her death, but Paul and Anthony are not excluded. And if George doesn't have children, it will come back to Paul and Anthony, or their offspring.'

'Another potential dilemma involving Andrew?'

Richard shrugged. He had expected the question.

'If we go on regarding Andrew as a Belleville, then I don't think there'll be an issue. Catherine didn't tell George about him. We didn't think it was necessary at this stage.'

'You're probably right,' Alice conceded.

'And then I had a few days in Sydney. I saw Susan. She announced she's going to come up here for Christmas, which surprised me.'

'That's good. You haven't had Christmas with her for a very long time.'

'It's great. Catherine said she'll put up with the heat for a few days too and come up here. I've promised to get some air conditioning units installed in my house.'

'You'll have to get onto that quickly. Perhaps Nathan can help,' Alice said, nodding in the direction of the building work that was now well advanced.

'I can see that's going well. What about everything else?'

'No outbursts, if that's what you're worried about. Alex and Amanda are now well established together, I believe. Paul spends a bit of time with Marianne which has been helpful for her. He's very good with little Mel. And he's been collecting his two from Amanda a couple of afternoons a week and bringing them to Marianne's place. Marianne tells me that Linda Kent is moving in with him soon. Nathan has given her a job that will start in the New Year.'

'So it's sorting itself out, in some fashion.'

'I think so,' Alice said. 'I hope so. I had a word with Alex. And I had a word with Amanda separately. I told them they would always be welcome at Prior Park.'

Richard was stunned by Alice's unexpected revelation but he knew he shouldn't have been. Alice was always the peacemaker. Always the person who wanted the family to be on good terms with one another.

'How did William take that?'

'I didn't tell him until after I'd had the conversations.'

'How did Alex react?'

'He was grateful. He gave me a hug, which is unusual for him. I said it wasn't so much that I forgave him for breaking Marianne's heart but that I understood he had made a choice he believed in at the time.'

'And Amanda?'

'She just smiled and thanked me. She knows what she did in trapping Paul into marriage was wrong. But I've always felt sorry for her, having to live up to her father's expectations and not having a mother to give her some advice. Both of their lives would have been different if they'd had proper parents. We can't judge them for how others failed them.'

Richard listened intently. It was a long speech for Alice but he understood it was important for her to explain why she had reached out to them.

'You did well, Alice. Very well. I would have been tempted to do the same but somehow it wouldn't have come out quite right. Women are so much better at handling tricky situations.'

Just then, he heard the sound of his brother's footsteps walking purposefully along the verandah from the direction of his office.

'The wanderer returns,' William said, shaking his brother's hand. 'I take it Alice has filled you in on everything.'

'She has. Things seem a bit more settled which is good with Christmas approaching.'

'I guess so. Did she tell you your son's going to have a girl living with him?'

'I rather expected that. I'll probably get grief from her father about it.'

'I'm told it's the modern way. Marianne thinks it's fine,' he said doubtfully.

'Well, given Paul's romantic history, I think it's much better he establishes a relationship before he heads up the aisle again.'

'You're probably right, brother. By the way I think the accountants have some things you need to attend to. Some cash investments falling due at the end of the month and other issues you need to deal with.'

'I'll see them on Monday,' Richard said, as he finished his cup of tea. 'I thought I might ride around the cattle today and catch up with Charlie Weir.'

'Good idea. Paul actually took Andrew for a ride the other day. Just a short ride. He loved it. Did he tell you he's not giving permission for them to change the father's name on his birth certificate?'

'He did,' Richard said. 'I was wondering how that issue has been going in my absence. If Paul's come to terms with it. What do you think?'

'Well, the boy still calls him Dad. And as far as I can see Paul hasn't changed his approach to Andrew at all. In the end, does it matter?'

'Does what matter?'

'That he's a Fraser and not a Belleville. We will all know but he can just grow up as one of the four. Between the four, they'll inherit Belleville interests and Robinson interests.'

His brother's attitude surprised him. But he was relieved too. Alice and William were the very beating heart of the Belleville family. Their acceptance was crucial.

'And Marianne? How is she getting on? Is she coming to terms with everything?'

'She is, Richard. She's very resilient,' Alice said. 'The baby looks so much like Mel.'

'That's good. She'll find someone else eventually,' Richard said. And then he noticed William and Alice exchange glances.

'I think Nathan Flynn has hopes in that direction. Paul told me he asked him about Marianne,' William said.

'I hope Paul told him to be patient and understanding.'

'He did,' William said. 'He seems like a nice bloke. Little Mel is full of Nathan this and Nathan that. They've just about finished her little house. His father helped out for a few days. I met him. Nice bloke. Just retired. He came up to visit his son.'

'Well, I hope Marianne gets to move on from Alex,' Richard said. 'It would relieve my mind. I sometimes feel I've been responsible for the entire Amanda and Alex debacle.'

'I think we all have to move on, Richard,' Alice said. 'That's the past. It can't be changed. And there are four children we can never regret. Two lovely little girls. Two great little boys.'

He smiled and nodded. Alice had an unerring ability to put things in the proper perspective.

He stood up then and headed towards the boot room to change into riding boots. He desperately needed to feel the sun on his back and forget the disappointments of a turbulent year, now almost at an end.

35

New Year's Day 1977

JUST AS THEY HAD on Christmas Day, the Belleville family gathered at Prior Park to welcome the new year. Christmas lunch had effectively been a trial run for Alice and William hosting the family that included the divorcing couples. Now it was generally accepted that Amanda and Alex would sit alongside one another on one side of the table while Paul and Marianne sat on the other side.

Only this time two new faces had been added to the guest list.

Linda Kent sat nervously alongside Paul while little Mel demanded that Nathan Flynn sit beside her. It was only Alice who noticed Alex's fleeting look of annoyance at his daughter's obvious closeness to the new man in her mother's life.

Andrew Belleville, about to turn seven, sat beside his mother and surveyed the gathering of people around the table, unaware he had been the cause of so much upheaval in the family in the past year.

Silence now surrounded the topic. Paul would not speak of it. Amanda, taking her cue from him, did not speak of it. Alex, aware of all this, remained mute on the topic, letting his actions speak louder than words.

He was the one teaching Andrew to ride. He was the one

teaching him the skills he thought a man would need. Andrew was becoming as familiar with Armoobilla as he was with Prior Park.

For Alex, it was the opportunity to guide the child as he wished a father might have guided him. He was becoming a father to him in all but name.

But seeing little Mel's untroubled acceptance of Nathan Flynn, Alex felt a surge of impotent anger. He was no longer seeing her every day, no longer part of her daily routines, no longer welcome in the house except for brief visits. He'd known there would be a price to pay. It was a disappointment he had to live with. For the children's sake. Marianne had made the rules and he could not unmake them.

It was the first time in more than a year that Joel Tynan had accompanied his wife Pippa and their little daughter Jessica on a visit to Prior Park.

'I'm pleased you could get the time off,' Alice said. 'It's lovely to see you up here with the rest of the family.'

'It's good to be here,' he said. 'I've never been part of a large family. I had a couple of aunts who my mother rarely spoke to and a few cousins but there was never a big get together. Not that I remember.'

'It's nice to have family around us,' Alice said. And then she smiled. 'Even if they give us a lot of trouble at times.'

'Pippa told me everything,' he said. He did not add it reminded him of his own first marriage where the child he thought was his turned out to be fathered by another man.

'Well, two divorces coming up. At least it's easier now,' Alice said.

He looked across the room to where Andrew stood alongside Alex.

'Parentage is sometimes hard to hide,' he said.

Alice followed the direction of his gaze.

'Yes, it had to come out sometime, didn't it?'

'Does the boy know?'

'I don't think they've told him. Not yet.'

'It will need to be soon,' Joel said. 'Children have an instinct about these things.'

Alice listened intently. She liked Joel. He spoke good sense. He was calm and reassuring. She lowered her voice.

'Can I ask how Philippe's marriage is going? I can never raise the subject with Pippa.'

Joel smiled, an almost conspiratorial smile.

'I think Karen has everything in hand. She manages Philippe very well, from what I've observed.'

'We're pleased Julia has this project with the new house to take her mind off her divorce,' Alice remarked.

'I know it hit her hard,' Joel said. 'Karen is a force of nature, I'm afraid. Once she had decided Philippe was going to be her husband, it was just a matter of time.'

'Julia's brother Richard was always worried about her in the background.'

He nodded. He knew the story well.

'Anyway, this is a new chapter in Julia's life. She seems to have recovered her spirits. When I see her here, I know where she belongs,' he said.

'Yes, it's strange, isn't it? Prior Park always drew her back. I hope the new house is a success. You'll be staying there next time you come up, I imagine.'

'Well, the house looks great. Not far off finished, I'd say. I think we're going to hear a handover date today, in fact.'

Alice glanced in Nathan's direction, wondering if he was making the announcement, or Julia.

'Are he and Marianne getting together?' Joel asked, following Alice's gaze. 'Pippa hears from Marianne but she's been very tight-lipped about any new romance.'

'Early days,' Alice said, although she was hopeful something might come of it. Both she and William liked Nathan. He seemed sensible and steady.

'You know if this family gets much bigger, you'll need a bigger dining table,' Joel said, looking at the chairs ranged on both sides of the table.

'Yes, seventeen adults and two children, plus three little ones who don't quite make the big table yet,' she said. 'Once Anthony gets married, that will be another one.'

'I've met Victoria in Sydney a couple of times. She's very nice. I'm pleased it's working out for them. I thought she might be here with Anthony?'

Alice shook her head.

'They're keeping a low profile until after her divorce. He sees her but in her professional work. There'll be plenty of time for us to host her once they can be together,' Alice said.

'That's a good plan,' Joel said. 'Anyway there's been enough change for you to cope with this year, just looking around. Paul moved on quickly.'

'Very quickly,' Alice said.

Joel smiled at the emphasis on the word *quickly*.

'Pippa told me. She keeps me abreast of the Prior Park gossip.'

'Well, it caused a scandal for a while, I can tell you. He wasn't very discreet.'

'Reacting to his disappointment about the boy, I suppose?'

'I'd say so. A few months back he had a go at Alex. Except that William and Richard intervened, it would have been an ugly incident.'

He nodded. He would have been surprised if there'd been no response from Paul. He'd felt the same instinct himself towards his first wife's lover. He had restrained himself with difficulty.

'I must see to the lunch,' Alice said, turning in the direction of the kitchen. 'My housekeeper and her two nieces are managing everything but I have to keep an eye on it.'

As Alice bustled out of the room, Susan accosted Joel. They had met only once before.

'Pippa said I should talk to you about what it's like to be a doctor,' she said.

'Bloody. Bloody awful at times. Rewarding. Sad. Stimulating. And hard work,' he said, looking critically at the girl. 'It's not pristine white coats and easy consultations with patients who have nothing more than a stomach ache.'

She looked him up and down, trying to decide if he was being serious. But there was something genuine and kind about him, she decided.

'Well, that rules out medicine,' she said, with a shrug of her shoulders. 'I can cross that off my list.'

'Your list of possible careers?'

She nodded.

'It's getting shorter by the day,' she said, with a sigh.

'You could work up here alongside your father surely?'

'My problem is I've been brought up at Berrima Park with my mother but I don't really belong to them. And yet I feel like I do. If I do something independently, I can continue to live down there and then continue to visit up here.'

'Well, there are other professions. Anthony did architecture. What about that?'

She shook her head.

'No, it would look like I'm following in my stepfather's footsteps. My father wouldn't like that.'

'An allied health professional such as a psychologist?'

'And listen to people whine about their lives? I'd tell them to make the best of it and get on with life. No, I don't think so,' she said, ruling out another suggestion.

'Law?'

He was running out of ideas.

'Possibly,' she said.

'What about a pilot?' Paul asked, as he inserted himself into the conversation.

'That would be fun,' she said, 'but would that get me a job? Men tend to reserve all the good jobs for themselves.'

'That's true, but I have a feeling they'll be no match for you, my dear sister,' he said playfully. 'Linda's doing what used to be classed as a man's job.'

'Does she like it?'

'I think so,' Paul said, 'but she'd prefer to be a pilot.'

'My daughter been interrogating you, Joel?' Richard asked. 'It will be decision time soon for university.'

'I think it's good to ask around,' Joel said.

He wondered if Susan knew how fortunate she was. She could choose any course and her father would reach for his chequebook to pay the fees. He'd had to work hard to get a high enough pass to ensure he was offered a scholarship.

Now he was part of the moneyed world. Little Jessica would never want for anything. Her mother's wealth would eventually dwarf that of her Belleville relatives but he had seen the dark side of wealth too. It could destroy a person's character, hollow out their soul.

But he did not see that in the Belleville family. They were grounded, honest people. There were no displays of wealth of the kind he had seen on Long Island.

'Unfortunately, she's torn between two camps,' Richard said. 'Her Berrima family and us here.'

'I think she's making a good fist of it, Richard,' Joel said. 'She's had the stability and security of that family as she's been growing up, while always knowing you were there for her too. She seems to have a very independent streak, if I may say so.'

'Well, a determined streak. Last time she was here she announced I was buying her a car for her seventeenth birthday. This time, she announced I would be taking her to visit Catherine's home in England. If you remember, she was the one who missed out on the trip when I remarried Catherine. Kate thought she was too young.'

'You'll have a busy year. At least one wedding. Possibly more?' Joel asked.

'Paul says not. I hope Anthony's wedding goes ahead. I think he really needs the stability of marriage.'

'Is Linda happy with that arrangement?'

'I think she is for now,' Richard said. 'Her father isn't but it's not up to him, is it?'

'She seems a nice girl. Paul's probably quite bruised by everything that's happened. I can understand his reluctance.'

'Were you reluctant to enter another relationship, Joel?' Richard asked. 'Pippa had told her mother about your first marriage. Julia told me, probably to reassure me Paul's not the only man to be duped in this way.'

Joel paused. He hadn't known his past had been the subject of discussion in that way, but he could see Richard was genuinely interested in his answer.

'I was devastated, Richard. I had no idea, not until I saw my wife's lover on the floor of our house, urging my daughter to come to him, saying *come to papa*. I was tempted to kill him on the spot but I resisted the temptation. My wife accused me of being a neglectful husband. The marriage had been a mistake almost from the beginning. I knew that. She threw an African artefact at me. It caught me a glancing blow on the head as I walked out.'

'But you got over it.'

'I did, but it took a while. Paul's situation is different. The child will always be part of this family group. It's going to be tough for him at times. Just give him some latitude.'

'I will. I just hope Linda does. He shares a family trait among the men. Women trouble.'

Joel laughed at the description.

'Well, you don't look like you have women trouble now. Catherine would see off any rivals, I would think.'

Richard smiled. Their re-marriage had been a success. She was the woman he loved beyond all others.

'Well, you and Pippa look ideally suited,' Richard said. 'We are so relieved. We were worried she might get hooked up with an American.'

'She has her moments,' Joel said. 'Deep down, she can't forget she was given away as a baby. It was merest chance she found her real family.'

Richard shook his head from side to side. How long ago was it? He calculated quickly. Nearly thirty-four years.

'It's the family's enduring shame,' Richard lamented. 'I can't believe my mother did that. If I had been here, it would never have happened. I know it's easy to say that, but my mother would not have gone against me. I simply would not have let her do what she did.'

'But we can't change the past, can we?' Joel said, just as Julia came within earshot.

She slipped her arm through her brother's.

'My big brother,' she said. 'He was always my protector. Always picking me up when I fell over. Or standing up for me when my mother got annoyed with me. I know he would have stood up for me then. And he took care of me when Philippe abandoned me. Remember the dinner with you and John Bertram. It was the day the lawyer brought around the divorce settlement for me to look at. Life moves on, doesn't it?'

'New houses can help with that,' Joel said.

Julia brightened at the thought.

'It's going to be finished ahead of schedule, according to Nathan. Work is starting on the interiors after the New Year break. And the landscaping will be done by the end of the month.'

'Is Anthony going to announce the completion date today?'

She nodded.

'I've given him that privilege,' she said smiling.

As if on cue, Anthony called for silence. As the hum of conversation died down, he cleared his throat.

'I'm delighted to announce that the new Prior Park house will be ready for its new occupant by the middle of March,' he said.

There was a general murmur of approval and delight at the news. The tragedy of the fire would finally be consigned to history.

36

March 1977

IN THE GLORIOUS AUTUMN sunshine, Julia's new house stood ready. A beautiful phoenix had risen from the ashes of a fire that had consumed everything in its path.

It was as if Anthony, having summoned the spirit of his great grandfather Louis Belleville, had finally laid to rest the scandal of his grandfather's making. It was now part of the family's story which would slowly but surely slip into history.

'It looks magnificent,' Richard said, as he stood alongside his sister. 'I almost feel when you open the door, we'll meet our mother coming down the stairs.'

'I get that feeling too,' she said. 'It looks like the old house in many ways and in other ways, it doesn't. I love it.'

He gave his sister a gentle hug. Her memories of the original house were mixed. The new house held none of those reminders.

'I expect it cost more than you thought it would?'

She laughed.

'Of course. Don't tell William. He'll think it's a waste of money.'

'It's not a waste of money if it's what you want.'

'It is,' she said. 'After what I've been through, it's wonderful.'

'And James?'

'In the end, I think we're both happier just to go on as we are.'

'That's probably wise,' Richard said. 'Have you told him?'

'Yes, we've discussed it. He's happy with that. He knows I want to keep my independence. I think you understand what I mean.'

'I do,' Richard said, relieved she had felt able to make a decision that he thought would disappoint James.

'I keep remembering back to the time you went away to join up. I was just turning eighteen. You missed my birthday party.'

'I missed a lot of things,' Richard said, 'and then the years just rolled along.'

She turned towards him then.

'What do you regret most from those years?'

For Richard, it was a tough question. An unexpected question too.

'The obvious things. Breaking up with Catherine the first time. How I dealt with Alistair McGovern. And then how I interfered in Paul's relationship with Amanda.'

He could tick them off mentally. These were the things he would change if he could wind back the clock.

But he hesitated to ask the same question of his sister. Knowing this, she smiled.

'I know you wouldn't ask me because you know what I would say. I would have stood up to my mother and refused to give my baby up.'

'It's something I struggle to forgive my mother for,' he said.

'And our father?'

He was grim-faced, thinking of the consequences of their father's actions.

'Hard to forgive. Very hard to square it away with the man we knew as children. Later, I had an idea he wasn't the man I thought he was. But I never thought of what that might mean.'

'That's life,' she sighed. 'The good and the bad.'

'It is indeed,' he said.

'Have you noticed how much closer Andrew has become to Alex?' she asked.

'I thought it would be inevitable,' Richard said. 'Alex dotes on him. And of course he's with Alex a lot more now he and Amanda are together.'

'I guess you're counting on Paul's relationship with Linda enduring.'

'I think it will,' Richard said. 'I really like her. I always felt Amanda was too ...'

Words failed him. All he really wanted to say was that they hadn't been well matched. Julia filled in the blanks.

'Feisty? Independent? Wilful? Challenging?'

'All of those things,' he agreed, 'but I've always liked her. But Paul, in his own way, is quite fragile. He needs a caring partner. Linda is ideal.'

'Do you think she might be wearing a diamond ring soon?'

'I'd be surprised if she isn't. I think her father might relax a little bit if Paul pops an engagement ring on her finger.'

He looked around then.

'It looks like the crowd is about to descend on us.'

In ones and twos the extended Belleville family began to arrive at Julia's front door, eager for a tour of the house and the champagne supper that would follow.

Finally, Julia flung open the front door and welcomed her family to her new home. Anthony and Victoria were close at hand, Anthony to talk about the inspirations from the old house and Victoria to talk about the interior design.

To Richard's relief, the interior of the new house bore very little resemblance to the stolid elegance he remembered. This new house was light and feminine. Pretty in parts, elegant in others.

He caught James Fitzroy's eye and whispered.

'No dirty riding boots in here, James,' he said, smiling.

He rolled his eyes.

'And the beer will be served in fine glassware I imagine,' he said, warming to Richard's theme.

'Oh, I think you'll have to upgrade to fine wine, don't you?'

But Richard was relieved to see he seemed relaxed and happy with no obvious signs of disappointment.

'It's a lovely house,' Catherine said. 'Victoria has done a wonderful job with the interiors. She has a great eye for colour.'

She turned to Richard.

'Don't you think it's time your house had a makeover?'

He groaned. He feared that would happen.

'Of course. But just remember, it's an old Queenslander. It needs to remain an old Queenslander.'

'Of course,' she said.

But he could see she was already mentally preparing a brief for Victoria.

Little Mel looked on in wonder at the beautiful big house. Her own little house was her domain and she loved it, but to her the new house looked like a castle. Baby Laura, now nine months old, sat happily in her mother's arms, eyeing the lights.

As the champagne corks began to pop, William and Alice hung back, taking in the house from all angles.

'It's different,' Alice said. 'It's lovely. Anthony has done a marvellous job. And Victoria too.'

William, looking around him at the extravagance of the interiors, put his arm around his wife.

'I'm pleased it's different from the original house,' he said. 'What it tells you is we were right to build a different home after the fire. We made the right decision.'

'We did, William. This house will take effort to live in. Our house is more robust, if I can use that word.'

And then she laughed.

'James isn't going to get away with muddy clothes or dirty boots.'

'No, indeed,' William agreed, as he accepted a glass of champagne. It was not his drink of choice but he had been told to join in the celebrations wholeheartedly.

Paul stood beside Linda at the back of the room surveying the scene. He followed her gaze. Amanda, arm in arm with Alex, was deep in conversation with his father.

'He always liked Amanda,' Paul said. 'I think he's relieved though that the truth came out.'

'Would your marriage have survived if Andrew had been your son?' she asked, unexpectedly.

Paul shrugged noncommittally.

'I don't know.' He paused. It was time for honesty. 'I think eventually she would have gone back to Alex. He was always her first love. Finding out for sure who Alex's father was actually changed everything for her I believe. She had an excuse to bring Alex in as her partner. It was a cunning manoeuvre.'

It was as if he was realising for the first time how separate their lives had been. They had in fact shared little beyond the children.

'My new boss is trying hard with your cousin,' Linda said, having shifted her gaze away from Amanda.

'He is. I've noticed. He seems to have won little Mel's heart. Marianne might be a tougher assignment.'

'Why do you say that?'

'Because she's devastated with what happened with Alex. He'd lied to her about his earlier relationship with Amanda. Marianne had been brought up in a very sheltered way. She didn't realise he was such an opportunist when he romanced her.'

'A different upbringing from you?'

'Very much. My parents divorced. My father got remarried. I have a stepsister. I went away to school. None of these things happened to Marianne. She went to school locally. She lived with her grandmother while she did that. She never lived away from her parents or got a job. And the world has changed a lot but they've hardly changed at all.'

'We all have to move with the times,' Linda said. 'That's why I pushed to go away to university. I didn't want my life to be narrow.'

'And now?'

'I still don't want it to be narrow.'

'Meaning tied down to domestic routine?'

She shrugged.

'I haven't really thought about it except I really want to do more flying. Nathan thinks I can combine the two things – my civil engineering career and my flying. They often hire a plane to fly out west to inspect projects they might bid on or projects that are under way. He said I could take on that role if I want to.'

'You know your family is going to expect me to put a diamond ring on your finger very soon,' he said.

'I'll stall them,' she said, with a smile. 'There's no rush. Besides we have to live our life together the way we want to, not the way they think we should.'

At times there was something about her that reminded him of Amanda. Single-mindedness. An inner strength. And best of all, she wasn't pressuring him. Whatever it was, he loved her for it.

Across the room, his half-sister Susan stood alongside Marianne.

'He's keen,' Susan said in a lowered voice as together they watched Nathan with little Mel.

'Not you too,' Marianne groaned. 'I'm not even divorced yet.'

'He's nice, though, isn't he?'

'Yes, he's nice. And before you say it, I know he's good with the kids.'

'How are you getting on with your ex?' she asked.

'It's tense but polite.'

'But he's still included in everything?'

'Well, it makes sense. His daughters are part of the Belleville family. Amanda's sons are too. They'll always be around the family.'

'But Andrew … ?'

'Will always be regarded as a Belleville. Didn't your father tell you?'

She shook her head.

'It could be an interesting question for the future of the Belleville inheritance,' Susan said.

'Well, I'm not going to challenge it if it's what your father wants,' Marianne said.

'But when the older generation has gone, surely it will be our generation that decides,' Susan said.

'Well, I wouldn't go against their wishes. Besides, at this stage, it's just the four of us. Your interest is being managed by Paul I understand.'

To Marianne, it seemed a strange conversation to be having with a sixteen-year-old.

'My Dad's coming to Sydney after Easter to go shopping for a car for me,' she said, changing the subject. 'I bet he'll want to buy me something that's boring and practical.'

'Probably,' Marianne said. 'That's what parents do.'

'You won't get away with that with little Mel,' she observed, as the little girl came running up to them. She turned then and headed towards her father who was busy subduing an unruly Andrew who decided it would be fun to run at full speed through the rooms.

'Interesting,' Susan said. 'Alex is really acting as Andrew's father by the looks of it.'

Marianne simply smiled and laid a hand on Susan's arm.

'It's best not to talk about it, Susan,' she said. 'Everyone knows. We don't need to be reminded.'

She looked at Marianne then, realising for the first time how the truth about Andrew's parentage had broken her heart.

'I'm sorry. I didn't think.'

'No, you didn't think,' she said, feeling a gentle rebuke was in order. 'As you get older, you'll realise you have to be more thoughtful about what you say.'

'I know,' Susan said. 'I know that. My mother's always telling me that.'

'She's going to be a handful for her parents,' Nathan said as he joined Marianne and together they watched Susan walk away. 'What's her mother like?'

'Kate's lovely,' Marianne said. 'We all missed her when she broke up with Uncle Richard. Then for a long time we hardly saw Susan at all.'

'She looks headstrong to me,' he said.

'That's one way of describing her. She told me she already has a boyfriend. He's twenty-four. She's only sixteen and still a school-girl. It worries me. Her parents don't know.'

'And I suppose she made you promise not to tell her father.'

'You guessed it. If she was twenty-one and he was twenty-nine, it wouldn't seem so bad but I don't like the sound of it.'

'Nothing you can do about it,' Nathan said. 'Hopefully he won't push the relationship too far.'

She knew what he meant.

'How are you feeling this evening?' he asked quietly. 'I know it's not easy for you having to see your ex-husband with someone else every time there's a family event.'

'I'm getting used to it,' she said. 'Thank you for being here for me.'

'I'll always be here for you,' he reassured her. 'You know how I feel about you.'

She smiled and slipped her arm through his.

'I do. I just need time to let go of my old life. Slowly but surely, it's happening.'

'That's good,' he said, sensing progress in their relationship.

Across the room, her mother and father watched on.

'I think that relationship is progressing just a little bit, don't you?' Alice said quietly.

William shrugged. He was less certain than his wife so he said nothing. Catherine, standing alongside Alice, agreed with her.

'They certainly seem to get on well and he's so good with her children,' Catherine said. 'I hope it comes to something, for Marianne's sake.'

'I hope so too, Catherine,' Alice said. 'I think only then can she move on from Alex and put the past behind her. She feels like she failed because she should have realised what he had told her about Amanda wasn't the truth.'

'Well, she's not the first woman to be taken in by a smooth talker. And she won't be the last,' Catherine said, as she reached for another glass of champagne.

Yet for all their criticism of Alex's behaviour, no one in the Belleville family actively disliked him. His charm, it seemed, had won the day as he continued to move easily among them all.

'I suppose you're disappointed your mother and father aren't tying the knot again,' Richard said.

John Fitzroy shrugged his shoulders.

'It was always unlikely. My mother values her freedom now. Whatever he promised, I think the old man would still have expectations of what a wife should be. They're happy. No reason for them to change now.'

'I agree,' Richard said. He too was relieved at his sister's decision. 'It's good to have you on board to under-study William looking after our cattle business.'

'I enjoy it,' John said. 'I can learn a lot from him. He wants me to come on the next trip with Paul.'

'Good idea,' Richard said.

'And Susan? I know what Marianne does and where Paul and Anthony are likely to fit into the business but I was wondering what role you see for Susan.'

'Well, that's a vexed question. I think time will tell. She seems keen on doing law at the moment.'

John raised his eyebrows.

'Is that because she's keen on a lawyer?'

'What do you mean?' Richard demanded.

'Just that I heard her talking to Marianne about her boyfriend. He's a lawyer, apparently. She seems a bit young though to be seeing a guy who must be well in his twenties.'

'She certainly is,' he said, as he scanned the crowd for his daughter. 'I can't imagine her mother knows about this.'

'I didn't mean to get her into trouble. Go easy with her.'

But Richard was in no mood to take John's advice. Having spotted his daughter with Anthony and Victoria, he headed in her direction. As he approached, she rolled her eyes and appealed to her brother.

'Here comes trouble,' she said quietly. 'You've got to back me up here.'

Anthony looked perplexed but Victoria was quick on the uptake.

'Boyfriend issue?'

Susan nodded.

'Someone's spilt the beans.'

She laughed.

'You'll be fine. You'll tie him up in knots.'

'I can do that but I've just got to stop him ringing my mother and telling her.'

'We need to have a quiet word, you and I,' Richard said to his daughter.

'What about?' she asked innocently, not moving towards her father.

'Don't try that innocent line with me, young lady,' Richard declared. 'A little birdie whispered in my ear that you are seeing a young man much older than you. It's just not on. Do you hear me?'

'Why?' she asked.

'I think you know why.'

'Because you think I'm still a child. Well I'm not. I've passed the age of consent so you don't have to worry there. He's really nice. We have fun together and he teaches me stuff about the law.'

She eyed her father up and down.

'I'm not going to get pregnant if that's what you're worried about. It's easy to prevent that now.'

Anthony, desperate not to laugh, decided it was time to intervene.

'She's winding you up, old man,' he said. 'Take it easy or next thing we'll be gathering for your funeral.'

He searched the room for his mother. She however had been alerted by the raised voices and wondered what all the fuss was about.

'The old man is just about to explode at Susan,' Anthony explained.

Catherine put her hand on Richard's arm.

'What's up?'

But instead of Richard, it was Susan who explained, giving a slightly different version of the story she had told Marianne.

'Well, probably not ideal boyfriend material for a sixteen-year-old,' Catherine said, 'but at least he appears to be teaching you something. I'd keep him at arm's length if I were you. It would hurt his career if there was a scandal with a schoolgirl.'

'Of course it would,' Susan said.

She looked at her father then.

'Winds of change, old man. They're blowing like a gale through society. You need to catch up. You're still stuck in some 1950s time warp of virgin brides and women tied to the kitchen sink. It's not like that anymore.'

Richard groaned. He knew his daughter was right. He looked around him. Easy divorces. Couples living together instead of marrying. Children in blended families. Winds of change indeed, he thought. Even the Belleville family is not immune.

He relaxed then. Nothing will ever be the same again, he decided. He simply must accept that.

'It's been a tumultuous year,' Richard said, as he stood beside William and Julia in front of their mother's grave.

The graves of their parents had been repaired and a new fence erected around the two.

The new house stood majestically some distance away, not quite dominating its surroundings as the old one had done, but making a grand statement, nonetheless.

He shrugged, thinking of everything they had learnt about their history.

'We're not the family we thought we were,' he said. 'It was all a myth created by an adventurer.'

'Does it matter?' William asked.

'Not really,' Richard agreed, 'but we are the people we've become because of what went before.'

'But we had the same ambition as our grandfather,' William pointed out. 'Secure the future for our families.'

'And we've done that,' Richard said, satisfied they had made good decisions to lay strong foundations for the future of the family company.

'It's good to have you as part of it,' Richard said, turning to look at his sister.

'I always felt I belonged here,' Julia said. 'I felt I was happy in my other life but looking back, I'm not sure now. Prior Park will always be my home.'

'You know it feels to me we've finally settled with the past,' Richard said. 'I felt as if there were unfinished chapters in our lives that needed to be brought to an end. And now we can look forward.'

He paused.

'My daughter talked about winds of change blowing through society. I think we've endured our own winds of change and we've survived as a family.'

'We have,' Julia said, linking arms with her brothers. 'We have survived. But we've done more than survive. We've created a legacy for our children and for their children. And for those who come after them.'

She leant forward then and placed a bouquet of roses on each of their parents' graves. For the three of them, there was – finally – an acceptance of who their parents had been – their father flawed but charming; their mother domineering but loving – each capable of decisions that had echoed down the generations with catastrophic results.

Yet their children had survived and thrived. And the bonds of their sibling love had held fast. As it would for the rest of their lives.